To Anne

Exactly 23 days

by Jayne Higgins

☺ Smile always

Jayne Higgins.

Published by CompletelyNovel.com

First published in the UK in 2015 by Completely Novel

www.completelynovel.com

ISBN 9781849147293

Printed in the UK by Lightning Source International

To women everywhere.
You can break a woman but a strong woman will always pick up the pieces, rebuild herself and come back stronger than ever.

CONTENTS

CHAPTER 1

Learning to love again

Fiora had left him in Devon to make his own way back to Manchester but not to their home, she had removed his front door key from his jeans. He wouldn't come through her front door again. Ever.

The irony of the lyrics blasting from her car radio, informing her of learning to love again! She drove with fury as the voice pelted out the song and the tears poured down her face. "Fuck off" she screamed, pushing the off button on the radio in her temper. "Why the fuck would I want to love him again? "FUCK OFFFFF" she yelled at nobody and everybody at the same time, followed by "and where the hell are you when I need you Mother?" She realised she was becoming hysterical whilst in charge of a vehicle and that she was driving dangerously too. Pulling over onto the next petrol station car park, she undid her seat belt and slumped over the steering wheel and sobbed. Oh boy, did she sob? Gut wrenching, heart jolting, unendurable sobs, barely taking a breath as mucus ran from her nose and mascara stained her pretty face. Fi used her shirtsleeve as a handkerchief, wiping away the conjoined messes, in readiness for the next deluge to arrive. She had no idea how long she had been there, when she heard a gentle tapping on her window and as she looked up to her right, a smile crept across the woman's face as she mouthed something through the window, that Fi couldn't hear. She pressed the electric window button to reveal a softly spoken voice saying, "Are you okay dear? You've been here awhile." Fi replied, "No I'm not, but I will be, thank you very much for asking," she said, "I will use the toilets to freshen up and then get myself a drink and be on my way," she continued, before finally adding, "I've had some upsetting news but I will be fine, thanks again for your concern." The woman walked away and Fi promptly burst into tears again.

Some time later she opened the door to step out of her car and realised that she was still wearing her slippers, as she recalled the behaviour that had led her to flee the caravan in such a hurry that morning. "Bastard," she thought, "fucking bastard," he was the one who had been deceiving her and yet there he was, nose to nose, yelling at her with such vitriol and hatred that she could feel his spit on her face, as he continued to behave in that all too familiar way when he couldn't handle conflict, being verbally abusive, with the threat of violence. He had done the one thing he had sworn, during their short lived time together, that he would never, ever do, he had finally admitted having an affair and yet he was treating her in such a violent manner. Yes, she had been scared and yes she had been shaking inside with fear and yes she had fled wearing her slippers.

Fi shook the recollection from her mind and quickly changed footwear before going into the public toilets. When she looked in the mirror the pain was clear to see, although there were no visible bruises from his failure to batter her physically, the emotional bruises were there nonetheless, in her heart, in her soul, in her eyes and in her swollen face from the hours of tears already shed. She threw cold water over her face repeatedly to shock her into the present and to allow herself to take stock and make decisions. The realisation, that it had all been a lie, was, without putting too finer point on it, shocking to her. He had started their relationship lying when he told her he had three children but then later on in the relationship confessing to having six children. However, Fi eventually found out that he did have seven children! Now here he was, ending their relationship 5 years later and still lying, when she had finally gotten him to admit to his affair. She also realised as she stood there looking at herself in the mirror, that the other woman wasn't called Chloe and that she wasn't a sales rep that he had met in his role as a postman, because she also knew for sure that they too were lies. The last 5 years had indeed been one big lie and 'Do you know how I know he's lying?' she asked herself, 'because his fucking lips moved!' she answered!

She rearranged her mane of curly hair into some sort of acceptable state, ready for her to face civilization again on the other side of that toilet door and she put her sunglasses on to avoid eye contact with anyone, whilst hiding her pain. She took a deep breath, opened the door and walked out into the bustle of the petrol station shop, grabbed a coffee and muesli bar and paid at the check out. In her haste to reach the safe haven of her car, she bumped into the kind assistant again as she was exiting the building. "You take care" said the woman, gently touching Fi's arm, "thank you," Fi replied as tears teetered on the edge of her eyelids, ready to flow down her cheeks and open the floodgates again. 'Deep breaths, deep breaths, deep breaths' she told herself as she quickly walked back to her vehicle, just managing to stem the flow of tears, for now anyway.

Fi sat and ate her snack and drank her coffee whilst checking her many emails, messages and voicemails. She had informed her nearest and dearest via text message and social media messaging what had happened, as she could not possibly face the relentless conversations needed to explain the micro details of yet another ending of her marriage to this fucking crazy arsehole. Her received messages were asking her to contact them all ASAP whilst supporting her decision to take his house key off him and "leave the tosser in Devon to get wherever he was going." Via all this multi media contact, Fi's supporters wanted to: "fucking kill him," "be there with you as soon as possible," "help you get him out of your life for good," "dump his shit on the drive," "take his shit to the tip," "slash his shit so he could no longer wear it," "sell his shit to pay for a quick divorce," "put itching powder in his shit!" "take great pleasure in telling his naive kids what a fucking tosser he was, is and always will be," "make sure his work 'mates' got to know the real truth and that his name be mud," etcetera, etcetera. All of this support from her friends and loved ones made her feel great in the moment of course but that was just it, 'THE' moment. A single, solitary, stand alone, fucking moment.

She sent a further blanket message to them all, telling them she was going to Plymouth to be with her son Calum (who had been injured in an accident and was undergoing surgery that day) and that she would be in touch when she got home to Manchester in a few days time. Her nearest and dearest were not going to accept that briefest of contact of course but for now she had at least replied to them all. She decided however, that she needed help with a specific issue and so she answered yet another call from her friend Tracey, one of her 'tell anything at anytime and not be judged, coffee o'clock club members'. Tracey listened intently to Fi as she sobbed, as she conveyed the story of how his affair had been revealed whilst providing as much reassurance and comfort as she could to her friend within the constraints of being 300 miles away.

Tracey said goodbye and set about dealing with the required task of finding dog friendly hotel accommodation for her, near to her son's university halls. Fi made her way to Plymouth with, "Bastard! Fucking bastard," being her mantra for the full length of the A38 from Exeter, with the odd, "fucking arsehole!" thrown in for good measure. Even the poor DJ got an ear bashing as he attempted to deliver his daily pop quiz through the airwaves, as she screamed at the radio, "You can fuck off as well!" as she pushed the off button for the second time.

The lack of radio noise however, allowed the pinball machine inside her head to start up, and start up it did, with a million realisations and questions about the past five years. More importantly though were the questions about the past few months. When had he been phoning, texting and seeing his trollop? Who was she? Where was she from? Where did she work? Why? After all he had said about having affairs, in conversations with his wife, would he do that to her? The sickening thoughts of his double life and of his changing patterns of behaviour, over the past few months, were jigsaw pieces of the affair and the pin balls continued to clatter and batter the inside of her head. Clang, clang, clang before being dropped into the many holes, which were nanoseconds of relief in her mind, only to be replaced with further balls entering the relentless noisy, head banging, crazy making games machine that was her mind.

The lies emerged, the pretence emerged, the additional fake affection towards Fi emerged and then steadily 'the facts' emerged! The fact that there was extra long dog walking in a different direction from his usual walk in the park across the road, the fact there was the sudden new habit of staying up later than her, (obviously to make calls and send texts to trollop) the fact there was the bizarre day when he went Christmas shopping in July! (on his Friday day off) for an extra special present (that needed to be ordered months in advance for her, he said), the fact there was the lack of bank statements coming to the house, the fact there was the lack of mobile phone bills coming to the house, the fact he was having ‘extra’ late shift duties, as well as the usually scarce rostered ones, the fact of the smell of alcohol on his breath when he came in from the ‘late’ shifts! (I’ve just had a quick one with Andy and Dave, he would say), the fact there was the smell of smoke on his clothes when he came in from work from these late shifts, when he didn’t even smoke, the fact there was now silent mobile phone tones, (it no longer rang or beeped when a message came through), the fact he slept with his mobile under his pillow (so he could quickly turn his alarm off, so as not to disturb her, he said). The facts, the facts, the facts but the only fact she needed to concern herself with was that he was a lying, cheating, thieving, con-man who had bled her of everything, her love, her kindness, her soul, her inner peace, her health, her happy home and her money. She had been the ultimate meal ticket and the throbbing pain inside her head was too much for her now, as she screeched her vehicle to a halt, opened the car door and vomited.

Fi arrived in Plymouth in the midst of a deluge of torrential rain but the dogs still needed walking and so she had no choice but to face the rain. What did it matter anyway? The deluge from the sky would mingle with the deluge from her eyes. Nobody would know she was sobbing again. She parked near the hotel and put the dogs on their leads and headed through the park gates of the Hoe. She walked across the parkland towards the Belverdere, down the steep steps and onto the road before turning left and walking past the Tinside outdoor lido, which she noticed had it's own wave machine going on due to the horrendous wind and rain. On she walked, down to the harbour, past the cafes, bars and shops and along to the very end bar where two days before, she had sat all Sunday afternoon with her husband and her son, enjoying people watching whilst laughing and drinking with her two favourite men. She just had to go there again today, she had to see the last place she had enjoyed laughter with him, the last place she was ignorant of his betrayal, the last place she had been happy with him. She certainly didn't want to invest in a pity party for herself by coming here, oh no, she merely wanted to sit there again in that outdoor space, under the warmth of the outdoor heaters and watch the waves clipping the harbour walls and remember, just remember.

One day you have a husband and the next day you don't, simple as that. Fi sat there awhile but soon began to feel her wet clothes affecting her body temperature and she decided to retrace her steps across the Hoe back towards her hotel. Upon arrival she checked in at reception and was shown to her room. She shut the door and dried the dogs off, fed them, made a cup of tea and for the second time that day, there was a deluge of water mixing with her tears as she took her shower. She tried to sleep but couldn't, the dogs kept barking as they were not used to confinement and with every noise disturbing them, she was conscious that they in turn, were disturbing the rest of the hotel.

Fi decided to make some calls accepting that she couldn't put it off any longer, she spoke to her son Calum, her daughter Louise and her best friend Julie. There was nothing anybody could say to her to comfort her and so they listened, whilst she talked and cried and talked and cried some more until in the end she was done with talking and she said her goodbye's. However, she hadn't done with crying. Sleep still eluded her and when it was light, she got up, took a shower and got dressed. She skipped breakfast and drove over to her son's uni halls to find Calum looking pale and tired, just like her. He was in pain from his operation but he hugged his mum with his untrussed arm and held her whilst she cried, yet again. He had had to endure that dick head's behaviour for far too long now and was seeing again, the aftermath of his shabby treatment towards his mother. He gently coaxed her into sitting on his bed and went off to make tea for her. It took a while with one hand in plaster but when he returned to her and she was still crying, a surge of anger evolved inside of him and he acted on his emotions and left "ugly conk" as he now referred to him, a voicemail saying, "Why Robert, why, you sat there with me and mum on Sunday, playing happy families when you've been doing this behind her back, why? She didn't deserve this treatment and you fucking know she didn't." There was of course no return call. He didn't want one. He knew the truth of what his mother had had to endure for 5 years. He was, after all, the only one of the other 23 people within this crazy step family scenario that had lived under the same roof as his mother and her mad husband. He knew her pain all right and he was so angry and for sure, he was one of the growing queue of people who wanted to punch Robert to make themselves feel better.

Fi spent a couple of days in a blur whilst in Plymouth but she wanted to make sure her son recovered well enough from his operation and to ensure there was no reaction to his anaesthetic nor any signs of infection from his wound. The ex nurse in her was alert for such issues. She did her best to contain her tears as she didn't want her fragility to overshadow his need for recovery but when she was satisfied he was okay, she had a very tearful goodbye with him and set off for the long drive home. Surprisingly she managed the journey without tears and tried to focus on the positives of this opportunity she had to finally be rid of this crazy tosser. The journey was uneventful as she sang loudly to her favourite music as she drove, stopping twice to use the service station bathrooms, get refreshments and walk her dogs, before she eventually arrived home six hours later.

She sent a text to Julie who was at her door in an instant. Living two doors away meant they could be there for each other twenty-four-seven. Julie made a drink for them both and offered Fi food before they sat to discuss the past few days. Of course Fi cried as she repeated the finer details of the painful events, as well as describing Robert's callous and abusive reactions following his declaration of betrayal. Their conversation regarding his behaviour was splattered with hatred, anger, pity, relief and much bad language on both sides. Julie and her husband were also in the 'punch him queue' and were furious, to see their friend going through unbelievable levels of emotional pain at the hands of this maniac, who had only 12 months ago, promised he would never inflict such pain upon her again. Hours later, Julie encouraged Fi to try to rest and assured her friend she was there whenever and for whatever she needed. "We'll get you through this," she said as she hugged her friend and left her on her own. The house was silent and hollow and empty, every inch of it reminded her of him. She couldn't face sleeping in their bed and so she dragged a mattress from storage in the spare room and lay down on it. Again she couldn't sleep and the pinball machine in her head was in overdrive mode. The next day

Fi changed her home and mobile phone numbers to avoid any attempts by him or his family to contact her and to avoid the trauma of thinking it might be him when her incoming calls and text message tones bleeped. She would never speak to him again.

That pinball machine continued to drive her crazy for days, every waking moment and in every dream state too. It stopped her thinking straight, it stopped her feeling, it stopped her loving herself and others. It stopped her taking pride in her personal care, it stopped her eating properly, it stopped her drinking properly. It stopped her reading, it stopped her writing, it stopped her enjoying her favourite TV and radio. It stopped her caring for her dogs properly (but it didn't stop them being loyal to her), it stopped her socialising and interacting with her cherished coffee o'clock girls and her bestie (but it didn't stop them interacting with her), it stopped her being a mum (but it didn't stop them being her children). It stopped her everything. Fi stopped. The days mingled into weeks, which were a blur for Fi, with her repeating herself to anybody and everybody who contacted her and who was prepared to listen. She called it her parrot phase!

She accepted her good fortune in life being inundated with different people calling in person, ringing her, texting her, emailing her, sending her flowers and cards, letting her know she was loved and that they were there for her. Her best friend Julie, worked with a woman who was married to one of Robert's colleagues and it was quickly established that it was a neighbour from around the back of her house that he was having an affair with. "How shallow can the bastard get?" she asked Julie when she was given this news, "a 'neighbour,' a 'fucking neighbour,' he is 'fucking my neighbour,'" she added, "can this get any worse?" she sobbed, as all her neighbourly possibilities loaded themselves into the pinball machine in her head. She needed rid of this prick and fast. She likened him to a piece of the filthy chewed chewing gum he so often left lying around the house, as she kept finding him stuck to her and unable to get rid of the mess left behind. Well, no more, she screamed inside her head before collapsing on the sofa, where Julie left her and where she remained for two days in a zombie versus pinball machine state.

Fi's friends and her cousin Jen decided to pay for a private detective to secure evidence to obtain a quick divorce from Robert and finally allow her to be rid of him for good. Everybody had had enough of seeing her in repeated pain. She had taken him back repeatedly and now they all felt the same way as Fi, no more. No fucking more. He was a psycho, no other words could describe him, he was a psycho and he was killing their beautiful Fi, steadily, he was killing her, from the inside out. Her physical health had deteriorated so fast during her time with this wanker. She was ill enough. She had Lupus and all the challenges that that entailed.

Fi and her friends had to do some of the initial "undercover" work themselves, to supply the detective with dates, times, vehicle registration numbers, address details, phone numbers etcetera in order for him to then go on to collecting photographic and video evidence. Julie, Tracey, Pauline and Fi laughed as they acted like the characters from the Yorkshire pudding advert, stalking the neighbourhood and speaking to the potential trollops neighbours, to clarify information, eliminate certain people and eventually identify who the woman was. This involved late night and early morning surveillance, staking out both him and her, in different locations and included a few bungled efforts and a couple of hair raising moments when they were nearly seen. By the time they handed the matter over to the detective they were satisfied that they had progressed to the competences of their given nickname of the 'Whitefield Angels'. Fi managed to find odd moments of laughter in all of this mess, but she also had a growing list of questions that would remain unanswered, as she had already decided that she would never ever speak to the cretin again and why would she want to?

Paul, the detective from Pinnacle Investigations was both proficient and fast. She was amazed how quickly he was able to supply her with updates and he sent her daily reports containing any evidence he had collated. Julie insisted on being with Fi whenever she opened these reports and it was on one of these occasions that she heard Fi gasp, "Julie, she's called Fiona," Fi said sadly, to her friend, as a tear rolled slowly down her cheek, this was surely a nightmare and she was going to wake up from it all soon wasn't she? "She has the same name as me, for fucks sake," before adding, "NO! Julie it gets even worse, she was born in Salford where I was born and she works in a Mental Health place where I used to work 10 years ago," she paused before saying, "jeepers fucking creepers, what are the chances of that?" pointing at each of the similarities to her own life on the screen in front of her. She sighed before asking, "Is he really that callous?" but she didn't really need an answer to that question did she? It made her feel sick, reading it all. This was like reading a far-fetched movie script but every detail of it was true, he was having an affair with her neighbour, she had the same name as Fi, she was born in the same town as Fi and she was working in her former place of work.

They decided to check out her Facebook page, which displayed images including one of her dressed as a dog! "Oh the irony," said Fi as she and Julie laughed. The profile contents and videos revealed her to have all the attributes of a chav, a loud mouthed common chav, who spoke like a chav, looked like a chav, had a stereotypical aggressive chav dog, dressed like a chav slapper, and swore like a 'foul mouthed' chav in her Facebook postings. She looked and acted like a trollop! Fi had done some swearing lately but in the comfort of her own home with her friends and in her head too but to behave like that on a social media forum for everyone to see, yuk. There she was on the screen right in front of her, 'the cow' without a shred of decency and loyalty towards women. A fellow member of the sisterhood without a moral compass, who had quite willingly participated in an affair with a married man and choose to wreak havoc upon other people's lives. He had chosen well, as he too had no moral compass. "Well, at least he won't call her the wrong name when he's shagging her and he's coming, will he?" said Fi, as they burst into laughter "Bastard!" they both yelled at the same time which made them roar laughing, bringing a brief respite from the reality of Fi's nightmare. Not a sleep induced nightmare but a real life one. The chav blocked Fi's access to her Facebook page a short while later too! Now why would you block somebody, who isn't even a Facebook friend, who you don't know? Unless you are trying to hide yourself from that person, for some reason, mmm! Yet another clue that the thick fuckers left for the Whitefield Angels!

During the next few days Pinnacle Paul, as Fi and Julie nicknamed him, also provided information regarding Robert's current location together with photographic and video evidence to place before the courts to prove his adultery. Fi also obtained his mobile phone records for the past 18 months. The detective was hired in case Robert decided to deny his affair by lying again, which given his track record was highly likely. This whole trauma really was a crazy making time for Fi, whilst she attempted to come to terms with the what, when, where and whys of her husband's affair, as well as accepting all the madness of her 5 year relationship with him and his equally mad family. On one particular day however, the crazy scale was about to shoot to the moon, as the reality of the information staring at her from her computer screen hit Fi like a punch in her stomach. As she typed unknown phone numbers from his mobile phone records into Google and as she read the words jumping out at her,

'ESCORT GIRLS, MASSAGE PARLOURS, OUT OF HOURS SERVICE, FULL RANGE OF SERVICES ON OFFER, SCARLETS, KAREN'S, JACKIE'S, NORTH MANCHESTER, SOUTH MANCHESTER',

her ear piercing screams were heard by the neighbour's who ran to assist her as she fell to her knees yelling, "NO!" They tried desperately to make sense of what she was attempting to convey to them, amongst her incoherent mumblings and her agonising sobs. The pain of him having an affair paled into insignificance at this realisation that he had been having regular, long standing, late night and early morning contact through his mobile phone with a host of massage parlours in both North Manchester where he lived and South Manchester where his mother lived. Fi ran to the bathroom and vomited. Julie left her for a while to weep and when she went in later to see her friend, she found her sat on the floor where she had slid down the wall and collapsed in a heap. Julie felt that she could literally see Fi's pain but Julie felt her own pain inside of her too, as she heard that all too familiar sound of gut wrenching sobbing coming from her friends broken, wracking body. In her imagination, Julie now formed a queue of willing 'killers'. A punch was no longer good enough. What else was this fucking wanker going to do this fragile soul? Her beautiful friend was deteriorating by the day and Julie was scared for Fi now, for she knew, without doubt, that her friend simply couldn't take anymore, she just couldn't. Fi was in so much emotional pain, with her physical pain levels quickly gathering pace. She was literally in a state of shock.

Julie sent Tracey a text who living locally too, was there within five minutes. Together they put extra layers of clothes on Fi as she sat shivering uncontrollably. They made her hot tea with honey and brandy, before putting her to bed with a hot water bottle and Milly the cat. Milly would not take no for answer, Fi would get company, love and affection whether she wanted it or not! She was that kind of cat. Her beloved 'coffee o'clock' girls never left her side for a week, taking it in turns to sit with her day and night, whilst she slowly ebbed back into existence. Not life, just existence. Louise, Fi's daughter then arrived from London and spent two weeks with her mother. She too was in emotional pain, flitting between seething rage and blubbering sobs at having to watch her mother, "Her give everything to everyone, never expecting anything in return, selfless mother," crumble in front of her, yet again, at the hands of this knob. Whilst her mother rested, Louise took great pleasure in spending hours, literally hours, speaking on the phone to Tom, (her step brother) and Robert's eldest son. During several phone calls, she told him everything from day one of this crazy relationship and how his father had behaved towards her mother. Toms' standard question, (as she relayed the many scenarios to him) was, 'Are you fucking kidding me?' As he too, joined the rapidly expanding 'wanting to kill him' queue. His own son said the words, 'I'm going to kill him!' Tom offered all the support he could but deep down Fi knew that blood was thicker than water with Robert's family and she would never be able to sustain the lovely relationship she had had with him, his beautiful wife and their gorgeous son Freddy, Fi's grandson. Yes, to Fi, he was her grandson and she really did love that little boy (although other members of Robert's family cruelly reminded her, that as Freddy was not a blood relative, then he was not her grandchild). She did however know that separation and divorce went way beyond the immediate two people involved, especially, when naivety and ignorance were part of the equation. She decided she wasn't bothered about the loss of his other children and their families, she had tried to embrace them all over the years but now she accepted, they had never liked her and they never would and she accepted that she was finally okay with now being able to admit, that she had never liked them either! On reflection, the loss of the wider crazy family was easier for her to bare, but losing Freddy and his parents, now that was another heart breaker. No more Granny Fi. How cruel can people be?

Fi eventually began to emerge from her pain and as the pinball machine began to slow down in her head she was able to contend with difficulties a little better with each new day. There was of course, the ebbing and flowing of the emotional tide but she slowly found she was crying less often, thinking about the trollop less often and talking about Robert less often. She began to eat a little better, although it was a limited diet of paninis and vanilla yoghurts and to be frank she was eating because she had to and not because she had any appetite. She began to drink her favourite Nespresso decaf coffees again and her lemon and hot water were again part of her daily routine but she decided to avoid alcohol for a while, such were the depressive effects it could have upon her. Fi found that she couldn't venture outdoors very often but she could at least look out of the windows and appreciate the variations in the weather, admire her beautiful garden that she had designed and completed in the summer and finally appreciate that she had, had a miraculous escape from the 'mad one.' His trollop had inadvertently presented her with a priceless gift in finally taking him away from her for good. Was she relieved she asked herself one day whilst watching the rain run down the French windows, "absofuckinglutely" she was.

When she had enough emotional strength to deal with issues without crying, she had two urgent things on her to do list. First, she used an old SIM card and compiled a 'send to many' text message for all his kids, his trollop and himself, stating:

"I have had a private detective working on you and your trollop and I have your mobile phone records, photographic and video evidence amongst the extensive report I have in readiness for the divorce court. It would appear you have been contacting massage parlours, namely, Jackie's, Karen's and Scarlet's in both north and south Manchester over a significant time, day and night. If I find out from health testing that you have further compromised my already fragile health, then god help you. There is already a growing list of people who want to punch you. You started this relationship lying about your 7 kids and you ended it lying about your trollop. I have sent a copy of this text to her and to all your children, who now, all have egg

on their faces, do they not? They are all complicit in your deceit of others but they've had a bloody good teacher. Yuk. You will rue the day you EVER thought it was okay for you to treat me like shit, you despicable, vile, scumbag."

His subsequent mobile phone bills indicated that upon receipt of that text message he made attempts to contact all his children and his trollop. Fi didn't need to ask herself why! Liars always frantically try to cover their tracks! His son Tom was also instructed by text message to reiterate to his father, that under no circumstances was he to EVER get in touch with Fi again. He would hear soon enough by way of the courts regarding the divorce. She also bundled all his mail together and placed it in a larger envelope and redirected it to him at: No Morals Lane, Arse Hole Village, D1CK 4EAD and hand delivered it to the mail office where he worked!

Second, she contacted a local solicitor Wendy Worsley and discussed at length, on what grounds she would divorce Robert. There was so much evidence compiled from their five years together, that it was a pick and mix scenario of any of the legal options available by way of the courts.

They decided upon the best options for Fi, with all legal and court costs being sought from Robert and she was tasked with compiling a written statement of her marriage and the reasons for wanting a divorce. They scheduled their first meeting for the following week. Fi relished the task of compiling the report. She had compiled hundreds of court reports in her role as a Probation Officer for several years before retiring and it would be a pleasure to compile this final one. Although it was emotionally hard for her to recall and catalogue the vast amount of evidence, she also found it reassuring to know that in a matter of months, this would all be over and she would no longer bear that shitty surname. According to Fi's written evidence, he appeared to be spineless, had no balls and come to think of it, did he even have a dick, she wondered? Well, certainly not with her during the past few weeks but then she should feel relieved she thought, given that he was shoving it into his trollops, as well as multiple prostitutes, orifices. Yes, okay, if she was being really truthful, she was feeling just a tad spiteful, but who cared, he certainly didn't feel spiteful when he was shagging her namesake and his massage parlour escorts and putting her health at further risk. She made a note to get a sexual health check ASAP. What the hell had she seen in him? She wondered, as the report shot out of the printer and onto her desk. She was a confident writer and she recalled that after her speech at their wedding, she had been told by several people that it was the best 'wedding speech' they had EVER heard. She had had a standing ovation for it and Robert had been so embarrassed at his own pathetic effort (that somebody else had written for him the night before) that he had refused to give his grooms speech at his own wedding! So yes, she was a confident writer all right and whilst editing her latest work, it was very evident to Fi that the document she had produced did not make for pleasant reading and he certainly would not be portrayed in a good light when he appeared before the magistrates in a few weeks time. However, it was an essay of HER truth, which was more than he would ever be capable of, telling anybody the truth. On paper, as well as in reality he would be exposed for who he really was, a liar, a man who spent his entire life lying, to his wife, his children, his grandchildren, his parents, his friends, his work colleagues and his bosses. He had regularly brought mail home from work that he should have delivered to people's homes and burnt it in the back garden or taken bin bags full of it to his parents house for them to dispose of in communal skips. He was a snide, in all aspects of his life and his nickname at work was 'Bullshitter,' 'I wonder why?' Fi thought. He had no scruples whatsoever and literally did not give a shit, who he shat on.

He was a man who embezzled money from his elderly parents by scamming them with lies too, thousands of pounds of their hard earned pensions, he was a man who failed to contribute to his marital home financially, he was a man who manipulated his whole family, parents, children and grandchildren against each other to ensure they were always on his side, he was a master manipulator. He was a man who ridiculed Fi for having medically retired (through her incurable, challenging illness) and accused her of financially burdening the family, when, virtually since the day she had met him, she had paid her way and then some! She bought everything in his life, every god damn thing, presents for his 23 family members for every occasion (including birthdays, Christmas, Easter, weddings, anniversaries etcetera, etcetera), every item of his clothes and footwear, (he was a scruffy, unkempt, unstylish man when she met him) and she had done a great job of styling and grooming him over the years. She also paid the mortgage and all the utilities, she bought the groceries, she paid for their holidays, she paid for their social life. Indeed Fi had paid for everything in his life during their time together. He was also an emotionally unintelligent man who didn't have a clue how to operate in a relationship or a marriage with any moral decency and his having at least two affairs (as she subsequently found out about 'Angela' too), together with using massage parlours, proved that beyond doubt. There was nothing he wouldn't lie about. Nothing. It was such a relief for Fi to know that the truth was finally out there, through her daughter telling his son Tom all the details of his Father's sickening behaviour and through the courts having such a comprehensive piece of evidence placed before them. He had tried to rob her of everything, absolutely everything, but he didn't quite manage to steal her self-respect and pride, which she was fiercely clinging on to.

Fi had embraced 23 people in this relationship and he couldn't even manage to embrace Fi and her two children but as Louise said, "who cares mum? we didn't need him to embrace us, we couldn't stand him, he's a knob, a first class knob, our truth is mum, we never liked him, we TOLERATED him, for you," she said, as she hugged her mum, "and when you go to court, there will be a crowd of us there right beside you, all your girlfriends and family ready to cheer and CELEBRATE you and your bravery at finally dealing with the scum bag as you have, kicking him to the kerb, big style!" before adding, "and after court, we'll be in a bar, chinking champagne glasses, in readiness for your new life". Cheers dears, Fi thought, as she tried to imagine that day, which wasn't, in all honesty, too far away and she agreed with Louise, why settle for being tolerated when you should be being celebrated!

The next task facing Fi was his personal belongings. What to do with them, she wondered. She was certainly aware of what other people thought she should do with them, through her many conversations and messages. One day, as she and Julie began the task of sorting out the bedroom and loft areas, with "The Power of Goodbye" playing on full volume and with Fi and Julie's 'singing' setting on full volume too, a wave of anger suddenly hit Fi, as the first of her “what to do with his shit” ideas came into her head! She began to sort his clothes into two separate piles. The first pile was for the ‘shite’ he had come into her life with five years ago, (shite sounded angrier than shit and she was feeling VERY ANGRY at this point) including his unstylish, well worn, damp smelling, must ridden clothes, coats, footwear, his underwear with holes in and his odd socks. This first ‘shite’ pile was placed in black bin bags along with all his younger sons belongings to be collected later by his family. The second ‘good’ pile was the clothes that she had bought him over the years, including designer suits and shirts, shoes, boots, vintage trainers, stylish jackets, cardigans, jumpers, designer boxers, silk socks, belts and cufflinks, on trend outerwear and scarves. The good stuff went into the boot of her car ready to go to charity shops, dress agencies, and to the recycling bins at the tip! No way was he going to be walking past her house, with his trollop on his arm and her getting the benefit of him being dressed in smart and trendy clothing at Fi’s expense! “No fucking way” she said to Julie, “no fucking way, indeed!” Julie replied as they gave each other a high five, had a girly hug and a giggle, as day one of ‘shite shifting’ was finally done! They opened a bottle of wine and clinked their glasses, “Who the fuck is Robert, Julie asked?”

The following day they got back into the loft and with the help of some ‘guy muscle’ from Julie’s husband Andy and Sam, one of Calum’s mates, they emptied it of his vast collection of football shirts, records, CD’s, dvd’s and computer games. His precious record player and amplifier somehow happened to bounce down the stairs, smashing to pieces as it went, whoops! How the hell did that happen? They all worked really hard cataloguing the bar codes from the CD’s, dvd’s and games onto a music website that bought such items. They then boxed them all up, ready to be collected in two days time. The vinyl records were sold on specialist websites and in local record shops and the unsaleable ones were given to charity shops. All his paperwork was shredded, including his birth certificate, driving licence and passport, which Fi had paid for.

His general crap, that was not fit for any purpose whatsoever, was also loaded into her car for the refuse tip, which incidentally, took two trips, such was the quantity of the 'shite' he had placed in the loft!

The next day as they were disposing of the said, 'shite,' one of the men working at the refuse site said to the girls, "Oh, there's some anger mixed in with that rubbish girls!" to which Fi smugly and proudly replied, "you bet there's anger in there mate, that's my ex husband going in those skips!" The site man replied, "Well we don't have a skip for recycling 'arseholes' girls!" and they all roared laughing. The drive home from the tip felt so cathartic and the radio was again blasting out on full volume to Hard Fi, "Watch me fall apart," Julie and Fi sang along with gusto as they pelted out the lyrics at the top of their lungs! "Could have been written for him, that song!" said Julie, as she pressed repeat and the girls laughed hysterically, as they sang it all again. It had been a good few days.

She loved him more than he loved her. She cared for him more than he did for her. She had hopes and dreams for "their together forever" more than he did for her and when the temptation presented itself to him he took a trip to the skip and threw her away.

CHAPTER 2

If only

Life eventually began to get back to normal for everybody in Fi's life. Louise went back to London, Calum was of course in Plymouth and Julie went back to her work at the school after the half term holidays. The personal visits from her coffee o'clock girls were noticeably fewer, as were the phone calls, text messages, emails and deliveries of flowers and cards. Her supporters were satisfied that healing was slowly beginning to happen in Fi's life and the world outside her front door carried on as always. Life couldn't suddenly go back to normal for Fi. Not yet anyway. Robert may have been able to throw his love for her away but she couldn't do the same, not with the same selfish disregard. It would take time and she would not be 'throwing' her love for Robert away, she would be letting it die. In her mind, she absolutely knew this had all happened for the best but she needed time to let go properly. She flipped in and out of the stages of her grief and the loss of the love she had felt for Robert. As she sat in her bedroom one afternoon crying, she was no longer sure if Robert had ever loved her, 'you don't behave like that to people that you love, do you?' she wondered. 'No, you don't,' she answered herself, 'that wasn't love from him,' she thought as she began to feel herself entering an angry phase of grief. She sat and tore up every photograph that reminded her of him as she reflected on their five years together.

As much as she would like to, she couldn't possibly rewind that five year tape, erase it and act upon the many 'if only's' that had come into her mind this past few weeks. If only she had not asked him if he were in a relationship and when he said no, asked him for a coffee date. If only, she had trusted herself when she told him 'he wasn't for her' six weeks after she met him. If only, she had not given him a second chance when he had popped a note through her door a few weeks later. If only, she had remained steadfast in her desire to end the relationship when she caught him lying about his three/six/seven kids. If only, she hadn't planned such a spectacularly unusual way to propose to him, on his birthday, during their romantic weekend away in the beautiful Lake District. If only, she hadn't married him. If only, she hadn't taken him back repeatedly, when he had repeatedly walked out on their love and their marriage, (as his way of attempting to resolve a conflict). Only to want to come home again the moment he had gone. If only. If only. If only. The list was endless but at the top of it was 'if only, she hadn't fucking met him,' but met him she had. If only she could get rid of this emotional turmoil but she knew that there could never be any 'e-baying,' 'charity shop donating' or 'dumping in skips' of the 'rubbish' that was inside her head, as there had been with his personal belongings. If only, it was that easy.

Everywhere she went in the house there were memories, his presence remained and yet his absence crushed her. How can somebody be present and absent at the same time? She honestly thought she would never be able to escape his ghostly haunting of her life and her abode. She couldn't understand the power of his aura emanating such negative emotions in her once happy home, why, she wondered, was he still so invasive? He hadn't had any influence whatsoever in any of the design aspects of her home, not because she hadn't wanted to include him in such decisions, because she certainly had but more for the reason that he was a yes man when it came to such matters, "Whatever you want love," "Yes it's really nice," "If you want that, you get it," "Have I ever stopped you getting what you want?" he would say when she asked his opinions on such matters. Robert was always a people pleaser about their home, be it a paint colour, wallpaper choice, crockery set, tap design, lampshade style, garden furniture buy." Whatever, whatever, whatever, he had no desire to participate but simply to enjoy the results when a project in 'their' home or garden was completed. She had tried so hard to include him in design and decor decisions because she wanted it to be 'their' home, even though he came into her life 11 years after she had bought it. He just wasn't interested in embracing the home making aspect of their relationship, stating frequently that he trusted Fi's design and decor choices. She was struggling, as part of this aftermath, to identify which aspects of their relationship he had embraced. So if the design matters were all her choosing why was his presence still so prominent? She broached this subject with Julie one day (who, despite her return to work, still maintained her daily contact with her friend in some form, even if it was just a "how are you chick?" text message) asking her, "why can I sense him here all the time Julie, sometimes I can even sense his smell in the house, am I mad?" Julie's response was as blunt as ever when discussing Robert, "The only smell you'll get from 'im, is eau de shite!'" which caused Fi to splutter her mouthful of drink back into her cup and they broke into a fit of giggles. They discussed the matter further and came to the conclusion, that it was the absence of her daily routine with Robert that was making his presence felt and so they hatched a plan to get a brand new routine to eradicate his negative aura and stinking 'eau de shite' out of her life and her home.

The first change was a small one but it made a huge difference to her mood. Fi put a radio in every room she went into and each morning she switched them all on when she got up, leaving them on all day until she retired to bed. Robert hated her favourite radio station and Fi admitted to herself that she had allowed him to dictate the station of choice in the house because in the end, she couldn't be bothered to keep resetting the radio station and so she chose instead to listen to her playlists and CD's when he had the radio on. 'Not anymore though,' she thought to herself. Her radio was 'back in the building' with a vengeance and as DJ's humour and new music echoed in each room, a different atmosphere and mood swept through the house and she began to find herself slowly emerging from the confusing fog. Fi found herself buying music again for the first time in years and she was enjoying using the repeat button to replay her favourite tunes, or to listen again to inspiring lyrics, probably, to the great annoyance of her neighbour's.

Her dance moves were re emerging too, as she boogied to whatever sounds bounced from the speakers and reignited the embers of her diminished appetite for a bop round the kitchen or an impromptu chasse in her lounge or hairbrush and dance combo in her bedroom. Over the coming days her heart began to dance a little too, as she fell in love with her music all over again. Oh how she had missed this 'radio lover' and she felt caressed increasingly each day, by the beauty of its varying moods. 'Dare I admit feeling moments of happiness again?' she pondered one day, as she listened to 'Heartbeat' by Andy C and Fiora (great name she mused) whilst she bounced around the kitchen waiting for her Nespresso machine to deliver her a cappuccino. 'Yes, I dare,' she told herself.

Decorating was also a plan and Fi set about revamping her bedroom, "No way can I sleep in that room again until it is no longer 'our' room," she said to Julie one night over a glass of wine. "Right, well we can get that done in a week, I'll get Andy to strip the walls for you and we'll get it done, boom boom, brand new room," and they laughed and clinked their glasses and toasted the prospect. Fi loved interior design and took the time to enjoy searching for inspirational ideas. She eventually settled on a theme and colour scheme and took great pleasure in the hard work it took in reaching her final decor decisions. Her 'Boutique Hotel' haven was admired by everybody who saw it but especially by the coffee o'clock girls, who gushed over the silver and white tattooed wallpaper design and the bold, dark blue ceiling. They "wowed" at the cracked glass shade that reflected a beautiful pattern onto the dark ceiling when lit and they sank onto her bed as the luxurious white bedding and silver accessories enveloped them. They felt the sensuousness of the silver silk curtains as they ran their fingers along the fabric and they marvelled at the creativity of the various mirrored textures displayed throughout the room before sitting on the thick white shag pile rug. They also admired the striking unfinished painting hanging on the wall. A treasured friend had died before he had had the opportunity to finish this wedding gift for Fi and Robert but she couldn't contemplate parting with it and had put it in the loft, hoping to be able to find somebody to complete it one day. It now took pride of place upon her bedroom wall. She no longer wanted a finished painting, Fi thought it was absolutely perfect as it was, depicting a faceless couple dancing and she felt it's significance in two ways. First, it was a reflection of broken love as the faceless couple danced and she took great comfort from the symbolism of not being able to identify Robert in that painting. Second, it also reflected of an unfound love between two people that she absolutely knew was on it's way to her. Even in her fragile state, in the aftermath of her own broken love she had absolute faith that real love had not eluded her altogether. "It's coming my way, I'll wait patiently as I know for sure that it's coming my way," she told herself and the girls as she proudly surveyed her efforts. "You need to get on some of the dating websites," said Julie, before suggesting, "Get on 'Plenty of Fish,' my friend has met a lovely fella on there," "plenty of sea monsters more like" replied Fi. "Well, you can't be wasting this room, it's a proper shag den now" said Julie and they all laughed as Fi added, "I 'kin wish" before adding, "give it time girls, no rush, I need to recover and get the 'Devon dickhead' out of my system," and they all burst into laughter again. It was no longer an unhappy memory ridden bedroom. It was now her den of peace. Who knew what that space would eventually become? They enjoyed a bottle of Prosecco and some Green and Blacks Organic chocolates and toasted two things, her beautiful room and the fading of the 'Devon dickhead' in her memory.

Fi made a mental note that her next project would be her son's bedroom but for now she had decided to devote some time to her physical and emotional wellbeing.

Concentrating on herself however, did not involve what she considered to be the usual sticking plaster approach to boosting your confidence, post relationship breakdown. She would not be getting a radical new haircut, or drinking herself into oblivion every weekend in a quest to relive her younger single life again, nor would she be revamping her wardrobe. No, she told herself. I like my lion's mane hair, I already consider myself stylish, I don't like getting pissed and I certainly don't like the hangovers afterwards.

Fi had health issues, which involved taking extra care with her dietary needs to manage her challenging illness. Improving her health was now high on Fi's agenda in her 'new me' plan. She joined a local gym, not because she wanted to throw herself with any gusto into a regime of weights, spinning or kettlebells classes in any post split effort to 'show dick head what he was missing'. No! She joined the gym to take leisurely walks on the treadmill and to participate in Pilates and yoga classes several times a week, with the specific aim of all the positive health benefits of exercising. She enjoyed choosing several gym and yoga outfits from her favourite gym wear designer and as well as feeling comfortable in them, she also felt as attractive as one can when wearing them, which was always an issue for Fi with her body dysmorphia. As reluctant as Fi had been to join the gym, she soon began to look forward to her three times weekly classes, followed by sessions in the Jacuzzi, sauna or steam room. It was only a matter of weeks into her gym participation before newfound friendships began to blossom for her and she was being invited to social gatherings outside of the gym. With each new day she felt stronger and stronger. As she drove home after one of her exercise sessions Joshua Radin sang 'Brand New Day' to her from her playlist and as usual when a positive song was playing, she pressed repeat and sang along to the lyrics as she thought to herself, 'Yes, I had to fall but it is a brand new day and I am definitely on the mend.'

Healthy eating was something that Fi was quite keen on prior to her marriage breakdown. She was an organic food fan, a reasonable cook and an enthusiastic baker and she had always fed herself and her family well. Fi was always happy to embrace new diet regimes, including, encouraging and supporting her daughter's almost lifelong vegan preferences, as well as trying immune-specific diets for herself. However, she knew she had really neglected her dietary needs after Robert had gone and she made a promise to herself to make an increased effort to make nutritious food regularly from now on. She visited her favourite Organic supermarket and stocked up on store cupboard essentials and a whole range of organic fruits and vegetables, as well as choosing some of their eco household and personal cleansing products too. "I am detoxing my house and myself," she told Julie in one of their daily contacts over a decaf skinny latte, accompanied by a vegan cake, (home-made of course). Fi had her own coffee shop at 'Number 9' now that she had her Nespresso machine and the 'coffee o'clock girls' all visited whenever they could.

Her time with the girls was a literally a lifesaver for Fi. They were her essential supply of 'feeling loved and cared for' now that her children had their lives away from her. It had been a tough year for Fi, losing all her loved ones in one way, or another. Louise left for London in June, Calum left for Plymouth uni in September and she had left dick head in Devon in October. The only love left within the four walls of number 9 now was her love for herself, which was seriously depleted in the aftermath of her receiving the series of shocking revelations. Her self-love 'meter' needed topping up and the coffee o'clock girls were exactly what best friends are in such circumstances, her lifesavers. What would she do without Julie, Tracey, Pauline, Jackie, Annette and Eve-Marie? All very different friends in terms of what they added to Fi's life but friends for life for sure. They were Fi's version of the 'Sex and The City' girls. She was also lucky enough to have long distance support too in her long time friend Kate, who lived in the Middle East. Fi had the added gift of having recently met a beautiful new friend from London named Jen, as well as having her wonderful cousin Jen, who lived in Newcastle, who all maintained phone, text message and social media contact with Fi. She knew she was fortunate, she had her fabulous girlfriends close by, she had her children and she had Kate Kuwait and the 'electronic Jen's' as she liked to call them, whom she seldom saw, but knew, were there for her too.

She relished an invitation with one or more (or on rare occasions with all) of the girls because it would always be a lovely event and she knew without doubt, there would be at least one belly laughing moment involved. There always was. It was on one of these occasions when Tracey, Julie, Jackie and Fi were off over to Chorlton in South Manchester for the day, to 'shite shop' and have lunch. Shite shopping is the girls reference to 'charity shop' shopping, whereby, they would go into the many charity shops and buy items, which were invariably other people's donations of 'shite!' They loved it and got many a bargain during these fun filled expeditions, picking up all sorts, from teaspoons, to potato ricers, to designer handbags, to shoes. Who knew what 'shite' they would find on these occasions, followed with a lovely lunch somewhere. What wasn't to like about these girly gatherings?

On this particular occasion they were meeting another friend Teresa, at The Lead Station on Beech Road, a particular favourite for all the girls, as it was a quirky independent bar that served fantastic food. It was Teresa's birthday and they were all gathering to celebrate. Upon arrival, they greeted their friend with hugs and Happy Birthdays, sat down at their table and ordered drinks. They then gave Teresa her cards and present, which she opened and promptly gushed over. A bracelet with 'True friends are the ones who never leave your heart' engraved on it, with a T charm attached. They all smiled and raised their glasses to the birthday girl as Julie made the toast, "Because we love you" and they all chinked glasses. Teresa thanked them all as she looked across and winked at Fi, knowing that she had found this unusual heartfelt gift. "What did Jim get you?" asked Tracey, "nothing yet, surprise when I get home," Teresa replied, "he'll be after HIS 'birthday surprise' more like!" said Jackie and they all burst out laughing. "Oh no, don't spoil my birthday, please!" Teresa responded, (not relishing the thought of any bedroom antics with her husband), as they all laughed some more. "Well get yourself 'birthday pissed' before you go to bed and think of some young hunk then?" said Julie, "I'm on 'Dry January,'" replied Teresa, (making reference to abstaining from alcohol for January and raising money for charity in the process), and Tracey quipped, "well can't you be dry at both ends then?" to which there was uncontrollable, tear rolling laughter for several minutes. Jackie then looked at Fi and said, "And you better hurry up and get on those dating sites 'an all, otherwise yours is gonna dry up and get dusty!" Tracey then added, "We should all be in the 'Rusty Crack' in Lanzarote with these fanny jokes," (referring to a bar) with the five of them then collapsing into incoherent mumblings and screaming laughter for what seemed like forever. Tracey was the first one to compose herself and asked with a puzzled look on her face, "Anyway how can you be on 'Dry January' in November?" Teresa promptly replied, "There's no way I am staying off the drink in January when I'm off to Lanzarote with the girls, so I'm doing it two months early!" and of course there was yet more laughter. They were on a roll for sure! "Will you be taking your dusty crack in the Rusty Crack?" asked Jackie and that was it, tears of laughter and Pirates of Penzance moments (girl speak for 'pee your pants') all round! When they stopped laughing, Fi revealed that she had once been in a bar in Spain called 'Bollocks' and the tears of laughter rolled yet again. The waiter eventually ventured over to their table and asked if they were ready to order, "I'd ask you to share the jokes ladies but I don't think that's wise," he said, "definitely not!" they all replied at the same time and set off laughing again.

No amount of anti-depression medication could help Fi's healing process like the support and laughter of her friends and that day as tears of laughter ran down her face, she knew she was healing nicely from inside, without the need for medication. Laughter with her best friends was her best medicine.

He was only ever going to have a temporary parking space in her heart and in her home

CHAPTER 3

Cock in a sock

"Hi chick, how are you?" said Julie, as she entered Fi"s house. "Not bad," Fi responded. "What's up? You look sad," Julie questioned, "I've just got off the phone from Eve-Marie and I was explaining to her about the loneliness of it all," Fi said. She sighed, "I know I have contact with various people virtually everyday Julie but the killer for me, is at night time, it's horrible, just horrible," said Fi as she wiped a tear from her cheek. "It's so lonely Jules, I can't wait for 8 o'clock at night and then I can give myself permission to leave the dogs, go to bed and hope that the loneliness leaves me as my sleep appears, IF? My sleep appears," she finished. Julie went over to her friend and held her, letting her know that in those few moments she was there for her. "It's driving me nuts Julie, I feel like I contend with difficulties really well during the day with all my distractions but the nights are really quite challenging for me."

Fi opened a bottle of alcohol free wine. She was on her health kick for a number of reasons, so alcohol was limited to protect her mood levels and her liver, (given her condition) and to assist with weight loss! As they walked into the lounge, Julie gushed at the major changes that were evident in the room, "Oh, wow, it's so cosy in here," she said, "it looks really homely, did you fancy a change?" she added, as she admired the new look. "To be honest, I could still feel him in here Julie, I could still see him sat right there on the sofa," she said as she pointed to his place, "and I was sick of seeing his trollop walk past my window virtually every bloody day!" They sat down as Fi continued, "It's like she is rubbing my face in it Jules, I have never seen her walk past here before I found out about them and then all of a sudden she's walking past here everyday! Now you're not telling me that that is not a deliberate attempt to goad me?" Fi asked. "Course it is," replied Julie, "well two can play at that game Fi," she added in an angry tone. Fi shot her friend a furrowed look before Julie continued, "The massage parlour news will be all round his workplace tomorrow, because I've told one of my colleagues, who is married to one of his colleagues about all his shenanigans!" "NO! You haven't?" gasped Fi as Julie nodded before replying, "too bloody right I have, she asked me how you were, so I told her what the dirty bastard has been up to, he won't get away with it Fi." She looked deep in thought before adding, "I can't physically batter him, for the never ending mental assault on you Fi, because that's not how it works, but I'll get him back for what he has done to you!" she added. "Oh I'd hate to be in his shoes with all the whispers in that place tomorrow," said Fi, as they both laughed at the thought of the fallout from the truth of his 'dirty dick' antics being swept around his work premises.

They chatted awhile about the necessities of each others lives before Julie said, "Anyway, I've been asking the girls at work about dating sites because one of them has met a really decent guy and she is so happy and I've got some names for you to try, so come on, get the laptop out and lets get looking!" Fi, raised her eyebrows at her friend, folded her arms indignantly and stated, "Firstly, I don't want a man and secondly, I would not be going on those dating sites to find one, even if I did!" to which Julie replied, "you don't have to date them, just get looking and maybe emailing them for a bit of company, come on, let's just have a look, if it's crap, it's crap, we'll give up, but lets at least have a look while we drink our wine!" As Fi opened up her laptop Redbone, "Come and Get your Love" came on her favourites selection, they burst into laughter before then bursting into song, whilst at the same time dancing round the room, enjoying the newly defined space. "See," said Julie, "karma is sending you love" before raising her glass and toasting the air, saying, "cheers karma."

Whilst sharing their bottle of wine they searched the recommended sites as well as looking online for forums covering dating agency safety advice. They checked out how the different sites worked, what were the pros and cons of each one and how they structured their subscriptions.

They laughed at some of the crazy names they came across with fuckaduck.com, hookmeandfuckme.com amongst many others, having them both in fits of laughter as they perused potential sites. There were even toy boy and sugar daddy dating sites! Fi decided on three very different sites from across the wide range on offer. She wanted to have access to a variety of men as well as fair pricing structures and to know how the money would be taken from her account and she wanted to be able to eliminate the crap ones as she went along. She decided to register herself on the chosen sites but she was not prepared to pay any fees at this stage until she was satisfied with the calibre of men she was communicating with on the sites concerned. She needed to be sure the site was safe, user friendly and value for money too, without having excessive subscription and cancellation penalties. She had, after all, seen first hand experience of two friends being hurt in very different ways on dating sites. One of them caught up in a fraud issue relating to mail order items and the second one experiencing domestic violence in her relationship. Fi was very wary and wanted to tread carefully in this minefield of online dating. However, upon registering, she found that some of the sites wanted her to subscribe immediately to allow her to 'access the men' and so reluctantly she opted for minimal subscriptions of between one month and three months dependent upon the site. They spent all evening collating her profile, choosing their words carefully to 'sell' Fi, without sounding desperate but making sure she was being completely honest about herself and what she was looking for in return. In the end she settled for a heading of **'I'mlookingformrniceguy'** and uploaded her 'script':

Friendly, happy woman who loves life. Wishing to find the same in a man. No baggage, my past has passed and I am looking forward to whatever adventures and curveballs life throws my way. I want to share life, love, laughter and the inevitable low times too with a man. I don't believe there is a ready made soul mate out there for me, I believe as with any other new friendship or relationship we will evolve into each other's soul mates. Why make it any more complicated than that?

I love interior and landscape design, cooking, baking, writing, nature (be it beach combing or walking in the woods), my family and my friends. A good belly laugh with the girls warms my heart and it would be fun to do that with a man in my life too. My social life consists of lunches with the girls, because I can, my classes in the gym several times a week, walking with my dogs in calming, interesting places and spending precious time with my children who have now flown the nest. I also

volunteer a couple of times a month. Kindness costs nothing and I try to give a little back to the world every day, as I am grateful for all that I have in life. Independent cafes, bars and restaurants interest me as socialising venues. I also love the 'jukebox' that is my vast music files and have a varied taste in music. Writing is a particular passion too. My interest in home and garden design has prompted me to restyle my kitchen and bathroom and landscape my garden in the last two years and I have just begun to restyle the upstairs of my home, keeping me very busy.

They then chose several photographs that were recent, which they felt reflected aspects of her personality and watched as they uploaded onto the various profiles. Within minutes she was getting a repeated pinging alert for emails and as well as the expected confirmation of subscription emails, she also had several messages from one of the sites telling her that several men wanted to meet her. "Already? Jeepers! 'kin vultures!" she said to Julie, "either that or flies round shit!" she added as she giggled. "Hey you! You're not shit! Far from it, you're gorgeous and these fuckers have all got to pass the Julie test. They're being vetted by me too!" replied her friend as they belly laughed again. They decided to go for a late night walk with the dogs and when they got back they made hot chocolate and had a quick check on the potential 'meets'

They logged onto the site, clicked the 'wants to meet you' file and clicked on the profiles individually:

Baldman1254 wants to meet you

Baldman was of course bald and 64, not that Fi had an issue with bald, far from it but there was just no attraction there at all, he had sent her a message saying, "hi," to which she politely replied, "thank you very much for your message but I don't think we will be compatible and I wish you luck in your search."

Manfromthecity wants to meet you

Manfromthecity was just not her type, not that she had a 'type' per se but there was no attraction there either. There was no message from him, he had obviously just clicked a button to 'meet her' and she promptly blocked him from any further contact. She wasn't here to waste her own, or anyone else's time.

Paul0987 wants to meet you **Paul0987** met the same fate.

Robertsmith27 wants to meet you

Robertsmith27 well this poor guy got an immediate verbal blasting as she stated incredulously! "And you can fuck right off with that name, some of us have morals you know! No way am I dating anybody called Robert, I don't care if he looks like George Clooney, he can do one!" They both laughed as Fi clicked the blocked button and switched the laptop off. They hugged each other as they always did when they said their goodbyes. Fi locked the house up and went up to bed, taking the cat with her, (who had taken to sleeping on Fi's bed each night, breaking one of her golden rules) but to be honest, she was grateful for the company.

The next morning she woke after a fitful night's sleep with memories of bad dreams about Robert and she told herself that he WAS a bad dream period! She had a busy day planned and so she jumped out of bed, turned the radio on and shrieked, “TUNE!” as The Avalanches, ‘Since I left you’ was playing. She had the volume on loud whilst showering. Since I left you I have certainly found a whole new world she thought to herself, as she sang along to the song. Simple lyrics that say it all she pondered as she dried her body and her hair. She then put on her make up and sprayed her perfume, dressed and placed her favourite bracelet on her arm. Today, she decided she would be wearing her ‘Mum’ charm to allow her to have her children near to her. She missed them both.

She went downstairs and completed her daily routine, just as she did, every other day. She fed the cat, changed the cat litter tray, emptied and reloaded the dishwasher, took the bins out, washed down all the work surfaces in the kitchen, vacuumed the two rugs and then steam mopped the floors downstairs. Fi then gave the dogs fresh water and biscuits, put the kettle on, brewed tea, took a brioche out of the cupboard, turned all the radios on and went and sat in the lounge. Every day. Same routine. Same order. It usually took her about 45 minutes and then she considered herself free to do whatever she wanted with her day. She wouldn’t be going to the gym today as she was helping her friend Jackie at the elderly peoples home. They were all going out for lunch and they needed volunteers to escort them there safely. Fi was happy to help her friend, as she loved seeing the pleasure the elderly people gained from such a simple outing as a pub lunch. What is more important though, she loved spending time with Jackie. They had been friends since they were teenagers when Jackie’s parents had bought the house next door to Fi. Fi’s stepmother had just died and Jackie and her family became a wonderful distraction. She had fabulous memories of the kindness that enveloped her life when her new neighbour’s arrived. Theirs was a house full of fun, laughter and food whenever she was in their company. She knew for sure, where Jackie got her kindness and sense of humour from and so she also knew today would be filled with fun, as always, whenever she was in her company. It would be a very welcome distraction away from her house, where the ghosts of the past few weeks still wandered.

As she sat listening to the radio, she checked her emails and found that she had the usual marketing crap, which she promptly deleted with a repetitive click, click, click into the trash bin. She also noticed she had a Facebook message from her beautiful friend Kim in New York:

Dear Fi, I'm thinking of you and hoping all is well. I am seeing some posts you have been making that would indicate that all is not OK. Would you enable me to catch up with your news? I'm really sorry for any trouble you might be having. I'm sending you good thoughts and big hugs, my friend.

Fi replied:

Hi Kim. My husband has been having an affair as well as accessing massage parlours. I have discovered he has had at least two affairs during our time together. It has been the craziest five years ever and to know he has been betraying me with one of my neighbours is particularly hard to stomach. I hold my head up high Kim. I was a good wife and he used and abused me from the get go. Again Kim, I failed to adhere to the red flag warnings that you and I have often discussed. I have had a private detective investigating them to get evidence, because I know he will attempt to lie in court and deny an affair as he always lies. I will get a quick

divorce due to his incessant, unreasonable behaviour. He really is the most, vile specimen I have ever met. I am hurting and I am lonely Kim BUT I am free and I know I will be okay. Thank you as always for your kindness. I hope all is well for you in NYC.

Kim responded promptly:

Dearest Fi:

I am so very, very sorry to hear your news. My words for your soon-to-be ex: return to sender, address unknown. You are right to want rid of him and to start healing from his chaos when you can. What he did is a reflection of who he is as a person and has nothing to do with you. Surround yourself with those who love you and seek out positive reinforcement. Sending you my love and good thoughts always. Kim

Fi sent a final message saying:

Thank you so much Kim as always. You are such a beautiful soul. Xx

She sighed as she drank the final dregs of her tea as a tear rolled down her face, a tear for her pain but a tear also for the beauty of such a kind and sweet woman as Kim. They had met on the internet and become firm friends, being supportive of each others struggles' over the years but Fi was so glad that Kim was now very happy, had a wonderful husband and a happy life and Fi was pleased for her beautiful friend whom she had never met face to face. One day she thought to herself, I will have the money to be able to go and see my lovely friend. Inside and out, she was so beautiful. How fortunate she was to have found her. She was so grateful for all her girls, both near and far. Fi also noticed that she had a few emails from the dating sites. They can wait, I want to savour the love and care contained in that heartfelt message from Kim and I want to wait for Julie to read them with me too, she thought. She got her coat from the hall, made a final readjustment of her make-up, kissed her dogs goodbye and got in her car to drive to her friends. It wasn't long before she was singing to her music as 'Se a Vida E, by The Pet Shop Boys' blasted out of the speakers. Such a happy tune and she hadn't heard it for ages and of course, it went on repeat for the twenty minute drive to Jackie's.

Jackie was happy to see her friend, as always. They hugged, swapped compliments of each others attire and Jackie promptly put the kettle on. Fi told her friend the latest news regarding herself and her recovery from the madness, her upcoming divorce and news of her children. Jackie then conveyed news of her own friends and family including an update on her little grandson. They chatted some more, before going over to the elderly peoples home. They slowly walked with them to the pub next door. Everybody enjoyed a hearty lunch as a treat from the proceeds of the autumn fair, which Jackie had helped to organise and much laughter was heard around the tables. It was a welcome change of scenery for the residents and an enjoyable social gathering that they had all looked forward to. Many of the elderly people were enthusiastic in their appreciation of Jackie and Fi's efforts and as the girls were leaving Oak House, a woman thanked Fi for giving up her time, to which Fi replied, "you are very welcome, this seems a lovely friendly home to live in," and the woman answered, "yes it is, but the problem is, there are more men than women here now," "oh," Fi responded, "sounds good to me, I think I'll put my name down," and she and

Jackie chuckled. The woman laughed before replying, "Don't bother, they'll be no good to you love, you have to lift them on and off!" and there was uproarious laughter throughout the communal lounge! Laughter, you can't beat it Fi thought, young or old, it's so infectious. She and Jackie said their goodbyes and Fi drove to meet Julie for a shopping trip en route home.

They met at a local shopping centre and went into their favourite shop, perused the racks of clothes, selected a few items each to try on and went into the changing rooms. "Do I really need it?" Julie asked Fi as she held up a lovely blouse, which she said she would wear for work. "Do we ever really need it?" asked Fi before adding, "it's retail therapy and girl time." Julie nodded and paid for the items and they then went into a coffee shop. Fi told Julie over the coffee and cake that she had a 'man selection' waiting at home in her inbox, Julie laughed and said, "You wish! If only you did have a man selection for your in box!" and the girls fell into a fit of giggles. Julie smiled at the thought of Fi 'shopping' for a man.

When they got back home they sat and 'sifted' through the list of messages:

Lalala21 had clicked the 'wants to meet you' button and the 'send a flirt' button, which sent an automatic "hi" message.

Lalala21 received a message from Fi thanking him for his time but she did not think they were compatible and wished him luck in his search.

Studman wants to meet you. **Studman's** profile image was one of him without a top on, stood in front of his bathroom mirror, taking a selfie, with a 'pretentious prick pose.' Fi said, "Dick" and blocked **Studman** from any further contact as she and Julie giggled.

Just as she was about to click on **Mark333's** profile, she received a notification that she had a response from **Lalala21**. He said, "You shouldn't judge a book by its cover."

Fi said to Julie, "I'm after a first edition best seller, not a second hand paperback! Cheek!" and she blocked **Lalala21.**

Mark333 had clicked the 'wants to meet you' button and sent a message, which, when she opened it read, "I'll cut to the chase here, I am after sex, are you available now?"

Mark333 was sent a 'polite' written message saying, 'no thanks.' In addition he got a much 'less polite' verbal message, (which he wouldn't hear of course) as Fi said to Julie, "Dirty bastard!" as she clicked the 'block user' button.

They sifted through another 6 emails and dealt with them by using either a block user or reply to message option if, it was someone they decided was a 'no chancer' but required a polite response. They had a similar experience on the next site before they decided to go on the Kiss or Miss App on Fi's phone which finds you potential matching profiles near to where you live. If you like the look of them you click kiss and if you don't like the look of them you click miss. If they've 'kissed' you too, then great, you get a 'puckering lips' cartoon onscreen, with a kissing sound and then you can message each other:

Tony, 47, from Runcorn, likes drinking and having a laugh and was displaying a profile picture of himself with a big fish. **MISS.**

Scott, 51, from Sale, likes motorbikes and Sale sharks and was displaying 3 profile pictures of his two motorbikes and a dog. **MISS.**

Aaron, 102, from Frodshaw, doesn't like anything according to his blank profile and was displaying pictures of a man in his early 20's. This was obviously, just young men uploading each other's pictures. **MISS.**

Robert, 54, from….. Fi didn't give a shit, **MISS.**

Dave 63, from….. "Who cares, too old for me," said Fi, **MISS.**

Bob 52, from Leeds, likes cinema, eating in or out and displaying pictures of himself with his 'cock in a sock' charity picture and his midriff hanging over the sock! **MISS.**

Julie and Fi were by now crying with laughter at some of the sights they had just seen, "Unbelievable, and you think I'll get a decent guy from all this shit?" Fi asked, before adding, "NEVER! I'd be better off at the Post Office on pension day, at least I might find one with a bit of money! Jeepers Jules," as she shook her head and they laughed some more. Welcome to the world of Internet dating.

She'd much rather be 'single and sane' than 'partnered and in pain'

CHAPTER 4

Cheeky bidders

As the days passed her by, within her routine of dog walking, gym sessions, coffee o'clock dates and the occasional shopping trip for treats, Fi tried to reintroduce some of her hobbies and passions back into her life as part of her recovery process. She began looking for inspiration for her next decor project, which was to be her son's bedroom. She was aware that although she was enthusiastic to start this major project, she was also saddened at yet another potential 'loss' in her life. That had been Calum's room for 15 years since she bought the house and the prospect of claiming the space for a different purpose was quite a wrench to contemplate. It was not only a reminder that she was emptying the nest, by having lost her children on their own life journeys but she was re-feathering the nest too, which meant getting rid of the remains of his presence in the room and that added to her sense of sadness. Still, she felt that if she was to move on in her head and her heart, she must also move on and revamp her surroundings too, therefore overhauling all aspects of her life.

After giving it some thought, Fi decided she would be reclaiming the space for her true passion, writing! Within her role in the Criminal Justice Service, Fi was the author of hundreds of pieces of work from that period in her life but recently, she had come to realise that since medically retiring from work two years ago, she had missed this almost lifelong passion so much. It also hit her with such a stark realisation (as she planned her new space in her head), that she had somehow lost her way along this particular leg of the journey of her life and she no longer knew what her purpose was. Her 'only' purpose in life after she retired, seemed to have evolved into that of being a devoted wife and caregiver to the unappreciative masses but that role had been snatched from her now and she reminded herself again, that she was so glad that her marriage was finally over. As she stood in her son's room, she recognised how much of a mess her marriage really was, how unhappy she was, how much of her life had been wasted on Robert and his family and how much she despised him. She smiled to herself and in her mind she raised an imaginary glass to 'The Dickhead and The Trollop,' saying, 'Cheers you wankers! You deserve each other. Meeting him was a mistake, a huge mistake!' She was filled with hatred for them both and despised these inevitable intrusions into her inner peace but also accepting that they were necessary aspects of the long haul to healing a deep and troublesome wound. At this moment she was okay with her hatred and the fact that she had no room whatsoever for forgiveness.

Fi made herself an herbal tea and opened her laptop and set about searching for ideas for the creation of a mood board for her writing room. She researched fabric swatches, paint colours, accessories, textures and furnishing options to bring the theme together. This was the first part of her redesign project and she was delighted with her eventual final choices as she set about ordering samples and swatches online. Fi then contacted her builder for quotes for ripping out the old built in furniture, re-plastering the walls and building her a new desk. She also got quotes from an electrician to redirect electrics for her lighting, computing, printing and internet needs, a decorator for decorating, a plumber for plumbing in a stylish new radiator and a final quote from a local blind company. When she had negotiated the prices with her team, she then set a date for the work to begin early in the New Year. She was glad of this new focus and was looking forward to her creative den emerging. Fi was very excited about the prospect of what she might create in this space.

Fi also tried her hobby of reading again, to reignite the embers of her diminished sense of purpose and self-worth but she found it hard to absorb the words and often found herself rereading pages, to concentrate on the subject matter. This was a disappointment to her, as books had always been a huge source of pleasure in her life. She even tried audio books, but that too proved difficult and so she shelved the books both metaphorically and in reality, until she was ready.

Her efforts at renewing her interests in sewing and craft work were equally thwarted, with too many ruined projects amongst her efforts and so she made the decision that they too, were to become shelved hobbies for now. She did however enjoy her cooking and baking and she continued to make herself nutritious food nearly everyday, as well as baking scrumptious vegan cakes and cookies, which she shared with Julie's family and her immediate neighbours. She also helped her daughter's friend Felicity make cakes for her celebration cake business, enjoying the distraction and challenges of sculpting things with fondant icing, which really fed into Fi's flare for creativity. Generally she was progressing slowly and she acknowledged that given that Robert and his entourage had taken five years to chip away at her self worth, she wouldn't get that back overnight. It was taking its time to reemerge and she accepted that. It was all part of the journey back to herself. She was glad she had morals. She was glad she had the emotional capacity to plummet to the depths that she had, because it meant she had great self-awareness and therefore the emotional intelligence needed to learn the required lessons from this relationship in order to climb out of the vortex.

Fi and Julie continued to meet as often as they could, checking the dating site information together as and when they had the opportunity to do so. Of course there was often laughter when they did, at some of the sights that appeared on the sites! As well as cocks in socks, they perused images of men posing with sedated tigers or crocodiles with their mouths tied trying to look macho. Men with varying sizes of fish, that, they had supposedly caught. “Why would you do that?” asked Fi, “that is surely the equivalent of a woman who bakes for a hobby, posing with different sized loaves of bread on their profile pictures?” she added questioningly, before shaking her head in dismay, before adding, “Who cares? For fucks sake!”

Mountains also seemed to be a theme with the men! As there were men climbing mountains, men on top of mountains, men on top of snowy mountains, men on top of mountains in Lycra, men on top of mountains in Lycra with their bikes. Fi also noticed that cars were often used in an attempt to lure women into their particular worlds, with images of men next to their cars, on their cars, in their cars, washing their cars and even under their cars! Again Fi was aghast with some of the images in front of her. There was also the ‘Jim at the gym,’ gallery, as Fi nicknamed every man pictured at a gym, which made them both giggle as they perused images of the men in the gym, men in changing rooms at the gym, men using equipment at the gym, men with bags at the gym and quite frankly a fair few men with sags at the gym too!! There were images of lairy men with beer bottles or cans in their hands, men in fancy dress, men sticking their tongues out, men running, muddy men running, men in half a wetsuit, men in full wetsuits, men under water in their wet suits, men on holiday in hotel rooms or sat at a restaurant table (probably their last holiday with their wife/partner) with the next picture of them wearing the same outfit with the wife or partner cropped out of the picture!. “Jesus,” said Fi on one of these many ‘flicking sessions’, “I’m supposed to be hunting for Mr. Right and all I can see is Mr. ‘kin Not Rights!” she laughed, before Julie replied, “he’s out there somewhere Fi, there is someone for everyone!” “Well I’ll tell you what Jules, I’m getting some tips from my ‘Sex And The City’ Dvd’s, at this rate, ‘cos this is shite”, replied Fi, before adding, “I’m fussy me Julie and all I’m seeing is desperate dicks!” as they laughed together at some of the rogues gallery who had viewed Fi’s profile. One hundred and sixty eight of them so far on this one site alone and she hadn’t been attracted to a single one of them. There was a never-ending chorus from them both, as they regularly perused the gallery, of, ‘no way’, ‘fuck off!’ ‘Too young’, ‘too old’, ‘cheeky fucker’, ‘high hoper’, ‘not bad’, ‘not good’, ‘knob’, ‘dirty bastard’, ‘ugly bastard’, ‘what the fuck?’ With the very occasional, ‘Ooh la la,’ or a ‘he’s not bad!’ thrown into the mix. They laughed so much to the point where they would be encouraging each other to stop because they were going to have ‘Pirates of Penzance’ moments.

If? And it was a big IF, Fi and Julie managed to get beyond the bizarre gallery selection, and click on an ‘Ooh la la’ or an ‘he’s not bad’ profile picture, then the next phase was sifting through the written profiles posted online. Fi was a reasonably intelligent woman and she was hoping to meet someone of at least the same level of intelligence to throw into the mix of a possible relationship, but the chances were slim, judging from most of the 'adverts' that men were posting about themselves. Amongst their bizarre 'selling credentials', potential suitors were posting headliners including, 'are you the sugar for my tea?' 'Do you wanna be mine all mine?' 'Looking for me? 'cos I'm looking for you', 'Hey baby, I'm all yours', 'come and get me', 'drinks are on you', 'stop searching in the haystack, I'm your needle,' 'red light says stop here!' 'Try before you buy.'

As if the headliners weren't bad enough, the 'looking for' criteria was just as cringe worthy in most cases, with suggestions of men looking for, 'someone who drinks, smokes and likes fishing', 'someone who likes climbing mountains', 'someone into motorbikes and fast cars', 'someone who wants to travel regularly to my apartment in Magaluf' 'someone who wants to come to my caravan at weekends', 'someone who likes going to the races,' 'someone who likes boating,' 'someone who likes bird watching,' etcetera, etcetera. "Boring, boring, boring, yawn, yawn, yawn, where are the interesting men?" asked Fi, taking a sip of her wine before adding, "I like doing some of those things but you're supposed to be selling yourselves to me here!" she shouted at the screen one evening in her frustrations at the lack of imagination in some of the profiles.

They laughed again at some of the amusing messages sent to her inbox, from straight forward requests for sex, through to will you meet me in the blah blah retail park for a coffee, 'cos my bus stops near there, too cocky younger men, as well as hopeful older men putting in a cheeky bid for a date. During one of their flicking sessions Fi had an epiphany but she just couldn't get her words out, as she sank into a fit of giggles, before she eventually managed to inform Julie, "We've gone from shite shifting to shite sifting" and they both collapsed laughing. A proper, belly laughing, tear rolling session. "Stop it you! I'm going to piss my pants," Julie said.

They were just about to log out of shite sifting for the day when 'ping.' The new message flashed in the corner of the screen, saying, **Lovingismyforte** has sent you a new message. Both the girls simultaneously said, "ooh!" and when they clicked on his profile picture Fi said, "double, double ooh!" and burst out laughing again. He was gorgeous. Correction! He was 'FUCKING' gorgeous!

Lovingismyforte is 51 and from Liverpool.

"I can do Liverpool," said Fi, "it's only up the road, not too far. An hour max. Used to do it all the time for work," she added. To which Julie replied, "Shut up babbling and read what it says about him!" Fi and Julie couldn't check his profile quick enough, reading together out loud in an almost undecipherable chatter, as they scrolled down the page squealing with delight as the image of this beautiful man and his beautiful profile jumped off the page at them! It read:

I am a successful businessman with my own business as a specialist antiques dealer. I will soon be retiring and my daughter will then take over my business and I will be free to concentrate on living my life, hopefully with a lovely woman. I am a happy man, with a good sense of humour, who loves to laugh. I love my life and the people in it but I miss having someone special in my

life since my divorce 8 years ago. I still believe love is possible and I am seeking a long-term relationship and hopefully my partner for life. I'm a 'young at heart,' romantic guy, whilst also keeping my feet firmly on the ground until a relationship has fully blossomed. I am also passionate and chivalrous. I strive to be a gentleman and take pride in treating women with dignity and respect. I like to treat other people, as I myself would like to be treated. I love to travel as often as I can and I am fortunate enough to be able to do so with my work. I enjoy researching and watching documentaries about shipwrecks and I am an active diver. It is my true passion. I love to read with a wide choice of reading material at my disposal. Music is everywhere with me too and I do have a very varied taste in music. I like to try new activities when I get the opportunity and I think of myself as an adventurous person. I am definitely looking for a loving, harmonious relationship to make my life meaningful and complete. I would like to meet a successful, kind, caring, responsible woman, with a sense of humour. It sounds simple but it's very important that if she makes me smile at the thought of seeing her, she may be on her way to winning my heart. Like everybody else, I am on here to get off here.

"Arrrrrrrggggghhhhhh!" squealed Fi, followed by, "oh my giddy fucking god, Julie, he is gorgeous!" "Just a bit chick, just a bit!" replied Julie, nodding her head. Fi squealed again and said in a very questioning tone, "And he has sent me a message!" "HIM, THERE, has messaged me! What the fuck?" she added pointing to the screen. She clicked onto her inbox on the dating site and there was his gorgeous avatar looking at her again, dark haired, tanned, beautiful grin, stunningly dark eyes, nice casual shirt, opened slightly, with a hint of a hairy chest and a thick silver chain around his neck, "Wowsers, wowsers, wowsers Julie, just look at him, I can't get over him, he is off the scale gorgeous", said Fi. She clicked onto the 'envelope' symbol next to his avatar image to open her message, which read:

11 November 2013 12:15

Hey, you are a beautiful woman and your profile made me smile. I can hear the happiness in your words. Wondered if you would like to chat. Bran.

They both squealed again and 'high fived' each other, Fi was physically shaking. "Oh my god, I need a drink," she said and promptly went to the fridge and opened more wine for herself and Julie. She came back and they clinked their glasses. Fi was thoughtful for a moment and said, "Now I know it is only a message and not a proposal of marriage but to me it might as well be, because THAT (and she pointed to her laptop again), has made my day!" She thought some more before adding, "I'm repeating myself Jules but a gorgeous guy, has liked my profile enough, to want to send me a message! Oh my fucking god!" To which Julie replied, "Too right he has!" before adding, "Robert, who the fuck is that Twastard?" and they collapsed in a fit of raucous laughter. When they had composed themselves enough Julie said, "I meant to say twatting bastard and it came out as twastard," and they both set off laughing with the tears rolling down their faces again. "That's his new name now Jules," said Fi as they kept repeating it like naughty toddlers, "Twastard, Twastard, Twastard!" they said, as they laughed some more.

"Are you replying then?" Julie asked Fi, when they had calmed down. "Not yet, I don't want him thinking I'm too keen!" Fi replied, "I'll take the dogs out and then reply when I come back," "okay, well I'm off for the night now, so I'll text you from work tomorrow, to see if he has replied," said Julie. "Okay, night Julie and thank you," said Fi and she set off giggling again for no particular reason, other than she was in a giddy mood. Julie walked up the drive and turned to Fi and shouted, "No more shite sifting, I hope!" and they both roared laughing again.

Fi was glad of the fresh air as she walked the dogs. She took deep breaths and composed herself as she did a double circuit of the local park, to tire the dogs out, before then choosing to walk the long way home, giving her time to think. When she got back into the house, she locked the front door, removed her coat and made a Nespresso, before going back into the lounge where she sat down at the dining room table and opened her laptop.

The dating site was still open on her desktop and she logged back in with her password, clicked onto his profile again and opened his images. There were three pictures, a larger version of his avatar which showed what she had admired before, but in much greater detail, 'wow' she thought to herself, 'he really is absolutely gorgeous'. She then spent time looking at an image of him in what appeared to be a car showroom or at a car exhibition, she wasn't quite sure which. He was standing with another man (who in all fairness was also very handsome). They had their arms around each other facing the camera and they were both smiling. He looked a happy man. The vehicle was some sort of American 'monster' jeep type of vehicle and she thought to herself, 'he probably has that type of vehicle for collecting and delivering all his antiques'. The final image was of him standing outside a grand building, it was a lovely sunny day and again, he had a healthy tan, he was smiling on this picture too and she noticed he had lovely teeth. Fi was a stickler for 'nice' teeth having been a dental nurse for 14 years she noticed 'nice' teeth straight away when she met people and she noticed 'not nice' teeth even sooner! In this particular image he was wearing a suit with a shirt and tie and he looked good, very good she thought as she nodded her head at the screen in front of her. She linked her hands as if to pray and rested her chin upon them as she sat awhile, taking in the three images, 'he is so handsome,' she thought and 'I don't know why I am thinking this but he looks sincere, how can you think that from an image?' she asked herself, but she did. She just had a feeling that he was a 'really nice' guy. Time would tell, she told herself as she opened his message to her and clicked on the reply button.

She wrote:

Hi Bran, thank you for your message and your kind words regarding my images and profile. Your profile made very interesting reading too and I also had a smile or two as I read it and viewed your images. I have to say this. You are a very handsome man! It would be great to chat. Fi.

She pressed 'send message' and went over to the sofa and curled up on it with her dogs as she drank her coffee and let her mind wander, wondering where his business was and where in Liverpool he lived. She imagined it maybe a beautiful waterfront apartment given that his images and his business description conveyed that he probably had money. Not that she was after money but he wouldn't live in a crap area would he, if he did have money. He certainly oozed class in his clothing choices. He was very well groomed. 'Oh well,' she thought to herself again, only time will tell. She switched on the TV and caught up with the day's news events for half an hour before deciding she was really tired and after locking up the house, she said goodnight to her dogs and went upstairs to bed.

The next day she was up early as she was off to get her annual flu jab from her GP and to ask for a sexual health check after explaining 'Twastards' history to him. He gave her instructions of where to go to get completely checked and then he said to her, "remember years ago Fiora when you told me you were paying for private therapy after that tragic family issue?" "Yes," replied Fi, with a quizzical look on her face, "well!" her GP replied, "it was worth every penny because you should be very proud of yourself, to go through what you have, at the hands of your husband and sit here with me, a matter of weeks later, as psychologically sound as you appear today, well done Fiora!" he added. She was astounded, "Thank you," she responded, "I don't know what to say to that," he smiled at her and responded, "say nothing, walk out of my surgery and hold your head up high!". She stood to leave in a state of disbelief at such a lovely compliment and said, "Thank you so much doctor," and as she closed the door behind her, she heard her doctor say, "pleasure." She was gob-smacked and elated at the same time, I'm doing fine she thought to herself, absolutely fine.

When she got home she had a quick breakfast of banana and goats milk yoghurt with a drizzle of honey and a cup of hot water with lemon and ginger. She quickly showered, changed into her gym gear, went for a walk with the dogs and dropped them back off home before getting into her car and driving to the gym. She sang along to Tegan and Sara, 'I was a fool,' as it played on the radio, she loved that song and she loved the video too. The girl was chucking her lovers' shite out after their break up! 'Sounds familiar, and yes I am holding my head high and it feels so good!' she thought to herself. She enjoyed her Pilates classes and rushed back home afterwards to meet Tracey for lunch. "6 weeks!" said Tracey incredulously, "is that all it is? It seems like forever Fi," she added as Fi prepared lunch for them whilst conveying the doctor story to her friend. "I know," said Fi, "and I haven't missed HIM Tracey, not one bit, he leaves such a bad taste in my mouth and he has brought so much crap into my life over the years," she added, "I missed the routine of him being around but I am more upset at the betrayals. It was such vile behaviour, but I really don't miss HIM or his baggage at all," she added, before Tracey responded, "I bet you don't, he's gross!" Tracey went onto tell Fi her own news, as they hadn't seen each other for a while and she couldn't wait to see Bran's images as Fi opened her laptop, logged into her profile on the dating site and enlarged the images for Tracey to see. "Jeeeesus!" Tracey exclaimed, "Wow, HE IS WOW, absolutely wow," before she laughingly added, "if you don't want him, I'll 'ave him. Oh my god Fi, he is so handsome," she said, enlarging his images. Fi was beaming, "I know!" she replied. "Well, get checking that bloody message while I am here," Tracey exclaimed as she noticed there was a new message waiting, "oh shit, I hadn't noticed that" said Fi as she opened the message, which read:

12 November 2013 13:16

Hi Fi, thank you for messaging me back. How lovely that you wish to communicate with me, I very much look forward to seeing where this may lead for us both. Is your name Fiona then? My name is Branimir but I prefer Bran as my grandfather preferred to call me that and I was very fond of him. Anyway, how are you doing on this site, how long have you been on it and how many dates have you had or are there too many to count? I would not be surprised, as you are a very attractive woman and you compose yourself well on here, unlike many of the women, I am afraid to say. What are you up to on this bright sunny day? Bran. I have attached another photo for you.

"Awhh, Tracey, he sounds lovely doesn't he?" said Fi, looking up at her friend from the computer screen. "He does sound lovely," said Tracey. Fi decided she would reply later when she was alone, giving herself time to think about what she wanted to say. She clicked on the image and Tracey gasped and said, "Bleeding 'ell Fi! He is so handsome! LOOK AT HIM!" as they both looked at the head and shoulders image of him in a pink striped shirt. It looked like he was sitting at a picnic table in a public space and he was cradling a little dog. Fi zoomed the image so they could look closer and as she admired his handsomeness, she turned to Tracey and smiled at her friend. "WHO the fuck is Robert?" asked Tracey exaggerating the Who. Fi then conveyed Julie's new name for him and there was raucous laughter coming from Fi and her friend again, before Fi closed the laptop and they chatted some more about anything and everything, as they so often did. Tracey left about 4pm to go back to work.

Later that evening Fi logged into the dating site and sent the following reply:

Hi Bran, thank you for your message, kind compliments and your photograph. The handsome and happy image was lovely and you don't look so bad yourself! I jest of course! The puppy is cute and you look happy and handsome.

My name is Fiora, which is a variation of Fiona. My wonderful Granny Rosie referred to me as Fi when she first held me and I have always preferred it to my full name. I have had a fun day at the gym and having lunch with my friend and I am now going to rest and watch a film, it's been a busy day. To be perfectly honest, I am not enjoying the Internet dating scenario. I liken it to 'ebay for humans', with some watchers, some pestering people asking for unnecessary information about me with some cheeky bidders too! I have, never ever had to 'shop' for a man and I must admit, I don't like it. I have not had any dates, just messaged a few people but nothing came of any of those communications. Enjoy the rest of your day and I look forward to hearing from you. Fi.

It's more than just dating

It's holding hands and kissing

It's accepting each other's flaws

It's about being yourself but finding happiness with each other

It's about seeing an imperfect person perfectly

CHAPTER 5

Mr. Antique

The next morning she felt tired and decided to have a lazy day, her body was telling her to rest and she knew from experience the requirement to listen to her body. She carried out her morning ritual of domestics to claim the rest of the day for herself. She liked a neat, tidy house with the laundry and all her 'house' chores completed before she embarked on the rest of her day. She felt that it added structure to her life and was good for her recovery to have a daily routine. After completing all of her tasks she then brewed her decaf tea and made hot water and lemon and helped herself to a vegan blueberry muffin from yesterday's baking session. She savoured the simple breakfast and decided to have a catch up day with some of her recorded TV programmes and films. She knew she was in for a cosy day. 'Lovely' she thought, as she got comfortable on the sofa with her big plump cushions, her blankets, her laptop and with her dogs curled up beside her. She unlocked her phone to check her emails and social media messages and noticed that she had a message from Bran on the dating website. 'Ooh,' she thought, as she opened it to reveal the following message:

13 November 2013 10:42

Hey Fi, how lovely to hear from you again. I loved your humour, you made me smile, and making me smile is a big bonus for me. I believe good relationships should contain smiles, humour and laughter. I too have just messaged a few people on this site but did not feel

enough connection to continue the conversations. I am searching for somebody very special and I am happy to wait to find the right person. I find the delay factor in the messaging system on here frustrating and was wondering if you wanted to chat off the site. Let me know how you feel about that. Bran

How did she feel about chatting off the site she asked herself?

Just then she had a text from Julie:

Julie: Have you heard from Bran?

Fi: Yes, he's want's to communicate off the site. Should I be worried?

Julie: You can never tell he seems a decent guy at this stage. I can't see any harm chatting by email at this point, are you worried?

Fi: No, not with just swapping email addresses.

Julie: Go for it then! Coffee later? X

Fi: Yes, I'll need to let you know the details. X

Fi replied to Bran for the last time on the dating site: 13 November 2013 11:01

Hi Bran, I agree with you it's worse than having a 'satellite link' phone call, communicating on here! My email address is Fioraburton@mail.com

Hope to hear from you soon. Fi.

She indulged herself in her lazy day, enjoying the lack of pressures. No gym, no lunch dates, just an appointment with nothingness, she loved it! She had her fill of skinny decaf cappuccinos and some of her Green and Blacks Organics mini chocolate selection. She watched continuous episodes of one of her hero's 'Oprah,' followed by her favourite film of the moment, The Holiday. Can you really fall in love in two weeks she wondered as she joined the character 'Amanda' in dancing frantically around her own lounge to the sound of 'The Killers, When You Were Young,' only to be startled by a loud knocking on the window. There stood Julie pointing her finger and raising her eyebrows at Fi in a questioning look? "Oh fuck, you caught me in a mad moment" said Fi, as she opened the door and the girls walked into the kitchen. "Coffee o'clock Jules?" asked Fi as she took the cups down from the shelf before continuing, "I've made your Bradley some banana muffins," she said handing her friend a tin containing some of her recent baking efforts.

The girls went into the lounge and Julie asked, "Have you heard from Bran?" to which Fi shrugged and said, "I don't know, I've not checked since this morning when I sent my email address to him," Julie encouraged her friend by saying, "well! Check now while I'm here!" Fi picked up her phone and said, "I've got 16 emails," she opened her inbox and quickly scanned the contents, "shit, shit, shit, Jules, this must be him, I don't recognise the email address, oh shit, I've got a message, Jesus, my heart is racing," she opened the mail from Branimir Rodrigues which read:

13 November 2013 15:10

Hey Fi, How are you doing? This is Bran from the

dating site. This is just to check on you and to know how you are doing? Thanks for the message and it will be much better this way. Do let me know if this gets to you... Have a good Thursday! Bran

Julie smiled at her friend, Fi was in a kind of semi numb state, almost disbelieving, not that it was anything exceptional, it was a simply worded email but she felt something. She just couldn't possibly explain what. Julie asked, "Are you okay Fi?" "Yes fine, just got the weirdest feeling, don't know how to explain it Jules, I'm not even going to try. Weird!" she replied. They read the mail together again and as she reread the email address, Fi said, "Bran. What a great name." The girls chatted about Fi's lazy day, Julie's house decor plans and other trivia, before Julie got up from her seat and said, "I'm off to make tea for the boys," before adding, "Andy's not home tonight, come round in a bit if you like." "Will do, thanks love," replied Fi, as she kissed and hugged her friend. She locked the door and was about to put on her music whilst she did some hand washing in the kitchen, when she remembered she hadn't replied to Bran. She opened his email and clicked on reply:

13 November 2013 16:04

Hello Bran, how are you? Thank you for your email. Yes, I am sure it will be much easier to chat on here now. There is just one problem with emailing though I don't get to see your handsome pictures as I type! I have had a busy day doing nothing! I had coffee with a friend and just enjoyed a rare day of completely relaxing. It has been lovely. What did your day entail? I hope to hear from you soon. Regards. Fi.

Fi fed the dogs, showered before putting on some cosy gym gear and taking the dogs for a walk. She returned home to find she had a text message from Julie:

Julie: Dinner's ready at No 11 in 10 mins. X

Fi: Thank you! X

Before she left she checked she had her phone with her, as she was expecting Louise to call and she then went to Julie's house. They had a lovely meal of Italian chicken, vegetables and potatoes. After she had eaten her food, Fi said, "That was lovely Jules, can't believe you made it so quickly!" to which Julie replied, "I didn't, the pinger did it!" and they both laughed at Julie's reference to her microwave. After clearing the dishes away they had just sat down to watch TV and chat, when there was a scribbling noise coming from Fi's phone, "What the 'kin 'ell's that?" asked Julie, "it's my email alert tone, it's the sound of someone signing their signature!" replied Fi. 'I thought it was a fucking mouse," laughed Julie as Fi opened her email. "Well! Is it from Bran?" Julie quizzed. "Shit, yes," replied Fi, as she opened the mail to reveal his latest words, which she read aloud to her friend:

13 November 2013 19:30

Hello again, Thanks for taking some time to respond to my email, I really do appreciate it. I am home at the moment, also trying to relax, just got back from Cardiff earlier today. I will send you some photos on here, which I also expect you to reciprocate because I wouldn't want to go to the dating site all the time to see your pretty face. In the meantime why don't we get more acquainted, tell me more about you, your family,

lifestyle, job and interests.

Speak soon. Bran

Fi felt giddy. Why? She asked herself. She also felt sick and told Julie so. "Why?" asked Julie, "I don't know, probably nervous energy," Fi replied. She sat and thought awhile before suggesting, "Maybe it's mixed emotions, end of one, beginning perhaps of another?" She answered. She thought some more before adding, "This might sound mad Julie but I feel like I am betraying Robert," Julie's jaw dropped and her startled eyes spoke for her, but she vocalised what she was thinking anyway. "You what! Are you kidding me? He wasn't worried about betraying you, when he was sticking his dick in the bacon slicer!" and they set off howling laughing at Julie's reference to Peter Kay the comedian and his bacon slicer joke. "Julie, what would I do without you?" Fi asked. " Likewise bestie," Julie replied and they hugged each other before Julie added, "now piss off and let me have a peaceful bath and don't you dare EVER! Have any qualms about moving on from 'Twastard'" she said, emphasising the name 'Twastard' just because she liked the sound of it. "I am still so angry with him Fi, I hope I bump into him because when I do, I'll have him," she said, before pausing and continuing, "I don't care where it is and how I humiliate him. I hate him, for what he has put you through and I'll have him." There was so much anger in her voice but even more pain in her heart for her friend as she allowed a tear to roll down her cheek. As Fi opened the front door to leave, Julie said, "Now get chatting to Bran and keep moving forward and don't let him or his crappy entourage poison 'ANYTHING' in your life ever again!" Fi entered her own home, locked up and sat down and replied to Bran:

13 November 21:42

Hi Bran, Thank you for your message. I am sat here relaxing, listening to the wind outside and I am glad to be cosy and warm. I am drinking my favourite decaf coffee, eating cake (I love vegan baking) and flipping between the TV and my emails. I live alone now as my children have left home. I have a daughter who is 25. Her name is Louise and she is a delight. She is beautiful, full of fun and very intelligent and a 'get go' girl. She has a degree in photography, a teaching qualification and she was head hunted by her current employers to the head office in London and she is now the photography manager for their website. She has a very active job based around style and fashion and is a very creative young woman. She is a lovely daughter and watches out for her mum all the time. I speak to her nearly every day and I am going to London later this month for a few days to see her. Can't wait! I also have a son Calum, who is 19, who has always been sports crazy since he was a toddler. He too, has followed his passion through his studies and he is now at a specialist sports Uni studying Sports Science. He is also a special child and of course that makes me a very biased mother! He is quieter than Louise but he is also very supportive of his mum and checks up on me regularly. I was with my children's father for almost 20 years but eventually I left the marriage due to unresolvable issues, despite our efforts to make it work. However, for the sake of my children I have a very amicable relationship with him now, which I believe is beneficial to the children. I remarried again in 2011 and in July 2013 I discovered my second husband was having an affair with one of my neighbours as well as indulging in other infidelities too.

I believe that if two people love each other then every problem in life is solvable within the realms of compromise and respectful negotiation but I have always been adamant that I could never, ever recover from infidelity and so here I am looking for that decent man who I absolutely know is out there. I have faith that that is true. I am a good woman and I only want the same from my man.

I left school at 16 and became a dental nurse for two years and then became a student nurse in a local hospital. After qualifying, I specialised in oral surgery and dental nursing and spent 14 years in that field of work. When I separated from my children's father, I was determined I would not live on my salary topped up with state benefits and so I studied for a professional qualification by training to become a social worker, which took me 5 years. I worked with people with addiction issues before applying to work in the criminal justice arena, where I worked specifically being as a court report writer for the latter part of my career. I am now retired for the past two years and have spent that time and much of my money on my home. I have designed and refitted my kitchen and bathroom as well as landscaping my back garden. It's been a busy couple of years for me. I am just about to revamp the whole of the upstairs rooms now that I have an empty nest! I have two Shih Tzu dogs and I have acquired a cat from my daughter when she left for London!!

I have a group of close female friends whom I have acquired from childhood, at the school gates when taking our children to school, or through my various working roles and as neighbours too! I adore them all

in very different ways and spend as much time as I can with them. I also volunteer with helping children to read at the local school and at a local elder persons home when I can. My hobbies are reading, writing, creative interiors and garden design. I love baking, cooking, fashion and my favourite hobby of all, 'belly laughing' with the girls till tears roll down my face!

I hope you like my short tale of some aspects of my life and I will sign off now and I look forward to hearing from you again. I have to confess I had a sneak at your profile again on the dating site just so I could see your photographs! I have sent you two new images of me. The first one was taken yesterday. Fi.

She then went upstairs to bed and slept very well for the first time in a long time. The next morning she awoke refreshed and full of zest for life. She completed her 'tasks' and showered, and drove to the gym for her Pilates class, choosing to listen to a calming piece of music on her playlist for a change, she hummed along to the beautiful sounds of Air: 'Ce matin La' echoing soothingly from the speakers. She felt cuddled by the tones. After her class, Fi spent the afternoon in the back garden collecting the fallen leaves and apples and was impressed with having put the effort in to reclaim her outside space from nature. She adored that outdoor room so much and intended to spend every possible moment out there come the spring and summer. It really was a wow factor garden that everybody admired whenever they saw it and Fi was looking forward to filling this space with fun again.

It was then time to make herself some food and as she selected her 'Happy' playlist, she began to bop round the kitchen to Agnetha Faltskog's, "Dance your pain away!"

'Oh my, that's a positive one,' she thought to herself and hit the repeat button. Why not? This was after all her medication and she was attempting to dance her pain away, just as the song instructed! She prepared and ate dinner for one, before deciding to shower and groom the dogs. Fi then spent the evening flicking through the TV channels watching nothing in particular. Julie called about 9 o'clock, for a 'nightcap coffee' with a drop of Bailey's in it! They chatted about their respective days and Julie jumped again, when she heard the 'scribbling' sound letting Fi know she had an email. "Ooh, Bran's writing to you!" Julie teased, as Fi grabbed her phone, opened her inbox and discovered that sure enough, he had 'written' to her! She clicked on the email and the girls read it aloud together:

14 November 2013 18.42

Wow Fi! Thanks so much for letting me into your world. It would be great if you wrote a book. Lol. I think you write beautifully. Maybe it was an advantage of being a court report writer. I truly enjoyed reading it! Wonderful. I love the photos. You look beautiful I must say. Is that your daughter? I will just take some time now to write a little about myself and I hope you don't get too bored.

Family is what I haven't been so blessed with in life, but I'm very grateful for the little I have. I have just me and my daughter. We have Danish roots but I grew up in Maribor, Slovenia. I had an elder brother who was killed in a car accident at a very tender age. Dad was away working in Slovenia, but it was a matter of time before mom and I had to move and join him. The family were not so good to us back in Copenhagen. So

my Dad, he lived without his family the rest of his life, as we literally never went back to Denmark. We moved back to Slovenia for good.

I don't know how I ended up with Kate alone, maybe that's destiny I don't know! I know in my heart I would have cherished a larger family circle. My parents are both dead now from cancer of the lungs as a result of heavy smoking! I don't condemn people who smoke, if one has a will to quit, I try to help out but I personally don't smoke! Kate is in her final year in Kingston Uni in London. She might still do her masters in London, most likely!

I work in Cardiff. Monday to Wednesday, sometimes Thursdays too on a busy week and I am back home in Liverpool for the remaining days of the week through the weekend. I have been living in this area 5 years full time now. I have also lived in Germany and Scotland due to my education/work. Click the attached link to take you to my direct business web page to get an idea of what I do for work.

Divorce - It's been 12 years since my divorce and I am proud of the point I am at right now with my daughter. I look at her and it makes me feel very happy inside. She is doing great at uni and wants to take on my business after I retire. We don't keep in touch with her mum or know her whereabouts and that suits us both well. She cheated in the marriage too and started using drugs with her new beau at the time. It was a horrible time and I couldn't let my daughter grow up seeing all those terrible things. My ex became very violent as well but that's in the past, her loss not ours! Life is good today and my daughter wants the best for me. When

Kate comes around for rare weekends, it is usually shopping, cooking, chatting, cinema and just enjoying being at home for the weekend. Taking after my footsteps is her dream and yes she will definitely live it soon!

Desires - There are lots of things I am still looking forward to in life and I don't know which to mention first LOL! When I meet my Queen! I'm sure we will work out between us what we enjoy and do those fun things together. I wonder if you dive or would like to?

I like Thai, French and Italian recipes and 5 star restaurants I love, love, love! I love red wine if I am to take a drink. I love anything that makes me laugh when it is funny without hurting others. A simple smile on your face, quick email or call from someone just to say they care would make me smile too...that's me!

Moving on - I am more of an extrovert but I also love the quiet times too with someone special to share weekends or at night with a glass of wine and just romance the night away into some breathtaking moment Mmmmmmm! Dancing wise, I enjoy the salsa and the waltz and I am quite good too! How about you? Do you dance?

I strongly believe our paths crossed for a reason, so I look forward to what fate may have in store for us. I love taking walks, especially on a beach holding hands with someone special! They say nothing good comes easy in life, I believe that. I am a 'True Romantic' and I believe in chivalry. I want someone who can be my all in one. My friend, soul mate, partner and lover! I want all the good things a relationship has to offer, someone

to travel with and to have fun with. One thing you must know is that I give my best effort in whatever I want to do to make it work. So be sure I will do the same for us if fate takes us there.

PS: I am the little one next to daddy in the family picture...such a retrospect! I miss them all so much!

Kate is the girl in the middle. Her friend Dora on the right is a cancer survivor. I am very proud of that girl and happy for her. Oh and we are Elvis Presley's fans. You can tell from Kate's photograph, ha ha! Have a good day, stay in touch and keep smiling. Enjoying getting to know you. Regards Bran.

The air was punctuated with all sorts of verbal drivel between the two of them, none of it making much sense, except to the two of them, as they read and reread the email, "Oh he likes your writing! So he should, you're brill!" said Julie. "Ooh, Danish and Slovenian, he'll have a sexy accent then!" Fi said and they both giggled. "Ah, sad, he's lost his brother very young," added Fi. "Sounds like a good dad," said Julie. "Oh, no family to worry about!" said Fi, "thank fuck for that," she added, "you'll get some bloody peace now," said Julie and they laughed again. "Hey, he works part time by the sounds of this, whoopee do, high five!" added Julie, "good, more time for me!" Fi answered, before continuing, "His daughter's in London too, good, we can go down to London together and see our daughters!" and they burst out laughing again. "Divorced, no mad ex-wife, thank god!" said Julie, "daughter taking over his business so he can retire, it's getting bloody better by the minute," said Fi. "He wants a Queen does he, I'll be his bloody Queen all right!" she scoffed and this time they cracked up laughing. "Moving on!" Fi said in a sarcastic voice as she laughed again. "What is wrong with you?" Julie sniggered, "You've set me off now," and they were in hysterics laughing at nothing whatsoever, except themselves. "Let's try again?" Julie said as she read on. "He likes Thai, French, Italian," she paused, before adding, "and 5 star restaurants he love, love, loves! "Does he," she continued, "well he won't be coming to tea at number 11 then will he?" she blurted out and that sent them both over the edge as they just creased up laughing, stopping and starting, stopping and starting, howling with laughter. Eventually they composed themselves when Julie said, "RIGHT! Let's stop pissing about now and get this read." "Right!" said Fi and took a deep breath before continuing to read aloud, "He can have his red wine, while I have my white," she said, 'he's a true romantic is he, well I'll be the judge of that!" she added as they sniggered again, "STOP IT!" Julie said sharply, trying to keep a straight face. "Yes, mother," replied Fi, "friend, soul mate, partner, lover and all the good things a relationship has to offer, yes PLEASE!" Fi raved as she read on, before adding, "Someone to travel and have fun with and he gives his best in everything and will do the same for us, if fate takes us there!" "Well, PRETTY PLEASE, shit, shite and cacky, I have died and gone to heaven Jules," she stated. After pausing, she added, "He sounds a dream, too good to be true, there's got to be a catch," before repeating, "there's got to be a catch Jules."

They spent the next hour, looking at the additional images he had sent, together with all the information contained on his website, where they were met with yet more images telling them about him, his life and his business. After they had finished, Fi brewed tea and as they drank it, they chatted some more as Fi tried to figure out what was wrong. They discussed everything they saw, his writing, his childhood photographs, the photograph of his daughter, various photographs of him in pleasure and business settings, a very professional looking website with his images clearly contained within it, prices of very expensive antiques clearly visible and a contact us page too. They were struggling to find a catch and they came to the conclusion that they thought it was genuine and above board. Fi decided that she would have to keep a check on her hyper alert sensitivity and suspicion of men. In that moment, she really hated Robert for making her doubt herself and others. She needed to be able to trust men otherwise she could never be a part of a happy relationship. She needed to be able to trust Bran she thought as she chinked her coffee cup with Julie's before holding hers aloft and saying, "Well Mr. Antique, welcome to my world!"

Just chuck it

in the fuck it

bucket

and move on

CHAPTER 6

Dare I dare to dream

After Julie had left her house, Fi decided to get some air, to clear her head of the giddiness and the lingering doubts. It was a wet night so she chose outdoor attire to protect her from the elements, before putting the dogs' coats on and setting out on her walk. She had her music set to shuffle on the classical playlist. She welcomed the calm surprises in her ears distracting her as she walked for over an hour before she eventually turned into her lane and headed towards home. As Fi walked, she used the time to reflect on everything. Why she had doubts, where they had come from, who contributed (including herself), what she was going to do about them as and when they came into her head, because for sure, there would be more of them! They were deeply entrenched in her psyche and needed to surface. Fi so far felt fairly certain that Bran had not given her any evidence to doubt him. So she decided that she was 'looking for problems' considering what she herself had been through, what she had seen her friend's experience with online dating and as a result of the 'mountain of men on mountains' and the other crap she had so far experienced in her own online search. She acknowledged that that wasn't fair on him and it wasn't fair on her. She pledged that she would go with it and that if she had any waving 'red flags' of nagging doubts and 'intuition alarms' ringing in her ears, then she needed to trust those thoughts and feelings and act upon them when they arose. 'So,' she thought to herself, 'relax, take a deep breath and enjoy.' She was glad of her walk and the clarity it had provided but she was equally as glad to be in her warm cosy home. The weather was wicked! She took off hers and the dogs' wet coats and hung them up to dry, made a Camomile tea and sat down to reply to Bran. It was late but she wanted to do it while her mood was lifted and whilst she felt positive to do so. She opened his message in her inbox, took another look at all his photographs and clicked on reply:

14 November 11:58

Hello again Bran, thank you so much for your story. I really enjoyed reading about you, your family story and your life with your daughter. What an absolutely stunning little boy who became a stunningly handsome man. I literally said, "Wow" to myself when I saw your photograph on the dating website! You resemble your father, as I resemble my mother and I will send you a picture of her when I can. I too, have a very sad childhood story to tell, which I will do when I feel the time is right. My family story also involved alcohol and severe violence and although I enjoy a glass of wine or my favourite Gin and tonic, I am very aware of excessive drinking outcomes on family life.

You are right, that is my daughter Louise in the photograph, it was her birthday that day and we were having Champagne and cupcakes treat! Karen is a beautiful young woman and you are right to be proud of her, her achievements to date and her dreams for her future as she follows in your footsteps. Your website is creative, professional, informative and unique all at the same time. I could almost see you on an antiques TV programme, which I love watching by the way. Isn't it lovely when you get to enjoy what you

do every day? How lucky we are in that respect.

I like what you desire in your future, I believe in fate and paths crossing for a reason. I believe in working so hard, forever, to achieve my goal of a happy, fun, spontaneous, loving, sensual, supportive relationship. I do not believe in the fairy tale ending. I believe in the reality of creating what you want in a relationship, you are not responsible for my happiness and I am not responsible for yours. We are both responsible for a fifty, fifty, shared goal to create our 'us' if that is what fate has in store for us. I give my all in my relationships too and I am not a "taker" creaming off what I can. I love to invest in my lifelong friendships and fully intend to do the same to create a beautiful future with somebody. Maybe that will be you. Who knows?

I am not the type of woman who goes looking for men (neither when I was a younger or as a mature woman) and so I find the dating website scenario very strange as I have said before. I have never given my body away unless I am in a loving relationship but when I am ready to do so I love the healthy pleasures associated with such. Mmmmm indeed as you said in your profile! I am enjoying exchanging words with you and hope to hear again soon. Fi.

She reread it before she was prepared to send it and she did so for a couple of reasons. She did not want to sound 'desperate and needy' and because she wanted to be completely honest in her writing. Was there any other way to behave she asked herself? Of course not, a relationship has to be based on trust, in other words the 'base' of it has to be about trust from day one, she told herself, 'I need to put my head on my pillow each night knowing I am being completely truthful and as long as I can do that, then the rest is outside of my control.' Her purpose for the content of her reply was to convey her thanks for his message containing his life story, answer some of his questions and clarify points he had asked her. She also wanted to convey a message to him that she wasn't a trollop, never had been and never would be BUT she also wanted to hint, without sounding like a 'trollop' that she loved, yes loved, healthy sexual relations within a healthy relationship. In other words, just a tiny flirt! Had she managed that? She reread it a third time and finally pressed send in answer to her own question. Fi considered herself a woman who, now in her middle life years and like many women her age, wanted to have 'better than ever' and more frequent sex. Women nowadays, thanks in part, to creations such as Candice Bushnell's, 'Sex And The City,' had permission more than ever before, to be open and honest about their wishes and desires to be more sexually adventurous.

Fi had a peaceful sleep and lay in a little longer than usual the next morning. She showered, ironed and put on her clothes, for her day ahead. She was helping Felicity (her daughter's friend with the cake business) decorate some cakes and it was a big order, so they were in for a long day. The dogs had a quick run in the park and Fi made tea and grabbed a cereal bar for breakfast before checking her emails. She gave a little 'ooh' when she saw Bran's name in the inbox and clicked on the message, which simply said:

15 November 2013 06:45

Good morning Fi

It contained an attachment and when Fi opened it, it made her gasp as it revealed a picture of him. He was sat in a bar looking straight into the camera, he was wearing a beautiful smile, and she could see the details of his eyes, his eyebrows, his clean shaven face, his perfect 'clean' teeth, his well-cut and nicely styled hair, his smart but casual clothes which were fashionable but not too 'young' for him, he dressed very well she could see, she could really see HIM and he was stunning.

She sent a quick reply before dashing out of the house for her day with Felicity:

15 November 2013 09:42

Hi Bran, Thank you, what a beautiful photograph. You really are a stunning, handsome man. I said wow to myself when I opened my email. Fi.

Did she sound desperate, needy, clingy even, she asked herself after she had sent it. She then answered herself, 'my intention, was to say thank you and to compliment him.' Simple. Would she have done the same to Robert, hell yes! She told him all the time he was handsome and that he looked good when he had gotten ready to go out and she was just as honest telling him when he didn't look right in an outfit too. Honest? That email was honest, she told herself. He was stunning.

She drove over to Sale whilst listening to her calming classical music, there was somehow a requirement for soothing music, as she knew she had a frantic day ahead of her. They were scheduled to prepare several dozen cupcakes as well as adding the intricate finishing touches to a very large wedding cake for a celebrity client. They were sworn to secrecy though. After their mammoth day at Felicity's business premises and after delivering their secret cakes, to the secret celebrity, to the secret location, Felicity said, "Come on Fi, lets go for a coffee, my treat, we deserve it!" Fi replied, "Oh that sounds great, as long as there is no cake involved, I'm caked out after today!" and they laughed. It had been a very busy day and they were glad of the chance to sit and relax in the bar overlooking the canal, as dusk descended. It had been a crisp cold day and snow was forecast. It was a wintery scene outside and the girls sat and admired the view, framed by the large plate glass window, overlooking the candle lit courtyard and out onto the canal, where several barges were moored and lights flickered in their tiny windows. "It's lovely, its such a cosy feeling with the log fire lit, I could stay here all night," said Fi. They chatted about Felicity's healthy order book and how her hard work had finally started to pay off. She had recently earned herself international award winning acclaim for her cake making and decorating skills, having won gold and silver medals at an international cake show and her website was now fully launched too. With the odd celebrity order now coming in, it was indeed, an exciting time for Felicity's creative career and Fi was glad for her daughter's friend. After they had been sat for an hour or so, Fi saw the first flurry of snow appearing and as she stood to leave, she said, "I'm off now, don't want to get caught in the snow." Felicity thanked her so much for her hard work and as they said their goodbyes, Felicity added, "Good luck with Mr. Antique, let me know how it goes, so excited for you!" Fi promised that she would keep her informed and she set off for the short drive to the other side of Manchester, taking over an hour for a normally 30 minute journey.

Upon arrival, she was greeted with Julie shouting from her front door, "Oi, Mrs. Have you heard from Mr. Antique?"

"Yes," Fi shouted back, "just to say good morning and he sent me a photograph too," she added. "Nice?" asked Julie referring to the photograph, "just a bit," Fi laughed. Julie gave Fi a thumb's up as she shouted "I'm coming round in a bit to check," and with that Fi gave her a wave and closed her door. She checked her paper mail, which was lay on the mat behind her front door, fed her dogs, made a pot of herb tea and crashed onto her sofa to check her electronic mail. After dealing with her inbox, she settled to watch TV and it wasn't long before she fell asleep, such was the level of her exhaustion. She was woken by the 'scratching signature' sound of her email alert. What time is it? She wondered, 'Jesus, its 11:30' she said to herself, 'I've been asleep for over two hours'.

She had a text from Julie:

Julie: Called round. You were zonked. Catch you tomorrow. X

Fi: Just woke up! See you tomorrow. X

She then checked her emails and amongst the usual marketing crap, which she systematically deleted, was a message from Bran, which read:

15 November 2013 22:19

Hello Fi, This is just to let you know that you are my last thought before bed, I hope you've had as productive a day as mine. I will definitely write more tomorrow, you have a wonderful nights rest and make sure you dream of butterflies, or do I say see you in dreamland? Lol. Bran

She gulped, realising that she felt very upset inside, not

because he had sent a thoughtful email, it was nothing whatsoever to do with Bran. She was upset because she realised, that when Robert had admitted to his affair and she had left him in Devon, all the simplicities of a relationship had disappeared with him too and such a sweet email had suddenly made her realise that. There is so much to miss when a relationship ends but the adrenalin rush of the past few weeks had masked the niceties of being in a couple. Dare she trust somebody to say such a simple thing as goodnight to her again and wish her sweet dreams. God, this is hard, she thought as she screamed in her mind at Robert, telling him to 'FUCK OFF.' He will not rob me of anymore, he's had enough of me, she thought and she clicked reply and wrote:

15 November 2013 23:51

Hi Bran, You have such a lovely name. I meant to say that to you the other day. I do hope to see you in my dreams, that is a touching thought and I wonder what we may be doing if I do see you there? Sleep well too. Thank you for your lovely words. I am going to dreamland with a glowing smile. Fi.

That too, was her truth. She attached two beautiful photographs of her mother, one was a facial image and the other was one of her mother's modeling shots. She had modeled tights and stockings for a well-known manufacturer at some point in her young twenties and this was one of their promotional shots. She looked amazing in the picture and she had great legs too! Fi loved those photographs. They were all she had of her mother. She pressed send and switched off her laptop.

Fi let the dogs out in the garden, put the cat in the shed to use her litter tray, made herself a special hot chocolate by dropping some of her Green and Black's Organic dark chocolate with ginger into the hot milk and luxury hot chocolate powder. She let all the animals back into the house, locked up and went up to bed. She took her medication and vitamins with a glass of water and then settled to read her online newspaper whilst savouring that heavenly chocolate drink. Dare I dare to dream, she thought.

The next day she woke about 10am and felt so refreshed and as was usual when she sat with her first drink of each day, she checked her emails. She sifted through them and trashed all the 'trash' ones, before clicking on Branimir Rodrigues! 'Ooh,' she thought to herself as her stomach flipped a little. 'What was that for?' she wondered. She wasn't exactly sure but suspected it might be the beginnings of excitement!

16 November 2013 09:48

Hey Fi, I must confess, I am also enjoying exchanging these lovely letters that we are sharing, thanks for letting me know so much about you. I think you stole so much of your mum's beauty. Those pictures are stunning. How old is Louise? She is a beautiful young girl. Kate (not Karen) will be 21 come February. I am so sorry about your growing up but it is good you have really moved on past all that now, I am happy for you that you are now in a happy place. I hope you don't mind a few questions, and please, do ask whatever it is you want to know. Throw your questions at me because I am like an open book, what you see is what you get.

So here are a few questions for you.

Are you high maintenance, low or somewhere between both?

What turns you on and off?

3 things you can't do without?

If you had just one day left to live, how would you live it?

The type of fragrance you like to wear and what do you like to smell on your man?

Do you like lace or silk underwear?

You are always free to throw some back at me anytime you like.

My 'turn on's' comprise of the physical aspect, the good looks, appearance, the appealing smell of their body and their perfume, dressing nicely with fashionable and good quality clothing. Trashy women don't appeal to me. I like honesty, sincerity, kindness, a good kisser and romance thrown in too and of course a beautiful smile and much laughter. These are such a huge turn on for me.

My 'turn off's' are just the opposites and looking to fall in love to me, means hoping to find a mate to touch my soul rather than just seeking an already made soul mate which most people believe is common. I think discovering each other and building a steady relationship as time goes on is so beautiful. The one thing I am not looking forward to is to start and then

have cause to want to withdraw, which is why it is necessary to be open to each other rather than have secrets that may not be such a good surprise later. I think you agree. Yes?

My requirements are not much. My woman should be romantic, enjoys intimate conversations in quiet times and not 'too shy' behind closed doors (ha I really don't think at this stage in our lives one should be, as there should be nothing new other than the newly found love but you never know). Someone who could just challenge me to a pillow fight and then we go to extremes in the bedroom hmmm! A woman who loves being sexually active!

I am not a jealous type of man. I am open and honest as long as I trust my woman as much as she does me, then fine. I enjoy traveling a lot and due to the nature of my job I get to do a lot more than most people, hence my love of diving all over the world, but there is a huge difference between work travel and traveling for pleasure. It is better still to have a pleasure trip with 'special someone' by your side. I would like to visit CAYMAN ISLANDS and BRAZIL (Rio de Janeiro) for pleasure soon but this time it has to be me together with someone special. I want to be there and share the beautiful experience with someone who values me as much as I'd do her. Bran

She picked up her phone and sent a text to Julie and Tracey which read:

Fi: Oh my giddy fucking god, coffee o'clock time girls! X

Fi went upstairs changed her bedding, cleaned her room and ran a bath and just lay there awhile, soaking away the inevitable invading concerns. Gradually, calm, replenishing thoughts emerged as she relished the smells of her luxuriously fragrant bubbles and bath salts. With her tranquil calming music playing, she pondered on the contents of her reply to Bran. She finished her pampering session with a long overdue leg shave, then soaked her body in her favourite body lotion, painted her fingers and toenails and dressed in cosy casuals for the day. She wasn't planning on going anywhere. She took the laundry downstairs, put it into the washing machine and switched it on before brewing a Nespresso. As she prepared lunch she sang along to Closer by Tegan and Sara and she really did start to think about being underneath him! She took her courgette soup and sandwich into the lounge to hear her text message signal beeping:

Julie: WTF. What? X

Fi: Mr. Antique has written to me! Come round after work! X

Julie: Will do! Sooner if I could! Intrigued. X

She then read Tracey's message and replied:

Tracey: OMG. Whats happened? You okay? Can be at yours in 10, is that okay? X

Fi: Mr. Antique has written to me! Nervous and giddy! Lunch will be ready. X

Fi quickly prepared lunch for Tracey too and 10 minutes later they were sat in her cosy lounge and Tracey listened intently, as Fi read the latest email from Mr Antique out to her. “Fi, he sounds absolutely AMAAAZZING!” said Tracey, exaggerating the word for effect. Her eyes were startled and she was shaking her head in wonderment as she looked over at Fi and said, “Unbelievable, I don’t know what else to say, except wow.” “I know” Fi replied, “it is unbelievable isn’t it?” before adding, “I don’t get why but the majority of men on all the sites I have had contact with, turn out to be weird in some way or another.” Fi pondered for a second before speaking again, “It really is like looking for perfection, because I absolutely know what I do and don’t want!” “Well, it’s looking like you may have found perfection Fi?” said Tracey, before continuing, “I mean, how many men have you had contact with?” Fi thought some more and said, “Well from the three sites, hundreds! Looking at their profile pictures, clicking on their profiles to read their ‘selling’ blurb and deciding between those two criteria if I want to take it further, yes, it’s hundreds!” She paused to drink some of her coffee, before adding, “Then, IF, and it’s a big if, I want to message them to start chatting, as I am with Bran, they act weirdly, in the main.” She took another sip of her drink and explained, “They either just talk shite with no initial spark in the conversation, or they are too sexually suggestive from the get go, or they speak to you online for a while, indicate they want to meet up, MAKE ACTUAL ARRANGEMENTS to meet up and then all communication ceases! She pondered before adding, “All kinds of weird men Tracey.” “It’s not pleasant being online for dating purposes and overall, I wouldn’t recommend it from my experiences so far,” Fi said, “I mean, I know we have screamed laughing from our girl’s perspective but when you’re really looking for someone, it’s a shit way to find a man to be honest.” Fi told her friend. “However, Bran seems so different,” she added whilst smiling at Tracey, before continuing, “gorgeous, intelligent and knows how to communicate so far!” “Do you know what you are going to reply?” asked Tracey, “I’m just going to answer his questions honestly and be myself and hope that that comes across but the written word IS harder to convey isn’t it?” replied Fi.

“Right, you look at his website and profile again to see if you can see anything I have missed, because in all honesty after all the ‘shite sifting’ I have done with Julie, I’m a bit overwhelmed that someone so gorgeous, wants to communicate with me,” said Fi. “I’ll just go and make us another coffee,” she added as she walked into the kitchen. Tracey double-checked the website and his previous communication and found nothing untoward. They spent the remainder of Tracey’s visit discussing other aspects of their lives before Tracey had to leave to return to work. As they said their goodbyes at the door, Julie pulled up in her car and the three girls chatted for a few minutes and giggled about the prospect of Bran being in Fi’s life. They were all enjoying the distraction and fun that this Internet dating and in particular ‘Mr. Antique’ was bringing to their friendship. The girls went into the kitchen and they discussed Julie’s day at work and her family issues of the day, Fi reported that she had booked her train ticket to London to see Louise. She couldn’t wait. It had been many years since she had been to London and as well really looking forward to meeting her new friend Jen again, Fi also wanted to see a West End show and visit the Tower of London. Fi brewed tea for herself and made coffee for Julie and then read the contents of his latest email to her friend. “Fi, just go for it,” said Julie, “he just sounds a really lovely guy.”

So she did when she replied to him an hour later:

16 November 2013 16:11

Hi Bran, It's so lovely to hear from you again. There is a sense of anticipation wondering what treasures, pleasures and surprises I may find within the words you write. I do apologise for writing Karen instead of Kate (I failed to edit my own writing) yesterday! She is a beautiful young woman and it must be such a delight for you both to share a love of art and antiques with the aim of her taking over your business. What a joy for you as her father? It is a reflection of the selfless, rare and priceless father and daughter bond you have instigated as her single parent, that has then developed between the two of you. I admire that selfless quality so much in you. It is quite rare in a man. How are you today, how has your day been, what have you done with your day?

Now to answer your list of questions:

Are you high maintenance, low or somewhere between the two?: Honesty within communication is paramount to me.

I am not quite sure what you mean so I will answer as I have interpreted the question. I will tell you now I have an illness that comes under the umberella of "auto immune diseases." I inherited it from my mother and it is called LUPUS. There is no cure but it is NOT terminal. It is manageable. Very manageable! I take full responsibility for it and I see my specialist twice a year and I have very mild medication for it (prescribed high dose iron and Vitamin D for the symptoms). I also have an irregular heart rhythm as a result of the LUPUS and take a heart tablet daily. I live as normal a

life as possible, I go to the gym, eat and sleep well and take additional vitamins to ensure optimum health. I follow all medical advice and research and I challenge the medical professions when I have questions, to ensure I have access to knowledge and up to date treatment options. I may get slightly tired if I am having a flare up and I can also get breathless if my heart rhythm is having a blip. I also have to be careful in the sun using strong sunscreen. My illness rarely affects my daily life and it certainly doesn't stop me trying to do anything I choose to do. I absolutely do not believe that my illness requires high maintenance and whilst having an illness that has no cure sounds scary, I am certainly not fazed by it. I listen to my body and act accordingly. I would not want you to be worried about it. I have been diagnosed since 1999 and I am fine. Stress has to be avoided.

I have my own hair, naturally curly, my own hair colour and have it cut by my long-term hairdresser and friend Debbie-Jane every 6 to 8 weeks. I do not dye my hair and nor do I have extensions. My beauty regime is showering with luxury products from one of my favourite toiletry stores, together with body and face conditioning again using simple but quality products.

I have a subtle make up regime that I have followed for years which I believe works for me. I am a stylish woman rather than a follower of fashion. I only ever buy what I like and what suits me. I like to buy the best quality pieces I can personally afford to wear and am not a labels person, nor a slave to having to follow the fashion crowd. That is not to say I don't have my favourite designers, I certainly do with a certain crazy

Frenchman being my absolute favourite. I love elegance rather than dare I say it a "slutty look" and I have never been a fake tan fan due to my skin sensitivity issues. I love having my nails done as a treat and I have a range of everyday and evening fragrances in my collection. I love good fragrances and I wear my perfume where I like to be kissed!

I like to wear matching underwear always and I prefer silk to lace. I like a specific style of bra to enhance my shape without being a tart and beautiful lingerie is a guilty pleasure when I want to treat myself.

I love, love, love stylish unusual shoes with what I call a feminine heel, rather than sky scraper heels that don't suit me. I also like clothes that say wow to me that suit my body shape. My all-time style icon is 'Carrie' aka Sarah Jessica Parker from Candace Bushnell's 'Sex And The City.' She can wear anything and look amazing. I believe I am low maintainance because I believe less is more but I also believe that my 'less is more' philosophy regarding my own style, delivers a wow result.

What turns you on and off?

A smile across a crowded room.

A look that says, "do you want to make love?"

A slow, delicate kiss that crescendos and takes my breath away and enhances my desire to make love.

Bathing in a candle lit bath together with music, champagne, chocolates and flowers.

A rushed, passion filled, love crazed shower before making love on the bathroom floor.

A walk on a cold, cold day with the prospect of making love in the glow of an open fire when we get back home.

The thought of making love under the stars.

Seeing the man I love walk through the door knowing I want him, all of him, right there and then in that instant because I have missed him so much.

Having the surge in my stomach when I hear his voice on the phone and having a tear of joy in my eye knowing he'll be home soon.

Seeing him across a crowded room and feeling so proud that he is mine.

The smell of HIM, on his clothes maybe, on his body as we take a shower together, just his very own smell. Mmmm.

A good scent on a man that suits him, as with women, fragrance is personal and should be worn because it suits you and not because it is an on trend fragrance. I wonder what yours will be?

Seeing him come out of a dressing room ready to take me out and he makes my heart melt and therefore we may not get out after all, or we may be very late!

Seeing my man behave beautifully with my friends and loved ones and admiring his behaviour, manners and rapport with others in his everyday life.

Turn offs:

Bad manners.

A bad attitude towards me as your woman.

A lack of respect for my opinions.

Failure to hear me (we don't always have to agree but I have a right to be heard too).

Violence. In any form.

Over indulgence in both alcohol and food (gluttony), moderation is my style. I love an occasional alcoholic drink as well as good food but I don't like excessive appetites for either.

Poor clothing style in a man, unhygienic men and a lack of regular grooming in a man.

3 things you can't do without?

My children, I have worked so hard as a single mum and am really proud of them both. Life without them is too much to contemplate.

My creativity and love for writing.

My positivity in knowing fate will deliver whatever is coming my way in life.

If you had just one day left to live, how would you live it?

I would wake up in my mother's arms as a baby, have

my first day at school with her there to see me at the gate, she would be there to see me graduate, see her grandchildren blossom and live fulfilled lives and finally she would be there as I turn around and see her waving to me with pride in her eyes and her heart as she finally gets to see me living the love filled life I have co created with my man, whoever he may be. She died when I was a baby and never got to see any of the above.

Here are some throw backs for you.

What do you like in a woman?

What turns you on and off?

Where would you take me on our first date?

What are your hobbies and passions apart from art and antiques?

I hope you like the attached photos. I look forward to your responses. I am loving our communication. Fi.

Was she flirting she wondered? Absofuckinglutely! She thought!

3 hours later he replied:

16 November 2013 19:21

Hey Fi, Wow! It is always amazing to read you messages I must say. I really enjoy the way you write. I am so sorry about your illness but it doesn't change a thing, I am willing to see where this all takes us and I want to be by your side if our journey leads to longevity for us.

I think your hair is rare and very beautiful and I see you take pride in your body and appearance too which I really like. Your list of 'turn ons' really strikes a chord for me and I really like all that you said there, very much!

If you had just one day left to live, how would you live it? All you said concerning your mother really touched me, I cannot imagine growing up without a mum.

As for me I am between high maintenance and low. I treat myself to special things and know how to maintain a relationship pace. I understand when my woman needs her time with friends.

Turn ons - A good smell from my woman turns me on, good hygiene, whispers in my ears...a stare in a crowded room with just our eye contact sending messages to each other without speaking....romance, yes candle lit dinners together, watching a romantic movie together, holding hands, playing with my woman's hair...it all turns me on.

Turn offs - Lies, no matter how little. Unhygienic, bad smells, unkindness, selfishness and self-centredness turns me off! Oh and yes bad languages too!

My 3 things I can't do without would be: Kate, my zest for life and love.

I currently wear a host of lovely smells but I do have my favourites too!

Not shy at all baby. I mean not at all! LOL! I am a Virgo!

August 28. Your star sign is?

One thing is certain. I certainly would make you remember the joy of being a woman. I have a soft spot for females. At this stage, I am not looking for a supermodel. I would just like to find that special person to grow older with.

About our first date. Mmmm?

I am thinking about doing something I like to do but I haven't done in a while, is there anything you are also looking to do that you've not done in a while?

I am thinking we could go dancing together, it's been awhile since I did that, what do you think about that? The normal dinner and coffee thing seems a bit boring to me, let's be spontaneous about it.

Apart from art and antiques: I like to write poems, I love diving and swimming, I enjoy singing as well and I love traveling to see new things and places.

I will be having a business meeting with some important clients for the next few days and I just hope all goes well. Bran. PS: Are you having a good day?

Fi reread the email and savoured his words before she sent a text message to Julie:

Fi: Julie he doesn't like swearing

Julie: Fucking tough!

Sometimes you just have to be brave and tear off the plaster

CHAPTER 7

Dancing and dog biscuits

Fi was intent on spending the next day cataloguing items to sell online. She had lost weight through the associated effects of the recent traumatic events and although she was not yet completely satisfied with her emerging shape, 'there was one certainty,' she was going to be preventing that weight creeping back on, especially now there was the possibility of a gorgeous man on the horizon! She would never be wearing those 'too large' items again she thought, as she viewed the pile on her bed next to other items that 'Twastard' had bought her. A faux leather jacket, never worn, red 'sky scraper' high heel slapper shoes, never worn, Christmas jumper, never worn, two watches, never worn, black dress, never worn, poncho, never worn, perfume (unopened), never sprayed, slippers, never worn. Jesus, she thought to herself, I spent five years dressing him head to toe in gorgeous, stylish clothes and all I'm left with is this 'Aunt Twacky' shite. She laughed out loud as she thought of her Aunty Mary calling things 'Aunt Twacky,' relating to old-fashioned clothing (apparently deriving from the word antique and originating from Liverpool!)

What was he thinking when buying her all this crap she thought. Good job she could style herself! As Fi listened to her music, the sound faded when an email came through and she gave a little, "Ooh," to herself as she opened the mail to see Bran's name and her stomach flipped! She clicked on the email and read:

17 November 2013 11:37

C'mon you look beautiful..... Your smile is so cute, oh my goodness! Where have you been?

She fleetingly wore a beaming smile, before quickly allowing the doubts of low self-esteem to creep in. She looked in the sent file and clicked on the attachment of the photographs she had sent him yesterday just to check. 'Oh yes,' she thought, 'nice smile,' as she scrolled down to the next one, 'nice smile, beautiful outfit, pretty face, okay,' she thought again as she scrolled down to the final picture, 'smiling eyes, happy image' she thought, and went back to her inbox and re-read his message:

17 November 2013 11:37

C'mon you look beautiful..... Your smile is so cute, oh my goodness! Where have you been?

'Jesus,' she thought, 'this guy really likes me.' She clicked on reply and wrote:

17 November 2013 11:48

Thank you so much. I could say exactly the same. Fi.

She finished organising her wardrobe and made a mental note to ask Louise to do a 'proper' wardrobe revamp next time she was home. Louise worked in retail! Louise knew how to make a wardrobe 'shout' when you opened its doors!

Fi showered and changed into her gym gear and set off for her 1pm Pilates class. She was happy to see some of her new friends and after their class they all enjoyed an hour or so in the Jacuzzi and steam room area, chatting away and introducing their lives to each other, as new friends do. Fi then showered again before having her nails done in the beauty salon. She was due to meet Tracey in the reception area at 5pm so they could have an hour together before Tracey's class at 6pm. They greeted each other enthusiastically and Tracey was of course, eager for all the gossip.

Having checked her wifi connection, Fi opened her emails and shared the last couple of day's communication she had exchanged with Bran, with her friend. Tracey read them all and 'oohed and aahed' at their contents before putting the phone on the coffee table in front of them and commenting, "well he sounds like he's a good father and a man who likes to groom himself well and smell good, which is always a turn on," she said, raising her eyebrows, "he has a really interesting job and nice hobbies independent of you and he wants to take you to the 'kin Cayman Islands!" She laughed before adding, "He's really into you and he's selling his sex appeal, AND his appeal for sex!" They laughed together and Tracey said, "Fi, I love it, this is getting so exciting for you," "I know," said Fi, "BUT, am I getting too giddy and ahead of myself, we're only emailing each other!" "FI!" Tracey said with incredulity, "He is REALLY into you!" and at that point an alert sound came from Fi's phone. She checked her inbox and there was Mr. Antique, "Oh my god, he's messaged me again," squealed Fi with excitement, "what's he said?" asked Tracey and Fi read out loud:

"How are you today? Kind of missed you though, been having you in my thoughts a lot today. Kiss" she said before Tracey replied, "SEE! He is REALLY, REALLY into you!" "He is isn't he?" Fi replied and followed with an “arrrggghhhh!” and they both laughed again. “Listen, I’m off to my class now but keep me up to date and I am so pleased for you Fi, after all you have been through, not just with Robert but since I have known you from our boys being five years old, you have had SO MUCH PAIN!” she emphasised, “this is so exciting and I am so excited for YOU!” “Text me with updates,” she called over her shoulder, as Fi waved to her friend.

It was nearly 7pm when Fi got home after doing a quick grocery shop. She fed her dogs, cat and herself and then settled on the sofa to catch up with the world news before calling her cousin Jen. Jen had been so good to Fi, calling her, texting, emailing her and sending her flowers and cards to help keep Fi’s spirits lifted and Jen was pleased that her cousin was starting to turn a corner. She confessed to Fi that even as she participated in hers and Robert’s beautiful wedding celebrations in such a stunning setting that she had commented to her husband Bill at the ceremony, ‘I don’t like him, there’s something not right about him, I don’t know what it is but I just don’t like him.’ She was right to trust her instinct. Fi found it very telling that her cousin was not the only one of her nearest and dearest to declare their dislike of Robert. Nothing pleased Jen more than to hear Fi laughing about her ‘Whitefield Angel’s antics with all the girls and as Fi told her the events of the dating site, they laughed hysterically about some of the metaphorical ‘Cocks in socks and pricks and dicks’ she had come across. She then began telling her cousin the in depth details that she knew about Bran. She sent photographs as they spoke on the phone and Jen commented on him being a ‘gud looken’ fella’ in her lovely ‘Geordie’ accent. She advised Fi to be careful and to leave details with her friends when she went on dates with him to ensure her safety. Fi promised she would and they ended their call to each other with, "Lot's of love" as they always did.

Fi opened her mail, clicked on create new message, typed in Br and the auto fill did the rest and she wrote in the main content section of the template:

17 November 2013 21:23

Hello Bran, how lovely to hear from you on both occasions today. Thank you for emailing me during your busy day with clients. I have to say that you have been in my thoughts a lot today too. Lovely thoughts. I loved your likes and dislikes lists and the thought of dancing together on our first date sounds exciting. I cannot dance formally but I do think I have rhythm, so maybe that will be a good start! I am certainly willing to learn and I absolutely love watching others dance. One of my favourite pieces of art is a painting called "Dance me to the end of love" by Jack Vettriano.

Thank you for asking about my day. I have had a busy day with one of my friends. I have also bought myself a beautiful item of clothing that I may well wear on our first date! I thank you for not passing me by due to my illness, as I say, it does not faze me and I am hyper sensitive to my symptoms and well-being, to allow me to stay around as long as I can! I am excited by your mutual list of what turns you on and agree with you regarding turn offs. I believe if you live your life the right way, then everything falls into place and I give myself wholly in a relationship attempting to fill it with fun, support, respect, compromise, sensuality and love. Perfect ingredients I believe. I hope your business meetings go very well and I look forward to hearing

from you soon. It is such a joy to receive your messages and read your lovely words. I feel like I could go on writing to you forever, I don't want to finish writing once I have started and I don't want to stop reading your emails when I receive them. I may catch up on Strictly Come Dancing on the TV now and pay closer attention to the Salsa and the Waltz! I absolutely love seeing to Andre Rieu in concert. He is the King of Waltz music I believe and I have been lucky enough to see him live on two occasions. Until I hear from you again, take care. Fi.

At 21:53 she received a reply:

17 November 2013 21:53

Hey Fi. Hello again. It is amazing that we have mutual interests. I am glad you like the idea of dancing on our first date and do not be worried. As long as you can move your body it starts from there and I am willing to teach you now that you are willing to learn. I am so much looking forward to that lovely day. I can see us dancing and laughing in my mind as I type. I see you've had a lovely day and did a little shopping too. Wow, now I can't wait to see you in that dress, hold you close while we dance, watch you smile and enjoy laughing together. Now we will have to pick a date and place also, do you have any place in mind you'd like us to go, there's this new place in town, I can't remember the name now, but I will let you know when I do and see what you think.

Thank you so much for wishing me well concerning my meetings, I really hope it all goes in my favour. It is wonderful how much we have exchanged and know

about each other already and it makes me wonder where you've been all this time. I would like you to go and listen to 'Wonderful Tonight' by Eric Clapton if you can and make sure you have a good nights rest. Bye for now and speak soon. Bran.

Fi put 'Wonderful Tonight' (with the lyrics visible) on her laptop and didn't know what she was feeling other than whatever it was it felt lovely, really lovely. She smiled a happy smile as she took herself upstairs to bed and she did have a wonderful night's sleep and she did meet Mr. Antique in her dreams.

When she woke up the next morning, the 'lovely' feeling also awoke within her as the memory of last night's message re-entered her mind and a happy smile crossed her face again. Her audible email alert scribbled a signature across the room and she wondered if he had written to her. She smiled when she saw his name in the inbox she clicked on his name and read it:

18 November 2013 07:21

Good morning my pretty one, how are you? Bran.

"Jessssuuuuusss!" she screamed inside and she was grinning from ear to ear as she ran downstairs to start her morning routine. The kitchen entertainment that day involved louder than usual volume on her music player and in her singing voice too and the dancing was certainly worthy of a 10 from Len. Oh my god was she happy! Fi prepared breakfast, which was substantial today, by her standards, as she had arranged to take the dogs for a walk along the canal with Pauline. As she ate her bananas yoghurt and honey, followed by scrambled eggs on toast washed down with lemon and hot water and her decaf tea with skimmed goats milk, she thought how much she was enjoying feeling the benefits of 'spring cleaning' her life. As she listened to her 'Happy tunes' playlist, she got to thinking, 'I wonder what kind of music Bran likes,' and so she decided to ask him:

18 November 2013. 10.10

Hi Bran, thank you for your lovely email. It brought a smile to the start of my day! I am just sat here relaxing and scrolling through my playlists and I got to thinking, I wonder what kind of music Bran likes? So I have decided to set you a challenge. Please go through your music selection for me and choose 10 pieces of music that you like the most. Send me an explanation telling me why you have chosen those pieces, what they say about you and your life and the final part of the challenge is to select a piece of your music just for me and again telling me why you have selected it for me. I will do the same for you and I will send you my selection soon. Have a lovely day, Fi.

Fi picked Pauline up planned and as they drove over to Dunham Massey, Fi told her friend all about her contact with Bran through the dating site. She also told her about the 'sights for sore eyes' on the site and how they attempted to sell themselves and they laughed at the comedy of it all. Pauline was hanging on her every word as she described exactly how Mr. Antique had arrived via cyberspace and she too was delighted for her friend. They had been work colleagues and shared an office for many years and had remained firm friends. Pauline had a beautiful caring soul and Fi loved people who oozed goodness and Pauline certainly did that. She would do anything for anybody and spent her life caring for others, be it her three lovely girls, her grandchildren, her neighbours, her family and her friends and Fi was grateful to have such a wonderful 'role model for goodness' in her life. They enjoyed a long walk along the canal on this bright, sunny but cold, frosty day. It was threatening snow according to the weather forecast but they were wrapped up warm and the briskness of the walk maintained their body temperatures for them. They stopped and admired the scenery, the bare trees, the grass coated in frost, the fields out across the horizon and the clear blue sky. They spotted a heron on the opposite tow path, searching for a catch, before it was startled by Fi's dogs barking at it with gusto from the opposite bank of the canal and then they watched, as it soared into the air making its ascent into the skyline. "Beautiful site," said Pauline, "what a lovely treat," she added and Fi replied, "absolutely, now lets go back to the village and I will treat you to lunch," "ooh, lovely," Pauline added.

They walked back along the canal exchanging greetings and discussing the lovely setting with some of the barge owners they passed en route. They made their way past the field with the horses which one of Fi's dogs always tried to enter, in his effort to play with the animals but she was savvy to his playful ways now and had him firmly on his lead, by her side. They walked into the village and called into the 'Swan with Two Nicks' pub. It was dog friendly and the dogs were immediately greeted with a warm welcome, a bowl of fresh water and some dog biscuits! "Are they for me?" asked Fi, as she, Pauline and the woman from behind the bar laughed together as the dogs lapped eagerly at the water. The log fire was roaring away, which was a wonderful site, in contrast to the cold outside and the girls took their coats off and sat at the table nearest to it to feel it's benefit. They each ordered the same thing from the menu, as it sounded so good and they sipped at their hot Cappuccinos' as they waited for their food. The atmosphere was cosy and warm and Pauline commented that Fi was 'glowing,' just like the fire in front of them. She too, had seen her friend frozen in time with the ravages of some of life's cruel lessons and she was delighted to see her friend thawing and emerging from her protective hibernation. Just then Fi's email 'signature scribble' sounded from her phone and Pauline laughed as Fi explained what the strange noise was.

There were 3 emails and she clicked on his name:

18 November 2013 12:01:

Hey Fi, oh my, I just got your message re the music challenge. I will do that tomorrow for sure. Bran.

Fi smiled as she relayed the contents of the message to her friend, whilst explaining the significance of the challenge to her. She had realised during her hibernation period that she needed musical compatibility too, to an extent, no more heavy rock and 'twingy twangy' country dominating the house for her, she thought. Each to their own of course but she was choosing that she didn't want it in her life anymore and she hoped Bran had as an eclectic taste in music, as did she. She was hopeful, given the Eric Clapton track sent to her the previous night. Their food arrived and the girls devoured it heartily, soon revealing empty plates. "I was so hungry!" said Pauline, "me too, that long walk gave me an appetite!" replied Fi as she paid the bill as they put their coats on to leave. Fi was conscious of having to disturb the dogs, sleeping in front of the log fire. The woman behind the bar came for a farewell cuddle with the dogs and they all said their goodbyes and Pauline, Fi and the dogs headed back through the grounds of Dunham Massey Hall to Fi's car. As they drove home they chatted about ex work colleagues they had shared their careers with and their respective children's lives, catching up on each other's news. Fi dropped Pauline off at her home before calling into the organic supermarket near to her own home to stock up on items for her planned new juicing regime. She really was on a health kick now!

When she arrived home she put her shopping away, read her 'paper' mail, made tea and sat down to relax after her long walk and sent the following reply to Bran:

18 November 2013 16.11

Hi Bran, Thank you for your messages today. I hope you are well. Here is a list of music for you according to my challenge. I wonder if my list will be as you imagined it would be and what will it tell you about me? I have had a lovely day and it was all the more pleasant with the thoughts that I had of you.

1) Sanctus. Libera. I take's me back to my school days when I was in my church choir, my school choir and my town choir too. I love singing and this is such a beautiful calming piece of music.

2) Because I know that I can. Andy Burrows. The title says it all. I know I can do anything that I want to.

3) Beneath Your Beautiful. Labrinth and Emile Sande. Stunning song and beauty is inside of us primarily. In our souls.

4) Sunshine in the Rain. BWO. Such a happy, happy

tune, when driving in the car, roof down, sunshine pouring down on me, this song on so loud and I'm singing along to the words and feeling HAPPY.

5) Brand New Day. Joshua Radin. Fantastic lyrics. My favourite line invites me to make sure my past is passed. So inspiring.

7) The Children of Piraeous. Aroma. Taken from the sixties song by the Chordettes "Never on a Sunday." Well wouldn't that be nice to kiss you on a Monday, Tuesday, Wednesday, Thursday, Friday and a Saturday. I have a confession though, I am greedy, I would want the kiss on the Sunday too!

8) Pie Jesu. Andrew Johnston. I am a sucker for choirs and this is simply stunning.

9) Wonderful. Gary Go. Affirming song telling one to look in the mirror and tell yourself you are wonderful, when life is throwing you one of it's many curveballs. Uplifting tune.

10) Happy Birthday. Altered Images. A happy song I always play to myself on my birthday. Which is incidentally, the 15th of February. Just missed being a Valentine baby.

A piece of music for you: The Cinematic Orchestra. Arrival of the birds.

I have chosen this for you and for us. Because, I have imagined you and I, making love to this beautiful piece of music. I am taking a risk telling you that Bran but it is true, I have. I hope my imaginings one day come true. I have just listened to Eric Clapton again. It's

such a beautiful song. Thank you. I also hope that one day you will think that of me too. I am so enjoying our lovely writing to each other. Thank you. Until I hear from you again. Fi.

Fi rested a while on the sofa before she was woken from her catnap with a text message alert from her cousin asking her to ring her when she was free. Fi went to use the bathroom, freshen her face with cold water and rang Jen. “Hello Pet, how are you?” asked Jen, seeing her cousin’s name in the caller display. Fine thanks Jen, everything okay with you and Bill?” “Champion, aye, smashing, nothing to report from here, just wondering if you’d heard from Mr. Antique?” Jen replied in her lovely Geordie twang. Fi laughed, “ Yes I have heard from Bran!” “What’s he called, Bran?” asked Jen, before adding, “what kinda names that? that’s a foreign one isn’t it?”. “It is,” replied Fi, before adding, “he is half Dutch, half Slovenian.” “Eeeh man, well he’ll have a canny accent mind, to go with those looks!” laughed Jen. “I hope so,” said Fi before telling Jen all about his emails from the past couple of days, filling her in on what he did for a living, his family structure, his ex-wife status, his hobbies and his hopes within a relationship, and she also told her about the cute emails regarding Eric Clapton and good morning pretty one! “Eeeh man,” said Jen, “he sounds a dream, you’ll have to get yasell practicing some moves fa ya dancing date, you could do with some lessons, mind.” All the time Fi was laughing at the lovely Geordie accent and the funny images Jen was igniting in her imagination and she said, “I could do with living closer to you and then you could teach me!” (Jen is a past ballroom dancing champion) and they both laughed. “The waltz is easy enough, man” said Jen, “it’s just one, two, step to the right, one, two, step to the right, one, two, step to the right," and Fi joined her cousin both verbally and with her feet, trying to move to Jen's instructions, "one, two, step to the right, one, two, step to the right, one, two, step to the right ooh shit!" and she burst out laughing as she tried to tell Jen in between giggling that she had kicked the dogs biscuits all over the floor as Jen joined in the laughter too. "I've heard of tantrums and tiara's," said Jen, "but you've got dancing and dog biscuits to contend with!" and they both broke into laughter. After composing themselves, Jen said, " 'Eeh god, you'll have to improve your dancing, otherwise you'll be there in your sequins standing all o'er his plates of meat!" (Geordie speak for feet) They both burst out laughing again. Fi added, "Yes but will I get a ten from Jen?" and they cracked up laughing again. They finally composed themselves enough to say their goodbyes and Fi promised to keep her cousin informed of any developments as Jen said finally, "I'm really, really happy for you pet, it's lovely to hear you laughing after what that Tosser put you through! Lot's of love" and they ended their call. Fi made dinner for herself and watched a film before sending Bran an email and going to bed for an early night:

18 November 2013 22.22

Hi Bran, I was thinking of you and thought I would say hello. I hope you have had a good day today with both business and pleasure successes. I have had a long dog walk by the canal and a restful evening with music and a movie. I have had some verbal instruction today from my cousin (who is a past dancing champion) in readiness for our dancing date! I have missed your 'informative' messages today. Fi.

She sent the message and then reread thinking, 'shit' do I

sound too demanding on his time, what I meant was I have missed our detailed messages which I really love reading, oh bollocks, bollocks, bollocks! Oh well not a lot she could do, it was flying through cyberspace now, on it's way to him!

Why walk when you can dance?

CHAPTER 8

Fuckety fuck fuck fuck

The next day, Fi heard nothing at all from Bran and given her previous history of "The Case of the disappearing Man," she was not surprised and as she went to bed that night she felt sad and miserable. It didn't matter how much she tried to rationalise it all with perfectly explainable excuses why Bran may not have contacted her, nothing soothed her low mood and she considered that she was somehow allergic to good men or vice versa. Not surprisingly she didn't sleep very well.

When she arose the next morning she showered and went straight out with the dogs. She threw them in the car and drove off to The Lake, a local beauty spot. She had to clear her head. That horrible shitty throbbing questioning felt like she was on the cusp of THAT pin ball machine switching itself on again and she had to avoid that at all costs, she couldn't bear it. Sometimes she questioned if she could EVEN survive that level of pain again. Could she? She always said that because she had been left behind by her own mum, in reality, she knew that she NEVER would take her own life because she also knew, from experience that, 'the pain' does always pass, but Jesus, it fucking hurts like hell. Far, far worse than any physical pain could ever hurt, she'd had two children remember, she knew physical pain!

She marched round the lake with the determined mindset to get the fuck away from her mind games, she had her music on the highest volume, and she pressed the repeat song option with, 'Coldplay's, Viva la Vida.' She could not hear an outside sound and she was hoping that by the time she had done a full circuit of the lake she had fucked the pinball machine off good and proper! She got back to her car, took her phone out of her pocket to put it in the dashboard tray and she heard the scribbling pen sound! She opened her emails and it was from Bran. 'Oh here we go, he's going to tell me to jog on,' she thought as she gave the dogs a drink of water in the hatchback area of the car and sat in there with them looking out onto the lake. She clicked open the email with her heart racing as she realised, she felt sick. She put her glasses on and read:

20 November 2013 10:08

Hello 'Pretty One,' I sent you an email yesterday before heading out but it seems it didn't get to you. I have had a failed message alert. I really missed you! I will resend to you now. How are you doing this beautiful day?

Here goes my top ten music challenge.

Mmmmm, I liked your number 11!

1, Happy. Pharrell Williams; When I think about all I have been through and where I am now, it really makes me happy, though still needs that special person to make it a complete package. Will that be you?

2, Make you feel my love. Adele; Because it sounds more like a poem and I love poems, I write some myself and in time I shall share some with you.

3, Lady in Red. Chris de Burgh; It has a very good

story line that I like to follow, Lady Diana and all that.

4, Wonderful tonight. Eric Clapton; It is a song I am looking forward to singing to that special person, maybe doing a karaoke or perhaps playing my guitar.

5, I swear. All for one. There is just something about that song that I like so much.

6, Move closer. Phyllis Nelson. Yes, please!

7, Candle in the Wind. Elton John. Just a great song and I love Marilyn too.

8, Turn out the light and love me tonight. Don Williams. Maybe for the open fire moment you mentioned!

9, Missing you. Michael Bolton. A beautiful song to sing when you are missing someone.

10, Colour of Love. Boyz to men. Lovely love song.

Well, I had a business meeting today and as a result of it, I have two days to prepare for New York and I was like no way! Why now, I ask myself?

Normally my clients are to tell me what is highest on their demand list in the art and antique world (what they need at any given time), then I figure out which country is best to get them and off I go to source the items for them. So that is the major part of my job. You will find out more as our time goes on. I just hope you can hang on there for me I will be gone for just over a week.

So do you have any other guys you're talking to from the site apart from me? I have talked to about 5 women on there but not exchanged my emails with more than two and you are now the only one I talk to. The rest for one reason or the other didn't strike the right chord with me. I don't go on the site often now as you may have noticed. As a matter of fact, if you and I make it, then it's the end of the site for me. I swear I'd like a date with you soon, can't wait to meet you now! Something I can't explain about you when I look at your pic and read from you. I have had one major relationship since my divorce. I had another very short relationship soon after but soon found out she was a liar!

My free times these days as a single man isn't so much fun as when I had or if I had a partner. I like to cook, sometimes with my daughter, go to good restaurants, to the park to people watch, I love museums and cinemas. I also enjoy reading, keeping up with current affairs, watching sports, and oh, of course, I love my diving and sea swimming in summer so much. Hand in hand beach walking and feeling that sea breeze, I love that too. Do you have any favorite pastimes you want to share with me?

I am the type of guy that takes pride in his appearance. I brush up well I have to say. I like to smell nicely and stay healthy. So you will be having a real man for yourself if we hit it off, hopefully we will. Lets just say I have big enough shoulders for you to lean on anytime you need me. I was thinking to myself this morning, how much I have missed being with someone special. You know those lovely late night summonses to be together because you miss each other. Often made by

telephone arranging spontaneous liaisons on an ad hoc basis (times when we just can't help it anymore, you just need to be together). You know what I mean, when you are in love nothing is impossible. I want all that back again.

My last relationship ended over a year ago year. So I can honestly say to you without being bashful over it that I have been M.I.A and I have not been with anyone intimately for a year plus now. I just channeled all my energy into my business and tried not to think of what's missing. I am happy in my own skin now but that obvious someone is missing. We can all be happier when we find that special someone. A truth we cannot deny! I think I would sweep you off your feet. I feel very close to you already and don't know how best to explain that. You see, normally it's kind of difficult to feel that synergy with someone you haven't even met, but it's not the same with you at all. I'm being honest, as deep down, I know there is something working together for our good somewhere and I am positive about us at this point. Is it fate? Anyway I think it is time to hear your voice, drop me your number and a good time to call you and we will speak soon. Bye for now. Bran.

PS: That's a picture from our business meeting yesterday.

Fi felt a sense of relief inside of her. She had been on a downer for 24 hours because of a failed satellite issue. 'WTF,' she thought as she locked the dogs safely in the hatch and got in her seat to drive home and put a particular track on her playlist, loud and on repeat of course! 'Happy' by Pharrell Williams, because now she felt happy as she drove home for coffee o'clock without any of the girls! At home she just wanted to have a chill out day, she was emotionally exhausted, 'why couldn't people have mind transplants to erase all trauma?' she thought. It would be so much easier. She opened the mail again and played all the tunes on his list, some she had heard and others were new to her, but she enjoyed his selection very much, she could live with that music taste she thought, definitely. She also reread the details contained in the email and allowed her thoughts to flow as she imagined him. It was great to know that he was being exclusive to her, after all, she was doing the same but she couldn't have demanded that from him could she, they were, after all, only emailing each other at this stage and it had actually only been for a few days. She liked his list of hobbies and would definitely enjoy all of those pleasures with him, except the diving, they would have to discuss that one but she was certainly not declaring it a complete NO. She could certainly tell he was a guy who liked to look after himself, she could smell his sex appeal through her laptop, the look of him alone turned her on and that was a very good starting point! There appeared to be no lingering ex's, which was also good but what the hell does MIA mean? She Googled it and found that is meant 'missing in action' as in, he had not had any sexual relations for over a year! Good, she thought, he's obviously not a promiscuous man but wait till she got her hands on him, she thought, 'Jesus'. The thought of him sweeping her off her feet sounded very appealing indeed and she ebbed and flowed in between enjoying the thought of that prospect and needing to keep her feet firmly on the ground. Her capacity to trust was shot and she hadn't met him yet! She then sat and observed yesterdays photograph for several minutes. The date and time the photograph was taken were clearly visible. He was pictured with another man and they were shaking hands. He was wearing glasses and he looked so handsome as he smiled, not a happy wide grinning smile but a small smile showing some of his teeth. He was wearing black trousers, a white shirt, a black waistcoat and a short black wool coat. It was very much a business photograph but a nice image, nonetheless. 'Mmmm,' she thought, he is seriously hot. She clicked on reply and typed her response to him:

20 November 2013 12:26

Hi Bran, how lovely to hear from you. I really missed your messages yesterday. I have listened to your tunes this morning. I love your selection. I have just had a request to meet a friend for coffee at 2 so I will dash off and get a shower now. I cannot wait to hear your voice but here is another challenge for you to find within all of my previous writing to you. You already have my number! Can you find it? Time will tell! I am excited for you going to New York. I have a beautiful friend in New York, her name is Kim and I have never met her in person only online but she and I have a beautiful friendship and one day I hope to meet her in her hometown of New York. She has such a beautiful soul, as my intuition tells me, you have too! I cannot wait to see where all this takes us and I assure you, if we get to that stage, I will give you and us my all, without being a clingy, jealous woman. I just want to be myself with a beautiful man, creating a beautiful life together and I have happy feelings about you. I am not on the dating site anymore, other than to reply to a couple of emails when I have politely declined other men's contact with me. I have integrity and have been treating you online as I would want to be treated. I cannot possibly speak to you as I have in a genuine way, if I was emailing

other men too. I could never, ever behave like that. Be assured I am in contact with only you. I am excited about what/when/how our adventure will evolve, as it has, after all, already begun. Your picture is beautiful as always and I cannot wait to hear your voice now, and before long see your eyes looking into mine, taste our first kiss, feel the strength of your arms around me, laugh with you until I cry, etcetera, etcetera. I cannot wait! Thank you for responding to me on the dating site. You jumped off the page to me for a reason. Fi. X

He responded within minutes:

20 November 2013 12:45

Hey Fi, now I will have to search for your number. I love your challenges. I cannot wait to hear your voice either. I am on my way to London to see Kate, as I fly to New York from there and I will phone you from her home later. You enjoy your time with your friend. Bran.

Fi showered and changed for an afternoon out with Julie, they were going to a DIY store followed by coffee at their favourite garden centre, where the Christmas decor displays, were both fabulous and famous! In Bury anyway! They chose paint, paper and brushes ready for Julie's decorating project and then off they went to devour a huge slice of cake and enjoy a hot coffee on this cold winter day. They perused the decorations and filled their baskets with Christmas trinkets and gifts and joined the mammoth queue to pay for their goods, before driving home for yet more coffee and chat as Julie caught up on all the emails of the last few days. She was delighted for her friend that things were progressing as they were and they were so giddy at the prospect of where the first date might be. Fi imagined what she would wear and they laughed together about her 'telephone dancing lessons' and her new sequined shawl. Fi imagined herself having dinner with him in Liverpool somewhere, dancing in a club afterwards and then what? Should she drive home, should she book a hotel for herself? Who knew? She discussed with Julie that she suspected he perhaps had a waterfront apartment in Liverpool, as he somehow seemed an apartment kind of guy. Julie agreed. It was all very giddy again at number 9 as Fi pondered over what a difference 24 hours makes! The girls chatted some more about Fi's impending trip to London, her excitement at seeing Louise and doing the things together that Louise had planned for Fi. Fi would be happy to see Louise's 'base' in London and then she could finally feel at ease with her daughter's decision to move to the capital, to further her career! She just needed to know she was in a happy and safe living environment, because she already knew she was doing really well in her new role for her employers and that she was enjoying this huge career leap she had taken. Julie discussed her plans for the evening and they then said their goodbyes. Fi fed her dogs and then sent a quick email to Bran:

20 November 2013 17:19

Hi Bran, How are you? You may call me whenever you chose, to suit your busy schedule. Did you find my number as per my challenge! Guess what? I found yours! I am so looking forward to hearing your voice. Enjoy your time with Kate. Until I hear from you, I will say bye for now. I had to Google MIA by the way as I didn't know what it meant but it made me smile.

Let's hope neither of us are MIA for much longer! Mmm! Fi.

Just after 6pm the landline rang and she knew it was Bran, she had only recently changed the number to stop Robert contacting her. Nobody else rang that number! She was so nervous as she went to answer it:

Fi: "Hello,"

Bran: "hey Fi," she laughed, a nervous laugh,

Bran: "who is this?" he teased her,

Fi: "it's you," she laughed again,

Bran: "who's you?" he asked and he laughed,

Fi: "It's Bran," she laughed again,

Bran: "hey, how are you?" he asked,

Fi: "I'm good thank you, a little nervous but good, it's great to hear your voice, you have a lovely accent,"

Bran: "Thank you, you have a beautiful voice, you speak well," in her mind she was thinking, 'fuck!' as she nervously marched around the room, whilst she spoke to him.

Fi: "How was your drive down to London?"

Bran: "Good, I have had a good conversation with Kate and she is just making dinner and then I will finalise things for my journey tomorrow."

Fi: "well, I appreciate the call and I will email later and hopefully speak to you from New York, yes?" she said questioningly.

Bran: "sure, lovely to put a voice to your beautiful smile, you take care and we will speak soon, okay?"

Fi: "you have a safe journey tomorrow and we'll talk soon, I want photos please!" she laughed,

Bran: "me too, cheeky!" and they both laughed together, a hearty happy laugh.

Fi: "bye Bran, take care of you."

Bran: "bye baby, kisses to you."

She pressed the red button to end the call. He called her baby, Robert called everybody baby, she fucking hated that word didn't she? Err NO! Not the way he had just said it, Jeeez, that was hot to hear!

She sent a text to Julie:

Fi: Fuckety, fuck, fuck, fuck.

Julie: What?

Fi: Mr. Antique just rang me!

Julie: Fuck, fuck, fuck, I'm there, get the coffee on.

Fi went into the kitchen and hadn't even lifted the coffee glasses down from the shelf, when there was a loud banging on the front door. She ran and opened it and Julie rushed into the hall and they both squealed, really squealed, “Tell me, tell me,” screamed Julie. Fi conveyed the phone call to Julie, describing in detail the dialogue, his accent, the depth of his voice and his laugh. They both squealed again before Fi said, “Oh my god, Jules, he’s real?” and with that a doubt crept into her mind and she ran to get the phone, pressed 1471 and noted down the number in her mobile, it was definitely a London number (and she mentally crossed it off her list of doubts) and she saved the number in her phone as Kate Rodrigues. They had a quick coffee and Julie left to take her son to his football practice. Fi sat down again on the sofa and sighed, she took a few minutes to calm down and compose herself before she emailed him:

20 November 2013 18:46

Thank you for calling me Bran. That moment, when I first heard your voice is a keeper. That is in my memory forever and ever. Beautiful moment. Have a lovely evening and a safe journey tomorrow and now I cannot wait to see you in person, Fi. X

It had all just stepped up a notch for her now. ‘Game on’ she thought, she was now giving herself permission to go for it. It was real and that is why she had finished her email with a kiss. Game on indeed. He was a man all right. Jesus. She was shaking with excitement. She took the dogs for a walk and took the time to listen to classical music, to help centre herself. This was excitement on a big scale again. She hadn’t had that for a long, long time, she had never had it with Robert. She had had episodes of excitement in her life in relationships but THIS was off the scale ‘buzzing’ excitement. ‘OMFGG! Oh my fucking giddy god!’ she thought. When she got back home she settled on the sofa with tea, her blanket and her dogs beside her, when an email alert came through on her phone, it was from Bran:

20 November 2013 20:16

Hey baby, you adding your voice to our messages we've exchanged, makes a whole lot of sense to me now, all that is required is adding the physical to it. It is such a shame it cannot be now, how I wish we could have met before this business trip. I must say, you have a good voice, a lovely accent and you speak well and I can hear the fun too. I want to listen to you repeatedly now. I want to wish my time away in New York, as I have a sense of excitement inside of me but I will stay grounded and get my business done and count my days until our first date. I hope you are having a wonderful evening. Bran.

Fi replied:

20 November 2013 20:26

Hi Bran, having to take our time to meet will make it all the more special when we do finally see each other. I know! Don't ask me how but I do, that you are just as beautiful in your physical sense and as a person, as is conveyed in your photographs and beautiful writing. I am so, so excited about whatever is coming our way. Where have you been indeed? Wow. I have a happy contented sense inside. Hope you are having a lovely evening. Fi. X

Fi watched TV, nothing in particular though as she was too excited and couldn't concentrate and as she flicked through the channels she got an email alert again:

20 November 2013 20:55

Hey Fi, I will definitely keep up with you all the time from the USA and make sure I'm not too far away from you. I am having a lovely evening. It would be better if you were here too. Ha, ha! What are you up to now? Bran.

Fi replied:

20 November 2013 21:15

Hi Bran, I have had a visit from my friend Julie as she was excited to hear about our call, if that is okay with you, I have told her all about us? She said she would like to thank you because you have made me smile again and she hasn't seen me smile for 18 months. Thank you for making me smile. I have been out with the dogs and I think I will have an early night and dream of my Mr. Antique. I will send you some more pictures tomorrow evening. I will be out most of the day with my friend Jackie who I have known since I was 15. Her daughter is off to Australia for 12 months next week so we are all going to an Italian for lunch. Then I will be volunteering for a couple of hours with some elderly people. When I get home I will search through my photographs. Sleep well and safe journey tomorrow. Fi. X

She got ready for bed, made sure the dogs and cat were fed, watered and toileted for the night, made herself hot milk and honey and took herself to bed to read the newspaper. She was tucked up and content and thinking of her bedroom being more than a sleep space, when she had an email alert flash on her screen. It was from Bran:

20 November 2013 21:40

Hello Fi, of course it's Okay you telling Julie about me and I am glad she is happy for you. I am starting to tell my friends about us too. It is safe to do so I think now. I think you have also made me smile in recent times and Kate has certainly noticed a change in me she says. She wants to meet you when the time is right. I want as many photos I can get of you, I am having to wait longer than I wanted before I get to see you in person and so I will not get tired of seeing your pictures. Okay! You have a good day planned tomorrow, which sounds lovely. Have a great time and keep yourself safe for me. Keep smiling that beautiful smile, have a good nights' rest and we will meet on the other side as usual. Bran.

She lay in bed smiling, thinking of him, with stirrings of excitement as she imagined herself meeting him when he was home. It was getting nearer.

She sent a reply:

20 November 2013 21:49

Hello Bran, When you see movies and couples are talking on the telephone and they don't want to say goodbye or disconnect the telephone line. That is how I am feeling. I don't want to stop writing to you. I will say goodnight now but please will you give me a quick message tomorrow to let me know you are safely there in NYC. Please say hello to Kate for me and I very much look forward to meeting her AFTER I have met her father of course! Ha. Sweet dreams my Mr. Antique. Fi. X

Today is a page-turner she thought.

The next day was a quiet day for Fi as Bran was up in the clouds somewhere but then again so was she, sat on cloud 9!

The following morning she woke up to the sensation of the cat licking her face. Her phone was on her bed next to her where she had dropped it as she drifted to sleep. She checked her emails and there amongst the usual crap was his name, his writing jumped off the page too, as his dating site image had. She was so excited to receive his emails now, she recognised that stomach flipping excitement at the beginning of a relationship, when it is mutually stepping up a gear. She tapped on the mail and she gasped, there was an image of him in casual attire stood in Times Square. "Oh my god, oh my god, oh my god," she said aloud, "OH MY GOD," she repeated, "that guy there, YOU! Are mine. What the fuck?" "Arrrrgggggghhhhhh!" she screamed in her head whilst dancing in her bed as she lay there, staring at his image.

After a few moments admiring the image she sat up bolt upright to make herself comfortable to read, after noticing the date and time on the photograph:

22 November 2013 5:45

Hi dear, Firstly, I must apologise for not writing before leaving, I am so sorry. I am here safely now. I truly really wished you were with me while flying. I don't like lonely flying, especially, long haul. Wifi is working fine right here and I will write more when I am more settled, the time difference is so crazy you know, it takes some getting used to. Beautiful things they say

happen to beautiful people, you have happened to me and I am looking forward to beautiful things with you. Its just a shame business came calling now. I am looking forward to exploring the world with you, it is a very strange feeling like I have known you forever, it still always brings that question to mind "where has she been all this time?" Now I know my coming to the dating site isn't a waste, I just hope you don't get stolen before I get back home. Lol. Bran.

PS: The photo was taken today by a tourist, after I also did one for him too, I really need some rest now.

Fi tapped the reply button and typed:

Hi Bran, rest well and know that I have already been stolen! BY YOU! I am so ready for this beautiful adventure we are already on together. Until I hear from you again.

Take Care. Fi. X

I want to be wrapped in your arms skin against skin let me in

CHAPTER 9

The Twins

That day was filled with the pinball machine on full pelt but this time it had been loaded with happy balls. Fi was so high she was almost touching the sky. It was unbelievable how much a picture, a few words and a sense of what was on the horizon, had done to lift her spirits. Her emotions were suddenly soaring again, instead of the all too familiar plummeting. Is this happening after just two weeks, she asked herself?

She put on her happy tunes playlist as she had so much energy and she had decided to clean her house from top to bottom. She took her tunes with her into every room and sang her heart out scaring the shit out of the cat in the process as she ran away and into her shed to shelter from the madness. She felt so happy inside and sang along to all the songs including Kim Wilde, 'You came,' Tommy Sparks, 'She's got me dancing,' The Pet Shop Boys, 'Always on my mind,' Abba, 'Our Last Summer' and whatever else 'shuffled' into her home. She danced like she had never danced before to Animal Kingdoms, 'Two by Two' as she really was feeling ecstatic. She had been to two extremes recently, mad with pain and now mad with ecstasy and this wasn't the illegal ecstasy either, this was the real deal. Endorphines. Just after 11am she took a decaf coffee break and sent an email to Bran:

22 November 2013 11:24

Good morning beautiful man, that Times Square photo is wow. Thank you. I am sat here relaxing with my

favourite coffee listening to my music and I heard a song that sparked my interest so I checked out the lyrics. There is a verse that got me thinking of your reference to clandestine phone calls and spontaneous meetings, when in a relationship and made me feel warm inside! Taken from Dangerous by David Guetto. Take a listen! Mmmm. I also was thinking about my little quirky traits and what you would think of them and so I thought that I would tell you of a few:

I drink decaf tea with goat's milk and honey.

I like to drink from China cups or mugs.

I love a Gin and Tonic with good quality gin, ice and a slice of lime.

I like bottled beer on occasions with a wedge of lime.

I like to drink white wine, not too dry.

I love unusual glasses for my alcoholic drinks.

I love to eat my breakfast outdoors and have made my garden into an outside room to allow that in the summer.

I love to feed the garden birds and I have done since I was a little girl and have all manner of them visiting my garden.

I love music and prefer it to television most of the time, I have recently re discovered my favourite radio station and I am absolutely loving it!

I love singing loudly to my music but especially in the car, to a great happy tune!

I really like cooking and baking, with vegan cakes being my baking fad at the moment. I would like to be able to cook Chinese food as it is my favourite cuisine, although I also like Indian, Italian and a good English or French restaurant.

My favourite chocolate is Green and Blacks Organics. It is sensuous as well as delicious in the mouth.

I adore fresh flowers in the house with Lilies being a favourite. My daughter often sends me flowers from London, which is a lovely treat and I often buy them for myself too as I love the welcome, the smell and the beauty they add to the decor in my home.

I take ages and I mean ages brushing my teeth! Being an ex dental nurse makes me extra vigilant!

I am a sucker for unusual shoes, lovely lingerie and stylish clothes.

I love handbags but like to source items that are different from the crowd.

I love fresh bedding after a lovely sensuous shared bath and all the lushness of making the bed messy again with a never-ending love making session.

I love waking up tired after such a night and relishing all the thoughts of the previous evenings' events. Mmmmm. I wish you were here now! Anyway I will dash off now as I have just had a text for a shopping trip into town with Tracey. Maybe Lingerie is on my list! Until I hear from you again. Take care. Fi. Xx

Attachments: Photos as promised.

Tracey called to pick Fi up for a coffee o'clock afternoon and Fi was delirious as she conveyed what had happened over the past few days, including detailed information of his phone calls and emails. She showed Tracey this morning's photograph and her response was, "Jesus Fi, HE is gorgeous," before adding, "you can tell he's got money, even his casual clothes, reek of class." They both agreed as they discussed his attire in more detail and how thoughtful he was to think to send her an image of himself before he had even had any rest. Just then Kim Wilde came on the playlist again and Fi said, "Listen to the words'" and they agreed that he had come and changed the way Fi felt, as they sang along to the lyrics together. Fi suddenly burst out laughing and said to Tracey, "He'll be 'coming' all right when I've finished with him, can't wait, literally can't wait," and they burst into laughter, "Jesus, it turns me on just thinking about making love to him!" Fi added before Tracey asked, "Won't you be nervous?" "NERVOUS! NO WAY!" Fi replied, before adding, "we need a Trafford trip though, I need a whole new lingerie revamp!" and they both laughed some more as Tracey agreed, "too bloody right you do," (glancing over at the clothes maiden in the kitchen where some of Fi's underwear was drying!) before further adding, "it's SO exciting and I'm so happy for you Fi and I'm saying it again but I've never seen you look this happy EVER!"

The girls drove to the Trafford Centre listening to the radio and singing along to the music in between chatting about general life issues. Upon arrival at the shopping centre they had a lunch and drinks in readiness for a long shopping venture. I have 'special presents' to buy, as well as a couple of items for London, Fi thought. They toured the specialist lingerie shops as well as lingerie departments in the large chain stores, looking for Fi's specific requirements, but she was disappointed. She just didn't want 'pull your lumps and bumps in' foundation wear, even though she was conscious of her own lumps and bumps, as she had had two children. She wanted 'Teddies'. She loved them and used to wear them all the time years ago, having them in an array of colours. They are an all in one garment, like a swimming costume but lingerie, they are very comfortable to wear, they flatter your shape and they used to be very sexy on her and very well received too! She knew she didn't want anything else but those. She found the odd one or two but either the cups or the fabric just weren't right for her. Most departments they went into had all in ones in stock but they were the regular nude, black or white very unsexy, foundation wear. 'NO THANK YOU!' she thought, before deciding she would wait until she was in London, feeling more confident that she would find what she wanted in the capital. Fi went to the perfume counter and treated herself to all time favourite, expensive but worth the price, wow perfume. "It turns ME on, never mind him!" laughed Fi as they both doused themselves, when spraying it from the counter display bottle. They then drove over to Chorlton to have a glass of cider in the Lloyd's pub and ended up chatting to a guy named Gary, who sat at a nearby table and introduced himself to the girls. Tracey noticed how confident Fi appeared, chatting to a member of the opposite sex again and she was so glad to see her friend recovering so well from her trauma. She wasn't 'recovered' by any means but she was on her way and it was great to see. Whilst the girls were sat in the pub Fi received a 'signature scribble' email alert and they both raised their eyebrows as Fi opened her emails and nodded at Tracey. She clicked on his name and read:

22 November 2013 11:02

Hello sweet one. How are you doing today? How is it over there? I just had a well deserved rest. It's about 11am here now. It is so good to know you are ready for the sweet and beautiful things coming our way, it has been a while that I have felt this way you know, and I am very positive about us.

I just got to see the photos you sent, oh goodness me, you look amazing, like you were having a modelling shot on the one where you are wearing the white bikini? I would like to see you in that outfit! I can't wait. Right now I am waiting on the agent who will come and take me out, so I can have an idea to what to expect and that's what my day will consist of. Then I can have a little more rest and tomorrow I can start getting what I want. Oh my goodness, I see we share some traits. Ha.

Quite regular hobbies of:

Singing loudly in the car, I would love to do that with you.

I love the birds too but I have never tried feeding them before, now I am looking forward to doing that with you as well, sounds like a lovely hobby.

Quite, (no not quite, 'VERY') sensual hobbies of:

I love fresh bedding after a lovely sensuous bath too and all the lushness of making the bed messy with a never-ending love making session sounds just perfect.

I love waking up tired after such a night and relishing

all the thoughts of the previous night, me too. I am definitely looking forward to our time participating in those hobbies whenever we decide that may be. Yum. I have gotten a US line now. You can reach me on that if you have international call time it will be cheaper for you, I really would like to hear that lovely voice of yours. Let me say, you just have a way of turning me on with your messages. You can call me at about 9:30 to 10:00pm UK time, I will be back in then or I can call you if you let me know a suitable time. Bran.

PS: I hope my woman is having a good time with Tracey, you can also get the lingerie for when we spend our first night together. What do you think?

Fi chuckled to herself as she read but she couldn't share it aloud with Tracey as Gary was on the next table and it was a girl's only conversation! She would save that for later. She tapped reply and typed:

22 November 2013 16:33

Hello Bran, Glad you had a good rest. I am having a lovely time with Tracey. We are just in our favourite part of Manchester, in a place named Chorlton. The lingerie was not to my taste or standard and so I will have a search when in London at the weekend. I so look forward to our sensual creations together too. Wow. The thoughts of such are sending my stomach crazy! Have a good business venture today and I will call you later to hear your lovely voice, Fi. X

Fi received a text from Julie:

Julie: Fuckety, fuck, fuck, fuck!

Fi: What?

Julie: Is Mr. Antique at yours?

Fi: No! Why?

Julie: Posh car outside your house!

Fi: I wish!

The coffee o'clock club came to a close for another day and as they drove home Fi filled Tracey in on the last email and they giggled about his comments re her hobbies. Fi couldn't understand where her sensuous behaviour was coming from and Tracey thought she'd remind her, "Err hello, look at his pictures again, what normal red blooded female wouldn't want to be sensual with him?" "Yes, but I've never even met him Tracey," said Fi, "do you think I'm being slutty, teasing him, sending him things like this via email," she said, Tracey replied, "don't be stupid, YOU slutty, NEVER, we are in the age of modern women now, with sexual freedoms as well as freedom to express ourselves more. You've got no choice but to express that to each other through your writing at the moment, maybe on the phone too, now that you have a number but it's normal sensual behaviour between two people who have got the hot's for each other, now shut the fuck up and enjoy it!" "Okay mother!" laughed Fi. "I won't be doing any 'Sex And The City,' phone sex though!" she added as they laughed. Tracey dropped Fi off about 6:30pm that evening and after saying their goodbyes, Fi let herself into her house, fed her dogs and walked them for an hour, relishing in the euphoric delirious joy that she felt in her head and she believed that she was also beginning to feel seeping into her heart too. What a day and she'd not even met him yet. She got home from the dog walk, poured herself a glass of wine and put on another episode of Sex and The City, to distract herself until she would be calling him. Maybe that choice of Dvd wasn't a good idea though. All the girl talk of men, desires and sexual positions added to her own desires and as she lay on the settee thinking of them together and how they would fulfill their first night of love making, her landline rang and startled her out of her fantasies. She knew of course that it was Bran:

Fi: "Hello"

Bran: "Hey Baby," (Jeepers, that was so, so sexy she thought, his voice, his accent, the way he say's baby)

Fi: "How are you? Did you have a good day?"

Bran: "I'm okay, not a good business day though, didn't locate what I'm looking for, when out with the agent. I'm meeting him again in the morning and hopefully will be a better day tomorrow. How was your day? Sounds like it was fun!"

Fi: "It was a great day, thank you, great fun with Tracey."

Bran: "Who is Tracey, how did you two meet?"

Fi: "Well we met through our boys who are the same age and have been friends since they were five years old so almost 15 years now. She is so lovely, been there through the tough and tender times and many tears and giggles along the way. She is a beautiful friend Bran, inside and out. She's gorgeous looking."

Bran: "I look forward to meeting her too, she sounds

like she is part of your happiness now."

Fi: "Too right she is! We tell each other everything!" (He roars laughing at that comment)

Bran: "What will you do with the rest of your night?"

Fi: "I am feeling quite tired Bran, so I'll go to bed soon."

Bran: "Well before you go to sleep listen to Shayne Ward Breathless, (as he began to sing some of the lyrics to Fi) have you heard it before Fi?"

Fi: "Oh that was so good, the way you said my name, (she laughed nervously) no I haven't heard it before."

Bran: "Well put it on, close your eyes and I am singing those words to you as you go to sleep."

Fi: "I will, thank you, have a lovely sleep and thank you for calling me."

Bran: "I couldn't wait any longer to hear your voice baby, have a beautiful sleep and I'll meet you on the other side, okay?"

Fi: "Okay, thank you (she had tears in her eyes), talk to you tomorrow maybe but I will email you anyway. Good night Bran."

Bran: "Night Fi, Kisses to you baby." The line went dead.

She sat down. She NEEDED to sit down she thought as she took some deep breaths, due to her feelings of being overwhelmed. He was so sweet, so gentlemanly, he had lovely manners, he was interested in her, he was caring. It was too much. The joy inside her was unbelievable. She put Shayne Ward on her laptop and tears rolled down her face, it was a beautiful song, she had never heard it before and it left her both 'Breathless' and 'Speechless'.

Fi sent him an email:

22 November 2013 23:11

Thank you for the lovely phone call. I want to see your handsome face as I speak to you and as we laugh together even more now. I am so looking forward to that day. Enjoy your dinner, have a restful night and I will see you in our dreams again.

I believe that laughing is the best calorie burner

I believe in kissing, kissing a lot

I believe in being strong

I believe that happy girls are the prettiest

I believe tomorrow is another day

I believe in miracles

I believe in you and

I believe in us.

Goodnight Mr. Antique. Thank you for the joy you have already brought into my life. Wow. Fi. X

He replied almost immediately:

Good night sweet one, I just can't stop smiling now. I will be thinking of you. Good night and sleep tight! Bran.

Fi listened to Shayne Ward again and emailed him a final time that day:

Goodnight. That song just brought a tear to my eyes as I close them to find my sleep. Beautiful. Thank you for sharing it. Fi. X

He was her last thought as she drifted off to sleep.

He was also her first thought the next morning when she awoke and she smiled as she stretched out in her bed wondering what it would be like waking up with him. She imagined him turning over as he heard her stirring and whispering, "good morning baby," (she could hear his beautiful accent, and the way he said baby to her, driving her crazy, turning her on) as he leaned over her and kissed her gently on the lips and then with increased passion as his hands moved down her body in an effort to waken aspects of her body! She would startle him by jumping out of bed and invite him into the shower because she hated making love, if she wasn't clean. They would enter the shower together with him kissing her whilst holding her hands above her head as he pinned her against the shower wall and the extremes of temperatures (the cold of the tiles on her back and the warmth of the water flowing over her front) shocking her in and out of her desire. He would take her shower products and wash her gently, enjoying the emanating fragrances, adding to the sensuousness between them as he lathered her body. All her body! Then it would be his turn and as he turned his back to her she would gently caress and wash him everywhere too, before stepping out of the shower and continuing their journey to love making on the bathroom floor. Mmmm! She thought as she lay there on her own with him on the other side of the world. Can't wait! She decided to email him:

23 November 2013 08:33

Good morning Bran, I hope you had a beautiful sleep. Just wanted you to know I really did meet you in my dreams. Have a good business day. I read about the very heavy snow so you take care out there! I am going to the gym this morning, then my friend Julie wants to go to a local cafe. Lucky me. I look forward to our next contact and the hours are getting closer until I get to look into your eyes.

Enjoy your day, Fi. X

PS: I enclose a couple of photographs for you

The photographs were one of Fi and her daughter many years ago on holiday, Fi liked it for two reasons, it was a rather flattering shot of her then athletic body and her daughter was wearing a t shirt depicting the words 'girls club' on it and Fi was looking forward to the 'girls club' reunion in a weeks' time. The second image was a recent photograph of Fi lying on her bed, no make-up on, her glasses on, her bra straps visible under her vest top and she had her head tilted to one side in a coquettish pose. She wasn't very good at taking flattering selfie's and this was one was no exception but it was recent and a reasonable image of her, so she sent it.

She got up and took a lonely shower, dressed for the gym and did her daily chores with the accompaniment of music of course. She made breakfast, gave the dogs a twenty minute walk on the park across the road and drove to the gym. She felt content. She enjoyed her class followed by an herbal tea and a chat with a couple of the women and then she drove home, to clean out her kitchen cupboards. She hated that job, but tackled it with gusto and finished the job by polishing all the black polished door and drawer fronts, until they were spotless, she then steam mopped the floor, cleaned the kitchen window and rang the oven cleaning firm to book an appointment for them to come and clean the oven, hob and cooker hood. "There," she said aloud as she surveyed her hard work. She made a coffee and took a cookie from the jar to have with it and as she sat to enjoy it, a call came through on her mobile, she didn't recognise the number.

She answered:

Fi: "Hello"

Bran: "Hey baby"

Fi: "Oh hi, what a great surprise, lovely to hear you!"

Bran: "I am wide awake thinking about you and your email came through and I thought I'd ring you. Am I disturbing you?"

Fi: "Not at all, well, come to think of it, yes you are, you're distracting me from thinking about you and I'd much rather hear the 'real deal' talking to me than emailing me!" (They both laughed)

Bran: "Real deal heh?" (He said questioningly)

Fi: "I hope so!" (He laughed at her comment)

Bran: "Me too! It's feeling like the real deal to me anyway"

Fi: "Good."

Bran: "Thank you for the photographs. You look so sexy in your glasses, I must say, with your mane of hair spread out everywhere, very provocative shot!"

Fi: "Well I assure you, it was not my intention to be provocative, I wanted to take a selfie and I have to admit, I am rubbish at taking flattering ones and that was the best I could do."

Bran: "Well you look beautiful and so do the twins."

Fi: "The twins? What twins?"

Bran: "Your boobs, they look very enticing hidden away under your top and big too!" (Fi laughed)

Fi: "ME? BIG BOOBS! No! Are you looking at the right image?"

Bran: "I am looking at it right now, lay on your bed, glasses on, hair everywhere, brown vest top with just a hint of what might be hidden underneath and from what I can see of them, the twins look damn good!" (They both laughed heartily and she replied)

Fi: "Well I have never heard them called twins before, that's funny!" (And they laughed again)

Fi: "Well if you think I have 'BIG twins' perhaps I

should be buying Bridget Jones underwear instead of beautiful lingerie?"

Bran: "No way. I want my baby way more sexy than Bridget Jones." (They laughed again)

Fi: "How come you cannot sleep, is it the time difference?"

Bran: "A little baby, that is true, but I cannot stop thinking about you, you are in and out of my mind all the time. I feel we know so much about each other already."

Fi: "We do, it's really weird, I have never done this before, dated somebody when I have never met them."

Bran: "I suppose we are having conversations online and on the phone that we would be having if we were living local to each other and meeting for regular dates."

Fi: "Well, that is true: I feel like I get to know you a little more each day."

Bran: "Sure, me too."

Fi: "Well Mr. Antique I am loving it so far!" (They both laughed together again)

Bran: "I am going to try to get some sleep now baby and I will speak with you later, if we have the time, okay?"

Fi: "We will have the time, I'm sure."

Bran: "Okay sweet one."

Fi: "Sleep well and meet me in your dreams."

Bran: "I'll try, take care of you for me."

Fi: "Okay and you for me. Can't wait to see you face to face, can't wait, can't wait, can't wait." (She gushed, and they both laughed)

Bran: "Bye baby, kisses to you." **Fi: "Bye Bran, kisses too."**

She pressed end call and the line went dead.

Fi sat and pondered how lovely he was, she felt so at ease, he was so easy to talk to, no awkward silences, he spoke well, he was really amusing, his writing was always interesting and well what else could she say? He WAS shaping up to be the 'real deal.' She finished her coffee and cookie whilst listening to the radio and a song came on that simply blew her mind. She had never heard it before and as usual she found it on her laptop and checked out the lyrics to make sure she had heard it correctly. Wow, it was written for them, after her imaginings earlier today, together with his flirtations with her about 'the twins' and she emailed a link over to him and added it to her playlist and of course put it on repeat:

23 November 2013 13:17

This is definitely the music to match my thoughts this morning and our earlier phone conversation! Wow. Very evocative piece of music! Take a look at this video. Arianda Grande. Love me Harder. Just perfect. Fi. X

He responded twenty minutes later

23 November 2013 13.38

Hey Fi, wow, oh my, very apt and very sexy tune. I love it. Bran

She continued with her day as planned, meeting Julie for their afternoon tea, which was an expensive but rare indulgent treat. Slattery's never failed, their food was delicious and the girls relished the savoury and sweet treats with a pot of tea and a glass of champagne. Fabulous! Fi brought Julie up to date with everything and Julie was so excited for Fi as the time drew near for her and Bran to finally meet. They laughed about the twin's reference and Fi told Julie about her amorous thoughts that morning. Julie commented, "Too right, you're going to be having thoughts like that, brand new relationship, great communication between you, plenty of flirting between you both, why wouldn't you think like that and I bet he's doing just the same Fi. I bet he can't wait for a playdate with the twins!" and they both giggled at the thought! "Yes, please," said Fi, "jeepers, Jules, the thought of it sends me crazy!" It wouldn't be a Fi and Julie get together without them crashing into fits of laughter. It was part of their friendship DNA. The girls paid their bill, went into the bakery and shop attached to the cafe and bought both baked and chocolate goods before walking the short distance home. They said their goodbyes and Fi shut her front door on the world, ready for yet another lonely night on her own. Not for much longer she thought, not for much longer.

At 21:30 she dialled Bran's number and as she was waiting for an answer, she realised she was nervous but wasn't sure why, was it the 'new' nervousness that one feels at the beginning of a relationship, or was it excitement?

Maybe it was a combination of both.

She didn't know but her thoughts were interrupted when she heard his voice:

Bran: "Hey Baby!" (With an emphasis on hey, which sounded like he was pleased to hear from her)

Fi: "Hi Bran, how are you?"

Bran: "I'm good now, so good to hear you, I've not had a good day business wise so feeling a bit frustrated baby."

Fi: "You and me both love!" (She chuckled and it was a naughty chuckle too) He obviously got the gist of her joke and laughed too, replying,

Bran: "Oh are you now?" he said with a hint of playfulness in the way he placed the question

Fi: "Yep, how can I even think like this when I have never even met you? This is crazy, a good kind of crazy, but still crazy. I have never behaved like this face to face with a man in the early stages of dating, or felt as attracted to a man before, to be honest."

Bran: "What are you feeling?"

Fi: "That you're driving me nuts with feelings of arousal and I can't wait to see you, what the hell is that about? I'm turning into a real flirt! A really

frustrated one at that! The thoughts I had this morning were sending me crazy, I so wish you had been here." (He laughed again).

Bran: "Do you want to tell me about them?"

Fi: "No I don't, not over the phone, I watch Sex And The City you know! I don't think I'd be keen on phone sex! Not a lot of point in that is there? When you're already frustrated" (they both laughed together) **"but let me just say, the thoughts were mmmmm!"**

Bran: "Well I'm flattered you are having such thoughts and desires for me and us, any way, how are the twins?" (And they laughed together again)

Fi: "They are wonderful, thank you for asking, they are happily tucked up warm, they are rarely on show. I'm like Michael Jackson me, keeping my kids covered up." (And they both burst into laughter!)

Bran: "You are comical Fi, I can tell, we are going to laugh a lot!"

Fi: "Just a bit, a day without laughter is wasted. I want you to know that right now this minute, I really would like it if you were here. I'd like to be in your strong arms right now, that's all, nothing else, stood here in my lounge now, just that" (and a tear rolled down her cheek as she described that simple gesture. She took a deep breath and exhaled loudly and he must have sensed something)

Bran: "Are you okay Fi?"

Fi: "Yes, thank you" (her voice quivered and her silent

tears now flowed freely)

Bran: "I can hear your tears and sniffles baby, what is wrong?"

Fi: "Emotions surfacing Bran, it just feels so good between us and it feels too good to be true."

Bran: "It already is good isn't it and we have only just begun. Trust it baby, don't be afraid of me," (that comment just sent her over the edge and her tears were streaming now).

Fi: "I am going to go now, and compose myself, but it is lovely to hear you again and I hope we get to talk tomorrow."

Bran: "We will baby, listen to me please, are you listening?"

Fi: "Yes, I am listening"

Bran: "I am sending you that hug with my arms around you, right now, and I am kissing away those tears. Go to bed and listen to Michael Buble, Close Your Eyes" (and he started to sing it to her and she couldn't control the fresh flow of tears)

Fi: "Thank you." (She mumbled through her tears)

Fi: "I'll speak to you tomorrow, I have to go now. Bye Bran."

Bran: "Bye Fi, kisses."

The line went dead as she pressed end call. She took

herself off to bed early that night and as she sat with her pillows propped behind her head for support, she wrote to Bran:

23 November 2013 22:16

Dear Mr. Rodrigues, I need you right now to hug me to sleep. I relish the thought of falling asleep in yours arms whenever we chose that moment. Thank you for our lovely chance to talk again and your sweetness to me in the call. You are too far away from me and I really want you to be nearer. I hope tomorrow will be good business wise for you. Look after you because I need you here soon, I feel like I have waited too long.

I am so surprised by what is happening between us. From seeing your stunning photographs on the dating site to speaking and writing as we do now, it is so surreal. I feel like I have known you forever. I don't know how I know but I just do, that this is all going to be so good for us both. I will give my all to us every day because that is the way it should be in a relationship. That is always the way I behave. I want the calm tranquility, the respect and support in the tough times, the fun, the laughter, the caring, the sharing and of course the tenderness and the sensual pleasures too. Everything. I want it all with you. I can tell you for sure, I am already so proud to show my friends your pictures and tell them you are my man and to tell them with confidence that you are just as beautiful inside. How do I know that? I have no idea. The great part is that they all truly believe me and are so happy for me and for us. Remind me tomorrow to tell you a funny story about Julie that occurred yesterday. Sleep well Bran. I miss you. You are bringing tears of joy to my

eyes again. I feel blessed that you chose me. Thank you. Fi. X

PS: I hope you are not the kind of parent who favours one child over the other because they twins require equal treatment!

As she thought through the day's events and told herself it was all going to fine and to trust her intuition, she heard the all too familiar scribble and opened her mail to read:

23 November 2013 22:51

Sure the twins require equal treatment, ha, ha. Just start counting your days and I will be with you before you know it. I am sat here and just thinking away. I just so much want to be in love again. I see love as a planted seed. First you need that seed and that is (us), then you need a good garden to plant the seed (our hearts), then the seed needs time to germinate (the time it takes to get used to each other), then it needs nurturing to grow well (the daily connection between two hearts, expressing, showing and letting the other heart know how much they mean to each other and also to make them feel secure in their new love). Then after these processes, the small plant grows gradually to become a big tree with branches. It even bears fruits and looks beautiful (now that is love at it's peak) That is what I seek and how I want it. I believe any normal relationship built on these foundations would hardly ever fail. I see us on that path already Fi. You do remember those feelings of being in love, feeling comfortable and safe with someone but still getting weak knees whenever you hear from them and see them, especially when they smile at you. I am not

perfect therefore I am not seeking perfection in anyone else, just seeking to see the imperfections as perfection in our own way.

I want romance, honesty, understanding, care, love and respect from a woman and they say respect is reciprocal so that means I would give all back equally to you. When in a relationship I always have a high libido. I get attracted to my woman easily. She could be in the kitchen cooking and I could just go behind her neck and kiss away and we end up anywhere we chose in that moment. I am that kind of guy and very spontaneous and I am very open to trying new things with my woman as long as we both want whatever it may be. Okay, if I am talking off key here just say shut up but my gut is saying let it out! It's my truth.

I think I am very much an easy-going type of guy. I am fun to be with, free spirited, and always a shoulder to someone that needs one, especially my woman. I don't distinguish between races, cultures, etc. Nor do I class people due to how wealthy, or how poor they are. I believe all are not equal and everyone can't be the same but I respect everybody I meet. The life I seek is a happy life filled with love and romance with the right woman. As long as she has a good heart and kind deeds and we fancy each other then I am for her. That already feels like you. I am going to treat you like a woman should be treated because you are one heck of a woman, honestly from what I see already, you are a good woman! Though some women make men forget this, I believe that you are one of those rare women out there and you deserve to be treated to the fullest. I hope you are smiling now, no more tears baby. I hope you have a wonderful nights rest and at least think of

me before you close your eyes, you do have enough photos of me already but here's a latest for you! Bran.

PS: I really would love to know what Julie said to you and of course I will remind you tomorrow. I feel more blessed having met you. I hope you get the kisses I am sending.

Fi could hardly read the words as her eyes were blurred with the tears sitting on her lower lids ready to fall down her face. She took a tissue from her bedside table and dabbed her eyes and took a good look at the photograph he had sent. He was in the sea with his arms resting on a harbour wall and she could see a rusty chain attached to the wall underneath his folded arms, he had obviously just emerged from the sea as droplets of sea water ran down his face and his upper body, his smile was breathtaking, literally breathtaking, it was by far the best photograph she had of him and the others were off the scale gorgeous. Wow. Just wow. She put a message on her Facebook timeline:

Could somebody pinch me please because I haven't got a clue how this has happened?

Tracey left a comment:

What a change 13 days can make to someone. From being the lowest you could ever feel. To being giddyagain.com, if I could bottle and sell what you have at this moment Fi, I'd be retiring very soon.

Fi text Tracey and said I am awake if you want to chat and Tracey immediately rang her friend:

Fi: "Hi Tracey, how are you?"

Tracey: "Good thank you, are you?"

Fi: "I've got so much to tell you we need a coffee o'clock."

Tracey: "Well okay I'll come round tomorrow in my break."

Fi: "Good, I can't wait to tell you, he's just been singing Michael Buble, 'Close your eyes' down the phone to me."

Tracey: "Oh my god, has he? I love that song."

Fi: "I didn't know it till he sang it."

Tracey: "The words are gorgeous, oh Fi, how fabulous."

Fi: "I know" and tears rolled down her cheeks.

Tracey: "Are you crying?"

Fi: "Yes, happy crying." (She sniffled into her tissue)

Tracey: "Oh Fi, I can't tell you how happy I am for you, see you tomorrow at 1 okay?"

She pressed end call and the line went dead.

You sometimes meet people under the weirdest of circumstances and they make you feel like you're alive again? Was it a coincidence, fate or luck? Whatever it was, she liked it.

CHAPTER 10

A present in return

Fi awoke to the sound of the dogs barking downstairs and went to investigate the noise. It was very windy outside with a severe weather warning having been given the previous day. She drew back the curtains in the lounge and pulled the blinds in the kitchen to find her treasured gazebo had become a victim of the high winds. She loved that gazebo, it provided shelter from the sun (which is essential for people with Lupus) and she also loved using it as a writing den, weather permitting, during the spring and summer. Fi went outside to see if she could rescue it but it was snapped in several places. 'Hey ho! I will have to treat myself to another one, I need that outside room, my shade and my 'outdoor' creative den too, absolute essentials!' she pondered. She would wait until her son came back from Uni to help her remove it from the garden but in the meantime she made sure it was a 'dog-safe' space, as they loved the garden too.

After completing her morning chores, she made herself a healthy breakfast of porridge with pears, decaf tea and her usual lemon and hot water and she listened to her radio whilst enjoying both her breakfast and her thoughts, which of course, had wandered to Bran. She wondered what he would be dreaming as he slept over there in NYC. She thought how strange it seemed that two people she was very fond of but had never met (Bran and her lovely friend Kim) were both in the same city on the other side of the world. She had met both of them online and not yet had the pleasure of meeting either of them face to face and yet she felt she had an evolving bond with both of them. It was strange indeed but beautiful people in both cases. After finishing her breakfast, she cleared away the dishes Fi went to have her shower and change into her gym gear. She was going for a yoga class today as she felt the need to centre herself after the past few days of euphoria. She walked the dogs in the park across the road and then sent Bran a quick email before heading out the door to the gym:

24 November 2013 10:09

Lonely showering is not recommended, how boring was that? Where were you Mr. Antique? Missing you. Fi. X

She went off to her class which she found blissfully relaxing and she came away from the gym a couple of hours later feeling calmer and ready for her girly afternoon with Tracey. She got home and changed into her favourite jeans and one of her Hawes and Curtis fitted shirts and her vintage green leather jacket, she put on her new black suede ankle boots, her big black scarf and quickly grabbed her gloves and bag. Just as she was about to descend the stairs she suddenly remembered, 'oh perfume' she thought, as she turned and dashed back into her bedroom and sprayed perfume on her neck, her wrists, behind her ears and a quick squirt on the twins too! Tracey sounded her car horn outside and Fi ran downstairs, locked her door and ran to her friend's car. "Hi Fi, how are you?" asked Tracey as Fi climbed into the car, "good thanks, how are you?" replied Fi. "I'm okay and I've finished work for the day now so there is no pressure on us to dash back," said Tracey, "oh good, more us time then!" replied Fi. She fastened her seatbelt as Tracey commented, "I like your jacket," "do you?" replied Fi somewhat surprised, "Louise hates it and is always trying to persuade me to send it to the charity shop" she said, before adding, "but I love it, I've had it years, it's battered as you can see but it's one of my favourites!" "No way do you get rid of that, it's gorgeous, too good for a charity shop!" said Tracey "and it goes great with your shirt," she added. "Thank you," said Fi.

Fi suggested going over to Chorlton as she wanted to call into the Chorlton Bookshop to choose something for her trip to London and then they could have lunch somewhere. Tracey was fine with that suggestion and as they headed over to the other side of Manchester, Fi told Tracey all about the emails and calls since she had seen her the previous day telling her friend about Bran teasing her about 'her twins' and his affectionate attitude when he heard her tears. Tracey said she fully understood the sheer overwhelming deluge of high emotions that Fi must be going through after experiencing the bottomless pit lows following Robert's affair and massage parlour shite. Fi fought back tears again as they discussed the pendulum of shock her body was going through. Fi agreed that it had been a roller coaster ride of tough, scary uncertainty, escalating over the past couple of days to euphoria and she felt she was beginning to get to a place of trust again. Could she let go of her doubts about Bran and just be herself, 'free of fear' and really begin to enjoy all that was to come?

As Tracey parked the car in a side street near to the book shop, Fi received an email alert and opened her phone and read it aloud as they linked arms and began walking down the street towards the book shop:

24 November 2013 13:25

Let me start my day by asking how are you? I hope your tears have gone. I wish I had been there with soft kisses to take them away for you. Enjoy your day Fi. Bran.

Fi smiled as she looked at her friend and Tracey said, "Aahhhh, see, he's just lovely, let yourself enjoy it Fi, don't let Robert spoil your dream." "You're right, I will enjoy it," she replied and dabbed a tear from her eye with her glove and took a deep breath to compose herself.

The girls went into the bookshop and Fi felt like a child in a sweet shop, as bookshops were yet another of her guilty pleasures, where she invariably spent more money than she intended. She perused the different sections, not really knowing what she wanted for her journey tomorrow, an autobiography? A novel? She took a few options from the shelves before looking at a couple of fashion and home decor books for her coffee table too. She opted for an autobiography as she loved anything that the author was in, her TV work, her film appearances, her drama's, her comedy and having read her previous book, Fi anticipated another really good read, with giggles thrown in for good measure. She chose two coffee table book options too and went to pay for her purchases. She had been coming to this bookshop for many years. She loved a good independent bookshop. She loved independent local businesses period!

They then went into Fred's dress shop a few doors down which was another independent shop selling women's clothes, that were always different from the high street stores and the owners clearly had an eye for stylish yet unique items. Fi and Tracey loved this shop and usually purchased at least one item of clothing each, whenever they visited Chorlton. Unusual clothes you were not going to see anyone else wearing, what's not to like? They rummaged through the rails for a while before they decided to try on their finds. Tracey tried on a fitted black dress, which looked amazing on her. The dress clung to her body and highlighted her fabulous figure. She worked hard at the gym and you could see the results right there in the mirror. "Fab," said Fi, "it looks fab," she added, before trying on a cream dress with a burgundy paisley print as Tracey helped her to fasten the zip. Fi looked at herself in the mirror and thought she looked lovely in the dress. Paisley print was always going to be a winner anyway. She loved it. Tracey agreed with Fi, "It looks really good on you" as she suggested accessories that Fi could wear with it.

Fi responded with a giggly quip! "Yes, but do the twins look big in this?" and they both burst out laughing. As they were paying at the till Tracey made a comment about her buying the new lingerie to go underneath it and the shop assistant advised them about a newly opened lingerie boutique just around the corner. "Ooh, music to our ears," said Fi, as they thanked the young woman and went to find the knickers shop!

It looked a dream shop and it was called "Underneath" which Fi thought was a simple but brilliant name. The window display was eye catching, with a chair positioned with it's rear facing the window with a nude mannequin sat astride it, replicating the famous Christine Keeler photograph. A very sexy bra and matching pants were strewn on the floor nearby. "Very effective," said Fi, "wowsers," said Tracey and they entered the shop 'oohing and aahing' as they did, not knowing where to look first. "I thought I was in 'the sweet shop' when I was buying books!" said Fi and they both laughed, "where do I start?" she added. They spent a great deal of time looking at every rail, choosing bras and matching pants, lace shorts and matching vests (for wearing in bed) and Fi was seriously 'wowed' with the selection of 'teddies'. "Wow, wow, wow," she said. "If we think they are wow, what the hell will Bran think?" said Tracey, "That it's Christmas and birthdays indefinitely!" said Fi and they laughed again before she added, "it better had be!" as they continued to laugh. Fi paid the bill, £385! As Tracey commented, "now that is what you call a present. Wow indeed!" and the girls laughed as the assistant wrapped it all up in tissue and tied the package with beautiful ribbons before placing all the items in a luxurious gift bag. "Gosh what a result," said Fi as they left the shop, "saves me searching in Oxford Street now," she added. Fi was just a touch giddy at the thought of all those items on her body and even more giddy at the thought of them being taken off her body. OMFGG!

The girls crossed the main road to the Lloyds pub, where, after finding a comfortable corner to sit in they chose a delicious sounding dish from the menu. They ordered butternut squash risotto with feta cheese, bottled sparkling water and Camomile tea. They ummed and yummed as they ate their food, it was just as delicious to taste as it had sounded on the menu. They chatted about their respective trips, Tracey was off to Fuerteventura with the girls and Fi was of course off to London tomorrow and by the time Tracey got back from her weeks trip, Bran would be home and Fi would be with him. "At last," Tracey said, 'it seems like you have known him months," "it does, doesn't it," replied Fi, "how weird is that, it does feel like we've been communicating for ages," she added. I think I will email him about his presents," she said, laughing.

She took her phone from her bag and opened her mail and wrote:

24 November 2013 16:31

Hi Bran, Thank you for your lovely message. You are so thoughtful. I am having a lovely day with Tracey, yet again. I bought you presents today! Wowsers! I love them and I am sure you will do too! The twins will love their play-date for sure! Can't wait. Making me fuzzy thinking about it all again. Keep safe. Fi

PS: I want a present in return please. You are to remove your presents!

The girls laughed at her teasing him and ordered more Camomile tea before they got chatting to a lovely elderly gentleman, who was sat nearby with members of a funeral party. He told them about his career in the navy and his retirement to Spain and that he was just over here in England for the funeral. He insisted on paying the bill for Fi and Tracey, too much torment from his fellow party members. "He's just trying to get into your knickers love," one of the women scoffed looking at Fi. Tracey replied, "Well he'll have to join the bloody queue," and they were off again, laughing hysterically. "Ooh! Scribble alert!" said Fi and opened her mail, "oh just marketing shit!" she said and had just put the phone down on the table in front of her when there was another alert coming though, "ooh, again" she laughed and saw his name in the inbox, "it's him," and opened it to read:

24 November 2013 16:55

Hey sexy woman, you tease me with your messages when I am so far away! I too had a lonely shower and you are right, it is not recommended. I don't want to be far from you now, I am frustrated that the business is not going well and I may have to move to LA tomorrow, so I have decided that when I am back in the UK I am taking a week off work just to focus on you and on us. I think you have been very patient and I thank you for that and I cannot wait to see you too! Presents! Oh my, oh my! Now I need to look for something for you too. Bran.

They said their goodbyes to the raucous drunken funeral party as they left the pub to drive home and as they parked outside Fi's house, Tracey wished her friend the best of luck, she wanted updates whenever she was free to give them and Fi teased that that would be sometime in the New Year then, as she anticipated being very busy! They laughed and wished each other safe journeys for the next day and had a goodbye hug and again Tracey expressed her delight for Fi. They waved to each other and Fi went inside and carried out her usual evening dog routine of feeding, followed by a walk in the park and she returned home a short time later to find Julie at her front door. "Hi, wondered where you were chick?" "I've just been out with the dogs but I've been out for the afternoon present shopping!" she laughed and told Julie all about her purchases whilst showing her friend the results of the day's shopping, as they waited for their tea to brew. Julie was very impressed with the dress from Fred's but she was in absolute awe at the underwear Fi had bought, "OH MY GOD! We swear and exaggerate all the time to describe things but they are just, OH MY GOD!" she said, before adding, “You are absolutely going to blow his mind wearing that lot, “Jeeepers, ‘kin creepers Fi, gorgeous, absolutely gorgeous!” “Thank you, they’re amazing aren’t they, I’m glad I hung out to find them,” said Fi. “You’ll be hanging out of them all right and he’ll be POPPING out of his, when he see’s you in them” and of course the hysteria button had been pressed as they collapsed laughing. They enjoyed their drink and then Julie went off to be with her family.

Fi decided to take a soothing bath with candles, music, sensuous smelling bath salts and bubbles and a glass of Prosecco. She relaxed and took calming breaths whilst she soaked ‘up’ the atmosphere in the tranquil room, as she soaked ‘in’ the actual bubbles and salts. She embraced the aromas of her luxury products and absorbed the soothing notes coming from her classical playlist. Just what a bath should be, she thought. She pondered on the events of the past few weeks and how dramatically her life had changed. It really was like a movie script and she certainly felt she had been given a leading role. After almost an hour in the bath she climbed out and wrapped herself with a bath sheet, that she had prior placed on the radiator, to enfold herself in its’ warmth, after her bath. As she pinned it around her body using a hair clip, she then sat on her bed to dry her curly mane. She coated her skin in body lotion from the body shaped bottle, filed and painted her nails, cleaned her teeth, cleaned them yet again and moisturised her face. She then put on her cashmere leggings and matching silk top that Louise had bought for her and lay down on her bed ready for him, only tonight it would just be his voice she would get pleasure from.

She rang his number:

Bran: "Hey baby" (Emphasising the hey)

Fi: "Hi Bran, how are you?"

Bran: (he giggled) **"I'm good thank you, I'm good. So good to hear your voice again."**

Fi: "Thank you, good to hear you too." Bran: "So you had a lovely day?"

Fi: "I did, I feel like I've had a busy day but very good. I have just had a bath and I am about to pack my bags for London."

Bran: "What time are you going?"

Fi: "I leave home about half eleven and my train leaves Manchester at one and I arrive in London about half three I think"

Bran: "Are you first class?"

Fi: "Do you need to ask me that, from what you already know about me?" (She laughed before adding) **"I'm a first class woman all right!"** (And he laughed too)

Bran: "You are too cheeky."

Fi: "Yes I am!"

Bran: "You have been spoiling yourself today then have you?"

Fi: "No, I've been spoiling YOU! And the twins!" (And they both laughed)

Bran: "I look forward to opening my presents."

Fi: "Well I wrap my gifts very well, let me tell you! AND! I am very particular about who I allow to unwrap them."

Bran: "That's good to know on both counts!"

Fi: "I've told you, I am not a loose woman and it is very unusual for me to be so flirtatious with somebody I hardly know and certainly somebody I have never met! What are you doing to me Bran?"

Bran: "I have no idea how this happened so fast but all I can say at this point, is that it feels good, you are beautiful and your beauty is everywhere, in your looks, in your body, in your words and in your sense of fun. I am loving you being in my life, it feels like it has been for months, it is so strange."

Fi: "I said exactly the same thing to Tracey today, I feel like I have known you ages."

Bran: "Oh, tell me about the amusing story with Julie, I've just remembered."

Fi: "Oh yes, well I had a text message from her asking me if 'Mr. Antique' was at my house and I replied to her, no why?, you know he is in New York, and she then sent one back saying, posh car outside your house!" (They both laughed)

Fi: "My friends and I think you might have a big posh car and so Julie assumed because there was a Mercedes parked outside, that it was you, even though she knows you are in America." (He laughed again)

Fi: "We thought it was very amusing." (They laughed again)

Fi: "Tell me about your day?"

Bran: "New York has been a disappointment and I am off to LA in the morning where I hope things will be much better. I am flying very early and I am already packed so I will be in the air when you are leaving your house tomorrow."

Fi: "Well I might not be able to speak to you tomorrow then?"

Bran: "We will try but at least we can email."

Fi: "Okay, well I will go and pack now too and you have a safe journey."

Bran: "You too and have a lovely nights rest and meet me in dreamland."

Fi: "Will do, I'll race you there shall I?"

Bran: "Awwhh so sweet, goodnight and kisses."

Fi: "Rest well, see you soon."

Bran: "As soon as I can Fi, it's nearly time."

Fi: "Good, I cannot wait."

Bran: "Okay sweet one, I have to go now."

Fi: "Bye Bran."

Bran: "Bye Fi."

She pressed end call and the line went dead and she let herself slump into her pillows as she replayed their conversation in her mind. She shook her head in disbelief, as a smile of contentment crossed her face. She was so calm and chilled out she could easily have drifted into an early sleep but she made herself rise from her beckoning slumber and set about packing her bags and 'just in case,' she packed some of his presents! She completed the nightly pet requirements at number 9, made herself a drink and went to bed happy. Just as she was drifting off to sleep she heard the 'scribble alert' and it was Bran:

24 November 2013 23:19

The time is near my sweet woman, I am thinking of you right now. Bran

Not only did she go to bed happy, she went to sleep happy too.

Fi awoke the next morning to the sound of her alarm at 8am and got up immediately. She had a lot to do and didn't want to risk being in a rush to catch her train! She dressed into gym gear, made a quick cup of tea, which she drank as she dashed around the house packing bags for the cat, who was going to the cattery and for the dogs, who would be staying with Julie and her family. She drove to the Cattery, saw the cat settled into her 'room with a view,' as Fi had agreed to pay extra for a window chalet for her! She then drove home and took the dogs for an extra long walk, to tire them out until Julie came to collect them after work.

Fi was really looking forward to seeing her daughter. She was also looking forward to seeing her new friend Jen again and her son Henry, of course, as well as taking in some of the sites of London. She was really excited for this journey but she was even more excited to continue the journey of 'her and Bran,' which would force them both to take a different route, when they finally met each other next week. What if he didn't like her, after all, he had only seen her in images and communicated with her through emails and on the phone. Well, she would have to deal with that one if it happened and why was she hanging her future solely on whether he liked her? She might not like him either but she dismissed her negative thoughts, by putting her music on full volume and playing her 'Happy' playlist as she took her shower, dried herself and put on her traveling outfit. She had chosen a black fitted mini skirt (she was confident in her figure again now to be able to carry it off) with thick black tights and a cerise pink long sleeved fitted t-shirt. She dried her hair which she had recently had cut, by her long time hairdresser and friend Debbie-Jane who was the only person Fi trusted to cut her curly hair well! She decided it looked fab as she finalised the styling of it with her trusted finishing products and her favourite hair slides. She made her face up with her simple makeup routine and sprayed her perfume where she always did, (where she wanted to be kissed of course) as her Aunty Mary had taught her! She finished dressing, by adding a bold necklace of oversized flowers in silver and pink tones and pulled on her short length, fitted, black wool jacket before finally throwing her cerise pink pashmina around her shoulders. She finished off the look with her new black suede wedge heeled shoes, black leather gloves and her favourite black leather handbag. She looked amazing, she decided, as she took one last look in the mirror.

As she locked her front door after saying goodbye to her

dogs, she pulled her oversized bag to the waiting taxi, just as one of Robert's colleagues was walking past her house, "Hi Fi, how are you?" "Very well thanks and you?" she replied, "I am fine thank you, are you off anywhere nice?" he added, looking down at her bag, "I'm going to London to see my daughter." "Very good," he said, before adding, "well you have a lovely time and do you know something Fi? Maybe I'm talking out of turn here but I have to say it, it's his loss, foolish man, REALLY foolish man," he said, before adding, "You take care." "Thank you," she said and got into the taxi feeling rather stunned with a mixture of sadness, (as a stray tear threatened to fall) smugness and self-confidence as she thought, 'yes, his loss.' She arrived at the metro station a few minutes later to hear delays being announced over the tannoy and she was glad she had given herself plenty of time for her journey to catch her London train. It took her almost an hour to get to the main Piccadilly Station and she made her way directly to the platform to the first class carriage at the far end of the train.

She placed her large bag in the luggage rack, sat in her seat and settled comfortably with her classical playlist and her book. The train was quiet and she enjoyed the tranquility and peace as she listened to soothing music. Her efforts to read were thwarted by the lovely thoughts ebbing and flowing in and out of her mind. Reality thoughts with reminders of what had been said and written between herself and Bran and imagined thoughts, with fantasies of aspects of his, hers and their lives! What would it be like to see him? Where would it be? Where did he live? What was his home like? Was he a tidy man? What would his smell be like? HIS smell! Not his aftershave. How would he sound in reality and not just over the phone? What did he drive? What was his antiques showroom like? What did he read? What was his music collection like? Did he have modern taste in decor? Was he a good cook? What would it be like finally looking into his eyes for real? How would he kiss? How would he hold her? How would he undress her? What would he say when he made love to her? Would he be a gentle lover? Would he be an exploratory lover? Would he be a selfless lover interested in her pleasure too? What kind of presents would he buy her? What would he be like with her children when he finally met them? On and on and on the thoughts came as she closed her eyes and allowed herself to wonder and her mind to wander. They weren't worried thoughts, they were wondering thoughts and as she was lulled, by both her thoughts and the motion of the train she fell into a soothing nap. When she was woken by the sound of rattling cups Fi was informed by the waiter, that they were only twenty minutes from London. What a waste of "first class" that was! She went to the loo and freshened her make up and after getting off the train she waited on the platform for Louise to find her and sent an email to Bran whilst she waited for her daughter:

25 November 2013 15:40

I have arrived in London. Hope my man is okay? Fi. X

She saw her daughter running down the platform and she practically jumped into her mother's arms as she had done as a child on many, many occasions. It was so lovely to see her again. It really was.

They walked through to the underground connection and Louise insisted on dealing with her Mum's luggage to enable them to rush to get the connection to get home to Blackheath, before the transport system became completely chaotic, by which time Louise figured her mother would not be able to contend with the rush hour crowds! They made all their connections and arrived home to a lovely warm welcome from Jen and Henry. Here again was a friend whom Fi had met under very unusual circumstances but without doubt knew they would be friends for life. Absolutely. Fi could definitely magnetise good, honest, loyal, decent women into her life, no problem, she had a string of lifelong female friends but she just couldn't do it with men? Why?

They made a collective decision to have pizza's delivered for the family evening meal, which they all shared sat around the large table in Jen's country kitchen, whilst sharing a bottle of Prosecco or two, conversation and laughter. It was a lovely dining experience for Fi, having eaten home alone for the majority of the past few weeks, IF, she had eaten at all. They retired to the large lounge and watched TV together, chatting some more about their families, friends, health issues and Christmas, which was fast approaching! Fi retired to bed first and when she had climbed into bed she sent an email to Bran:

25 November 2013 23:25

Hi Bran, I arrived okay as I said earlier. It is good to see my girl. Had a lovely family dinner tonight and I am in bed now, feeling very tired. I enclose a photograph for you as promised. Catch you tomorrow. I've missed our communication today. Fi. X

He replied a while later as the 'scribble alert' woke her up

25 November 2013. 16:51pm. USA time.

Look at that cute smile... I am smiling back at you. Gorgeous. I will speak to you tomorrow as you may already be seeing us in dreamland now. Bran

PS: I am thinking of presents for you.

She wasn't in dreamland, as his message alert had woken her and she was tempted to ring him to hear his voice but she was too tired, he would be working and it wouldn't be a quality conversation to speak with him now and so she went to meet him back in dreamland again. She would hear his voice tomorrow. The next morning she woke early at 7:30 but she felt refreshed after a good night's sleep and crept out of the room, so as not to disturb Louise. The house was eerily silent but beautiful and peaceful nonetheless. Fi made herself tea and went to sit in the lounge admiring the lovely street view and enjoying the blissful peace. She took photographs of the street to show Louise's dad. He was familiar with London geographically, from his work as a driver and he knew, as with most cities around the UK, there were good and bad areas to live. The pictures would ease his mind and reassure him that his daughter was living in a lovely part of London. She sent the images to him and her thoughts were correct, he sent an immediate reply saying, 'Brilliant.' He was a man of few words but he was a good dad to his children, in his own way. Fi often felt a sadness that they had divorced but at least they had an amicable relationship for their children's sake and she could never, ever fault his generosity to his children regarding money. Not that he spoilt them with it but rather, that he was always there to help financially when needed, always. He had even put £50 in Fi's bank account for her London trip so that she and Louise could enjoy a meal out together.

After about an hour's solitude Fi was joined by Jen who gave her a good morning hug and asked if she had slept well, "I have, thank you Jen, did you?" asked Fi, "I did. Would you like some lemon tea?" asked Jen, "regular tea please," said Fi and as their drinks brewed, these relatively new friends who had bonded (having met during terrible circumstances for Jen and her family) only a short few weeks ago, chatted about their respective families, lives and friends. The two women had recently experienced the empty nest phenomenon with their daughters leaving home for travel and career options and their sons having left for long distance university options. Louise was friends with Jen's daughter Chloe and was now living in London with Jen. Jen's son Henry had chosen to study in Manchester, so ironically two of their children had done a geographical swap! Jen was a lovely woman, kind hearted, welcoming and a very beautiful and very stylish, fashion conscious woman. She had an abundance of friends it appeared and she had a very busy social life with plenty of charity fund raising events to occupy her time and a very interesting job too. She lived in a beautiful part of London, in a gorgeous huge Victorian semi-detached house and all was well in the world for Jen, until that terrible incident a few weeks ago that had brought these two friends together. Fi knew that this wonderful woman would be in her life forever, she thought, as she sat sipping her tea with Jen and reflected upon why she always seemed to attract the wrong men into her life but yet she attracted females, with such beautiful souls into her world. Why? She wondered, and was all that about to change?

Those lingering thoughts prompted her to check her emails and sure enough there was his name in the inbox:

26 November 2013 02:03

Hey Fi, I have seriously missed you so much yesterday! I have just reread all our mail since day one, as I cannot sleep with crazy thoughts of you and reading them again brings me so much joy and happiness inside. The number you have from me is mobile so you can contact me anytime you like or let me know a good time to contact you. I truly miss your voice. Hope you're having a great time in London. Bran.

Fi replied:

26 November 2013 10:22

Hi Bran, How lovely to hear from you. Sorry you can't sleep through thinking about me! You wouldn't be sleeping if I was there right now, that is for sure! You were my first thought this morning too. I have been having a lovely chat with Jen this morning, as I was up early and I am now off to see the sights and sounds of London with Louise after a breakfast stop! I will send you photos later. Hope you manage to sleep and I send you a 'under the duvet' cuddle via cyberspace! Fi. X

Fi showered and dressed for the day ahead. She put on her jeans with a new black top Louise had bought her as a present, which was both stylish and warm, she finished the outfit with her black suede and jersey biker jacket, her cream scarf with feathers printed on it (Fi collected feather items in honour of her mum) and she borrowed Louise's short suede cowgirl boots. Very 'rock chick' she thought, as she checked herself in Louise's full-length mirror. She admired Louise's new BIG handbag (Fi collected handbags too) and negotiated a loan of it for the duration of her stay in London! They set off on the North Kent line, from Westcombe Park to London Bridge station, where Fi spotted the Borough Market nearby, "I need a mooch round there afterwards!" she said, before adding, "I've been to it years ago when I visited the London Lupus Hospital, it's so good," "okay, cool," replied Louise, "we'll come back this way after we've been for something to eat," she added. They joined the long queue, outside the breakfast cafe and chatted and chuckled with some young girls behind them, who were complaining that a guy one of them was dating, was a liar and they were wondering if it was an 'immature young guy' issue! Fi quipped, "Well I can assure you, they don't get any better when they are older, I've just got rid of the all time Billy Liar!" and they all laughed! They were eventually seated at a 'share' table with a young couple and Louise enquired, "Are we gate crashing a first date here?" to which the young girl replied, "not really, well kind of!" and they all laughed. Fi ordered Eggs Benedict and Louise ordered pancakes with maple syrup and bacon and they had fresh juices and decaf tea to drink. They took photographs on their devices and sent them into cyberspace to individuals and to social networking choices, before paying their bill and then going out into the rain. They walked all around the Borough Market and Fi bought an unusual combination of olives, risotto rice and wooden carved Christmas ornaments as a thank you gift for Julie! They called into a pub near the market and had a glass of wine before walking to the Tower of London, taking more photographs en route, which Fi sent to Bran. Fi and Louise jostled for positions to take good images of the Tower and of themselves in front of it and at one point Louise told her mum off for pushing into someone's camera view line, "oh I am sorry," Fi said to the lady holding the camera, "would you like me to take one of all of you?" as she realised there was a party of four, "oh no," replied one of the men, "we wanted you in the picture" and they all laughed! Fi let Louise continue to take more images (the photographer at work, she thought) and she stepped to one side to take in the history of the Tower and its significance. They went into a cafe for a hot chocolate and to get warm before making their way to the Oxford Street shopping area which incorporated a long walk, an underground journey followed by another walk, much to Fi's disapproval as she moaned incessantly at Louise, complaining of aching knees, hips and feet! They walked for miles, or so it felt like to Fi and in the end she decided to stamp her aching feet and refuse to walk another step, just like a naughty 53 year old! She was in pain and feeling a little breathless and knew she needed to rest. Louise went in to mobile phone shop and bought a new phone and they then made their way back home to Blackheath, no shopping and no champagne! The Oxford Street trip reminded Fi of the well-known t-shirt slogan, 'my Mum and Dad went on holiday and all they got me was this lousy t-shirt.' Their version was 'Fi and Louise went to Oxford Street, one of the most iconic shopping streets in all the world and all they got was a phone!' They had purchased food items from a store near to one of the stations before they jumped into a cab for the final leg of their journey home and were fully intending to cook a stir-fry for the family when they got there but Jen insisted that she cook it instead and why not? She cooks a rather good one! It was delicious and washed down with Prosecco and accompanied by more chatting and chuckling, they enjoyed another family and friends get together around the big table and they finished the evening with catching up on the dancing and 'talent' shows on TV and Fi retired to bed about 11pm. She was missing Bran and she wanted to ring him. She needed to hear his voice today. She had really missed him. She got comfortable in her pyjamas and fleece over-top and climbed into bed. The cold and damp of the day had seeped into her bones and she felt really cold inside. Louise had made her a hot water bottle and she snuggled up with it and dialled Brans number:

Bran: "Heyyy!"

Fi: "Hiiii! How are you?" (She felt him smiling back at her as she herself smiled at hearing his voice)

Bran: "Lovely to hear from you baby. I'm good, I'm good, can't tell you how happy I am to hear you!"

Fi: "Thank you, you too Bran. I've missed you yesterday and today, how can that be when we have never even met?"

Bran: "I understand the question but I don't have an answer, it is bizarre isn't it but I feel exactly the same way. Never met you but miss you too. I missed your lovely emails and hearing your voice this past couple of days."

Fi: "Was it a good business day?"

Bran: "Very good, an excellent day. I have finished for the day now and am just relaxing with a beer with the agent."

Fi: "Very good, have one for me, cold with a slice of lime! (She laughed) **Shall I let you go then if you are busy?"**

Bran: "No Fi, definitely not, tell me about your day."

So she did, she told him all about her day from beginning to end, including how he had woven himself in and out of her thoughts at various parts of her day and how she felt the poignancy of forming a relationship in writing, when she had been at the Tower of London. She brought him up to date with all her news of Louise and Jen and what her plans were for tomorrow. They had been on the phone for about 30 minutes when Fi heard Louise coming up to bed and so she wanted to end her call and said to him:

Fi: "Anyway I have taken too much of your time up so I will go now and hopefully we can catch each other tomorrow. I've loved our call."

Bran: "Me too sweet one, lovely talking to you. We'll speak tomorrow yes? Look out for your presents today okay."

Fi: "Okay, I will do, I am excited and intrigued but we will speak tomorrow, bye Bran."

She pressed end call and the line went dead. How could he send presents? He had no idea where she lived or where she was staying in London, so how could he possibly send gifts to her, she thought?

"Who was that?" asked Louise as she entered her bedroom, "oh a guy, I have met online." "Mum! What have I told you about those dating sites?" before continuing, "remember what happened with your friends!" "They're just full of dick heads those sites, dangerous people, you just never know who you are meeting, you're living on your own now Mum, Calum and I aren't there with you in Manchester to protect you" she finished, Fi responded, "Well I need to give him a chance Louise, he seems very decent and he is a successful business man and he behaves very well so far." "Yes, so he says online mother," said Louise, "how do you know any of it is true? Just be careful, is all I am saying," she added. "I will be careful," replied Fi before continuing, "Anyway, you have met your man online too, so I could say the same to you, I just have to have faith that I will meet a decent guy online and so far this guy seems decent." Fi showed Louise his picture that she had as a wallpaper on her phone, "Well he's very good looking isn't he?" said Louise, to which Fi replied, "yes he is!" and with that she turned over to go to sleep.

The following morning Fi again woke, showered and dressed before the rest of the household. She made herself tea and sat in the kitchen to answer her emails and texts. Her friends were all contacting her to see if she was having a good time and to catch up on the saga of 'Bran' but there was nothing much to tell them, as there was still no set date to finally meet him. She told them she was enjoying London, would be coming home on her planned return date and she would meet them for coffee o'clock catch-ups soon. When the rest of the family was awake, Louise, Jen and Fi decided to go off to Greenwich Market for the day. It was a bitterly cold day and pouring with rain and they were glad to get into the sheltered building to escape from the wet weather but the temperature still wrapped itself around them and they were in need of a hot drink. They stopped at a stall and had hot apple juice with brandy before wandering from stall to stall and looking at the boutique shops around the perimeter of the market. Fi bought an unusual funnel neck coat, with a patchwork effect design, in black, silver and red with multi coloured buttons, which she loved but Louise hated! She also bought two hand made cards for Bran from a stall called

Betty Etiquette which sold beautifully designed stationery and Louise bought a desk organiser from the same stall. After a couple of hours wandering around the market they decided they needed hot food and they went to the famous Goddard's Pie and Mash shop (as seen on TV! No less) that had been serving customers since 1890, so the sign said! The queue was lengthy but eventually they were seated at a table and they all chose vegetarian pie, mash and gravy and a cup of Camomile tea. They were so hungry and it was a delicious, warming and welcome plate of food served in a bustling restaurant that they thoroughly enjoyed. They then walked around Greenwich for a while, in and out of various shops buying trinkets and gifts for Christmas presents for various members of their families before taking all their bags back to the car and then going into the nearby 'Heaps Sausages' cafe. It is a quaint vintage fronted shop and cafe, in a back street in Greenwich, that sells sausages made on the premises, in a variety of flavours such as the Pork and Leekie, the Lethal Lucifer and the Sweet Italian, all of which had the girls giggling as they read the menu! They settled for tea and chocolate brownies!

When they got back into the car to drive home, Jen decided to take them through Greenwich Park. It was just getting dusk and as they parked near to the General Wolfe Statue, they could see the London skyline, which was quite magnificent, even on this gloomy day. Darkness was just descending on the view but she could clearly make out the landmarks of the London Eye, Millennium Dome, Maritime Museum, Canary Wharf and over to the far left was St Paul's cathedral. It was a lovely sight and they took advantage of being able to take photographs with the help of a gentleman who very kindly offered to take a photograph of all three of them together. Fi forwarded the image on to Bran as 'the girls in Greenwich' and he promptly replied saying, 'lovely smiles'. They drove the short journey home and quickly changed before going out for dinner to Zaibatsu, a local Japanese fusion restaurant owned by a Malaysian chap who was an incredible chef. It was a family favourite that they were happy to share with Fi and she was happy that they had, the food was outstanding and beautifully presented with exquisitely carved raw vegetables and orchids decorating them. It had been a food day for sure and it was a fantastic final meal with her London friends and her daughter before she headed home tomorrow, ready for her new adventure with Bran.

She may have bought him presents but she was wearing a gift from him too, a smile in her heart

CHAPTER 11

The Singing Chauffeur

The next morning Fi woke up and when she checked the time on her phone, noticed she had an email from Bran with the heading 'Presents'. As she opened it, her heart began thumping with excitement. She had no idea what it might be or how he would get it to her.

She gasped at what she saw in front of her:

An image of him stood on a sun drenched rooftop, standing next to an easel with a canvas on it. He had his right hand resting on the top of the canvas, he was dressed in dark jeans, a grey patterned shirt, he had an expensive looking stylish watch on his left hand and he had his left thumb hanging onto his jeans pocket and he was holding his sunglasses in the same hand. He was smiling and his smile matched the beautiful sunny day. There were advertising boards behind him, with a scaffolding tower in the background. He looked absolutely gorgeous and her heart was racing. The canvas was of a cartoon sunflower with a smiley face and written next to the cartoon image were the words:

A little gesture to say ...... You make me smile. Bran + Fi.

She was shaking, it was true, there he was with an image clarifying there was a connection between the two of them. Jeepers, it's so real, she thought. Then she read the words in the email that contained the image:

26 November 2013 17:00

Hi Baby, So I went to this art store which I found yesterday looking for gifts for you, based on what you have told me so far about yourself. There was nothing that I liked and so I then decided I could make something to send to you and at least return the gift you give to me without even knowing that you do, making me smile! It was a fun time at the store, the guys there had no idea what I was doing until I was almost done and then said quote, "She must be a lucky woman" and I said, "I am the lucky one!" So there you go. It isn't a big surprise, just a little one, to say you are not far from my mind and you have brought smiles back into my life. Also, I needed to add a little thoughtful and personal poem that I put together for you. Every word, line by line, is meant for you.

PLEASE TAKE THEM AS THEY COME AS THEY ARE ALL STRAIGHT FROM THE HEART!

Alone in this room I sit and contemplate,

The last few weeks and I patiently wait,

To see your face, to hold you tight,

To kiss your lips throughout the night

(I'm quite sure of that happening!)

For those special moments are oh so near,

With you my Fi I have no fear.

My body is yearning for your sweet touch

Making love all night long will never be too much.

(I just know you have one)

Exploring hands, lips and tongues,

The touches of passion will be oh so strong.

In the dead of night, or when the songbirds sing,

Lovemaking so fierce we will always bring.

In the cold, I will make you feel so warm

Making passionate love until the dawn.

Whether loving hard or loving tender,

Our bodies still entwined, in sleep we'll surrender.

I'll be in heaven waking next to you,

With my heart full of love and yours for me too

Darling Fi, as my heart beats only for you

I really wish all of this to come true.

I REALLY DO. You rock my world Fi.

I think MJ has a song like that and I love that song....Awwwoohhhh in MJ's voice lol!

Thinking of you and smiling baby. Bran. Xx

She ran from the bedroom down the stairs and into the front room, she knew nobody would be in there as they would all be getting ready to go to work. She sat and looked at it all and read it repeatedly. There were the two of them in print on a canvas right there in front of her on the other side of the world 'Bran + Fi.' He was telling her they really were an item. A serious item. He made references to them making love, to his heart being full of love, to wanting it all to come true and as she sat there and tried to absorb what was in front of her, she was completely bowled over. She was stunned. These were really serious, life-altering declarations for her. Was he really falling in love with her over the Internet? Could that really happen in just a few short days? She re-read everything again and tears slowly trickled down her face. Just a few short weeks ago they were tears of pain and now here she was with tears of absolute joy. Here was a gorgeous, stunningly handsome man who had expressed an interest in her (when she had no hope whatsoever of EVER trusting a man again) and was on an image in front of her telling her he wanted this to come true! Her tears flowed and flowed.

She felt like she was going to burst. There was no more space left inside her to accommodate the growing sense of happiness. It was unbelievable. She then found Michael Jackson, You Rock My World on her laptop and played it, paying more attention to the words than she ever had done before. She cried some more. UNBELIEVABLE and he had signed his email with a kiss for the first time too!

She went into the kitchen made tea for the household and a lemon and hot water drink for Jen and after a quick chat she said her goodbyes to them all as they left for work. She would miss her daughter and she shed a tear when Louise left. It's a Mum thing! Within half an hour the house was empty and she was alone, until it was time for her to leave to get her train. She took the time to compose herself, shower, get dressed and pack the final items into her bag. She played soothing music as she sat and waited for her time to leave. How did she feel, did she want it all to come true too? Absofuckinglutely.

She couldn't wait for coffee o'clock time with Julie later today. She had missed her so much, the laughing, the swearing and just their general bond. She loved her bestie and she really needed to see her. Fi sent her a text:

Fi: Fuckety, fuck, fuck, fuck with bells on!

Julie: WHAT?

Fi: Coffee o'clock at mine after work. Be there!

Julie: Jeepers, I've got a nervous stomach now.

Fi: Ditto!

Julie: What?

Fi: Its Latin! Meaning 'me too' (nervous stomach)

Julie: You're a div never mind ditto.

Fi: Thanks love, love you too!

Fi arrived at Euston with plenty of time to spare and so she sat in the First class Lounge for over an hour enjoying breakfast and tea. She put her 'Happy' playlist on and replied to Bran:

27 November 2013 10:47

You made me cry with happiness Bran. I cannot stop looking at my gift, at you and at your beautiful words. That is such a unique gift. You're wow in that photograph. Your gift is wow. Your words are wow. I am truly overwhelmed by your thoughtfulness and caring behind your beautiful gesture and it really touches me deeply. I know we are so very lucky to have found each other. I can't stop gazing at you in the picture, that you would think of me in such a way and do something as beautiful as that for me, is very overwhelming and humbling. You are already bringing such happiness, care and dare I say it the beginnings of love into my life and I have never even met you. Wow. I miss you so much. How can I miss someone I have never met? I long for so many things, to hear you, to see you, to hold you and to kiss you and all that will evolve from that beautiful kiss. Hurry home. Fi. Thank you so much. I really did cry with happiness. X

PS: Here is a picture of me as I was leaving London today.

Thirty minutes later she heard the announcement for her train, which was slightly delayed due to technical issues. She made her way to the platform and to the first class carriage. She found her seat and settled to listen to music. She had created a, 'Bran' playlist with all the music they had sent each other and she put that on repeat. She decided not to bother with her book, as she knew she couldn't concentrate.

She sent him an email as she was awaiting departure from the station:

27 November 2013 11:30

Hi Bran, sat at Euston ready to go home. For some reason it feels like I am on my way home to you and I suppose I am. I can feel the next chapter of our book of 'beautiful adventure' about to emerge onto the page. The first chapter has been so spellbinding for me. This book is going to be a page-turner, with many, many sequels. I just know it. I am so excited Bran. I am feeling nervous, happy, giggly, and amorous for our lovemaking. I am getting goose bumps thinking about it all. I am listening to Ariana Grande, which heightens my desire for you.

Hurry home beautiful man. X

He replied immediately much to her surprise with the time difference:

27 November 2013 03:30 LA time

I am wide awake Fi, cannot stop thinking about you. Do I still say good morning? Is it past morning time over there? It's a crazy world. The time is confusing me today. I love your picture this morning as you left. Beautiful smile and gorgeous figure in your jeans and leather jacket! Wow. Is she really my girl? I said to myself. I am so glad you liked your presents! I meant every word. Just a little gesture until I can give you the real gift I have bought for you today. It is lovely knowing you are on your way home now and it is my

turn to be home soon. I will be home very, very soon my dear one, as I will be rounding up today. I will write again later. Take care of you for me. Bran xx

She wrote back to him:

27 November 2013 11:46

Looking forward to all we have to give each other. '6 words' Wretch 32 is playing as I type. 'I've found a treasure all right!' Mmmmmmm. Until we speak. Imagine this hug I am sending you, I have my arms wrapped around your waist, you are nuzzling your face in my hair, whispering to me and I am wearing one of your presents. You smell so good, you feel big and strong and warm wrapped around me and I am so looking forward to what we are about to create. That crescendo kiss is about to happen after you have picked me up and carried me to the bedroom. We will make that imagined hug come true soon. Awhhh, 'Close your eyes' Michael Buble is now playing on my playlist.You are absolutely one of a kind Bran and I do feel safe to stay, finally. Fi. Xx

He replied immediately:

27 November 2013 03:48 LA time

My Fiora sure is a sexy woman! Ha, told you I like poetry!

I sincerely cannot wait to have you in my arms, kiss your neck and whisper into your ear 'let's make love honey.' I can't wait to see you in those presents. I am trying to imagine you in them, maybe you can take a pic in one of them and let me see, just being naughty

right here! What plans do you have for the evening? Bran. X

Hey cheeky, she thought, no chance! Before replying:

27 November 2013 11:59

My friends and family are already ringing and texting me, wanting news of how we are doing. I have already had 4 calls, how fabulous. They are all so, so happy for us. They are also in awe of your beautiful gift to me. I am a lucky woman. I feel like we are part of the script of a movie and we are writing our own script. What a great film it is going to be! I am not sending any photographs of me in lingerie because I am not that kind of woman, you will have to wait until I allow you to unwrap them and in any event I don't trust the Internet! I send a little tease for you. Black Lace is one of your presents. Look after you for me and it's nearly our time, at long last. Bye for now Bran until I can hear that beautiful voice again, I will have to keep listening to my voicemail. X

He replied:

27 November 2013 4:02 LA Time

Have a safe journey home and I will call you tonight 9pm UK time if that is okay? Every hour gets us nearer to each other but in the meantime click the link below for this beautiful Ed Sheeran track. Bran. X

Fi enjoyed the rest of her journey in a blissfully relaxed mood listening to chill out music and drinking boiled water and thought that she had wasted the first class facilities yet again! She arrived back home mid afternoon and took her dogs out straight away. She rang the cattery and extended her booking for at least a week and she relaxed on the settee waiting for her friend to come round after work and listened to 'Thinking out loud' by Ed Sheeran and watching the amazing video. Thought provoking lyrics!

Julie arrived at 3:45 to undecipherable squeals and a hug from Fi! "Could you slow down and say that in English," said Julie and they laughed, "I said, I'VE MISSED YOU BESTIE AND I'VE GOT SO MUCH TO TELL YOU!" said Fi exaggerating her words in a slow motion fashion, "fuck off" said Julie and they both laughed. Fi made a Nespresso for them both and opened her laptop and began to tell Julie the saga of the painting, showing her the image of Bran and the 'Sunflower Smile' before reading her the poem from the email. They discussed his gesture at length and Julie was equally as amazed as Fi, commenting upon the thought and care behind the presents and the impact it had quite clearly had upon Fi. Julie thought that Bran was no longer just 'really into Fi' but that he was now quite clearly falling for her too! Fi agreed that she felt the same way about him but was still baffled how that could be, when they had yet to meet each other. The comparison to the 'letters of war' came to her mind and she accepted that although it wasn't the conventional way to date and begin to have feelings for someone, it was not unheard of for correspondence to be the foundations for many a great love affair. Why should they be any different? If he was falling for her he was getting the real deal all right, as she had genuinely been herself throughout. Julie chatted some more about her working day and her family issues before the girls parted company and Fi shut the door on the world outside and got to wondering about her man, who, at this moment, happened to be on the other side of it!

Whilst relaxing later that evening she received a phone call from him:

Fi: "Hello"

Bran: "Hello Fi, how are you baby?"

Fi: "Oh Bran, I'm good. Thank you, great to hear you again. I don't know why but the time difference and the distance between us makes it feel like it's ages since we have spoken and it was only yesterday."

Bran: "The time difference drives me crazy. I'll be glad to be back to normality, I'm coming home tomorrow Fi. I seriously cannot wait to see you."

Fi: "And you too Bran. Thank you again for your thoughtful gifts, I was touched."

Bran: "That was the plan. I feel very touched by you already and I have such lovely feelings about us Fi."

Fi: "I'm glad you do because so far it has been really good between us and I am loving how things are progressing."

Bran: "I feel like you are driving me crazy Fi, in the best possible way and I'm confused how that can be, as we have not met and yet I feel like I have known you forever and yet in reality I haven't, it is crazy but nice crazy."

Fi: "I know Bran, so crazy but good crazy!"

Bran: "Sure. So I am coming home tomorrow and I will send you my flight details. I have to fly into Paris

for my clients and then straight onto a Cardiff flight a few hours later then home to Liverpool! Me and my Woman time!" (He laughed)

Fi: "I am so excited Bran and nervous too! So I may see you the day after tomorrow?"

Bran: "When I am leaving Cardiff, I will let you know and I'm all yours for a week if you want that too? However we want to arrange our timetable. We will discuss once I am back in the UK. Mmmm! All the pleasures I have in mind for my woman!"

Fi: "Sounds good to me, wonder what those pleasures will be?"

Bran: "Well I'll let you imagine and go now to finish my documentation for the cargo and my own packing, so a busy few hours for me now."

Fi: "Well take care, have a safe journey Bran. It's all going to be good!"

Bran: "I know, Goodbye dear one, Kisses to you."

Fi: "Bye Bran, kisses to you too, can't wait for the real deal kisses!" (They laughed)

She pressed end call and the line went dead.

Fi sat back on her settee and pondered the call. He was coming home tomorrow but the time difference and all the other stuff meant it was going to be a couple more days yet before she got to see Bran. Bran, her man! She made herself hot chocolate and sent text messages to the coffee o'clock girls:

Fi: Mr. Antique flying home tomorrow, I feel sick with excitement!

Julie: Fuckety, fuck, fuck, fuck. Get your presents on! X

Tracey: OMG Fi. At long last, enjoy! So happy for you Fi. X

Fi: I am meeting him in two days' time! Starving myself now for two days!

Julie: Can't believe it, at last! Can't handle the nerves. Feel like Princess Diana only there's 'four' of us in this relationship!

Fi laughed and sent a reply:

Fi: You are so hilarious! Night girls!

Tracey: Night Fi, get some bloody sleep because you won't be having any next week!

Fi: Due on my period in 3 days! SHIT!

Julie: Get to the doctors and get something, tell him you are going on your honeymoon!

Fi: I've only just told him I left the fucker in Devon remember!

Julie: Oh shit yes! What you going to do?

Fi: I'll think of some excuse to get a script!

Julie: I'll be round after work tomorrow.

Tracey: No dry January in November for you then!

Fi: NO! Wet December, I hope! (She laughed out loud as she typed)

Tracey: Really funny Fi!

Julie rang and there was just howling laughter on the other end of the phone, and neither of them could speak and tears were rolling down Fi's face before the laughter eventually calmed down and Julie said:

Julie: "You are so mad!"

Fi: "I'm not joking, it better had be! I'm going to the GP tomorrow, I'm going to say I'm going on a yoga holiday, (before adding) **I don't want to be on my period while I'm doing the downward dog!!"** and the peels of laughter echoed from both houses!

Julie: "Let's hope his 'snake dances', never mind you doing the 'downward dog'!" and there was absolutely no sense out of either of them for several minutes as they just howled and howled with laughter. The email alert brought Fi to her senses!

Fi: "Shit Jules, I've got his flight details!"

Julie: "What?"

Fi: "I've just got an email with his flight details from Air France. Oh my god!"

Julie: "Get Nessie on, I'm coming round!" (Nessie is the Nespresso machine!)

Fi: "Will do."

Thirty seconds later, there was a knock on the door and Fi let Julie in, made coffee and showed her friend the flight itinerary document from Air France. It showed his flight number, time of departure, check in time, his scheduled arrival time at Charles de Gaulle, departure from Paris to Cardiff and the flight number which was 'Fokker50' which sent them into hysteria once more as Fi said, "I'm finally meeting the Fokker!" and Julie howled alongside her friend whilst performing the, 'I'm having a wee dance' as she ran upstairs to use the bathroom. When she came back into the lounge, they looked at it all again and his name Branimir Rodrigues was quite clearly printed on the document as well, as the cost of the flight, which was $16, 332.46 USD. "Look at his name there Julie, he's real!" said Fi and "look how much it cost?" she added before Julie replied, "course he's real and Jesus, $16, 332 dollars, he is some businessman all right, those antiques must be worth a fortune!" Fi thought before adding, "gorgeous, successful and probably wedged, who the fuck is Robert?" and they laughed again before Fi stated, "Julie, I'm so nervous." Julie replied to her friend, "You'll be absolutely fine, when he sweeps you off your feet and starts snake dancing!" as raucous laughter filled the room. When they had finally calmed down Fi replied, "I really am nervous now!" the day after tomorrow, that's it, a game changer!" and Julie answered, "it is so surreal that it is finally here, I feel like we've all been in a TV Sitcom!" and Fi replied, "no, a romcom movie with a happy ending!" and with that, the girls hugged and said goodnight and Fi locked up her house and sent Bran a reply:

27 November 2013 22:08

Hi Bran, It is so real now, seeing your ticket. I want to cry. I am so thrilled that at last I get to see you. I hope I don't faint when I finally do. Wow, thank you for choosing me on the dating site.

Here is a little dedication to our pleasure:

What will my pleasure feel like? What will your kiss feel like?

What will your arms around me feel like? What will your undressing me feel like? What will your touches feel like?

Touching my hair, kissing my ears, kissing my breasts, caressing my nipples, licking my back as I lay on my front, teasing, as you trace a map upon my body with your tongue.

What will my pleasure feel like?

What will your pleasure feel like?

What will I smell like?

What will it feel like as I run my fingers through your hair?

What will my kiss feel like?

What will my tongue feel like as our gentle kiss rockets to passions of desire overtaking us?

What will it feel like as I gaze into your eyes as we remove each others clothes?

What will it feel like as I too trace a map upon your body with my tongue?

What will your pleasure feel like?

Your pleasure is my pleasure and my pleasure is your pleasure.

For your eyes only. This is for you. Have a beautiful sleep and a safe journey tomorrow.

However long you need to be in Cardiff and then finally get home to Liverpool doesn't matter. Whatever day that will be. I will wait. Fi. X

She went to bed a happy woman. She could not wait to share those pleasures. She was a woman who loved the sensual aspects of a relationship too. After all, they were part of the foundations. Sexual compatibility and sensual spontaneity were such an important factor in a relationship for Fi. How could two people 'grow' in love, if they couldn't create love together with their bodies, as part of their own personal recipe for love? They couldn't, she thought to herself.

As she drifted off to sleep she heard 'the scribble.' It was Bran:

27 November 2013 15:06 LA time

"Your pleasure is my pleasure and my pleasure is your pleasure." Oh my goodness, you really should write a book. You are so creative. You never told me such art attributes were inside you, wow, I truly love all that you write and it makes me feel that I want you on my arm right now, just the way a perfect woman should be

treated. We are going to be so, so good. As long as you want me, then let's get creating. I really am all yours for those pleasures and all the rest of us too. So I say to you now, see you soon my sweet one. Sleep well and dream of me. Here is a little video I just made for you while driving in my hire car. Kisses baby. X

Silent, gentle tears rolled down her face and she clicked on the video. "Jesus, oh my god," she said aloud. He looked gob-smackingly gorgeous. He was sat in a car which he was clearly driving, he was wearing a maroon short sleeved polo shirt, revealing his hairy chest and his 'manly' silver chain was visible around his neck, he was wearing designer sunglasses, and as she pressed play, he began to sing 'Love Never Felt So Good' by Michael Jackson and Justin Timberlake and he interwove her name into the lyrics as he sang along to the song playing in the background. As the song finished he blew her a kiss and said, "See you in two days Fi baby!" and the video ended. She was now bawling her eyes out. There was nothing else to do. He was hers. He really was hers! She replied:

27 November 2013 23:27

I just saw the video. Wow. The Singing Chauffeur. You look GORGEOUS! X

As he made his way across the ocean she finally realised that she had to go with the flow

CHAPTER 12

Touch base

Fi woke a couple of times in the night. She was both excited and anxious, as she no longer trusted aircraft to be a safe way to fly and she wouldn't be happy until his plane was on the ground. She had his flight number and she was able to track his flight as it made its' way across America and then out over the ocean and her excitement grew, as the tiny dot on the map moved closer and closer every time she checked it online. When she checked at 2am she noticed she had an email from him:

27 November 2013 16:05 LA time

Hey Fi, it's lovely to have so many people excited and pleased for us, I feel like so many people in my life are already a part of us, they are so excited to meet you because I am so happy. Again beautiful woman, you are in my thoughts as I wait to board my flight. I need to get some rest over the next couple of days because I have a feeling we're not doing a whole lot of sleeping next week! I am feeling, happy, excited, aroused, nervous, in fact a mixed cocktail of emotions. I cannot believe what has happened. It is so beautiful. I have tried to cancel my dating profile but it won't let me, so I have deleted my photos and profile info and I immediately delete all messages from other women, because I found the most beautiful woman in you and I am on the most amazing journey of my life. Coming home to you. It is truly wonderful. Thank you Fi. Keep yourself safe for me. I truly cannot wait to see you. How am I even going to drive home to finally meet

you? I will be so nervous. Loud music to distract me I think. I will let you know when I land safely in Paris for a few hours. Can I put Paris on the wish list for us? It's a beautiful place for me to share with you. It's been awhile since I have been. I wonder where in the world our journey will take us. One thing for sure, it's already an exciting one. If you were here now right now I would eat you. I am so glad we have so much time together next week. This is the longest first date ever. Until we speak I send you a tease! I think my head is under the covers kissing you! BBB. Bye Beautiful Baby of mine. X

Fi replied:

28 November 2013 02:23

Hi Bran, You made me cry AGAIN! I am listening to my 'Bran' playlist, as I cannot sleep and I just love the ED Sheeran song, especially the line that says your soul is evergreen. I already feel like you have a beautiful soul, as we continue on our journey to soulmate bliss. We have certainly found each other in a mysterious way. There are thousands of people on that dating site and yet we jumped off the page at each other. What awaits us is a mystery, for us to solve. Safe journey Mr. Antique. Fi. X

PS: Perfect Paris. Oh yes please. X

Fi decided she needed to let Calum know about her new man. She sent him a text as she knew he may very well still be up, it was part of student life was it not, to party all night and sleep all day!

She typed into her phone:

Mum: Hi Calum, just wanted to let you know. I was having a girl's night in with Julie a couple of weeks ago and she encouraged me to look at dating sites and obviously we had a good laugh looking at all the dick heads. Anyway a few guys contacted me and one stood out from the crowd. We have been emailing all day every day for two weeks and I am finally meeting him in Liverpool in a couple of days. He is 51. A specialist antiques dealer for very wealthy clients, currently in New York/LA on business. He is lovely, sensible and I have a lovely feeling about it all. All my friends Tracey, Jackie, Julie etcetera, are in awe of the way he behaves towards me and are so excited for me having got rid of Rob the knob. He has a daughter Kate who is really chuffed for her dad. Your sister is not keen because it is online dating but she has just met someone on Kiss or Miss, so Internet dating is Internet dating is it not? I am a big girl, I have met enough knobs through work and in my personal life to know that he appears a genuine man and I am very happy with how things are going at the moment. I know there are always risks but I can look after myself. I don't want any negative vibes from your sister to influence what you might feel Calum. He really is lovely, good looking, makes me laugh, and oh, wedged! His flight home today from LA cost $16,000 due to excess baggage of antiques! He is called Bran (Branimir). He is half Dutch, half Slovenian and I am having a good time so please, don't worry. I'm looking forward to finally meeting him after his business trip. Love mum. X

Calum: All right Mum don't worry about Louise, she's obviously just worried about you after what you've just been through and to be honest, I can't blame her because I'm a bit worried about you as well! I don't want you going through anything bad again after what that big nosed bastard did to you, I know you're a grown woman, so just be careful, have fun and make sure you still take caution going on dates or whatever! X Love you X

She shed a tear. He was such a calm, placid young man who took everything in his stride, unless someone rattled his cage and then he was like a roaring lion! He was especially defensive if someone rattled his mum's cage and he had seen enough of her pain over the past few years with repeated episodes from Robert and he never wanted to see her go through anything like that again. Robert was a first class bastard in Calum's eyes and he had said he would repay him for what he had put his mother through and Fi knew that he would. When the time was right.

Fi tried to sleep but it wasn't a restful night by any means and she got up the next morning feeling exhausted and decided to just have a lazy day in her pyjamas. It was miserable weather and she just stayed indoors all day with her blanket, her hot water bottle, hot drinks and her dogs. She tried to listen to her music, she tried to watch TV, she tried to read her book, she tried to complete her puzzles on her game console but she couldn't concentrate on anything. She fed herself by grazing all day on unhealthy snacks and she was even tempted to open a bottle of wine late afternoon to calm her nerves but in the end she decided to rest on her bed with her shamanic meditation cd. She absolutely loved the calmness it brought to her wandering thoughts and she eventually managed to sooth herself into a more restful sleep for a couple of hours. She woke up, showered, changed into fresh pyjamas and fed her dogs. It was early evening by now as she made a decaf Nespresso and sat down to check her emails and discovered that he had sent her a message:

28 November 2013 10:38 LA time

I feel so shattered..... Haven't been able to touch base before now. I couldn't get on the flight, as the crazy LA Customs didn't let me. They seized my goods and gave me an appointment to return to their office at 08:30am tomorrow. I had a hell of a night they were really fierce with me. CALL ME LATER HONEY. In an hour or two. I am exhausted. Bran. X

'WTF!' she thought to herself as she reread it to clarify the contents of the email again. He hadn't gotten on the flight. There was a customs issue. That was perfectly feasible. He was a specialist antique dealer, dealing with very, very, expensive antiques. He would be a day or two later than planned. Disappointing? Of course! But it is what it is and there is nothing I can do about she thought to herself! "We wait," she said aloud, as she sighed and sat on the settee to cuddle her dogs. She had watched the reality TV shows regarding customs and border control issues and she imagined all sorts of scenarios in her head but she was just guessing, it could be any number of reasons, why they had stopped him leaving LA and in any event, it can't be that serious, they had released him and asked him to return later that day. She reminded herself that she did not know this man AT all, other than through his emails and over the telephone but Fi had to be hopeful that he would be back in the UK soon, given he wasn't being held in custody regarding his customs issue. She rang him 2 hours later having decided to give him time to rest:

Bran: "Hey Fi, I'm so sorry baby, so disappointing!"

Fi: "It is Bran, what happened?"

Bran: "One of the pieces I have is from Canada and doesn't have they correct paperwork for export and so I have to get the correct permit before I can take it out of USA. It should be a couple of days and then I am clear to leave."

Fi: "So why was it horrible then Bran? In what way were they fierce?"

Bran: "Because there is always an assumption you are committing a crime and it is up to me to prove I am not and not having the correct permit doesn't help, but I was ignorant to this required document and acted upon the advice of the agent."

Fi: "Ignorance isn't a satisfactory mitigating factor though is it?"

Bran: "Exactly, how many people go through customs saying 'I didn't know' trying to smuggle items in and out of a country. I am not trying to smuggle, I am genuinely trying to buy items on behalf of clients and I have had to involve one of them in clarifying my story today, which I hated to do. Client confidentiality is everything to me."

Fi: "Well a hard lesson learnt Bran. Have you had any issues like this before?"

Bran: "No I have never bought anything with

Canadian connections before and so I really was ignorant of the requirements.”

Fi: “Well hopefully, all will be resolved when you go back there tomorrow.”

Bran: “I hope so. I just want to be home. Had enough here now, it’s been a bad trip for me personally, New York was a waste of time and now this at the tail end of the trip.”

Fi: “Well go and get some more rest and let me know how you go on at your meeting.”

Bran: “Okay. I will call when I finish with them. Bye baby.”

Fi: “Bye Bran, take care.”

She pressed end call and the line went dead.

Fi sat and pondered over the phone call. Was there anything to be concerned about? It all sounded perfectly feasible. Customs officials have a job to do and if anything isn’t right, going in or out of their country, it is up to them to investigate that. That is exactly what they were doing and Fi and Bran would just have to wait a while longer before they got to see each other. Fi was shattered too, as she realised the emotions of euphoria, excitement and now disappointment, mixed with trepidation to a certain extent, together with lack of quality sleep had sent her into a sluggish and chaotic frame of mind and she really needed to get some rest. She went to bed early and slept reasonably well.

She awoke at 6:30 and didn’t expect to get back to sleep

and so she showered, changed into her gym gear and drove to the gym. After a good hour long walk on the treadmill, Fi sat and had breakfast in the cafe as she people watched and noted all the 'workers' coming in and out of their pre work gym sessions. She was glad she didn't have to do that anymore, she had done it religiously for years in the past and was thankful that she could now please herself when she attended the gym, apart from her scheduled classes of course. She drove home and walked the dogs in Heaton Park, before returning to complete her daily chores. She was all done and dusted (literally) for 10am and invited Pauline over for lunch. She decided she needed the distraction. Fi put together an afternoon tea with all the usual suspects on the cake stand and a cold bottle of Prosecco decanted into the teapot! She needed the drink. What a crazy couple of days it had been, AGAIN. Fi and Pauline spent the afternoon catching up on their respective lives, families and general gossip, as well as enjoying each others company as they always had. As the girls were discussing the aftermath of Robert's behaviour and how, only a few short weeks ago, Fi had been so devastated and whilst laughing at their respective roles within the Whitefield Angels and expressing their excitement regarding Fi and Bran, a message came through from him:

29 November 2013 07:15 LA time

Hey baby. I know we can't wait to see each other, hug, kiss and all the other beautiful things we want with each other eventually but right now when I need you. I need you to know you have touched me so deeply. I am with you in spirit today. I'll be home before you know it, just let me just sort things out with customs today. I'm on my way to them now. Bran X

Fi discussed the contents with Pauline and felt happy that he would be on his way later today, after tying up loose ends and legalities, regarding his expensive cargo. She felt so reassured after receiving the email and the horrors of some of the reality TV customs and border control programmes could be placed at the back of her mind. She replied:

29 November 2013 15:40

Hi Bran, I am thinking of you, good luck and hurry home! Fi X

The girls decided to go to the cinema that evening and went into the city centre to the art and cinema venue to watch a romantic drama set in Paris. It was a good film and a welcome distraction for the girls and a change from their usual late afternoon get-togethers. Afterwards they went for drinks in a local bar, before getting the tram in opposite directions back to their respective homes. Pauline had asked Fi to promise her that she would keep her informed of the forthcoming events with Bran and she had agreed to do so. She wouldn't be able to resist sharing the events to come. When she got home she made coffee and checked out Liverpool hotels on Tripadvisor but she had no idea where he lived and so couldn't book anything, as she had neither a date nor a destination but at least she now had a few options to book if she chose to. It was all a bit vague. She went to bed at 10:30 pm and calculated it would be 11:30 am in LA. He had been in his meeting for three hours and she imagined him being interrogated, she imagined him being strip-searched, she imagined him having every item of luggage and cargo searched, she imagined him being handed papers and hand shaking and him being allowed to continue his journey. She was weary of imagining, she was really tired and so she sent him an email and put her phone on silent mode, she didn't want disturbing tonight.

She wrote:

29 November 2013 22:45

Hey Bran, I'm off to bed. I hope you are getting to resolve the problem. I've missed you today. Fi. X

She turned off the lights and drifted off to sleep with the help of her shamanic drumming cd and travelled into her lower world during her meditation. She awoke the next morning and checked her emails on her laptop and saw a mammoth one from him as she clicked open. Her heart began to race and she felt nauseous as she read its contents:

29 November 2013 14:30 LA time

You are the sweetest soul I know as of today!

Hello sweetie, Sorry I haven't been able to get back in touch with you before now. Very stressful times for me. So a payment made it to them before yesterday's working hours ran out and I was called to come to office! I got there hoping to get cleared and leave. To my shocking surprise, they told me it would take up to 10 working days to get the trade permit that would allow me to go about my merchandise how I want. I literally felt like giving someone a smack! After getting the money they needed. I mean they never said that to me before. They should have just said that upfront the other day! Anyway, their senior official advised me to go find an International Freight Company to come

pick my merchandise up as I can't leave until my license is ready as an option and as it is, they would mail the permit to me when it's ready!

So I went out on a quest for that and managed to strike a deal with a cargo company to go pick up my Items. That was what got me busy for the rest of yesterday. So they now have my merchandise in their warehouse out of the customs office to avoid their 5 working days law of confiscating any goods that exceeds that! So I have been trying to finalise our deal so they can ship out as we have beaten the custom's odds of confiscating the goods after 5 days in their possession! Now that these merchandise are with the Cargo company in their warehouse they won't now ship out until everything is sorted. As of right now, I'm in limbo. Go to this website, mouse to 'SOLUTIONS', under it click on 'LCL' customer page' and put in this code ARC1114 to access my page on the cargo web site. The total charges before they ship out is what's left, as they have refused shipping out and getting paid but they need all their balance here and now.

So again, I was left with no choice but to ask for more helping hands from clients to complete the shipment. But the way it stands, it's not good news. So much money gone already for this mess. Seems no one at this point wants to send any upfront payment. They would rather take their money elsewhere to buy from other dealers as it's a peak period for business. Everyone is giving one excuse or the other. And the irony of this whole thing is, the guys who I'd call top figures in all of this are the ones who have so many excuses to give. The guy I least expected was the one who turned up to save my goods from the customs and now he too isn't

turning up and I don't understand. I am becoming frustrated and really have tried all doors I know. I don't know what to do at this point. I have exhausted all avenues! For every day my goods spend with the cargo company the warehouse fee goes up $156 USD!

Although I am no in position to ask darling, I just wanted to ask if you could be of help to balance up the shipment costs so then I can leave and get to you. I stand here and would be willing to give anything confidential you might need from me to legitimize this. I have been thinking and it kills me to ask but just had to after some red wine. I so want this nightmare over so we can have our normal lives and get to be together and never talk about this. I'm quite stressed even as I type this. I'm needing $5,200 USD which is equivalent to £3,300 GBP sent to the company on my behalf with my REG number you will see on the web page and I'd sum up with what I have on me here to sort things so I can move on. All I'd need is about 2 days to settle and I will reimburse whatever I might owe. I can't wait to start selling and making money. Oh they got me this time real big! Spent too much capital this time plus what these bastards suck out of me. But if you are not in a good place to help, I will understand and wouldn't want it to stress you! I am just trying your door. My pride is shaken and I am quite down emotionally. It is what it is.... I wait to hear from you and hope you understand too! Fingers crossed. No matter what baby, please don't be mad at me. That would even hurt more. I have the rest of the money to sum up the amount owed you'd see on the site. What I'm asking is just what I need. You are too good to me. Miss you! Kisses Sweetie.

She was completely dumbfounded. Despite the number of

times she read it, none of it made any sense. It read as if he was pissed whilst typing it? All she really knew was that he was asking her for money. She rang Julie in tears because her head was now in pinball machine mode with panic:

Fi: "Hi Julie, please come round."

Julie: "What's up? On my way, two minutes."

Julie knocked frantically on the door and Fi opened it and Julie hugged her friend, "What on earth is the matter?" she asked, Fi replied, "I've had an email Julie and I think it's a scam, I don't think Bran is real," and she gave the laptop to Julie. "Why, what's happened, why do you think that?" she asked in an equally panicked voice, "Because he is asking for money," Fi replied. Julie suggested she calm down and together they made tea. Then they looked at the email again, they clicked on the website and did everything he had instructed and there he was, registered with the cargo company and he had paid $23,000 USD of a $28,000 USD invoice and the flight details suggested a destination of Heathrow and then onto Cardiff. They checked his website again, they checked his emails again, Fi checked his phone number and it was a US phone number, and the London one checked out too, she checked his photographs including his childhood ones, she checked his video sent only yesterday. Everything added up. He just needed money, BUT she didn't have it.

Julie and Fi were reassured that it wasn't a scam and so Fi phoned him but there was no answer. She left a voicemail:

Fi: "Hi Bran, it's me, I have your email. I am shocked and upset as you can hear, (she was weeping) **but I will send you an email. Please ring me when you can. Bye."**

She sent an email:

30 November 2013 09:02

Hey Bran, I am crying so much. Don't know what to do to help you. I just don't have any spare money. I have my little income and I certainly don't have major savings or a credit card to help. I am so upset for you, for me, for us. This has all been a nightmare. Are you stuck there now if you don't get the cash? I don't know how I can help Bran. I am not angry. I am sad. I want you here. Do you have to wait for the document? Can it not be sorted from the UK? I feel so stupid sending you lovely messages and you're stressed with this nightmare. I didn't know it was so bad for you. I feel helpless. I am sorry I have no money Bran, I don't know what else to do. You need me and I can't help, I am so sorry. Fi X

Julie left to take her son to football and said she'd call again when she was back home. Fi suddenly had a thought that might help and sent another email:

30 November 2013 09:33

Hi Bran, just a thought that might help you. What about sea freight as opposed to air freight? Will that be cheaper and allow your goods to be released? Would that work for you? Fi X

Fi heard nothing all day and by early evening she decided to send another email, she certainly wasn't ringing again, he had her voicemail, he knew she was trying to get hold of him, she had already sent two emails and no reply. Her message was short and sweet:

30 November 2013 17:07

Hi Bran, how are things? It's 5pm here. Worrying about you. I miss you. X

She spent the remainder of the night worrying as he didn't contact her and so as she retired for the day she sent another email. By now she was pissed off with him!

30 November 2013 10:56

Hi Bran, just wondering what is happening. It would be nice if you could contact me. I am beginning to wonder if I have fallen into the trap of another one of those online dating scams that I often hear about. I would like you to contact me to verify that our contact has been genuine. Thank you. Fi. X

He replied an hour later:

30 November 2013 15:48 LA time

I have been on a roll. Out of my mind and not been myself. I hated to hear you cry and all on my voicemail. I understand your point of view but somehow disappointed at your comment. Am I genuine? You tell me. If you have been a victim of an online scam or catfish. You tell me if after all you've known about me... It's not demeaning for you to even say that! I am not holding it against u. just saying how I feel. As of today Kate told me her utmost effort got her up to £2,200. I am £1,100 short and I can't stop

pinching myself as this is the most ridiculous yet painful situation especially about money I have ever been. Settle down and don't ever send such a demeaning message again... That hurt. Actually! X

He was pissed off now wasn't he? No 'Bran' signature, no xx's, just a blunt, pissy, 'annoyed with her' email. He had heard her voicemail and yet he hadn't phoned when he heard her tears? She was pissed about that. He hadn't phoned to reassure her when she suggested a scam, she was pissed about that too and he had told her not to send demeaning messages, she was really pissed about that. She replied immediately as she was furious:

1 December 2013 00:13

I am sorry if my message hurt you but I have seen my friends as victims many years ago Bran. You are not replying to my messages, I sent you 4 yesterday. What am I supposed to think? I am going out of my mind too. I have had the most blissful three weeks and then to hardly hear from you and in the midst of it all, you are asking me for a substantial sum of money, yes I repeat myself here, what am I supposed to think? I want more than anything to believe that that beautiful man I have had contact with this past almost three weeks is real, because I can tell you for sure that I am exactly who I have shown you. I am 100% that beautiful woman. This is hell for me too, I am supposed to be in your arms right now, REMEMBER! It is not at all like you to ignore my messages so to suddenly have no reply to my messages or voicemail was worrying for me. Why can't you send it sea freight? Surely, that would be cheaper? I just trust in my faith in the power of the universe and if we are meant to be,

this will all work out. I am sorry that I don't have money to help you but if you want to be with me then surely that means keeping in touch with me in the good and bad aspects of our contact so far. Don't ignore me to leave me guessing, that is not fair. I can honestly say you rocked my world too Bran but you also upset my world when you ignored me. Can I do anything to help you other than money? I am sorry I upset you but put yourself in my shoes please. You upset me too. If I am to be with you then that means by your side always, 'ALWAYS', and not just the gorgeous times. Stay in touch. I'm here for you and I hope that counts for something. To me, that is priceless! I am crying now. I just want you here so much and I am so angry with you right now. Fi X

Bran replied:

30 November 2013 16:36 LA time

Oh I am so sorry for the delay in my response to you, and I am sorry about your friend as well but I don't think I would do such to anybody. Never! I was only trying your door to see if that will get me out of here on time, it's unfortunate you are not able to help. It is a shame I got into this mess even at this time when I am supposed to be happy with you. Don't cry anymore baby, I hope I get help before the weekend is over. I am sorry I made you doubt me. Bran

"So you fucking should be," she said aloud as she read it! Before answering:

1 December 2013 00:45

Hi, take care of you. I wait to hear from you. I want that man back! Fi. X

He responded:

30 November 2013 16:52 LA time

I will let you know once I get good news. Thanks for your concern.

Again, no Hey Fi or Bran, or xx's contained in the email she noticed, he really was pissed off with her too she thought. She went to bed and slept fitfully and when she eventually rose about 9:30 am she made coffee and baked some banana muffins, did her chores and sat down with her laptop, her pen and her notepad. She combed everything, the dating site profile, every email, every music video, the video of him singing to her, his website link, the air cargo link, the Air France ticket, the photographs he had sent and finally she Googled his name.

She made reams and reams of notes before sending him one final email:

1 December 2013 13:02

Hey, obviously not the 'sweetest soul' enough for you to respond to my emails. I have contacted you many times since I spoke to you yesterday and it is most unlike you NOT to respond to me. I think I may have been gullible in falling for your charms and even more gullible thinking that handsome man on the pictures is really you. From my research this morning, I suspect a fake dating profile, a fake business website, fake Air

France and ARCargo documents etcetera to extract money from me. The lovely trail seems to have gone cold now that I cannot help you with money. I am too smart for that but other vulnerable women will fall for this scam. I believe in Karma and if this is how you chose to live your life, then you will be rewarded accordingly for sure. I know that you will have made yourself untraceable, as is usual in these situations but I will inform as many organisations as I can to try to stop people like you hurting vulnerable women. I am not physically harmed by this contact we have had but you have now made me wary of dating websites. Thanks for that. I am very angry with you for trying to dupe me and I am even angrier with myself for allowing it to happen. I really am the lovely person I have portrayed myself to be within our emails and I rest my head on my pillow every night knowing that. I can live in peace each day knowing I am a good person, people like you cannot. Enjoy your day my gorgeous, handsome, beautiful Bran. NOT. Don't know who you are and I don't really care. Fuck you. Fi.

From registering with the dating site on 9 November 2013 until 1 December 2013 it was 'exactly 23 days.' Did all that really happen?

CHAPTER 13

The real deal

Julie came round later that day and whilst sharing a bottle of wine together, Fi showed her bestie everything she had discovered and collated into a thorough portfolio of evidence, under the heading of 'Liar, Liar' which made them both laugh:

The fake antiques website:

His home page on his website is unedited with many spelling and grammar issues, which contrasts greatly with his 'get to know me' page which displayed appropriate spelling and grammar with minimal editing issues. Would a man of his credentials have such an unprofessional website, when dealing with supposedly high profile and wealthy clients? Hardly. The 'contact me' page had a spelling issue on the address, the phone number was for a mobile, with no landline and having checked the number and listened to the voicemail the voice is that of a male, with a non-European accent, Fi suspected. Google maps search revealed that the address is a terraced house and an additional online electoral role check revealed that Bran had nothing to do with that address.

"They are so fucking clever," said Julie, "well, yes and no," replied Fi, "otherwise I wouldn't have found this lot!" as they continued looking at the evidence before them.

The dating website profile:

His 'about me' and 'what I am looking for' paragraphs clearly worded to entice and gain an initial bite of the bait, once he had made initial contact with me.

His emails:

Inconsistencies in his style of writing, spelling and grammar issues to the point where the 'big one' asking for money was completely out of sync with ANY of his previous emails.

"It is so badly presented that this was the deciding factor and made me so categoric, that this is a scam!" said Fi to Julie, before adding, "AND, there was obviously a team of people involved here." "Julie, I feel so many things but mainly I feel so stupid" she continued and Julie replied, "one thing you are not Fi, is stupid, look at what you have already found out! You could get a job with Pinnacle Paul, never mind the 'Whitefield Angels,'" as she chuckled to herself. Fi wasn't really in a laughing mood.

His Air France itinerary email:

Obviously a scanned and copied document with quite obvious amendments and no booking reference number.

"Yes but just look how the scammers have very cleverly detailed information from the Air France document into my emails," said Fi, "look there," she pointed before continuing, "they've included the flight departure and destination details, a link to Air France's website which is a genuine link and even the flight number, which when I checked it out online, displays a weekly flight from LA to Paris, look," she added, repeating the link process for

Julie. “The sly bastards” said Julie. Fi clicked back to her ‘Liar, Liar’ document to reveal:

His AR Cargo web link in the ‘big one’ email revealed issues including addresses at two airports, one in London and another in an area of the USA that was nowhere near LAX. Also there was no contact telephone number for the company on their website.

“All the instructions contained in that email revealed details as he described, regarding the cargo of antiques,” said Fi as she opened the link and followed the instructions again to show Julie. “Unbelievable Fi, the cunning behind it all and some poor victims have handed their money over,” she said, “because they are not as smart as you!” “Can you imagine how many people, on how many dating sites, in how many countries, all over the world this is happening to?” said Fi, “scary, really scary, and what about the psychological damage to people too?” she added, before continuing, “some poor victims will be distraught, I had this for 23 days and I feel bereft, some people may be 23 weeks, 23 months, even longer!” She sighed before adding, “ The conning bastards, I just want to punch them, whoever they are and wherever they are.” “I know,” said Julie, “the conning, cunning, cunts!” and that just sent them into their world of hysteria and when they came up for air, when their laughter had finally subsided, Fi clinked glasses with her friend and said, “well Mr. Antique, you’re still gorgeous wherever you are!” and she raised her glass and said, “thank you, we had so much fun getting to know you, and somebody is a FUCKING LUCKY BITCH!” she screamed at the screen as they laughed again. They carried on looking at his photographs and at the video he sent of himself singing to Fi and decided that they couldn’t identify any issues, “But,” Fi said, "I bet Louise could spot all the 'Photoshopping' and video dubbing etcetera, a mile off!" "It's her job, after all." she added. "I bet," said Julie, "oh Jesus, she'll go mad at you for allowing yourself to be done by a scammer," she added, "oh Jules, don't, what am I going to tell her?" asked Fi. "Tell her the truth, you found out he was a scammer, before any harm was done!" said Julie. "Well, THAT, my friend, is the truth!" said Fi.

They talked for a while about other issues in order for Fi to take a break from it all and after Fi had answered a text from Tracey, who was due back from Fuerteventura that evening, her thoughts drifted back to Mr. Antique and Fi had an inclination to Google his name. She typed Branimir Rodrigues into the search bar and he appeared in the list as having a Google+ page. She clicked on it and saw it had been searched over 2000 times and said, "Oh my god Julie, look at this," as her friend came to join her on the settee. There he was in an image that was just so stunning, "What an absolutely gorgeous picture," said Fi, "talk about save the best till last," she added. "Isn't he JUST so stunning?" she added, before continuing, "Wow, wow, wow!" He was sat in a limousine wearing a suit that can only be described as the 'mutt's nuts', black fine stripe three piece, white shirt, cufflinks and a dark tie, hair immaculate, a wearing very, very expensive watch on his arm. He was also wearing glasses and his beautiful smile. "There is no way that that guy there, (she tapped the screen) would ever need to ask ANYBODY for money!" said Fi. "He must have Gold Credit Cards coming out of his arse!" she added as they laughed. "He is seriously wedged, LOOK AT THAT VEHICLE!" she continued. "That confirms it more than ever now, no way does he need money," she repeated! "Definitely not," said Julie. "AND," added Julie, "there is no way, he would be on a

dating website, he will have women dropping at his feet."
"Exactly!" said Fi. She shut down her laptop and they chatted a while longer before Julie said her goodbyes and Fi took the dogs out for a very late night walk. What a day! Please let it be a calmer night, she asked nobody in particular, as she climbed into bed feeling emotionally and physically exhausted.

Fi woke the next morning disoriented as if waking from a bad dream and it took her a while to get her head around what had happened over the past couple of days. She was still half expecting to hear 'the scribble' alert anytime now and being fairly certain it would be Bran. Of course that would be no more. She lay there for an age just mulling it all over in her mind. It was hard to comprehend she was in a scenario where, 'one day you wake up having someone significant in your life and the next day you no longer have them!' Here today, gone tomorrow yet again and the irony of it all, was that the relationships with Robert and with Bran were both built from the outset on 'foundations of lies' and both relationships had spectacularly collapsed. Liar, Liar, pants on fire, so the children's rhyme says. Well, her pants weren't exactly on fire but she had been bitten on the backside again, for sure. She got up and went about her usual morning chores after deciding that today was absolutely going to be a day of regrouping. She needed to come down off this emotional high. She played her music very loud (as the neighbours were out) as she enjoyed the distraction of singing along to Sigma, 'Nobody to love' and for sure she agreed with the lyrics that she was sick and tired of exiting a party without anybody to love. 'Jesus,' was she? It was a good song to have on the repeat.

She decided to contact her friend, who had an apartment in Bowness. She was going to go away on her own for a while. It was the best alternative she had to her all time 'dream treat' of two weeks at The Olive Retreat in Spain. One day, she sighed, one day. She emailed her friend and booked herself in for a week, leaving in two days time. It will hold memories of Robert, she thought as she recalled that she first took him there six months into their relationship and she had spent part of her honeymoon there too but she would not allow him to spoil forever, this little piece of Lakeland heaven. She had been coming to this part of the world since she was a small child and she had taken her own small children there too. Fuck him. No way was he robbing her of that peace. She guiltily booked the cat in the cattery and dogs in their boarding kennels for 8 days and she packed her bag with sensible outfits for walking, her gym gear for yoga, and a couple of pairs of jeans and tops for going out for dinner, if she felt like it, although the thought of solo dinners in public places was both terrifying and upsetting at the same time. She tidied her house, made sure all unused fresh foods, dirty laundry and dishwashing were dealt with, to prevent odours developing whilst she was away.

She was exhausted as the evening arrived and she took a two hour soak using all her favourite luxurious toiletries in the bath and she let the tears gently flow, mixing together with the bubbles and the bath water. How? Why? She thought to herself, as the sad, gentle droplets flowed down her face, (as she registered the fact) did she not have any issues whatsoever, (she repeated it) 'WHATSOEVER!' with her girlfriends? Yet, here it was, happening after a relationship with a man, again! She had to remind herself that she was never ever going to have a relationship with Bran, he was a complete and utter fabrication and that the real guy's images were probably on dating sites all over the world. He was a bigger victim than she was, she thought. At least she was in the privacy of her own home, he was probably in hundreds of homes and hundreds of hearts right now and completely oblivious to that fact too. It made her so angry that somewhere out there evil people were infiltrating innocent people's lives, when all they were doing was trying to find companionship and love. Sick bastards she thought. What kind of evil would you have to have coursing through your veins, to choose that you want to hurt somebody else in such a way? The reality was there deep inside of her, she WAS really hurting but she also knew that some of this was 'Robert shite' resurfacing again, after all how could she be hurting because of Bran? She had never met him. How could she express her anger at the scammers? She would never meet them to be able to do that. Her head and her heart were torn to shreds and she needed so badly to get away. The only gratitude she had, whilst she lay in the bath shriveling like a prune, was that the pinball machine wasn't switched on. She knew for sure that she would never be able to handle that machine switching itself on again. EVER.

Fi spent the next day doing a chore she was dreading, contacting her friends and family to tell them all the truth, it took her most of the day, as people were not satisfied with a simple text. They wanted full scale explanations and her messenger, text, email and telephone communications kept her busy all day. Thankfully, not one of them judged her, they had all shared in this potentially delightful story of happiness, borne out of the horrors of pain and were captivated in the ongoing details themselves. They were all part of the story of 'Bran and Fi' too, in their own ways. Fi was able to explain the differing after affects with them all and in particular with

Kate Kuwait, her longtime friend whom she very seldom saw these days but who had always, always been there for Fi. Out of all her friends Kate had seen Fi in far too many grief stricken bouts at the hands of men. Too, too many over the years and she vowed to be, 'here if you need me, my lovely.' Fi shed many tears that day, she felt like she had been emotionally raped. When a woman is sexually raped, she has something taken from her body and that is how Fi felt in her mind. She had had the fragile embers of her emotional well being, stoked to a magnificent skywards dancing flame of excitement, only for it to be extinguished in an instant as the excitement was cruelly snatched by another liar. Yes, her mind had been raped.

She was able to explain to her friends as they listened to her pain that the relationship was a fake from the beginning. She had been targeted and lies were used to hook her, dominate her and ultimately exploit her. It was very obvious to her and to those who had seen her portfolio of evidence that this had not been a lone 'wolf' snaring her, to try to get her money and not caring about any hurt or devastation they left behind. The bitterest pill to swallow, was the one that made her realise, that, although she had learned lessons from Robert and was certainly on guard in learning to trust her instincts with men in a live situation, this was the first time she had been duped in an online setting and her acceptance of her own naivety, was hard for her to take. Time would tell if there were to be any long term side effects of her encounter but for the immediate future she needed to concentrate on the short term effects and there were a few. She felt foolish, no matter how much her friends told her they would have behaved the same way in the same circumstances. She felt the loss of a potential love. She had lost Bran (just like that, lost another man in an instant AGAIN and that was very hard to take). Bran wasn't a Nigerian Internet dating scammer, he was that beautiful man she had had communication with every day. Well, he wasn't, (she knew that, in reality) but she had yet to get her head around that fact. There were now at least four people in this relationship, herself, the scammer(s) (who had suddenly invaded her relationship with Bran and pinched her man, just like the trollop had invaded her relationship with Robert), there was the 'Bran' in the images and the real guy too, whoever he may be. 'You thought you had issues with the complications of Roberts messy entourage?' she asked herself! 'Try working this mess out in your head,' she thought as she sent a text to Louise:

Fi: Binned Mr. Antique, not what I thought in the end. Never mind. Closed my account for a while. Need some me time. X

Louise: Why have you binned him? It's always good for a distraction but just have to be careful that people are portraying what they are not! X

Fi: Just didn't like some of the stuff he was saying online! X

Louise: Oh god, like that was it? That's shit Mum! X

Fi: At least I know now and not months and years down the line like the other wanker. X

Louise: Yeah, exactly! It's tough to gauge what somebody is like online!

Fi: Yes but at least I've not gone through all that meeting him, trying to analyse him, etc. Sussed him and binned him with the click of a button. Much easier

ha! X

Louise: Make sure you block his email address so he doesn't contact you again! X

Fi was glad of the minimum communication she had had with Louise regarding Bran and was happy to let Louise think he had been an online sex pest. It saved the hassle of a potential, 'I told you so,' which Fi didn't need, to be honest. She needed cuddles, reassurance and love and although she wanted that on an everyday basis in a genuine relationship with a man, she was now doubtful she would EVER trust anybody except herself, her children and the girls in her life. She took herself off to bed for an early night, she had a busy day tomorrow.

The next morning she was up, showered, had had her breakfast and dropped the animals off by 10am. She had a quick decaf coffee with Julie, threw her bag in the car and set off for her 'her' time. She played peaceful music en-route and she arrived 90 minutes later pulling into the car park before slumping over her steering wheel for a moment to think. She took some deep breaths and said to herself, 'come on let's get this over with and then I can enjoy MY time here, this is my peaceful haven not his'. She had many more memories here other than the ones she'd made with him. She would soon eradicate him from this space. She unloaded her car and took her belongings up to the upstairs apartment, placing them on the bed in the main room, she opened all the windows, put her music on louder than loud and of course on 'repeat song,' as she sang along to Michael Buble, 'It's a beautiful day,' The lyrics were so cathartic for her as she danced around each room and moved items to different locations so as to change the mood of each space. She placed flowers she had bought in the centre of the dining table and sprayed her favourite eco room scent as she continued to dance with glee. She poured herself a glass of wine and as she listened to the tune and paid more attention to the lyrics again, she acknowledged that she was so very relieved that she had got away from him. He had been metaphorically sucked out of the window, here in this peaceful haven and blown into the wind to carry on contaminating someone else's life and any day without him, really was a beautiful day. 'Who the fuck is Robert?' sounded like music to her ears!

She spent the afternoon walking around the lakeside area. It was quiet, due to the time of year and the air was cold and crisp but she was wrapped up warm and she soaked up the peaceful atmosphere as she sauntered across the public path to the small jetty area at the Hawkshead car ferry terminal. She sat and enjoyed a coffee, whilst watching people tending to their boats and was awestruck at the sight of a beautiful yacht that passed in front of her eye line. Wow she thought to herself, how the other half live eh! She sat for a while before eventually deciding to meander back the same way, stopping at The Old England Hotel for a late afternoon tea. This hotel had always been a part of her pleasure whenever she was in Bowness. She often relished in the treats of an afternoon tea if the weather or time of year prevented her from enjoying a glass of wine or a cold beer on the outside terrace, watching the sunset. Fi seated herself at a window table overlooking the lake with a spectacular view and ordered the Champagne Afternoon Tea. She was celebrating after all! She was celebrating this beautiful place that had been such a significant part of her life for so long. She had enjoyed her childhood holidays here, her romantic weekends here, her mini breaks with her own children, her weekends away with the girls, a lovely break with her friend David the artist and yes part of her honeymoon with Robert too. At the time she was happy and that too was part of her celebration of this breathtaking location. The waiter poured her Champagne and she held her glass up to the spectacular view in front of her and toasted all her memories of Bowness and mourned for the loss of those she wouldn't get to create too! She would have brought Bran here, for sure. She had even discussed with Julie about buying a weekend break for him as a Christmas gift, as she had absolutely no idea what else she could buy him! Cheers Bran, she thought as she rested her eyes and concentrated on her breathing for a few minutes to stem the flow of tears, before eventually opening her them to see an elderly gentleman stood near her, taking photographs through the window, out across the lake. He glanced over and smiled at her and said, "You looked so peaceful just then, with your eyes closed," Fi smiled and replied, "oh, I was just saying a final goodbye to a few ghosts." The gentleman laughed and said, "Oh the irony, I come here to say hello to a ghost," before adding, "my wife and I have been coming here for 64 years and when she died three years ago, I decided I would continue to come here by myself on her birthday, for afternoon tea," he said. "That is so beautiful" said Fi, "what a lovely way to remember her," she added, dabbing a tear. The gentleman held out his hand and said, "I am William, but I like Bill," Fi shook his hand and said, "Fi pleased to meet you Bill, I like Bill too!" she smiled at him before asking, "would you like to sit with me?" gesturing to the spare seat next to her, "thank you," he replied before adding, "I don't want to intrude on your tea." Fi said, "You are not intruding at all." Bill sat and said to Fi, "I hope you don't mind but I took the liberty of taking a photograph of you when you had your eyes closed, (showing her the image on his camera), I thought it would be a nice image to capture and also to paint it too, would you mind me asking your permission to use it for a painting, I am an artist." Fi took the camera from him and looked at the image, it was a side profile of her, with her head resting back in the chair and eyes closed and yes she did look very peaceful. She was in focus in the shot, with the lake and landscape opposite giving added tranquility to the image. "It's a lovely image Bill and I have no issue with you using it for your art but may I request a copy of the image for myself. This is a very poignant day for me too and that would be a lovely reminder." "Absolutely Fi, is it Fiona?" he asked. "No, it's a common assumption," she replied, "my name is Fiora but I prefer Fi," she said, before Bill added, "a Latin variant of Flora! It's beautiful," he continued. Fi smiled at him and said, "Yes, I love the fact it is different." Just then his afternoon tea arrived and Fi asked the waiter to place it down on her table, he poured Bill a glass of Champagne and Fi held her glass up and said, "To past and present ghosts!" and chinked Bills glass. "What is your wife's name Bill?" asked Fi and Bill gulped before replying, "Flora." as a single tear rolled down his cheek and he took a deep breath and added "and I miss her every minute of every day." Fi held her glass up again and said to Bill, "Let's propose a toast," and he picked up his glass and raised it too, as Fi said, "Happy Birthday Flora!" and they chinked glasses in celebration of his wife. They enjoyed their afternoon tea immensely but they enjoyed each other's company far more, as the time drifted away. Fi told Bill that she had been coming to Bowness since she was 10 years old, for twice yearly holidays as a child and for weekend and short breaks away from Manchester, for most of her adult life. She spoke about her childhood, her family and her work life, as well as her retirement from the Criminal Justice Service and of her newly rekindled fondness for writing and she told him briefly of her marriage and the farewell to old ghosts. Bill spoke of his life too, being born and raised in Bowness and of his life as a young man when he had met his Portuguese wife Flora, whilst he had been in Lisbon, serving with the Royal Navy. He spoke of enjoying his career and rising to become a Commander and how having retired, he had then become an artist, working predominantly from his studio in the grounds of his home, here in Bowness. He had one son who was a very successful businessman with businesses both here in the UK and in Europe he said and he had 3 lovely grandchildren, one aged 19 and 21 year old twins and he proudly showed Fi a recent photograph of them at the twins twenty first birthday party in Portugal. They discussed Bill's love of art at length and how fortunate he was to have such breathtaking inspiration right here on his doorstep, with this world famous setting. He agreed with Fi's comments regarding the areas beauty and tranquility and said he never took it for granted, as he felt blessed to have been here all his life. Fi told him about her favourite artist Jack Vettriano and how her friend David had started to paint a copy of 'Dance Me To The End Of Love,' for a wedding gift he was to present to herself and Robert. She spoke of her unfinished painting due to her friend's death and how touched she was every time she viewed the poignant piece of art that hung on her bedroom wall. They whiled away the hours and eventually they had finished their contact by wishing each other well and Fi had given Bill her email address to send over the image he had taken of her. What an absolute treasure of an afternoon Fi thought. Another Bowness memory for her 'lovely memories' keepsake box that she kept locked in her head. Fi was in a trance state as she exited the hotel, bumping into a gentleman in the foyer. "I am sorry," she said, "I was day dreaming," and as she walked out into the cold night air and on up the hill towards her apartment, she felt the most content she had in a very long time with the noted absence of hyper or hypo emotions to deal with. This WAS her Bowness and she slept soundly and peacefully at Flat 7 that night. Fi spent the next couple of days walking in the hills, reading, listening to music, enjoying Jacuzzi baths, lazy mornings and preparing herself nourishing food from a mixture of her favourite, vegetarian, vegan and Paleo diet books. She fully embraced the complete solitude of having 'thought' conversations, only with herself. Asking herself questions and answering them, working out a plan for her future wellbeing, making sure she had fully understood the lessons too be learnt from Robert and Bran and feeling grateful that things hadn't been worse with the dating scam scenario.

Whilst Fi was in the Lake District she intended to tie up the loose ends on the dating fiasco and logged into the website, with the intention of reporting the scam and closing her account. As she logged in, she noticed Bran's avatar in her messages inbox and clicked on it to open their initial communications to each other. It all seemed so surreal and so long ago but aspects of it still jarred her, reminding her of what she would never have. She went through the process online of reporting the scam to the dating site and before closing her account she reread his 'for sale' criteria and was sad for herself and sad for THAT guy, whoever he was. She decided to look at online scams to see if there was any 'help' websites, to report the issue, warn other women and hopefully prevent anyone else being hurt, both emotionally and financially. She hated anyone being hurt in life but she particularly hated to see women being hurt. When she typed romance scams into the Google search engine, she was met with a raft of choices, including actual scam websites and research papers that had been written about it. There were links to high profile crime agencies in the UK and in the USA, who, dependent upon the level of the scam and criminality involved, would contact people for further evidence. Fi had kept all the emails, telephone numbers and videos relating to Bran and was more than happy to share it with any agency who wanted it, if it helped other women. Her research proved a fascinating project for her and as she trawled through the reams of information, she discovered that it was not just women within heterosexual relationships. It was men in heterosexual relationships too, as well as gay, lesbian and transgender victims. The worldwide scale of it was really shocking to her and the different kinds of internet scams were almost never ending, it was far more than just romance scams and it had vast organised crime and potential terrorist funding links attached to it too. It really was scary and as much as she felt a victim, she was extremely grateful, that in retrospect she had been very lucky, judging by some of the cases she was reading about. One of the websites had an images gallery of photographs used in scamming, as well as providing images of some of the real scammers, who had been caught. There were hundreds and hundreds of images to filter through but she decided she didn't want to know what the scammers looked like, she didn't need to know that but whilst researching she did come across a link to a site which revealed an interesting and very useful tool. When you upload images into this site it then searches the 'world wide web' and compiles a list of where those images are being used. What she found using images of Bran was staggering: Fake antique websites in many parts of the USA including San Francisco, New York and

Miami, all displaying fake property addresses, email addresses, phone numbers and home page information.

Bran allegedly had antique businesses all over America and the UK and further research took her to different dating sites and links to different profiles, where his images were being used under many different names. His picture was literally being used all over the world in a fraudulent way. Fi was angry that such a seemingly decent man was being treated in such a way but the shocking realisation for her, was if they could use his images, to create fake profiles, then they could just as easily use hers. She became aware that all the words Bran had exchanged with her, were merely cut and pasted excerpts from other people's dating profiles, that the scammers were using and that in reality it was just a recycling process, with the odd attention to detail, re phone calls and personal information thrown in for good measure. Her beautiful words to Bran were now likely to be enticing some other man or woman to enter into an online relationship with a scammer and so the scamming wheel will keep on turning. Horrific and on such a vast scale too. No wonder organised crime agencies in the UK and afar were involved in trying to get to the root of it all. There were images of raids on Internet cafes in Nigeria with men and women being arrested and taken away in handcuffs. There were literally call centre type organisations with vast numbers of people, sat in front of laptops with several telephones on their desks. She was so angry with them but at the same time she was confident in Karma working, as it does, returning the favour on people who chose to live their lives in this way. She was a firm believer in the simplicity of 'you reap what you sow.' She also saw that there was advice regarding NOT confronting the scammers. She thought to herself, 'Whoops, too late' but in reality she was glad she had had the courage to confront her scammer(s).

She read that they often attempted to blackmail people who confronted or reported them to the various agencies and used compromising written evidence, images and videos in that blackmailing process. Fi was glad she hadn't shared anything of that nature, not that she had any to share, no way would she photograph or video herself in potentially compromising situations. That was purely for the bedroom, to be stored in her 'relationship' memory only, not in a hard drive, cloud or server memory.

After a busy day of researching all the information, reporting it to three different dating sites and agencies and having searched several websites that were displaying Bran's images, she noticed a blog link and clicked on it and as the images popped up, she gasped at what she saw in front of her. There he was, the real guy, she had found 'The Real Deal.' The first thing she did was Google his real name and she quickly found links to Facebook, Linkedin, Google+, Youtube, Instagram, Flickr, Twitter. Virtually every social media site she was aware of. UNBELIEVABLE. His name was Pedro Cruz and judging from the thousands of images of him on the various sites that Fi scrolled, he was a very high profile media man in Portugal (how ironic, she thought, after meeting Bill a few days previously with his Portugal connections). His video channel had dozens of uploaded media items of a sporting nature, he was also all over red carpet events, photographed with sports people of varying disciplines and often with very beautiful women too, which confirmed Julie's assessment that he would never need to be on a dating site! He was pictured in modeling shots where he himself was wearing sports clothing, he was pictured in sports departments in stores, he was involved in a high end designer brand luggage launches alongside other sports men, he was at launches for clothes, fragrances and all manner of attire, be it footwear, sunglasses or watches again with other sports people. He was involved in alcohol launches, music launches, movie launches, charity functions, hotel, bar and nightclub openings and again always with sports people. He was everywhere it seemed, smiling as always and 'absolutely gorgeous' Fi thought, as always! Really, drop dead, movie star gorgeous. There was one image that she saw as she was discussing it all on the phone with Julie, who was also viewing the same site from her home and Fi said, "I thought Mr. Antique was in the higher leagues, but Jesus, Jules, he's literally like a movie star in that picture," and he was. He was in the centre of the image, wearing a very expensive suit, surrounded by dozens of people. It was a roof top location on a glorious summers evening, the bar was obviously a luxurious establishment, there was a raised DJ booth in the left corner of the rooftop, huge giant plant pots containing ferns and palms, a stunning tiled wall depicting an ocean scene, sumptuous outdoor furnishings, a central circular bar with people sat on stools and waiters pouring cocktails and mood lighting from bar fittings, plant pots and candles that added to the atmosphere. Best of all was the view out towards the sea which was truly stunning on a summers evening, just as dusk was descending. Pedro commanded the audience that surrounded him, as he took centre stage in the shot. The bar was identified as The Angels bar on the rooftop of The Paradise Hotel in Portugal.

She had found 'Mr. Antique,' only he wasn't Mr. Antique, he was Mr. Sports Media. She was intrigued by him and spent hours looking at his life in pictures and saw how it contrasted so differently from the life she thought he led. His world was sports promotion, PR and communicating, which he did through various media formats and social networking platforms and seemingly very well indeed. She was also very aware whilst researching, that he was never ever going to be hers. He was a pure fabrication of others doing and she felt sad that this man was being 'exploited' to exploit others. Evil people were using his inner and outer beauty to hurt others, which was the complete antithesis of how he behaved on the social media pages he subscribed to. Fi requested him as a friend on Facebook and sent him a message through messenger and she also posted a handwritten letter:

9 Cottage Lane

Manchester

United Kingdom

01.01.2014

Dear Pedro,

I really don't know how to begin this letter to you.

I don't know whether I should be saying, "Hey Baby", as a welcoming gesture to you, as I have been exchanging emails with you for several days from 9th November 2013 until 1st December 2013. On the 1st December 2013 I found out that I had been exchanging wonderful emails and forming a relationship online with "your images" and NOT you. I have been the victim of an Internet dating scam where your images are being used to lure women, with the eventual aim of extracting money from those who are vulnerable.

Fortunately, I am savvy and did not part with any money but believe me I was floored by having been duped to such a great extent romantically. It really is possible to begin the process of falling in love with such a beautiful romantic man, when you haven't even met him! Crazy I know, but true. I really was so excited to hear the ping of an email alert or the telephone ringing in anticipation that it might be you. Hearing the music on the radio or my playlist that we had selected for each other made my heart skip and I even have a video sent to me, of you singing to me whilst on your business trip to America! Simply looking at your stunningly handsome face in any images you sent to me drove me crazy. As it all unfolded, I shared all this experience with my girlfriends and it really was like the Sex And The City series, in my world for a while, with all the fun and laughter we girls had. I have been sent images of you as a child, with your family members as a child, with other people, with you stood outside buildings, in Times Square, etcetera, etcetera, and I have since discovered that your images are all over fake antique dealer websites located all over America and here in the UK too, via the dating websites where the scammers are portraying you as a 'specialist antique dealer'. I, together with my friends affectionately referred to you, as 'Mr. Antique!'

We exchanged our childhood, relationship and professional histories, we sent each other songs and lyrics, we exchanged intimate details of our likes and dislikes and we even chatted on the telephone whilst you were away on business. Two days before I was due to meet you I found out it was a scam, when you asked me in an email to part with a substantial amount of my money. You were to take a week away from your

business and devote it entirely to me, and amongst other aspects of my excitement, I giggled with my friends and with you too, (or so I thought) as I bought beautiful lingerie in readiness for our first intimate meeting, whenever we chose that would be! It was all very, very believable but thank goodness I was alert.

I decided to spend today as a research day to try to locate the "real person" in the images. I have persevered in my research and eventually found you through Blogspot, Youtube and Facebook after using many web searches and finally finding out you are actually Pedro Cruz and NOT Branimir Rodrigues as indicated in our online contact. You even have a Google plus account in the name of Branimir Rodrigues with your image on it. It was placing your images in a specific site that led me to many more sites where your images are used in a fraudulent way and then eventually to your blog and the real you. My heart really did skip a beat at finding you for real, not from a romantic perspective, obviously I am emotionally aware enough to know and accept that I have been duped but just a feeling of wow. What a coup. It is like trying to find a needle in haystack and I found the needle, when I discovered who you really are.

You may already know all of this information of course but I am very happy to share all of 'our' correspondence with you in order for you to see exactly how your images and a fake persona of you, are being used to romance and lure women and men into parting with their money. I suspect they are probably Nigerian romance-scamming websites using your images as that is certainly where all the evidence is leading.

I wanted to contact you simply to inform you what is being done worldwide, with your images, that has allowed such an intrusion of my life, your life and the lives of your family and significant others. I am glad I have found you to let you know this information. I thank you for your time in reading my letter and I have to say this feels so surreal, I am writing to YOU and not an image anymore. One thing for sure, I will pay a visit to The Angels Bar one day and I hope to bump into you. How people can become so innocently snared is mind blowing. The depths of deceit are frightening and to know nothing about it was truly hurtful, when I eventually realised what had happened to me.

I love all your motivational messages on Facebook and I have a habit of posting similar ones myself too but my favourite is this one from you:

"If you are always trying to be normal, you will never know how amazing you can be." Words of wisdom from the great Maya Angelou. My motto for as long as I can remember has been, "I don't do normal!"

I wish you a happy 2014. You seem like a beautiful man, inside and out! It is sad that you too are a victim of these crimes.

My very best wishes to you. Fiora Burton.

She received neither paper or electronic replies to her attempts to contact him but she was now completely satisfied that she had drawn a line under her relationship with Mr. Antique, allowing her to move on in her life. One thing she was certain of, she didn't want a man at the moment and if she ever found that she did, she certainly wouldn't be shopping for one on a dating site. Fi follows Pedro through his various social media platforms, on his blog and in a column he writes for a sports magazine (yes, he writes for a living too) and he is an interesting and seemingly lovely guy. He appears to be motivated by sport, sport and more sport, sports science, health, good food, fashion, music, human rights but particular Lesbian, Gay and Transgender issues.

He has an affinity to beautiful people be they famous or not and he often posts motivational quotes to brighten peoples days! Now that ironically is not unlike Fi's Facebook timeline!

Of course she will be disturbed as her 'memory' ghosts appear but she will no longer be haunted by them.

CHAPTER 14

I am a writer

The next morning Fi woke up wonderfully refreshed. She had no idea what the time was, as her room had blackout curtains and there were no traffic noises outside for her to gauge the possible hour of the day. She opened her phone to see that the time read 10:45! What a treat, she had slept for over twelve hours for the first time in a long time! She got up, showered and put on her walking gear before drinking her tea. She then grabbed a yoghurt drink from the fridge, as she headed out of the door. At the end of Beresford Road she crossed over the main road and turned right down a narrow lane past the cottages and round towards the rugby pitch. She continued for a while before turning left and following the lane out to the A592 and turning left again, she walked past Fallbarrow Holiday Park where she dreamed of owning a lakeside lodge one day. Fi continued into the village meandering her way through the back streets, past the rear of the church, the Chinese restaurant, The Old England Hotel and around past the water's edge and bearing left to continue on the A592, eventually turning right onto the smaller road which lead her to the small jetty area at the Hawkshead Ferry terminal. She had a coffee whilst watching a couple of children manoeuvre a dinghy to the rear of their grandparents' boat and as she was finishing her drink, she noticed the luxurious yacht sailing by that she had spotted a few days before. It looked a grand site as it carved its path through the surface of the water and again Fi harked on the fantasy of how the other half lived. How come some people go through life with life long partners and yet others (like herself) had a cyclical pattern of relationships with men? It was a mystery how life dealt you cards that decided whether you are successful or not, happy or not, rich or not, owned a yacht, or not. Fi affirmed to herself as she sat there that she wanted only to be rich in happiness and love and she was going to concentrate on getting both from her self until she was confident that she could take a risk again with a man. If that meant the cold turkey effects of withdrawal from loneliness, now that she had an empty nest at home, then so be it. She would put arrangements in place to relieve the loneliness, as part of her 'looking after herself' plan. She had been lonely within her marriage to Robert and on reflection very unhappy too, even before his 'dick-dipping' shenanigans. Being lonely in isolation as opposed to loneliness within a marriage was preferable, she thought. Fi walked back around the lakeside, back onto the public path, around past The Ship Inn and along the water's edge before starting her ascent up the hill and stopping off at the Albert pub for lunch. On her way back up to Flat 7 she bought enough food supplies for her last couple of days stay.

Later that evening she made herself some tea and ate the carrot cake treat that she had selected from the deli, whilst checking her emails. She noticed that she had one from Bill:

Dear Ms. Burton,

Please see attached your photograph as promised. It was a delight to have your company and I would like to thank you very much for choosing to celebrate Flora's birthday with me.

My very best wishes to you.

Kind Regards. Bill.

Fi looked at the enclosed image and felt its' significance as she looked at it in detail. It really had been a cathartic few days and she clicked on reply:

Dear Bill,

Thank you very much for the photograph. You captured a very poignant moment very well indeed. It was my pleasure to have your stimulating and polite company and I am sure Flora would have been delighted to know you were celebrating her in such a way, in her favourite place.

My very best wishes to you too. Fi. X

She forwarded the photograph to her local photographic printers. She would have a copy of that image in a frame in her new creative den.

Fi spent her last two days in the Lake District planning her 2014. She was definitely going to write again. She had missed it so much. She ordered a voice-activated typing programme for her computer and booked her two old laptops into a computer repair shop, to retrieve her hard drives and the dozens of previous written works she had completed.

She then had an idea and placed a new status on her Facebook timeline:

I am intending to have some of my writing published for the first time and I am suggesting the following

experiment. I am looking for a first time editor, a first time artist and graphic designer for illustrations for my book cover as well as a first time publisher too. Hopefully this work will then be a complete team of 'firsts'. I welcome suggestions, so please share with your Facebook friends. A very interesting experiment, let's see if we can make it work. Trying to keep it local. Fi.

Fi was very excited that the builders and decorating team would have finished the new creative den, by the time she got back to Manchester and she also intended to press ahead and re-decorate other rooms in her house in 2014. There were aspects of her home she hated and as is so often the case, once you have revamped a room or an area of your home, it tends to highlight the areas still requiring work. She WOULD finish restyling her home by the end of 2014 she promised herself and she made a timetable of priorities and set about finding inspiration to create her mood boards. She listened to calming music, she watched TV and movies and as a final homage to her 'selfie' week, she took herself off to The Old England again for a spa afternoon, treating herself to additional treatments, after which, she sat and had a pot of tea in her favourite window seat and embraced the beautiful view one more time, for a while anyway.

After tidying Flat 7, she said, "Goodbye, my favourite place," as she walked out of the door and locked it behind her, she took her belongings down to her car and set off for the drive back to Manchester, collecting the dogs en-route. She didn't want to risk collecting the cat as well, for fear of a disturbance in her car between the animals. They did not like each other! She dropped the dogs off and collected Julie for the ride out to get the cat and they decided to call at Slattery's on the way home for coffee and a chat. Fi told Julie about her week and Julie commented that Fi looked really well. Fi felt well. It had been a hell of a few weeks but she really did feel like she had buried her past with Robert. She told Julie she would no longer harbour any grudges towards him, but she felt that some people are just too evil to forgive and she didn't subscribe to any religious intentions anyway and so she was okay with her decision not to forgive him. He was 'a nothing' and she was okay to dismiss any thoughts of him that entered her mind, by replacing them with positive thoughts of the 'gift' of him no longer being in it! Julie agreed with Fi. "I'm okay that I choose that only special people get a permanent parking place in my life from now on!" Fi said to Julie, as she smiled across at one of the few people who had a lifelong parking permit. What would she have done without this wonderful woman this past few weeks she wondered? As she decided to toast her, "to my Bestie," she said to Julie, holding up her cup of tea, "shut up you tart, you'll have me crying," replied Julie and they both laughed. Fi held her arms up in an exasperated fashion! She bloody loved that woman and she was glad to be back and she just knew that the future was going to be so good.

Fi continued to go from strength to strength emotionally and physically by just listening to her body and her mind each day. If she needed a "do nothing" day, that is exactly what she did, she made sure she couldn't be disturbed. When she chose to, she also filled her days with the gym, eating well, walking her dogs, meeting her friends and of course her music which had comforted, soothed and inspired her in equal measures, without doubt. These were all the new loves of her life and along with her 'repetitive laughter syndrome' with the girls, had all proven to be the best possible medicine. She was well and truly taking the right route on her journey to self-healing.

Fi successfully retrieved all her previous writing which included past journals, exercises from her creative writing course, correspondence to friends, family and past loves, as well as old business correspondence too. She found a copy of an old will and letters to her children in the event of her death, as well as her own eulogy, as she didn't want anyone else to have the hassle of such an upset, when she had gone. She also found the instructions re: 'What to do with her body,' post-death, as she had already made the arrangements herself, she was going to science! With her history of autoimmune disease, surely there would be something useful to share with others, in the field of medical science? She laughed aloud at the range of items she found, that she had forgotten about and her determination to make things easier for her loved ones, when she was no longer here! But the most important thing she found that caused her to pump her fist in the air and say, 'YES!' out loud, was her file labeled 'Children's writing.' Contained within it, were two series of books for children that were finished and as she skim read through them all, she felt proud of her past work. It was still relevant in the world of children's literature. There were rhyming books for toddlers, a counting book, an alphabet book, a 'finding' book and even a book of short stories based upon true events from of her own children's antics as toddlers. She loved reading that work again and now felt determined to let those lovely children's stories be cosseted by chubby hands, as babies and toddlers sat on their parents and grandparents knees enjoying them. She also imagined older children sharing her series on environmental issues, in the classroom with their friends and teachers, as they integrated her work into their own work, in the classroom setting.

Julie called after work one day to have a catch up coffee and Fi was excited to tell her that she had had many replies to her 'First' request, that she had posted on Facebook. She had received messages from friends of friends and was now in the process of replying to them all, asking them to tell her more about themselves and their history, to help with her search for the right people. It was so exciting to have so many enquiries and to have choices. This would give her a new focus and all added to her renewed sense of self and of finding her new purpose in life. She was a writer. "I am a writer," she told Julie as they chatted away and Fi felt fully justified in giving herself that title.

This was her new career.

Fi spent the next couple of weeks emailing Facebook contacts and narrowing down her search, arranging face to face and Skype meetings before eventually choosing her 'first' team, to allow her to achieve her goal of having her work published. She hired a team who were all agreeable to having their fees paid based solely upon the success of their collective contribution, as, after all it was a test of all their skills being used for the first time. In other words, if the published works were a success then they would all reap the benefits of that. It was a really exciting experiment and everybody was so enthusiastic to get going. She hired Annie Forrest as her editor, who had recently graduated in English from Oxford University and whilst waiting for a start date for her new job editing for a government department, had decided to take on some freelance work. She hired John Ashley to design her book covers, he had a degree in graphic design and had helped design websites, produced art for sale on his own website and was proud of the fact that the odd body or two was wandering the world decorated in his art, as a result of his unique tattoo designs. Finally she hired Carlos Carter to publish her work, he was an entrepreneur who had many businesses within the media and hospitality arenas throughout Europe but had just recently invested in a brand new publishing house in Manchester and Fi would be their first published children's author and in fact, he had been so intrigued by the concept she had posted on Facebook, that he wanted to call his new business 'First Publications'. He was also enamoured with her style of writing and the vision she had for her children's books.

She had done it. A team of 'firsts' and all local too which was hugely important. More local jobs for local people would hopefully be created from this exciting experiment too. Over the coming weeks she worked closely with all her team in meetings, in places of mutual agreement within the city centre, except for Carlos who would be away for a few months in Portugal! (How strange, she thought, when he had told her, three references to Portugal in a short space of time. Yet another coincidence, her life seemed to be full of them at the moment.) Carlos explained that he had a large pending project out in Portugal that he simply had to be there for, to oversee on a daily basis, as well as a personal issue keeping him there too but he reassured Fi that he was available for Skype meetings and telephone calls at mutually convenient times. He also told her in one of their Skype sessions, that he liked 'Carl' as opposed to Carlos and quite frankly, 'Who wouldn't like him?' she thought. The teamwork that developed amongst them all was so inspiring to Fi and she was soon engrossed in new and exciting ideas for further books for children as well as having a great idea for an adult novel too. This would be a huge undertaking for Fi, as she had never written any adult fiction before. She had written adult 'fact' for years in her court-report writing role in the Criminal Justice Service but never fiction and she welcomed the challenge.

Annie Forrest was clearly fascinated by words and language and enjoyed enabling Fi to make more sense of her text, to ensure it flowed more freely onto the pages. Not only was she proficient in spelling, grammar and composition but she was always willing to challenge Fi and use her judgement in suggesting what might be missing in the stories that Fi presented to her and she clearly worked well with the other members of the 'first' team too. This was a completely level playing field, with all of them needing to work closely together and Fi was admirable of Annie's capacity to think from both a writer's and reader's perspective and her 'devil in the detail' focus to her work. Yes, Fi was very impressed with this young woman's talents who without doubt, had a bright and creative future ahead of her. Over the course of them working together Fi had grown fond of Annie and they had enjoyed a few social events together too, even joining their local branch of the WI (Women's Institute). No more Damson jam and frumpy frocks here, definitely not! It was inspirational talks, outings to the theatre and erotic art exhibitions these days and Fi was surprised that she was the oldest member of her branch at the ripe old age of 54! Annie no longer had her mother in her life and Fi no longer had her daughter close by and they found that they filled a little void in each other's lives, when they met socially. Despite an age difference of over 30 years, they got on fabulously and Fi hoped that it would be a lifelong working partnership and friendship too.

John Ashley currently worked for a company that designed and printed branding for a variety of items from golf balls to glass balls and anything in between but he had never before worked on books and was enthusiastic about the challenge of the designing commission from Fi. Fi was attracted to John's work because his illustrations had drawn her into them, which is how she felt children's illustrations should be, having the capacity to engross a child as equally, if not more than, the words on the page. Upon graduating with a first class BA (honours) degree in Graphic Design from a well-known London College, John modestly told Fi he had built himself a reasonable portfolio, which enabled him to get an internship at one of the leading design agencies in London for 6 months. However modestly John wished to view his portfolio, in her opinion it was a very strong and impressive collection of work showing a wide range of skills in various mediums of art but in particular his chosen specialisms of illustrating for advertising, fine art and photography. He was proficient in design software and his enthusiasm was abundant in their two way and team meetings. He really was very skilled and in a matter of days was able to present the team with an initial collection of six cover options for the first series of books to be published and during a productive team meeting via Skype, (in order to facilitate Carl's participation and contribution) a decision was made for John to expand his ideas on four of those options and a further meeting was scheduled for a months time. Fi also found John to be a consummate team player and given that this was a 'first' team effort, she was delighted with how it was all progressing.

Fi's first impressions of Carl Carter were that his career credentials were impressive enough to prove to her, his more than sufficient wealth of business experience, which though not specific to books and publishing, was an indicator of his knowledge of marketing and market trends and he had certainly done his homework regarding publishing. He clearly displayed a substantial level of knowledge of foreign and subsidiary rights too, which were not even on Fi's radar and he impressed her with his contributions to their meetings regarding due dates, schedules for publication, deadlines and seasonal trends, as well as having researched printing options when they were ready for the production stage. To be frank he bamboozled her with timescales for re editing, page proofing, colour proofing, final design dates, print and binding approximations etcetera and she was glad she had chosen him for the 'first' team. She had absolutely no idea there were so many processes involved, after her initial part as the writer. Carl was a successful businessman, she thought. Carl was a very impressive team player, she thought. Carl was also very hot, she thought!

Fi filled her days being equally proactive in the team process by preparing for her launch date, scheduled for some months later. She wanted to make herself accessible to children in a book friendly space and so ideally it had to be a large library or a large bookstore. She wanted to be sat down at child's eye level and surrounded by children, as she read the first book in the series to them, she wanted John Ashley to be present and for him to be working on one of the illustrations, to enable children to see how the characters came off the written page and into the pictures. She also wanted Annie Forrest to be present and for her to be working on text and to show the children how words, placed within a sentence in a different way could change how a story could become more meaningful and make much more sense. She was hoping that Carl Carter would be there too but in reality why would he be there? He was an entrepreneur, none of that was his role but she would like him there anyway, as he was one of the 'first' team but she also knew that, that was highly unlikely! He had bigger fish to fry in his empire than her little book launch!

Fi also wanted to engage the children in their own book stories, when they read, why they read, who they read with, what do they like about reading. She was hoping to share her lifelong love of books and writing with the children and inspire them to write too and what better place to do that than the Central Library in Manchester. Wow. What a spectacular and exciting library for children to visit. She had been brought here many times as a child to both author and theatre events and had attended as an adult for both studying and social events. She was in awe of this magnificent home to words and was delighted that they wanted to be involved in her book launch event by hosting it. The local media had even printed a story about her 'first' project a week previously.

Local economy and small business principles were so important to Fi and so she also managed to secure an event at the Chorlton Bookshop two months later for her collection of toddler's books. It was to be an informal coffee afternoon. She didn't need the same approach she wanted with the older children of course. She just wanted to let the little ones enjoy the pictures, words and numbers. Nothing more. Pick up, put down and pick up again toddlers books. Fi embraced social media to begin to market her new ventures and using Facebook, Twitter, Tumblr, Instagram and Google+ to access her growing fan base. She also started a child friendly blog through

Blogger, providing a weekly diary of updates of the ongoing process for fans and bought a domain name in readiness for her website design process to begin. Children were undoubtedly her soon to be toughest critics and she felt the pressure of being a new arrival, in such a competitive market, especially considering her approach to the publishing process. Fi also contacted a local toy manufacturer and distributor to discuss designs for soft toy prototypes, production dates and subsidiary rights and health and safety issues of the toy production. She then passed the issue over to her lawyer, who was recommended to her by Carl.

Fi interwove all this additional work into her usual daily routine of caring for her home, her pets and herself, as well as maintaining her regular contact with her circle of girlfriends. They chatted, laughed and cried together, as they always did and Fi had even motivated some of them to diet, given her dramatic weight loss, "but I don't recommend the diet I've been on to anybody!" said Fi one day as she was chatting to Julie and Lisa over coffee and cupcakes, (vegan of course) before adding, "far too much pain and tears!" Lisa replied, "Well, I can recommend a better one! Yesterday was day one, of my intense diet and exercise regime." Julie asked, "What does that entail because I'm sick of eating soup!" Lisa continued, "I had boiled egg without toast and a Kiwi for breakfast" and Julie quipped, "man or fruit?" as they all laughed and Lisa added, "then, mid morning I had boiled water with lemon and then for lunch, homemade broccoli soup with no bread, followed by a mid afternoon snack of 2 cream eggs, large milky coffee, 2 sugars and 4 biscuits for dunking!" and they all burst out laughing again. "Wait! This is the best bit, my exercise routine was a walk to the post office, to buy the cream eggs!" and by now they were all giggling again, before Lisa finished, "I think it's going well, don't you girls?" and Fi and Julie laughed again. "Well, I might as well be on the drink your own piss diet, because that super green soup I made last night tasted like piss!" said Julie, which prompted Fi and Lisa to simultaneously shout, "Fourteen stone in a day! Fourteen stone in one day!" and they all howled with laughter. Fi made fresh coffees and they chatted and laughed about anything, everything and nothing in particular before Julie excused herself to go to the loo, as Fi passed her a plastic jug and they all burst out laughing again!

Her visitors excused themselves as a text came through from Carl for a Skype call, and the girls teased her, "Ooh! Carl's calling!" As they all started laughing. "Do one, the pair of you, he is married and married men who have affairs, have what Julie?" asked Fi, "Dirty dicks!" replied Julie and they set off laughing again as she said, "It's a good job I drunk that piss otherwise I would be pissing my pants now!" and they all collapsed again. "TALKING OF PISS, PISS OFF," said Fi, in a forceful voice before adding, "how am I supposed to have a business call now with all these giggles in my head?" "Just look at him and imagine him naked," said Julie, to which Fi replied cheekily, "I bloody wish!" Julie raised her eyebrows and scoffed at her friend, "Oh hello, she's getting better!" and as she shut the front door behind her, Fi could hear Julie and Lisa continuing to laugh as they walked up her drive. Fi sent a reply to Carl stating that she would be available in 30 minutes if that was convenient? "No problem," he replied. Fi took the dogs out for a quick twenty minute run and when she got home she swilled her face with cold water to shock the giggles out of her system as she had found herself still chuckling to herself whilst on the park with the dogs, as she had relived her conversations with the girls in her head.

Fi checked herself in the mirror, put on some lip gloss, scrunched her hair and dialled Carl's number from her Skype contacts list:

Fi: "Hi Carl, how are you?"

Carl: "Very good thank you Fi, how are you?"

Fi: "Good thank you, how's your day been?"

Carl: "Very busy day with the project I have out here but it is all getting near to the final stages now and we are ahead of schedule too, which is great!"

Fi: "Excellent, well what can I do for you Carl, then you can get on with your day?"

Carl: "Well, I was wondering if you could make lunch on Thursday this week, as I am in the UK for 5 days from Wednesday evening?"

Fi: "Just let me get my diary. Right. Erm. Yes, sure, that suits. It will be good to meet face to face finally and I can show you the contracts re merchandising and the final artwork for the covers should be ready for Thursday too. I don't think the book illustrations will be complete but we are on schedule with those I believe."

Carl: "Great, shall we say 1pm at the Great John Street Hotel?"

Fi: "That sounds great, good choice, see you then."

Carl: "I always stay there when I am in Manchester, it's a great hotel group."

Fi: "I know, I have stayed in two of them, they are fabulously luxurious!"

Carl: "Good, well okay Fi, until Thursday?"

Fi: "Yes, great, see you Thursday, bye Carl."

She ended the call.

Fi hated seeing herself on screen and would prefer to call without camera contact but she felt rude doing that to her team members. She couldn't even Facetime with Louise as she hated her on screen image so much!

Julie text half an hour later:

Julie: Well?

Fi: Well nothing Jules, business lunch for the team, Thursday! HE IS MARRIED! END OF CONVERSATION!

Julie: Okay. Just checking!!

Fi went to bed early to make notes, it was all very confusing to her, she was not a businesswoman and she was having to get her head around issues she had never come across in her working life before. She didn't want to look a fool with the rest of the team on Thursday, as they were all so competent in their roles and although she was absolutely confident in her writing, she was a little lost with all the other stuff, if she was honest. She now appreciated why other people went through a literary agent. Let someone else have the pressure, she thought.

She was genuinely surprised just how large a team is involved in the process of getting a book onto a shelf, be it in a library or in a bookshop or indeed online as an e published item, which was also outside of her domain and causing her concern.

Thursday arrived and she started her routine as she normally did by completing her chores, seeing to her animals and making breakfast before spending a couple of hours making sure she had up to date paperwork for her meeting. She took a shower and dressed in her new black skinny jeans, a bright yellow silk T-shirt with a large statement necklace in silver and black and her black suede boots. She wore her hair as she always did, wild and clipped in place on top of her head with a black jewelled hair clip. She sprayed one of her daytime scents and finished her ensemble with her black suede biker jacket. She grabbed her handbag and document case and locked her front door. She walked down the lane to the tram station and bought a return ticket to St Peters Square, just as the tram arrived at the platform and she managed to jump on it as the doors were closing, before arriving at her destination 45 minutes later due to delays, but she was still 15 minutes early! She walked down to the hotel and entered The Oyster Bar. Fi was welcomed by a member of the staff, "Hi, what can I get you a drink madam?" Fi replied, "Well I believe there is a table for 4 and I assume it is in the name of Carter," "ah yes madam, Mr. Carter is already here" and he led her upstairs to The Mezzanine, where Carl was sat alone at a table for two. "Oh," said Fi, "are the others not coming to the meeting then?" and she held out her hand and said, "Hello Carl, pleased to meet you at last," and she couldn't help wondering if she had met him before. Carl shook her hand and replied, "No, they were not available today Fi and this is my only time in Manchester, so I thought I would grab the chance to meet with you finally, I will meet the others at your launch if that is okay?" "Sure," replied Fi, secretly pleased he would be there. "Remote working and social media makes anything possible in business these days, does it not?" she added. "You have excellent taste, this is a beautiful hotel," she said. "I find this hotel group never fails to deliver, whatever the occasion," he added as the waiter brought their champagne and poured them both a glass. Carl held his glass up to propose a toast and said, "To Fi Burton's success as a writer!" and she clinked his glass with hers and replied, "to First Publications success too and to the 'first team' collaboration," she said, wanting to include absent members. They enjoyed a wonderful lunch, as she knew she would, she loved this group of hotels herself and she was spoilt for choice with them being right on her doorstep too. They chatted about their respective careers, children and life experiences, including their children and relationships, although Fi was very guarded in what she shared. Not that she wanted to hide anything but she had buried her ghosts and she was not going to invite them to anymore parties by speaking about them. If they chose to haunt her thoughts then so be it, she would deal with that as and when but she certainly wasn't going to openly talk about them, except in the briefest of ways, to kick them back into the past, where they belonged. Carl asked Fi if she would date again and she replied, "I cannot answer that Carl, I don't know the answer, but I do know for sure that there is a 'Do Not Disturb' sign on my heart and I have no idea when it will be removed," she replied. He looked at her intently for a moment before telling her about himself, his education at university in Portugal, how he met his Portuguese wife, about his children and their successes in university in Scotland and Lancashire, his father and the fact he too, no longer had his mother. He spoke of his love of sport, sports cars and Portugal and finally his love of business, investing and entrepreneurial challenges. He was a very interesting man and she was shocked how quickly the time passed and the fact they scooted over business issues and ended the lunch 'meeting' several hours later! He insisted on paying the bill that Fi had asked the waiter for and he walked her over to the station to catch her tram. As they waited on the platform, she gazed in awe at the sheer scale of the Central Library right in front of her and still could not quite believe that she would be launching her first children's book here in a matter of months. "You pulled off a major coup Fi, getting permission for a launch in there, a historical building of such high regard in the literary world," "I know and it isn't the first time," she stated "Really? I'm intrigued," he said questioningly. "Or does the tale involve a ghost?" he asked. "Yes it does but a friendly one!" she said and they laughed as she told him that she had married her children's father in the chapel in a nearby Tudor mansion and that they had been the first people in 25 years to be granted permission! "I'm impressed," he said and how did you manage that?" "I just asked and they said yes! After 25 years of saying no apparently and I have absolutely no idea why!" The tram arrived and they said good-bye and again, Fi thanked him again for lunch. "Next time it's my treat," she said. "Deal!" he replied and waved to her as the tram door closed, separating them. As Fi sat and daydreamed for her journey home she got to thinking about the many implications of the use of words. The thing that she now did for a living and the impact words could have upon peoples' lives. Be they spoken or written they had the capacity to evoke so many emotions and reactions in people, they can make one feel harmed, hurt, healed, helped, cuddled, loved, cared for, rejected, make them laugh, make them smile, make them cry. What else could you use that could do that? The power of words whether they are in speech, in song, in theatre, in film, in books, in newspapers, in texts, in emails, in documents. It was such a pleasure to be able to share them, in such a powerful way to bring emotions out in others. What a gift to have been given, her love of words. She loved her new career.

Her writing made her want to write more and the more she wrote the more she wanted to write

CHAPTER 15

Private function do not disturb

The team continued to work together to achieve the ongoing deadlines in readiness for the production process. Fi was present at the warehouse when the box containing the first published copy of the first book of her first series was finally opened. She felt proud. It was an unbelievable feeling to finally see her work in print. She took six copies from the box and signed them for Louise, Calum, Annie, John, Carl and herself. After having a celebratory Prosecco with Annie and John who were at the warehouse too, she broke a rule and had a Skype call to her children who were together in London, as Calum was visiting his sister and they both expressed their pride in their mother. "All those years of typing away studying to learn your craft, hone it and now finally, finally see it in print! I am so, so proud of you Mum," said Louise, wiping away a tear, before Calum added, "Well done Mother!" He was a man of few words but they were always heartfelt. She had a brief chat and they told her they were off to lunch together and so she said her goodbyes and promised to see them both soon.

Fi caught the tram to Chorlton and wandered over to The Lead Station where she had arranged to meet all her girlfriends. Julie met Fi at the door of the bar and she was in awe of the book that Fi held up to show her. "I'm so, so proud of you Bestie," said Julie. Fi opened a page and showed Julie an illustration and the words underneath it indicated to her friend that one of the characters in the book was a frog named 'Mark.' They held each other for a while as Julie shed a tear and said nothing, they didn't need to. It was a very private moment between the two of them. Julie inhaled and then exhaled a deep breath and said, "I'm going to the loo, are you coming?" Fi followed her friend upstairs and Julie whispered, "I'm just having a peep in this function room, I've never seen it before and as she opened the door to the Copper Room, there was a tremendous cheer and everybody burst into applause as Julie held the door open and gently pushed her friend into the room full of people. Fi was literally awestruck and as she gazed around the room everything seemed to be in slow motion, as she tried to take in all the faces in front of her. She saw Louise and Calum, Jackie and her brother James and their families, Tracey and her family, Julie's family, Pauline, her cousin Jennifer and her husband Bill (which made her gasp in delight), Jen from London with Henry, Kate Kuwait (who was back in the UK for a short while), Tanya, who she had not seen for years, her long lost friend Joanne from Burnham-on-Sea who she had not seen for 11 years, old friends from work including Eve, neighbours Annette and Tony who she was close to and Annie and John too. So many people and as she turned around to face Julie and say thank you, she saw Carl coming into the room. They made eye contact and she smiled at him. She was handed a glass of champagne and shown a huge cake shaped like a book which represented the exact cover of her 'first' book and she searched the room to make eye contact with Fliss, who she knew, had made this beautiful creation and she smiled across the room at her. Julie tapped her glass with a spoon and 'shsssed' the room into silence before saying, "We are all hear today to celebrate not only this fantastic achievement of your 'first' published work, as we know you will be far too busy on launch day to celebrate properly BUT, we are also here to celebrate the fact that all of us here in this room are enriched by having you in our lives and to watch you go through what you have over the past year or so and to see the tenacity and determination with which you have fought and won those battles and finally the war, that was inside of you, we cannot be prouder. To Fi!" and she raised her glass as everybody joined in shouting "TO FI!" and a round of applause followed. Fi was trying very hard to control her emotions and hold back tears, as she composed herself to reply, "Erm, thank you, I am almost speechless, so I will try my best to follow that and keep it brief," she said. "I agree, it was battle after battle, in what, at times, seemed like a relentless war but I WAS determined to heal without medical intervention and I grasped at the things that I knew would help me, I played my music loud and proud, I sang along to inspiring lyrics and cried at some of them too! I danced like I had the dance floor to myself, much to the cats and dogs bewilderment! (The room laughed) I laughed, cried and I laughed again, with not only my 'coffee o'clock gang' but my extended group of friends too, I decided to eat well, eventually, (more laughter from the room) and I joined a gym, and made it there, eventually, (yet more laughter from the room) I cherished my animals, I embraced the rare visits from my children and I threw myself into my new career as I wrote and I wrote and I wrote some more! However, I could not have done any of it without every card, every text, every messenger message, every Skype, Facetime and phone call, every email, every bunch of flowers, every knock on my door, every coffee shop date, in fact every everything! I really do thank you all for the parts you all played and I especially thank you Julie, through my pain you have become the most precious person in the world to me and our laughter and tears will always be in my heart. My soul and my spirit shut down for while but they are back now. My heart also took a beating for all the wrong reasons but it could never be fully broken because I have too much love 'from and for' every one of you stood in this room and yes, when I'm ready, I hope to fill it up with love from a special man too! Not yet though. Finally, I thank myself, I dug deep and I did it. One CAN and must recover from loss, even when it happens twice in quick succession. And believe me it's true. ANYBODY CAN RECOVER. It takes courage and it takes determination but you can and you will, because I did. Here's to you all, here's to me and here's to the writer and the 'first team' who helped me to get to the published stage! Thank you so much EVERYBODY!" and she raised her glass and swiped it in front of her, across the whole room as everybody clapped, with one or two of them visibly shedding a tear or two. The gathered crowd eventually scattered into smaller groups and Fi took time to mingle amongst them all as she wandered round the room. She laughed with her children about their obvious secret when she had spoken to them earlier that morning (when she Skyped them they were in Julie's house) Fi, joked that she thought she recognised the wallpaper. She was overwhelmed to see Jen and Bill, her seldom seen cousin and her husband. She was shocked and delighted to see her old friend Joanne and they had many life stories to catch up on as Jo was in Manchester for a week, en-route to Canada. Kate Kuwait was here for two weeks, so that was a girly date in the diary, for sure. She hugged her friend Tanya who she hadn't seen for 7 years and they too sat and caught up on each other's stories a little. They had met when both their son's were little 'boy George's' and had only managed Facebook contact for the past few years but Fi had always had a fondness in her heart for this lovely woman in front of her, who was, Fi thought, still stunningly beautiful. She caught up with her coffee o'clock girls too, as laughter could be heard travelling around the room. Finally she managed to grab time with her 'first' team too and learnt that within his plans for his new publishing business, Carl had offered both Annie and John a lead role in their respective departments within his Manchester based company HQ, which they too were delighted with, for their own career progression. Annie never really wanted the government job anyway, she said. The afternoon went by in a whirl and as always at The Lead Station, the food, the company and the sound of laughter was enjoyed by everybody present. It was a great tribute to Fi and a fond memory bank deposit for her, for sure, and as she left the Copper Room, Fi took the paper sign from the door that read 'Private function, do not disturb.'

Launch day was now a week away and Fi spent the next few days finalising details with the Central Library for the rooms that they were providing and when she would be allowed access to them to set up her display of marketing materials from the printers and publishing house. She liaised with Annie and John to ensure they had organised their own needs for the launch. She confirmed with the three local schools that would be bringing children to the event and finally she spoke to Lisa to ensure that the marketing strategies were being implemented too. With just two days to go, she was satisfied all was in place for the big day. She was hardly JK Rowling but this was huge for Fi. She didn't want to put on a big launch event she just wanted it to be a memorable one for the children. When she looked around the room the night before the event she felt impressed and proud. The room was set informally, rather like a reading corner in a classroom with extra large cushions, (depicting characters from her book) scattered about the floor on the left hand side of the room, there was a collage of illustrations of the characters and scenes from the book, a mini exhibition of framed illustrations, together with words from the book emblazoned across the length of the opposite wall for the children to absorb and there was a low but comfy chair for Fi to sit in, as she read her book to the children. Annie and John's equipment was set up in a connecting smaller room, to enable the children to wander in and out of each room and participate in whichever aspect of the process appealed to them at the time.

There was a very large low table which Fi had found in a junk shop and decoupaged with scraps of her book cover and on it were 'party bags' for each child, containing tiny packets of seeds to grow flowers to attract the bees and instructions on how to plant the whole, 're-cycleable' packet. These were a nod to one of the characters in this, the first in the series of environmental books, a beekeeper named 'Bumble Bill.' The bags also contained another gift for each child. Fi had ordered paper straws with a tiny copy of her book cover glued to the top, rather like a flag on a straw and again re-cycleable. Little gifts but hopefully enough to start conversations amongst the children about looking after the environment. She left the room feeling very confident that tomorrow was going to be a good day.

She arrived home an hour later to find a card through the door telling her that she had a flower delivery left at Julie's. She called in on her friend and discovered she had had the biggest bouquet she had ever seen delivered. "I couldn't get it through the door!" Julie shrieked. It was fabulous, green and white and full of natural accessories decorating the bouquet and it was in a re-cycleable container too, which Fi loved. She opened the card, which read:

Wishing you the best of luck tomorrow, here's to the success that is undoubtedly coming your way, from all the team at First Publications. X

"Wow, that's what you call a bouquet," exclaimed Fi, "and that's what you call a positive message too! Talk about the Law of Attraction, wow!" "Fantastic Fi, well done Bestie," replied Julie as she handed her friend a coffee, "thank you," said Fi. They sat down and Fi said she would send a thank you email to everyone but suspected that Carl was behind the gesture, "Well he's certainly behind the bill," said Julie and they laughed. Julie asked her if she was nervous and she responded, "Do you know what Jules, I'm not, I can hold my own with children, I wrote those books years ago and still believe in them, from an educational and combined pleasure perspective and I think tomorrow will be great fun for the children and the team." "Good, I want you to be proud, you've worked so hard," Julie said, "Thanks Jules, well I'm off for a bath and bed," before giving her friend a hug and a kiss, "catch you tomorrow," Fi added, "okay chick," replied Julie as she laughed at Fi trying to manoeuvre the enormous bouquet out of Julie's house and into her own front door! Fi ran a 'luxury bath' as she liked to call it, with her favourite guilty pleasure bubbles, candles and music. She opened Prosecco, poured herself a glass and climbed into the bath to soak her body and her mind in bubbles, as she felt the growing, calming effects of both the soapy ones and the alcoholic ones. She listened to the tunes of a relaxing playlist as they randomly played on her mini jukebox! She really did feel proud as she sang along to, 'Return to Innocence' by Enigma, and she agreed with the very powerful lyrics that this was not the beginning of her end, but of her return to herself. She went to bed early and slept well and was up early the next day taking the dogs out, showering and grabbing a quick but nourishing breakfast. She dressed in a new navy blue skinny leg trousers, a beige buttoned silk shirt from Hawes and Curtis, a broad tan leather belt, high heeled cut out black leather shoes with freshly painted matching toe and fingernails, before finishing her look with silver thumb and finger accessories, a silver Indian cuff on her left arm and a collection of bangles on her right. It was a bright and sunny day, but it was still spring and so she threw on her long length chunky knit cardigan, just in case the weather turned and her large frame sunglasses to block out the bright sunlight. She sprayed her favourite scent (it was a special occasion after all) on her neck, behind her ears and on her wrists and took one last glance at herself and set off for one of the biggest days so far, of her new career as a writer. She arrived at the Central Library and was greeted by their conference and events manager who took Fi to the event room and she was surprised that there was already a press presence, with over an hour to go until the first lot of the children arrived! She was even more surprised when a local television crew arrived a few minutes later. She was asked if she wouldn't mind giving a mini press conference before the event started and she asked them to give her five minutes. She checked herself in the mirror in the bathroom, retouched her lip gloss and hair and sent Julie a quick text saying, "shit, I'm going to be on TV tonight!" and then went out to participate in her first ever television interview. After asking the waiting journalists and small crowd of people to be kind to her, which raised a few chuckles, Fi said, "Hi everybody, thank you for coming today, welcome to my book launch for the first of a series of children's books, based upon a Village called Greenville, which has an environmental ethos. The books are designed to introduce children to the principles of learning to take care of their own environment," she said, before continuing, “and the characters in the village all have catchy, relevant names, such as Bumble Bill, (who is the bee keeper) that children will hopefully embrace and be inspired to follow in their everyday lives, thank you very much,” she took a deep breath and added “right then, questions please, fire away!” “yes, you in the red,” she said, as she pointed to a woman in a red shirt. She spent the next twenty minutes answering questions about her books, her writing history and her ‘first’ team principles and how she had recruited her ‘firsts’. She felt it was going well and wasn’t daunted by any of the questions and with 20 minutes before she was due to read to the visiting children, she halted the press conference and continued to ensure both she and her team were all ready to go when the children arrived.

As the children were welcomed into the room by the library staff, they looked around the room as Fi observed how they behaved concerning the displays and the setup of the launch. Some commented upon the tray of goodies, of course! Others commented upon the illustrations, others read the words that they could see, aloud, whilst others were excited to be having a story read by a ‘real’ writer. When all the children, staff and various other adults were all seated, Fi commanded the room once again by introducing herself and telling the children that she had written a series of stories for children and that this was the first one that had been made into a book and also that this was a special occasion that they were to be part of, because this was the first time that she had read one of her books aloud to children. The children were very impressed with that fact. Fi sat down in her chair and introduced the book, showing the children the front cover and describing the character in the illustration. She read the story and at each turn of the page, she showed them the new illustrations and explained the significance of each illustration to that pages text and when she had finished the story, she closed the book, as the children started clapping and as some of them stood up, everybody, joined in. She was deeply touched, what a memory bank moment that was, reading a book you have written, to a group of children, who are then giving you a standing ovation! Wow. “Thank you very much everybody,” she said, “I would like all the children to sit down and ask you if anybody would like to ask me questions then will you put your hands up and we’ll get through as many as we can!” “You first with the ponytail, hello, what is your name?” “Sadie,” replied the little girl, “well Sadie, you have a special name don’t you, because there is a character in the book with your name, isn’t there? Do you remember what she does?” asked Fi and Sadie answered her. “That’s right! Why do you think her job in the village is so important?” she asked the children. She then spent 15 minutes or so letting the children ask her questions about the book, about her life as a writer and about the rest of the series too, which some of them said they couldn’t wait to be released. Fi then let them look around at the display and take a closer look at copies of the book and help themselves to a ‘launch party bag’ and she then ushered them into the next room to meet John and Annie, saying thank you to every one of them as they left the room, some of them also thanked her and asked her to sign their party bags and some of them told her they couldn’t wait to buy her book.

When the room was empty Fi took the chance for a break to freshen up and to get some refreshments before the second batch of children came in and she repeated the whole process again, this time noticing that Carl was in the room too! It was very well received and this second class of children were equally as enthusiastic as the earlier session had been, with one little girl putting her little arms around Fi's legs and saying, "Thank you for writing a lovely story Miss Fi," as she was leaving the room, which kind of melted Fi's heart a little. When the children had gone Fi asked the waiting press if they had any more questions and after answering a couple more enquiries about the schedules for the rest of the series, she excused herself and left the room. She bumped into Carl who had waited outside for her. "Congratulations," he said, "I hear from John and Annie that the interactive stuff with them, was great too, fantastic launch idea, I have to say Fi, well done!" he added. "Thanks Carl, it's been really well received but we'll have to see what the press and book sales say about how successful it has really been but I am very hopeful!". "You were a natural in there, I thought you were fantastic with the press this morning," replied Carl, "oh, I hadn't realised you were there," she said, "yes I have been here all day!" he added "in fact the media and literary industry reactions seem very positive so far from my information gathering this morning," he added, "oh that sounds promising," said Fi. "Shall we go for lunch?" he asked, "Erm, sure," Fi replied. "I am due back in 90 minutes, so I'll say 75 for lunch," she added. 'I like her punctuality,' Carl thought as they walked out of the building. "Will the Great John Street be okay again?" he laughed, as he held her arm to help her safely across the traffic. As they entered the hotel they decided to eat on The Rooftop Garden as it was a glorious spring day, Fi ordered sparkling mineral water and Carl a glass of wine and they sat and enjoyed the sun as they contemplated the menus.

Whilst discussing the impending launch and print run issues they ordered lunch, which when it arrived, proved to be a delicious food treat. The surroundings, the atmosphere, the lovely weather and the stimulating conversation saw the time fly by and before she knew it Fi had to excuse herself to go back to the launch as she left Carl in the foyer of the hotel, with suggestions to liaise re ongoing issues. The afternoons session was equally well received and this time Fi was asked to have photographs with some of the children, to be used in the press coverage due for both print and online deadlines that evening. After thanking John and Annie for their tremendous efforts that day, she suggested that she treat them to dinner but they declined, due to other commitments but said they would liaise with her regarding the follow on books in the series which they were already working on.

As Fi was sat on the tram on her way home, she saw that a man sat next to her was reading a copy of the evening news on his tablet and he did a 'take two' as he realised he was sat next the person featured in the article. Fi smiled at him and blushed, but she felt so proud.

When she got home she had a text message from Julie:

Julie: Hey Mrs. You're in the evening news.

Fi: I know. I've just seen it!

Julie: Will you still be my bestie when you're famous?

Fi: Sure will, once a Bestie always a Bestie.

Julie: Coffee at yours, five minutes?

Fi: That'll be my five minutes of fame gone then!

Julie: Ha ha, get Nessie on!

Julie knocked and brought her friend more flowers, Champagne, and a bag containing two buy one get one free ready meals and a Congratulations card. "Who are the ready meals for?" asked Fi. "Me and you, who do think?" replied Julie. "What about Andy and the boys?" Fi asked in response. "What about them? We're celebrating tonight, girls night in!" Julie laughed and popped the champagne cork, poured two glasses and then put the bottle in the fridge. "Now get that pinger going," she said as she pointed to the microwave. The girls devoured their Spaghetti Bolognese. They were so hungry, they were scraping their plates noisily and Fi burst out laughing saying to Julie, "I've been on a strange food journey today," as she continued, "gourmet dine to plates that shine," as she lifted her plate to her face and licked it clean. They then collapsed laughing! "You can take the girl out of Salford but you can't take the Salford out of the girl!" said Julie as they were interrupted by the local TV channel's early evening news programme running a feature on Fi and the girls were laughing again as they couldn't quite believe it. It was surreal. She had written a children's book and now she was on the TV. Bizarre. They finished their champagne and chatted some more before Julie went home and Fi decided to open her card. It read:

There is nobody like you. You are everything to me. I couldn't be prouder. Julie. X

It made Fi cry. That girl is just amazing she thought to herself.

Over the coming days Fi received flowers and cards from her friends and family and there was a steady influx of requests for TV and radio interviews as well as newspaper and magazine article requests. The attention was heightened by the fact that this was a 'firsts project' and people were genuinely interested to see if an idea using new local talent and a newly formed business, could succeed. As well as the business idea intriguing people, the books themselves were selling steadily, with a week on week growth in sales and so a decision was made to bring forward the release date for the remainder of the series. The event at Chorlton Bookshop for the toddler's books also attracted media attention, as they too were captivating books for little ones, using rhyme, lovely illustrations, letters and numbers, together with a 'finding' theme, which toddlers absolutely love when they are reading. The combined sales increased steadily over the next few months taking the 'First team' into profit within their first year, which was a great achievement and there were discussions in place regarding foreign, USA and Canadian rights contracts. They had a winning combination on their hands and Fi couldn't be more delighted. She was already working on another series of 'fantasy' children's books with an environmental theme.

It wasn't long before the highly regarded Bologna Children's Book Fair and Fi decided to take herself to this annual event to devour all the information she possibly could concerning writing for children. She had a hunger to broaden her ideas and increase her knowledge for trends. She liked the idea of meeting illustrators, as well as other authors and to have the opportunity of attending workshops for any manner of themes related to successfully writing for children. She was particularly keen to explore all aspects of digital writing and how she could use the different social media sites to increase her profiles, skills and increase her potential 'book buying' traffic. The world of digital illustrating was now a huge market which was completely new to her own experience of the traditional mediums of children's illustrating and she was interested to find out more about the processes and how the different applications and computer programmes could be further incorporated into her own work and in particular to her forthcoming 'fantasy' children's eco books. There would be an illustrator's exhibition and translator and literary agent's centre too. It sounded like a children's writers heaven she thought, as she emailed the details through to Annie, John and Carl for them to consider their own potential gains from attending such an event. She was not surprised that Carl had already arranged to attend. He informed her he was keen to develop the use of the digital media within his publishing business, including App development for children, who are very technically savvy these days. He also wanted to get a more in depth insight into technical publishing solutions, as well as looking at interactive storytelling. Carl also said he relished the opportunity to increase his contacts with developers and device manufacturers at the same time. Who knew, thought Fi as she read his email, gone are the days of writing on a page, drawing a picture and sending it to the printers and bookbinders! It was a whole new world out there and it was moving so fast. One thing she did know as a writer for children, she needed to make sure her knowledge of their requirements kept up with this fast paced race and The Bologna Book Fair seemed like a good way to review her skills and knowledge. She booked her 5 day ticket for the show together with her hotel and flights and somehow she knew that this was going to be a hugely beneficial step forward in her new career as a published writer and she wasn't remotely apprehensive about traveling alone on this adventure. She was quite looking forward to it. On the return journey Fi would be going to Madrid for 4 days to stay with an old school friend, Katherine, who was now living in Spain, having married a Spanish man. They ran a small B&B on the outskirts of the city.

In the meantime Fi continued to go about her daily life but making writing a priority of each day, treating her time at her desk as a day at the office, a very stylish office but a day at the office nonetheless. She had to be disciplined in her time management, as she wanted to get the adult fiction book completed, before she embarked upon her new series of children's books.

The 'first' team continued to work well together and all excelled in their respective fields of expertise. Carl bought some business premises not far from the relatively new Media City area in Salford, to be 'closer to initiatives, innovations and facilities', he said. He invited all the team to be a part of the process of the design of the building and although Fi would not be spending her working days here, he wanted her to experience as a writer, what was in place behind the scenes, to bring her work to life. "Isn't that what publishing books is, bringing someone else's ideas to life?" he asked, as he showed her around. It was a very impressive and inspiring workspace, situated in an old warehouse, with a stunning view of the canal for all the employees. There were creative mini pods and larger rooms too, where they could work individually or in teams to inspire each other. There were quirky soft furnishings, the clever use of glass as dividing walls to allow light to flood the building, natural materials everywhere, recycled materials too, a huge open plan kitchen and lounging area for staff lunches, parties and meetings. It was a really stunning space and Carl explained to Fi at length, that having cut his business teeth in the old fashioned corporate structured way and having witnessed that it wasn't always the best way to create and achieve productivity and profit. He told her he felt that an, 'everyone is part of this' company ethos, proves to be a much happier, more productive and ultimately profitable way of working. He added, that by having a 'focus on everybody' mindset, in his opinion, helped to prevent employee angst, division and absenteeism. His aim was to create an environment whereby his employees were far more likely to make his company, rather than break it. Carl explained to her that the true values of his company are reflected in the way he treats his staff and his customers and he used the analogy with her that if you look in a mirror as you leave the house and don't like the reflection looking back at you, then it affects the way you feel about yourself, it affects your day, it affects your event, your 'whatever' it is you are doing that day, so in other words if he doesn't get it right for his staff and his customers then his business performance is reflected back at him! Everywhere Fi looked were inspiring quotes and memorabilia, such as, 'Every role is important here, that means yours too!' 'We are a TEAM,' 'Try it, it might well work' and the quote above his own desk read, 'Be passionate enough to keep it inspiring and creative'. He had certainly set out on that path with the ethos and design of his creative headquarters for 'First Publica- tions'. It was already a building filled with humour and fun, as well being a buzzing, creative hive and Fi was very impressed with his level of business knowledge and his enthusiasm to transfer his skills into this completely new venture for him.

The day before traveling to Bologna, Fi completed her usual pre travel tasks of taking her animals to their respective kennels and cattery, packing her case, ensuring her travel documents were to hand for the flight and her necessary household chores of emptying fridges, washing machines and dishwashers was completed before finally booking her taxi for 6am the next morning ready for her early start. She had a relaxing bath, went to bed early and had a good night's sleep. After her shower, she dressed both for comfort and warmth, tied her hair in a ponytail and put on minimal makeup, she sprayed one of her day perfumes and finally cleaned her teeth before putting on her trusty long length chunky cardigan and finally drank her tea as she sat and waited for her taxi to arrive. Her mobile rang and as she answered, "Hello," she heard, "hi, Gregg the cabbie for you," "thanks, I'll be right out," she replied. She picked up her case and her handbag secured the house with her alarm code, went outside and locked her front door. She had positive vibes about this trip. As she was getting into the taxi she heard an all too familiar voice shouting, "See you Dick!" The voice although she recognised it, stopped her in her tracks and laughing aloud, she replied "See you Fanny!" as she waved cheerily to Julie. They had named each other Fanny and Dick (when they were newly formed Whitefield Angels) and the terms of endearment for each other had stuck! After she had finished giggling, Gregg the cabbie chatted to her about her trip and she explained where she was going and why, "I am a writer, and I am off to a book fair in Italy," she said. They got chatting about her current adult fiction and he jokingly asked if he could be in the book? He was certainly impressed with the brief description she gave of the plot and said he would buy the book, as he was very curious. She suspected he was being polite, although she had had an amazing response from her reviewers, which included very positive and surprising reactions from the men amongst them! She enjoyed the journey without having the hassle of driving to the airport and after paying her fare and a tip upon arrival at the terminal, she checked in and made her way through to the departure lounge. Fi spent the next couple of hours enjoying breakfast, perusing the duty free shops and buying herself her favourite perfume, lip-glosses and magazines to fill her time on the flight. As the announcement of the flight came through, she made her way to the departure gate, joining the queue to board the aircraft and after finding her seat, she settled to listen to her 'favourites' selection and read her magazines. It was an uneventful journey and after the usual arrivals routine of passport control, luggage collection and finding a taxi, she was on her way to her hotel in the centre of the city. It was a small friendly hotel with a lovely roof garden and Jacuzzi area looking out over the rooftops and a short walk from the Piazza Maggiore and the Galleria Cavour where the best of the 'Italian' fashion houses have stores and where one or two none Italian ones did too, much to Fi's delight! That would be a special 'day trip' if the 'coffee o'clock' girls were here with me she thought, when she discovered it was in such proximity to her hotel. Still, even without her girlfriends, it was an afternoon she was really going to enjoy, alone! (It would be a Carrie and Vivian afternoon combined), she pondered, as she recalled her two favourite movie characters. She consulted her diary of events at the book fair, to ensure she slotted that most essential of girly treats into one of her afternoons whilst she was in Bologna. She unpacked her case and took a 90 minute rest, before freshening up and going for a walk, to get some fresh air and to familiarise herself with the route to the book fair in the morning. She wandered the streets taking in the atmosphere and some of the sights of this beautiful city including the magnificent Piazza Maggiore with its atmospheric bars and cafes. Many cities in Italy are renowned for their famous town squares and this one in Bologna was no exception. She toured the markets looking at local produce and revelling in the atmosphere of what the markets used to be like in the UK years ago, during her childhood. Bologna has many cultural places of interest and Fi intended to visit as many as she could during her stay here but on her first afternoon, she was content to just stroll around, to get her bearings. She noted where the Villa Griffone was, so she could take a trip out there to see this small museum paying tribute to the work of the inventor 'Marconi,' who was born in Bologna. She had dinner in a pizzeria just off the main square, which served her two freshly made delicious tasting pizza slices with local produce of strong cheeses, hams, olives and mushrooms and a traditional tomato, mozzarella and basil option. It was the best pizza she had ever tasted, she thought, as she left the establishment, even in the kitchen one can be an artist! She was also keen to try the local iconic Italian dish too, this was after all home to the famous Ragu Bolognese sauce, as well as trying some of the many other pasta specialties, before walking off the calories by climbing the 498 steps of the Torre Asinelli to witness the birds-eye view of Bologna or wander through one of it's many porticos. She had a lot planned and was relishing the change of scenery and inspiration she might find while she was here. As she walked the short distance back to her hotel she spotted Carl with his wife and children, sat in a restaurant window and she waved as she passed on by. Upon her arrival back at the hotel later that evening, she took herself up to the roof garden with a glass of Prosecco and sat there enjoying the bubbles of the Jacuzzi and the stars in the sky. Perfect nourishment for her soul she thought. She slept peacefully and soundly.

The next morning she was up early and after showering and dressing in a signature outfit of jeans and a shirt, she topped the outfit off with a cashmere jumper for warmth. Exhibition halls could be cold, especially in March. She went down to the dining room and ate a breakfast of fruits, yoghurt and a pastry and drank orange juice and tea before going back to her room, cleaning her teeth and wrapping up with additional layers with her oversized black cardigan and a bright orange pashmina. She took the twenty minute walk to the exhibition centre and having already paid for her ticket she was able to join a shorter queue to get in. She bought a programme, which included a timetable of events and a map of the exhibition layout and decided to go to a cafe and sit in a quiet corner, to plan her workshops for the next few days. She was startled out of her concentration by Carl, "Hey Fi, may I join you?" he said. The 'Hey Fi' jarred her soul a little but she responded, "Hi Carl, sure, please, sit down," she replied, gesturing towards the seat next to her, "how are you?" they both asked each other at the same time and laughed together, before he said, "after you." "I'm good, thank you Carl, excited to be here, I feel like a writer now," she laughed, before adding, "I feel like I am on home turf," and he laughed with her. They spoke for a while regarding their lives and then chatted about their respective workshop plans for the next few days and then went their separate ways to explore the vast exhibition. Fi was in awe it was so impressive. It really was a vast exhibition space with Fi wondering where to start. There were book publisher stands, from all over the world, displaying their books, with crowds of people filling each of their exhibit stands. People looking at books, people engrossed in reading books, people signing contracts to buy books. There were people in every square inch of space, so it seemed. She spent a couple of hours wandering from stand to stand, picking up books, making notes in her trusty notebook, taking photographs with her smartphone, looking for inspiration for ideas, words, images and themes for new books.

The morning passed quickly and Fi grabbed a quick lunch before wandering over to the Illustrators exhibition. It was a long corridor type space with exhibits lining the walls on both sides. People were walking down one way and coming back up the other way and so she decided to join the flow. She was looking for inspiration but she was also looking at potential artists to commission, to illustrate future books, she didn't want to be solely tied to a particular artist, she wanted to expand her own 'team' and network and form working relationships with other people too. The exhibition was very popular and too crowded for her to really appreciate the work on display and so she decided to come back again, when it was a little less crowded. She then looked at her map before walking into the interactive display area, which reminded her of a computer store, with tablets installed all around the room for people to 'interact' with, with children's stories displayed on them of course. She was intrigued to know more about this area of publishing as Carl had mentioned it as a potential growth area for 'First publications.' This area was also packed with people and she had overheard a man saying this was 'big business' for children's writers, as children were far more likely to have a tablet, than a book in their hands these days. That was a startling realisation for Fi! It was true though, on reflection she realised that any toddlers and young children she had come across these past couple of years were all tablet and smartphone savvy and not one of them had had any books in their hands. As she looked around her, there were smartphones being used as camera's, to send emails, to make notes, to speak to people, to upload and download information, to make videos, to use as voice recorders and so she asked herself, why would toddlers and young children be any different? Learnt behaviour was the obvious answer, modern children were copying adults, as they always had and electronic media had replaced paper, as adults were seen reading more ereaders and tablets and the younger market was definitely following suit. As if to reiterate her observation the school children at the exhibition, were far more interested in the interactive stuff than in the actual books! It made her wonder who was buying children's books these days and was the market in decline because this exhibition was predominantly full of paper books. She made a mental note that she needed to research the matter in far more depth, if she was going to make a career out of writing for children. Who were her target market and in what format or formats should she be addressing their needs? It had been worth coming to the exhibition for that alone. She had learnt a major lesson already and it was only the first day.

The remaining days in Bologna flew by and Fi filled her time, her mind, her stomach and her shopping bags with all manner of goodies. There was the cultural excesses to occupy her time, eating excesses to fill her stomach, children's book fair excesses to give her inspirational overload and of course the delights of Italian designer shopping that a girl can never, ever, do to excess! Fi had always had a policy of spending 10% of her monthly income on herself and the rest on the necessities of life. She treated herself on this occasion to a designer handbag and a vintage designer dress and she went slightly over her 10% budget. Just on this occasion! It really was a heavenly time for Fi in Bologna. She felt well, she felt inspired, she felt nourished and she felt a little lighter in her bank balance too but more than anything she felt happy that she was celebrating finding herself.

Just give time the time and it will help you heal

CHAPTER 16

Will you trust me to say that I trust him?

The flight to Madrid was uneventful and Fi felt overwhelmed to be greeted at the arrivals lounge, by her friend Katherine. She had not seen her for 36 years but had the fondest of memories of their time together in school and beyond when they had both trained to become nurses. She had thought of her regularly over the years and had tried to find her on Facebook and other social media but having no idea if she was married or had changed her name proved an impossible task. In the end Katherine had found her by searching Facebook. Luckily, Fiora is quite an unusual name. They had corresponded for a number of months through phone calls and Skype sessions and finally they decided to meet up again. Their school days and therefore their teenage years, were filled with talk of boys in their school, favourite pop idols, screaming at the TV when certain actors or idols appeared on the screen, bedroom posters, making pin badges of their idols, the traumas of fancying the untouchable love of another girl, plotting to steal the untouchable love of the other girl, make up, fashion, experimenting with alcohol, evolving musical tastes, youth clubs, sleepovers, your friend fancying your dad! Fancying your friends brother and choking on cake when he came into the room! Sneaking into pubs and nightclubs under age and eventually getting steady boyfriends. It wasn't the steady boyfriends that caused them to lose touch though, it was geography and not the fact that they once cheated in a geography exam and got exactly the same mark! No it was the geographical distance between them. Katherine moved to Brighton with her family and so their friendship dwindled, as is often the case when the distance is such as it is, between Manchester and Brighton but Fi never forgot her friend and she was always transported back to her youth whenever she drove past her friend's childhood home, in Denton, yes even 36 years later, she flooded to the fore front of Fi's mind whenever she drove past number 28.

When they got into the airport car park, Katherine introduced her husband Henrique and Fi shook hands but he immediately embraced her and kissed her on both cheeks and said, "Welcome Fiora, Katherine has told me all about you two and she has spoken of you now and again over the years, lovely to see you," before adding, "Katherine, you didn't tell me she was a beautiful woman too!" Fi blushed and as the girls climbed in the back of the car she said to Katherine, "Pwhoar Mrs, he leaves Oggy in the shade!" and they burst out laughing. Oggy was the untouchable boyfriend of another girl! Katherine and Fi had spent a large part of their friendship giggling, as they too had a wicked sense of humour when they were together as teenagers and this reunion proved to be a recharging of those 'giggling' batteries that Fi was missing, with her coffee o'clock girls. Katherine and Henrique lived in Manzanares el Real about 50 km outside of Madrid where the magnificent Medieval Castle of Mendoza overlooks the Santillana Reservoir. It was a beautiful site as they drove towards the town, viewing the reservoir with the castle on the opposite side of the clear blue water, with the backdrop of the mountains in the distance. It was a magnificent site. They arrived at Katherine and Henrique's home almost an hour later and Fi was shown to her room and told to come out onto the roof terrace when she was ready. She unpacked her case and organised her room and then went out to join her friends, where they sat and enjoyed the magnificent view and drank chocolate Caliente, a very popular drink that is a thick version of hot chocolate and it is delicious, especially when you dunk churros in it! “These are so yum,” said Fi, “Gracias Fi,” said Henrique, which caused Fi to splutter her drink as she burst out laughing and upon looking at her friend, Katherine joined in the laughter too which then escalated into hysterical giggles because Fi had translated ‘gracias’ into ‘grassy arse’ in her mind and the two of them were then uncontrollable for several minutes before Henrique himself laughed and said “sin alcohol Fi and Katy! Sin alcohol!” and Katherine jumped up and kissed her husband and said, “welcome to the world of Katy and Fi! We laugh at everything and nothing and grassy arses too” and the girls ventured off into their world of hysterics once more, Henrique walked over to Fi and hugged her and said, “I like you Fi, funny woman, funny Fi” he said in his lovely Spanish accent and Katherine replied, “Funny Fi, ha, ha, we used to call her that at school!” and they all started laughing together. After a couple of hours chatting and enjoying each others company, they all went up to their rooms for a siesta and Fi checked her emails, texts and missed calls and caught up with her children and her friends before she nodded into a blissful slumber.

After showering and getting changed for an evening out with ‘smart casual’ instructions from Katherine, they set off in Henrique’s car to attend a dinner party at friends of the couple. Upon arrival Fi was greeted with warmth and pleasantries from their hosts Carmen and Josefa, before being introduced to the other guests present. Everybody was offered San Miguel or Amontillado and plates of dates stuffed with Brie, pomegranates and pistaschios, cheese, spinach and quinoa bites and stuffed baby potatoes with chipotle cheese, which caused much conversation amongst the women who wanted the recipes and the men who wanted more! They all enjoyed each others company with everybody wanting to know about Fi and Katherine's history together from their school days and about Fi's life since she last saw her friend. People took it in turns to translate and Fi felt completely relaxed in their company. They sat down to dinner of 'steak' sandwiches with an orange, avocado, and pistachio salad, fennel and carrots in a pickle dressing, baby sweet potatoes stuffed with dried fruits, nuts and drizzled with a sweet syrup. It was a feast of unbelievable vegetarian foods and it was hard to distinguish that the 'steak' sandwiches were not a meat feast but a meat substitute. Everybody cleaned their plates, emptied the dishes on the table and could have eaten more but there was the delight of the pudding too, which was an equally as heavenly tasting, vegan sticky toffee pudding with vegan whipped topping, followed by cappucinos and vegan peppermint chocolate cookies! Fi complimented Carmen and congratulated her on years of perfecting vegan ingredients and recipes because her dedication and love of the vegetarian and vegan diet was clearly visible to see. Fi had a daughter who was a vegan so she knew the quality of these ingredients and the skill in the cooking. The food was truly sensational and everybody agreed. After devouring such delicious food Fi felt healthy inside and it is not often one can say that after having a bountiful feast. The friends all sat outside with a fire pit roaring away and blankets for additional warmth, with fairy lights, candles and Spanish music creating an ambience of conversation, laughter and fun, with everybody dancing at intervals and Fi attempting Flamenco with Katherine, Antonio and Isabel. It was a magical night and Fi was delighted to have rekindled her long lost friendship. It was almost one in the morning before they left and as she said her thank yous and goodbyes, everybody wished Fi well in her writing adventures and looked forward to seeing her again. "What beautiful people," she said to Katherine and Henrique as they drove back to their hotel, "we are so lucky to have such wonderful friends aren't we?" said Katherine agreeing with her friend. When they got back into the hotel, Fi said goodnight to her friends and went to her room. She got ready for bed and before switching off her lamp she checked her mobile phone. She had missed calls from Julie, Louise and Carl. She would contact them all in the morning she thought, as she drifted off into a blissful sleep.

Fi woke refreshed and content the next morning but was startled to discover it was the afternoon, well five minutes into it, to be precise. She was horrified but she felt so good inside.

She dressed and wandered down to the kitchen and discovered a note from her friend:

Fi, you were sleeping so soundly, I left you in peace, have gone out to the reservoir with the dogs and then we are popping to Manana's for coffee, come and join us. Down the road, turn left and it is across the road. See you there. K.

She poured herself some juice and sat on the verandah outside her room whilst she made her calls.

Fi: "Hi Julie, it's me."

Julie: "Hi chick, how are you? Oh I've missed you, it's been ages, even though it's only a week. How are you? you can answer this time," (she laughed realising she had interrupted her friend)

Fi: "Great Julie, the fair was brilliant and so worth the trip and I am having a really great time here in Madrid."

She told her friend all the news of her trip. She told her about the contacts, the culture and the couture in Bologna and about her reunion with her old school friend here in Madrid. They then chatted about Julie's family news before saying their goodbyes and Julie finishing the conversation saying:

Julie: "Hurry up home, I can't swear when you're not here!" and they laughed.

Fi: "I'll see you in three days Fanny!" and they were still laughing as the line went dead.

Next Fi phoned Louise and had the same conversation, with Louise then updating her mother with her own news of work, home, friends and relationship issues and Fi promising her daughter a trip down to London soon to have some quality Mum and daughter time.

Next Fi rang Carl:

Carl: "Carl Carter speaking!"

Fi: "Hi Carl, it's Fi here, just returning your call."

Carl: "Hi Fi, how are you?"

Fi: "Great thank you, I thought the book fair was very beneficial, how about you?"

Carl: "Yes, a fantastic networking and informative trip for me. I will take so much from it for 'First Publications,' which is kind of what I hoped for."

Fi: "It was more than that for me, it was inspiring too from a creativity perspective which I am really looking forward to starting, when I get back home."

Carl: "Are you not back in Manchester then?"

Fi: "No, I am in Manzanares el Real outside of Madrid for a few days with friends. They have a hotel here."

Carl: "Excellent idea, recharge your batteries ready for your next venture!"

Fi: "Yes, good location, good food, good company and good fun too!" (She laughed before continuing) **"Anyway Carl what can I do for you? I was returning a missed call from you?"**

Carl: "Erm, eh, well, erm!" (He mumbled). **"I have the strangest request Fi."**

Fi: "Really! I am intrigued! Fire away Carl, I'm all ears."

Carl: "Well I know from the brief interactions that you have had with me regarding your personal life, that you are very guarded in relation to dating again but I wondered if the time is now right in your life?" (Where the fuck is he going with this, he is a married man, she thought, as her heart was thumping in her chest as her anxiety levels soared) **"And if it is, then would you consider trusting me to set up a date for you?" "I know somebody who has admired you from afar, for a while**

now," (he paused before continuing) **"I absolutely trust him Fi, he has integrity, he has morals, he is well educated and has a very successful business empire, he is an honourable, single man and I would not contemplate recommending a date, if I had the slightest doubts for you Fi. I know that you have had more than your share of uninvited pain but he is a really great guy Fi. I have known him for over 50 years. Will you trust me to say that I trust him?"**

Fi: "Well, I am absolutely flattered and floored in equal measures Carl and very intrigued too but if you don't mind I need some time. I am enjoying 'me' being on my own and I don't know whether I am ready to complicate that yet, or if I ever will be. Thank you Carl, very much for thinking of me, I do appreciate it and when I am ready I will give you an answer."

Carl: "Absolutely, take all the time required there is no pressure or timescale involved."

Fi: "Thanks Carl. As I say, when I am ready."

Carl: "Take care Fi and carry on enjoying Madrid."

Fi: "Will do. Bye."

She pressed end call and the line went dead.

She text Katherine and said she would be 30 minutes and then she texted Julie:

Fi: FUCKETY, FUCK, FUCK, FUCK, WHAT DO I DO?

The phone rang straight away and it was Julie:

Fi: "Oh my giddy god with bells on!"

Julie: "What? What? What is it? Tell me, for god's sake Fi, tell me!"

So she did, every detail Carl had said, she relayed to Julie and when Fi had finished she asked?

Fi: "What do I do Jules?"

Julie: "Oh my giddy god with bells on all right! Who is he, where does he live?"

Fi: "Shit, I didn't even ask his name? Do I need his name if I am not going to meet him? Julie I would be terrified to trust anybody again."

Julie: "Hang on a minute, think about it carefully Fi, Carl has told you this guy has admired you from afar for a while, he is honest, he has integrity, manners and morals, he is well educated and has a business empire and he has known him for over 50 years and he is asking you to trust him, that he trusts the guy. Fi, do it! Just, do it!"

Fi: "Whoa Jules, I might not like him!"

Julie: "That's the whole point of a date Fi. What have you got to lose? He sounds amazing by the description but just go and see for yourself. One date. If you don't like him, that's the end of it. Do it Fi!"

Fi: "I will think some more on it Julie but thanks for phoning and listening. I am flattered and floored to be honest and a hornets nest has been disturbed in my head."

Julie: "Well he doesn't sound like he belongs in a hornets' nest, they are nasty, angry, scary creatures out to hurt you, it's down to you whether you trust Carl that he trusts this guy and that is for you to answer Fi, but my gut feeling as your bestie is, do it?"

Fi: "Thanks Bestie!"

Julie: "Love you." She pressed end and the line went dead.

Fi walked to meet Katherine and Henrique but he had gone off with the dogs again with a friend of his and Katherine was enjoying her coffee in the early April sun. Fi hugged her friend and told her of her sound sleep, her phone calls to family and friends and finally to Carl. Katherine was equally as intrigued as Fi herself had been and asked questions about the potential date and about Carl that Fi could not answer. Katherine also asked about Fi and her sense of self and whether her emotional awareness and emotional intelligence were at a level to contend with dating again. The girls spoke for over an hour and Katherine, just like Julie, felt that Fi should, 'do it!' Fi decided she would ring Louise later and think on it overnight and let him have an answer when she felt the decision was right. One thing she did know was that she was feeling more 'excited' by the prospect, than 'daunted' by it!

Henrique returned with his friend Alejandro and the four of them enjoyed coffees and beers before heading back to the hotel for an afternoon snack and sharing each other's company. They rested a while in their rooms before Fi enjoyed a bath and changed for an evening out at a local tapas bar, where they enjoyed a wonderful food selection consisting of tapas dishes washed down with jugs of Sangria followed by their chosen desert of a tart, made with apple biscuits and cream. The welcome was warm, the food fabulous, the company was fantastic and the music provided by band with a Catalan, Rumba, Flamenca sound (rather like the Gypsy Kings) created an atmosphere in the packed restaurant that was jovial and happy and everybody was dancing and clapping when they played their more lively numbers. It really felt like a true taste of Spain for Fi with authentic Spanish cuisine, local people in a local (off the beaten track) restaurant with authentic music and plenty of the traditional Spanish drink to add to the mind-altering ambience! "Fabuloso mis amigos, fabuloso mis amigos," said Fi as she danced around to the music feeling just a little bit tipsy! It was another late night and the three friends sauntered home happy and giddy too, as they meandered through the streets to Katherine and Henrique's hotel.

The next morning Fi awoke just ever so slightly delicately! She took some painkillers and a glass of water for her headache and sat out enjoying the fabulous view of the castle and the reservoir. She chatted to her friend as they spent the morning perusing Katherine's box of photographs, which helped her to reconnect some more, with her friend's life. It was a lovely bonding opportunity for the girls and one that Fi cherished, as she asked herself how had they ever lost touch. She was so glad her friend had found her. After a lunch of traditional Spanish Omelette and salad made by Henrique, Fi retired to her room and phoned Louise. Louise was exactly the same as always when it came to affairs of the heart connected to her mother:

"I want what you want mum, as long as it is safe and you are happy, then go for it, AND practice what you

preach, trust your gut reactions! If your gut instincts are warning you, listen this time!"

Fi promised Louise she would listen to her gut, her heart and her daughter and she would keep her informed.

She then rang Carl but it went to voicemail:

Fi: "Hi Carl, it's Fi, I have pondered on your proposal and although I have questions to ask, I would like to meet your friend. Thanks Carl, bye for now."

That night Fi and her friends stayed in for a quiet meal enjoying Henrique's fabulous culinary skills, each other's company and some good quality wine. It was another lovely night and Fi said her goodnight earlier than the previous two evenings to catch up on her sleep. She was feeling very tired. When she had climbed into bed she checked her correspondence and replied to non business emails including one from Carl:

6th April 2014 17:36

Hello Fi, Be assured he is truly honoured that you agreed to a date and wonders if you would consider a diversion to Portugal before returning to the UK? Please let me know and he can get in touch with you directly. Please be reassured that he is an honest and honourable man. Respectfully. Carl.

Ohhh shit, she thought and texted Julie:

Fi: Ring me when you are free please. X

Julie rang straight away:

Fi: "Hi,"

Julie: "What's up?"

Fi: "He wants to know if I'd like to meet his friend in Portugal before I come back home?"

Julie: "Do it!"

Fi: "Jules! You know what I have been through!"

Julie: "Yes and this time I don't smell a rat, now stop behaving like a Fanny and get yourself gone!"

Fi: "Okay. I thought I was Dick?" (They laughed)

Julie: "Stop worrying, because I'm not!"

Fi: "Why aren't you worrying?"

Julie: "Don't know, my gut tells me it will all be okay,"

Fi: "Okay, I'll let you know how I go on. Bye Jules."

Julie: "Don't worry, bye."

The line went dead.

She emailed Carl:

6 April 2014 20:23

Hi Carl, after some thought. Sure, why not? Portugal sounds good. Please can you send me contact details for 'the mystery man' and can you pass my details onto him. Thanks. Fi.

She closed her eyes and tried to sleep but it eluded her for a while, as she dealt with one or two old ghosts, to satisfy herself they were not going to invade her sleep and turn into nightmares. She was fine. She was in a good place emotionally and physically. She was recovering nicely. She was happy. She was ready to try again.

Fi was first up the next day and she made a continental breakfast for her friends and left it under a cloth on the kitchen table and walked down to the reservoir with the dogs, it was a beautiful morning and she power walked her way around the banking with the dogs keeping up the pace with her. She relished the exercise and the fresh air and couldn't help wondering who the mystery man was! On the way back to the hotel she collected fresh bread and milk after sitting outside a cafe for a while and enjoying a chocolate and churro's treat and the awesomeness of the majestic castle in front of her, wondering what stories it had to tell. The hidden stories inside buildings fascinated Fi and she was inspired to make notes when she got back to the hotel. "Hola Henrique, Hola Katherine," she said as she stepped in through the kitchen doorway, to see her friends enjoying their breakfast. "Hola Fi," they both replied and she began to tell them about her walk and her treat and the inspiration that came to her from viewing the exterior of the medieval castle and off she went to her room to make notes, whilst it was fresh in her mind. When she returned to the kitchen, Henrique said, "Gracias Fi," and raised his eyebrows at her as she and Katherine burst out laughing again. It was such a silly joke but amusing nonetheless. Henrique kissed his wife and went off to the gym. The girls sat out on the verandah again chatting and drinking coffee when the doorbell rang and Katherine could be heard having a conversation with a male who then drove off in a vehicle. "Delivery for Ms. Fiora

Burton," said Katherine as she brought the parcel to Fi. "For me?" questioned Fi, as she took the parcel from her friend and looked at it in detail, acknowledging that there was no post-mark on it, indicating where it may have come from. The paper bore the logo of a famous Madrid department store. The parcel delivered by a driver, had had to be signed for. They both looked extremely puzzled. As she opened the parcel, Fi saw that it contained two separate smaller parcels. The first was a soft cream protective bag and she untied the string to reveal a leather-bound compact personal organizer in purple with a silver feather embossed on the front and the initials FB in the bottom right hand corner. She undid the fastening and opened the cover and it was clearly a brand new item complete with an address book, diary and notes section. The ribbon had been specifically positioned in the diary section and as Fi pulled the ribbon to open the page it revealed the date of 9 April 2014 marked with a cross and she looked at Katherine with an even more puzzled look. "2 days from now," she said. Finally Fi took a black bag from the main parcel and they both gasped open mouthed with startled eyes, as they saw the name of the jewellers. Inside was a box bearing the jewellers name again and as she snapped the lid open, she screamed, as Katherine said slowly, "OH! MY! GOD!" They were looking at a gold bangle watch with a diamond-studded face bearing the time 8 o'clock. Katherine disappeared for a few moments into the kitchen before she came back outside with bottle of wine and she sat down at the table and poured them both a glass. "What does it all mean?" asked Fi, "well who do you know who would buy you gifts like that?" asked Katherine, "nobody, absolutely nobody," replied Fi, "right so it's from 'the mystery man' then, do we agree?" Katherine questioned, before continuing, "You have a diary marked for 2 days' time, you have a watch set for

8pm," Katherine offered, before continuing again, "so you have the day and the time, so where is the place?" she asked. " I have no idea," said Fi. Fi checked her tablet and found she had an email from an unknown email address:

7 April 2014 15:30 Tmm@portugal.com

Dear Fi, You have a beautiful name by the way! By now you will have received some gifts and you will know the date and time of our first date. If these arrangements are okay with you I will have a driver collect you from your hotel at 11am on the 9 April and take you to the airport in Madrid where my helicopter will take you to Portugal, where a driver will take you to your hotel. The staff will be informed of arrangements later in the day to bring you to our date venue. I am really looking forward to meeting you and trust this all meets with your approval. Until we meet. My best wishes. TMM

Fi showed the mail to Katherine and discussed her 'alarm bells' of the vagueness of the email id. "Why the secretive aspect?" said Fi, "I'm a bit worried now?" she added. They discussed it some more and Fi decided to email TMM:

7 April 2014 16:00

Dear TMM, thank you for the items. I cannot possibly accept such lavish gifts from somebody I don't know. An unusual and intriguing start I feel. I have history with secrets and lies and need to know I will be safe. Fiora.

He replied immediately:

7 April 2014 16:03

Dear Fi, We can discuss the gifts further when we meet. I was merely having fun with you. The Mystery Man!

Next she emailed Carl:

7 April 2014 16:08

Dear Carl, I have had a very vague email and some rather extravagant gifts sent to me from my date. I do not even know YOU well enough to be absolutely reassured that my emotional and physical wellbeing are safe with HIM. I need reassurance. Fi

He replied immediately too:

7 April 2014 16:11

Hi Fi, You have my absolute assurance that you are completely safe. Carl

Finally she sent the text to Julie:

Fi: Hi Julie, I've received a very expensive watch with time set for 8pm, diary with page highlighted on 09.04.2014 and email signed with initials TMM to say he has his helicopter and car picking me up! Scared. Fi

Julie: Stop pissing about.

Fi: Deadly serious!

Julie: You're hilarious!

Fi: Deadly fucking serious!

Julie: OMFGG. Then stop being a 'Fanny,' get on that bleeding date and ask him has he got any brothers?

Fi: Ha, ha. Yes, Dick! We've officially swapped have we? You're Dick and I'm Fanny now?

Julie: Well you're bloody behaving like one! A diamond watch! I'd be lucky to get a bleeding duff watch!

Fi: I could be going on a date with Europe's most wanted criminal here and you're telling me to go for it? He could be any Tom, Dick or Harry?

Julie: Ha, ha, ha, laughing out loud, if that T stands for Tom we would be Tom, Dick and Fanny! Ha, ha, ha, ha.

Fi: I'm laughing now too!

Julie: Good. Have faith. Don't let that lying twastard spoil what might be and who the fuck is Bran with his crappy painting? A diamond watch! Now that is a fuckety, fuck, fuck, fuck off present! Get in on your wrist and smile!

Fi: Will do bestie! X

Fi felt reassured and spent to the rest of the day wondering who the hell wanted to meet her so much that he would consider spending £4,000 on a watch! There were definitely two people that weren't on the list of possibilities. So that left her with zero candidates in mind, she didn't have a clue.

The timings are in place but will they have the chemistry?

CHAPTER 17

Absolutamente incrível

Fi spent the following day in Madrid City with Katherine for two reasons. First to do the 'tourist tour' and second, she needed to do a big shop she had told her friend. "A big shop?" Katherine shrieked as she set off in a fit of giggles, (and as she had one of the most infectious laughs Fi had ever heard) she too joined in the raucous laughter. As they attempted to cross a very busy road in Madrid City, a Limousine slowed to let the girls' cross and Fi shrieked, "Ooh I wonder if that is the mystery man?" as they continued crossing the busy road and giggling like the school girls they once were, and Fi turned and cheekily waved to the car as it slowly moved away from them. "Anyway as I was saying before Mr. Limo interrupted me! I need to do a REALLY BIG SHOP! Like I have never 'shopped' before! What the hell do I wear on my body that matches the four grand beauty on my arm?" asked Fi. "Classy though Fi, whoever he is, he has got great taste" replied Katherine as she admired the timepiece on Fi's arm. "Don't worry, we'll find you something to compliment that, I have a plan!" she added as she made a call to her friend.

Katherine linked Fi's arm as they set about their tourist and shopping tasks, starting with a breakfast and coffee at the Real Cafe Bernabeu! "Football! YOU?" said Fi when she realised where they were going. "Hell no, this is for you, I know you're a football geek, I remember you going to the Manchester United matches after school!" she added. "Yes, that was to see the fit blokes in shorts, that I had on my bedroom wall and for no other reason!" laughed Fi. "I know nothing about the rules! I was once shown the offside rule with my handbags and I still didn't get it!" she laughed again, "well it's 'offside, always disallowed!' in our lounge," replied Katherine, "Henrique has to go to the bar for his football fix," she added. She laughed, as Fi replied, "I bet that really gets to him doesn't it? Having to go to the bar, with his mates, to watch football and drink beer, how tragic!" and they laughed some more. They sat at a table and ordered coffees whilst they perused the menu, "Regular coffee for me please," said Fi, as Katherine raised her eyebrows and asked, "what happened to the decaf queen?" "I need the hit, I am a bag of nerves with nearly two days to go," she said, "I'm making my debut tomorrow night, 8 o'clock kick off with a record crowd of two!" and they both burst out laughing. They enjoyed a light brunch as Fi was conscious that she did not want a bloated 'food baby' belly on display tomorrow night! Katherine took the obligatory 'fan outside football stadium' shots before they headed for their more serious cultural experience of shopping! "That's me and culture done for today, I'll have to do the touristy stuff another time!" said Fi, "I'm too nervous to concentrate on culture." " Well an excuse to come back and see us again," replied Katherine, "with the mystery man! Although I have a feeling you might be having a suite at a very different hotel next time," she added, smirking at her friend.

Katherine had a friend who was a fashion stylist, a creative executive for a fashion brand and a successful blogger, who had, to her credit, styled the odd famous person or two for video shoots and she was herself a very stylish woman. She had kindly agreed to help Fi and met the girls an hour later. After a quick beer in the midday sun they set off on their expedition, stopping first, at a high profile hair salon, where one of their top stylists set to work on Fi. It was a fabulous head pampering experience and 2 hours later when Fi finally presented herself to Katherine and Sara, they were astounded with the transformation of the amazing haircut! She had worn her hair at shoulder length for a few years now and as she exited the salon with a staggeringly and radically different new style, they were literally gob smacked. Fi felt absolutely fabulous. The girls all continued shrieking as they made their way to the nail salon and whilst Fi was being pampered with a manicure and pedicure session, the other two went off to choose clothes and shoe options for her to try on. This is all so surreal she said to herself as she relaxed, enjoying a boiled water and lemon drink as she was having her hands and feet soaked, scrubbed and massaged. She then had her nails filed, painted and sealed with a 'diamond strength' top coat, "No way do I want chipped nails tomorrow," she told the young man who was completing her treatment! "No way, Signora," he laughed as he finished her treatment and she sat for a moment admiring her matching fingers and toes. Nothing prettier to complete a woman's outfit, she thought, whether it was a naked outfit, a lingerie outfit or a fully clothed outfit, a good 'mani, pedi combo' always completed the look! Fi met her friends in the famous Madrid department store. Now Fi had been to the famous London department store on one occasion and had bought the cheapest item in the store, just so she could get an iconic carrier bag! (She was only 17 at the time). Fi had been to the famous department store in Paris on occasions and had bought a designer suit and handbag (well actually, they were bought for her) and she had been to Galleria Vittorio Emanuelle 11 in Milan (probably the world's best covered shopping experience) and bought designer sunglasses and a handbag too, (well actually, once again had had them bought for her by the same man from the Paris trip!) so she had an idea what to expect from this renowned Madrid department store. She made her way to the women's wear floor and she was shown to a fitting room where her friends were waiting for her. She giggled as she walked in to meet them, "I feel like Julia Roberts," she said. "Yes, meets Sex in The City!" said Sara, "You're meeting 'Mr. 'Big' Mystery Man' tomorrow!" and they laughed as Fi did her own version of the iconic Julie Roberts line, 'error, humungous error', holding her bags aloft as she did so before then morphing into her version of Carrie, "I like my money where I can access it quickly, hanging in my wardrobe!" and they all collapsed laughing as the assistant glared disapprovingly at them all. "Whoops, sorry," said Fi, "let's get serious now," she said to her friends, as she raised her eyebrows and went into the changing rooms. As she tried on all the range of outfits her friends had chosen for her, they went through a range of, "yes, no, maybe's, too titty, too tarty," and a lot of giggling for the next hour or so before she eventually settled on a 'WOW' as she emerged from the changing room wearing an off white jump suit, by her all-time favourite designer, from his spring summer 2014 collection. If he was good enough for Madonna, then he was certainly good enough for her, she had adored his designs for years and the chosen outfit was indeed WOW as the fabric and her body simply spoke to each other. It was light, delicate, sophisticated, flowing and damn sexy. The lightness and flow of the fabric meant that it sat delicately at her ankles, caressing her silver, lattice effect, stiletto heeled, ankle shoe boots. The fabric grabbed her backside, as she sashayed the length of the changing rooms with her hands in her pockets and the matching fabric buckle belt snitched at her slim waist. It was a sleeveless out-fit, with a biker jacket style off centre zip fastening and a convertible style collar, with patch pockets and silver adornments of studs and buttons on the front. It could be worn as provocatively or modestly as she liked, depending on where she chose to stop the zip! It WAS gorgeous, she LOOKED gorgeous in it, she FELT gorgeous in it and it was a GORGEOUS price too but she didn't care as it would be in her wardrobe for years, she knew that for sure! She had no idea who she was meeting, what he looked like, what his dress style was like, whether he was in fact stylish at all (which freaked her out as she pondered that thought, as she had to have a stylish man, she just had to!) and she didn't know where she was going for her date and therefore she felt this outfit hit all possibilities, an intimate dinner, a bar, dancing, or all three! She loved it for its simple, yet elegant look and the girls agreed that she looked completely wow, with her new hair and the tangerine nails added to a great look. "Do you feel nice in it Fi?" asked Katherine, "I do," she replied, before continuing, "it caresses my body, it feels luscious and drapey!" she said, "droopy!" laughed Katherine deliberately misquoting Fi, "he bloody won't be when he sees you in that!" and they all collapsed laughing again, much to the disapproval of the sales assistant. Fi selected a very fine jersey hooded jacket to wear over her shoulders and protect her from the evening chill, and she finished the look with a small tangerine clutch bag with an un- usual chain and bangle handle. Perfect. She gulped as she paid the huge bill with her credit card and as they left the store to go for early evening drinks, she was on a high at the prospect of dating somebody decent. Let's hope he is decent she thought, as the ghosts of past disasters, started to creep out of their cupboards and dance their dance of doubts into her mind, but she quickly slammed the door shut in their faces as she dragged the girls into the first bar she saw. It was called 'Hola' and it was a really cool bar

Fi thought as they entered. It was subtly decorated with a Spanish feel to the decor with subdued lighting and candles and it was a foodie place too, which was good because they were all starving and they very quickly found seats and ordered food and beers. It was clearly a very popular bar and according to Sara served the greatest cocktails too and so the girls decided they would be hitting the cocktails list, post food! There was music playing in the background which added to the overall mood and to Fi's hyper excited state, as she checked her watch and realised that in 26 hours' time she would be meeting the mystery man. "To Fi and the mystery that is to come!" said Katherine as she lifted her bottle of beer in the air and the other two chinked bottles with her as Fi replied, "thanks guys, have to say, I am terrified, the nearer it is getting," "understandable," said Katherine. Fi pondered before saying, "Everything is a mystery to me, who is he? What does he look like? What does he do? How has he admired me from afar for a while without me knowing him? Where are we meeting? Why such expensive gifts? Is he a pretentious prick? I've got so many questions and nobody to answer them and a guy who I don't really know, asking me to trust his judgement and by tomorrow evening I am just going to be a complete wreck!" she laughed nervously. "Does the fact he has money intimidate you?" asked Sara, "not at all, I am me and I have been out with a money guy with his own aircraft and all the trimmings before, it's down to who they are as people at the end of the day, that's all that matters. Whether we are attracted to each other warts and all and for me that is looks, personality and style and it doesn't take money to be any of those three things, which individually are all huge umbrellas to stand under but together I know that is a big ask of one man but that's what I want, somebody who doesn't lie the minute they open their mouth, somebody who makes me laugh, somebody with compassion and soul, somebody who is interested and interesting, has morals and manners, has integrity, is a stylish, fashionable man with good self care, smells divine, has a smile to die for, you don't need money for any of that!" replied Fi before Katherine added "whoosh, that's quite a list," "yes but you take that list Katherine and tick off the ones that apply to Henrique and I bet it is nearly all of them, you probably have all that in your man without even realising it," Fi added before she sipped her drink and continued, "whereas, I have had to compile that list in my head because I am NOT settling for anything less, I am done with having less than, now it's time for more than." Katherine gripped her friends forearm in a show of comfort to her friend, "I used to hate it when I was on the dating sites and guys would say they wanted a woman who didn't take herself too seriously. EXCUSE ME! Are you kidding me? I have not taken myself seriously enough too many times now and FROM HERE ON IN, I am taking myself very seriously indeed and if you don't tick all the boxes, you're getting deleted into that trash bin and no amount of money is going to guarantee getting what I want and what I need, so to answer your question, money is nothing to do with it and it does not intimidate me in the slightest, absolutely not at all." Her friends clapped and Fi smiled, but it was a sad, forced smile, because inside, at that very moment, she wasn't smiling. She was sad at the wasted years spent on people who didn't deserve her time and she didn't want anybody who didn't want her exactly as she was. He had a lot to live up to, whoever he was and he certainly had many advantages over her. He knew what she looked like and a fair amount of other stuff about her too, by the sounds of it, if he had admired her from afar for a while! He was able to imagine tomorrow night in so much detail and yet she had absolutely no idea and that was hugely frustrating and so nerve wracking. She was beginning to regret agreeing to the date as her favourite Brandy Alexander cocktail took effect. The girls chatted about possibilities and Katherine asked, "is he young, is he old?" and they laughed, before teasing her, "Fi's getting a Sugar Daddy!" which had them all giggling, "ERR, no thank you, I want longevity!" and she smirked because she just knew Katherine's reply before it even came out of her mouth. "I bet you bloody do!" giggled her friend and they all laughed and carried on discussing the possible options of friends, work colleagues, and a number of other ridiculous options which had them laughing hysterically but it was no use, Fi was on the merry go round of 'no idea' and it was exciting, frustrating and damn scary all at the same time.

Fi and Katherine said their goodbyes to Sara and Fi promised to send pictures and news of the evening and the mystery man too and they then made their way home to see Henrique. Henrique greeted them by babbling away in Spanish at his astonishment at the transformation of 'Miss Fi!' as he had affectionately called her these past few days, "Oh, Dios mío, increíble, increíble, te ves fabulosa, fabuloso, sensacional, hombre misterioso se sobresaltó por ti, hermosa señorita Fi" which Fi understood to include, incredible, fabulous, beautiful, sensational and she was really very appreciative of the male perspective on her new look. As the clocked ticked towards tomorrow and the date was getting nearer, Fi felt the huge pressure of the event that was looming and was surprised at how nauseous she was feeling. Her heart was literally in her proverbial Salford gob! The three friends whiled away the next hour or so chatting, drinking chocolate, dunking Churro's and laughing, really laughing and Fi went off to bed very content and thankful to have rekindled this long lost friendship, that now had a new beginning.

The next morning she should have awoke feeling refreshed, happy, alive and full of hope but she didn't, she woke up feeling un-refreshed, nervous, scared and feeling sick! These were all symptoms of nervous energy commonly known in her language as 'cacking it!' She showered and dressed in her 'travelling uniform' jeans, shirt, v neck jumper and converse combo, she dried her hair, admiring her new 'do', grabbed her jacket and headed off out of the door with the dogs in tow. She walked. Oh boy did she walk! She walked with such power around that reservoir like she hadn't walked in months of her going to the gym! She was breathless mind you and she could feel her heart doing it's 'miss beating, thingymajig dance' BUT she needed to push herself and dispel some of this nervous energy. She used the time to think things through again and question how this had all come about, was she safe? What safeguards were in place with her friends for her safety if things weren't right? As doubts started to creep into her head, she put her headphones on, turned her music on, cranked it up loud and sang along to the shuffle selection of Christina Perri's 'I believe' and she knew that beauty would indeed emerge from her scars. She found the repetitive chorus at the end of the song reminded her that this was indeed her beginning and she realised that she didn't have to put this tune on repeat, the message in the chorus was loud and clear. She got back to Katherine and Henrique's place with moments to spare before a car arrived and she and Katherine just gawped in awe as Fi laughed, a nervous laugh but a laugh nonetheless! The driver emerged from the driver's side of the vehicle and opened a rear passenger door for Fi, "Bueno señora mañana," he said as he took her bags and placed them carefully in the boot of the car, "Buenos días," she replied to the driver as she hugged her friends. As Katherine held her friend tight, she said, "Go and meet your Mr. Big!" and they both laughed, knowing the innuendo Katherine had let slip. Fi sat in the rear of the vehicle as it drove off and as she looked out of the window waving back at her friends, she couldn't quite believe what she was about to do.

They arrived at Torrejon Airport in Madrid, which Fi assumed must be for private aviation and she was quickly processed through to her flight to Portugal. She was in awe of the whole situation, this was a crazy making scenario, beyond anything she had ever experienced. This really was Vivian and Carrie territory! The flight was a new experience for Fi in terms of aviation journeys for a couple of reasons, she had never been in a helicopter and she found that the journey resembled a roller coaster ride, that added to a never ending threat of the nausea developing into a sick bag episode at any moment and she had certainly never been transported to a date in a helicopter and that too was vomit inducing, the nearer it got to meeting the mystery man! She was glad when they landed and she was on terra firma.

She was processed through passport control and a driver met her saying, "Boa tarde Ms Burton," which she assumed must mean good afternoon and hoping it did she replied, "boa tarde," and smiled at the gentleman. He took her bags for her and walked her over to a big, 'dock off, massive, humungous', Limousine! 'Jesus,' she thought, this is too scary! She really did feel sick and it must have shown as the driver opened a rear passenger door for her and asked if she would like water, as he opened the on-board fridge and she laughed as she took the ice cold drink and said, “I’d prefer a Gin and Tonic,” and he smiled in response. She took deep breaths, trying to feel better as the vehicle began to drive off, but it wasn’t helping, she really did feel faint and she put her head down on the empty seat next to her to ‘ease the quease’ as she called it! She realised she was probably dehydrated from last night’s alcohol having had neither food nor drink so far today. She needed to eat, drink and rest before her play! Fi was prone to migraines when she was this nervous and she was anxious that she might have triggered one! She drifted from nausea to cat napping for an unknown amount of time, that seemed like forever, before she became aware that the vehicle had stopped and as she lifted her head slowly off the seat, she realised that they were in an underground car park. “Where are we?” she asked, trying to sound calm (but now in need of a bathroom) because she really was feeling sick, as panic was now added to her mix of emotions! “We are at the hotel madam but there is building work in the entrance and foyer and so the staff will show you straight up to your room,” he replied, as a young man in uniform came with a luggage trolley, collected her bags from the boot of the car and asked her to follow him. She took deep breaths as she tentatively followed him through what seemed like corridors of any old building and out into a lavish and roomy reception area where she was shown straight to the lift. She didn’t notice what floor he pressed, as she was still too busy closing her eyes and taking deep breaths to stop herself feeling sick but when the lift stopped and as the bell boy held the door for Fi to alight, she noticed that there was a single door at the end of the corridor. The young man used an electronic key to let her in and she gasped in awe at the site in front of her. She had to be in the presidential suite of somewhere, it was enough to snap her out of her nausea, it was unbelievable and as she gazed around the room, she was suddenly aware that she was being spoken to. "Oh, I am so sorry," she said to the bell boy, "could you repeat that please," and he told her where she could find all the gadgets for all the gadgets! The gadgets being, the media and music devices, the safe, the wifi, the lights and electronic blinds and he showed her how to operate the Jacuzzi bath too, which was enormous and big enough for a football team. Fi thanked him and gave him a substantial tip (by her standards anyway) and she sat down on one of the lavish settees to take it all in, it was quite overwhelming there was no other word for it. Every inch of space took her breath away with the lavishness of it all. It was magnificent with a capital M. Fi went into the bedroom and she was stunned yet again at the size of both the room and of the bouquet of flowers lying on her bed. They were staggering beautiful. She noticed there was a card attached to them, tied with colour contrasting ribbon and Fi untied it and read the message: Dear Fi, hopefully you had a pleasant journey. Until we meet. TMM. Also contained in the envelope was a booklet naming all the unusual flowers, rather like a box of chocolates information card, there were Cafe au Lait Dahlias, Lemon Leaves, Succulents, Hypericum Berries, Hybrid Ranuculus, Roses (four types), Gloriosa Lillies and Galax. She lay back and smelt the scent and closed her eyes trying for the life of her, to glean an insight into who the hell this man could possibly be. He was clearly very rich but she was so nervous in case he was a 'Costa del boy made good' type of guy! 'Please no' she thought to herself as she realised she was terrified now and she had five hours to go until all would be revealed. She rang room service and ordered a cured ham salad, sparkling mineral water and lemon tea. She then ran a bath, choosing bath salts and a bubble bath combination which immediately fragranced the rooms with the aromas of ginger lily and sea moss and she couldn't wait to tease away some of the tension she was feeling. She wished the time to meet him were closer and get it over and done with. Room Service called and served her food, which she devoured, rather than savouring, due to her immense hunger and she then climbed into her bath where she was able to watch a relaxing music channel on the TV, soak away her stress and have a massage from the multi, side, back and feet jets, which she set on spa mode for the ultimate bathing treat. Fi lay and pondered everything, AGAIN and so she decided she needed her friend and rang Julie, putting the phone on speaker, as she discussed her anxieties yet again. She was going over old ground and repeating herself regarding her fears and they both agreed that as she was now there in Portugal, it would either be okay or it wouldn't, end of, and that she could walk simply away if it wasn't okay and that in a few hours' time, she would finally know. Julie wished her friend well and asked her to text to let her know she was all right, which was their usual modus operandi when Fi went on a date. Fi promised she would as she climbed out of the bath, wrapped herself in her robe and went to lie of the bed. She read her book for a while before falling asleep only to be woken with a start to hear the bedside telephone ringing. When she answered, "Hello," a voice said, "good evening Ms. Burton, this is reception calling and just to let you know that a member of staff will collect you from your room at 7:50 this evening," "Thank you for calling," replied Fi. She looked at her watch and discovered that she had one hour and twenty minutes to go. She got up and poured herself a Gin and Tonic before attempting to open the outside shutters but the remote control wasn't working, either that, or she really was crap with technology, 'I was only wanting to check the view,' she thought. She still needed to chill as she was bordering on having a panic attack and so she put her happy tunes on her playlist and of course loud (well loudish, she didn't want to disturb other guests) and she sang and she danced a little while doing her hair and makeup (both of which she hated, as you do, when you're a girl getting ready and a special date is looming!). She dressed in her new underwear, (but not the presents, they would never be worn, they were somebody else's presents) her all time favourite perfume, (and not where she wanted to be kissed, nobody would be kissing her anywhere intimate for a while yet!) her jewellery, (but not the gifted watch, she was quite content to wear her own understated delicate silver bracelet watch with a tiny diamond at the top of the face) her silver bangles, including her birthday collection from her friends, which formed a beautiful collection on her arm. She was just about to step into her outfit when there was a knock on the door, 'oh bollocks, they are early,' she thought as she grabbed her robe and went to unlock and open her door and there stood a member of staff with a gift wrapped parcel, "For you Ms. Burton," he said, "thank you," she replied nervously, as she took it from him, before closing the door. 'Oh, Jesus,' she thought to herself, 'what now?' as she wondered if this was some needy nerd with shed loads of money trying to impress her, because she really wasn't in the mood, she was nervous and she was angry with him now too. She didn't have a clue who he was, the mystery had been going on for a few days, exaggerated gifts, humungous flowers, posh cars, helicopters, what the FUCK am I doing?' she asked herself as she then said aloud, "OK, I get it, you've got money!" and as she threw the gift on the bed she said, "AND! So what?" She felt really annoyed and it crossed her mind to sack it. She felt, 'crowded' with all this 'STUFF.' 'Who gives a shit what you have and haven't got, let me meet you first and decide for myself!' She thought. Fi picked up her drink and went and sat down in the lounge area but she was soon up on her feet again, pacing the floor. She needed a distraction and once she tried the remote for the shutters but still, she couldn't get them to open. "Bollocks," she said, as she threw the remote onto the chair in her temper. She went and sat on her bed again and put her meditation playlist on and took some deep breaths for a few minutes. She felt a little better and picked up the gift and read the card attached, 'you have the when, this is the where for you to wear?' "What the fuck?" she said aloud and rang Julie:

Fi: "Hi, it's me!"

Julie: "What's up?" (As she heard the panic in her friend's voice)

Fi: "I've just got another present with a clue written on a card, of where I am going!"

Julie: "What is it?"

Fi: "No idea, I haven't even opened it, I just feel annoyed, like he is just shoving his money in my face, so fucking what if he's got money!"

Julie: "You're sounding 'pissy' now, open it!"

So she did (giving her friend a running commentary as she did so and inside was a box from a company called Coordinates Collection. When she lifted the lid off the unusual box, she found a silver bangle with a set of numbers and letters on it. She did not have a clue what it meant.

Fi: "What the hell does that mean?"

Julie: "Well I vaguely remember using a compass and doing coordinates in the girl guides to find places!"

Fi: "Are you being serious? I know I'm wearing a jumpsuit but I'm not going on fucking Treasure Hunt!" and they set off laughing, realising Fi's reference to the iconic television programme of years gone by.

Fi: "Julie, it's NOT funny! Somebody is coming for me in five minutes and I have not got a clue what to do with the set of numbers and letters and he has sent some mumbo-frigging-jumbo card telling me this is the where?" They both giggled again, it was getting ridiculous now, thought Fi.

Julie: "Yes Fanny! Diary: The date. Watch: The time. Bracelet with coordinates: The where! Google it!"

Fi: "What? I'll google HIM! He'll be getting a kick in his Googles. I'm going on a date not an expedition! For fuck's sake! (And they laughed again) **Julie I am panicking now, shit, shit, the door, the door, I've got to go, I'm not even dressed, shit, I'm terrified!"**

Julie: "You'll be fine, you've got 10 seconds left" (and they burst out laughing again as Julie began the countdown) **10, 9, 8, 7"** (still laughing)

Fi: "Stop making me laugh, you're gonna make me wee! I'm going."

She pressed end call and threw her phone on the bed. She went to the door and opened it a touch saying, "5 minutes, I'll be 5 minutes!" She struggled into her outfit, tripping and skipping as she tried to step into it in the most inelegant way, 'shit, shite, bollocks,' she thought as she struggled with the zip, the belt and the shoes. As she grabbed her bag, scrunched her hair and looked in the mirror one last time, she really loved the look, it was amazing and she couldn't help smiling to herself, thinking of one woman in particular who would kill for that jumpsuit! She opened the door and said, 'I'm so sorry," to the gentleman stood waiting and as he escorted her down the corridor she suddenly remembered something, "Shit," she said before putting her hand to her mouth! "I'm so sorry," she added, "I have forgotten something important," and she turned and ran back down the corridor and as she got to her room she realised she had walked out without her key, "Oh fuck!!!!" she said, as she ran back down to the man waiting for her, she asked him with some urgency, "Do you have a key to my room?" and he as he escorted her back up the corridor, she noticed a wry smile on his face as he took what she assumed was a master key from his pocket and opened the door for her. She ran in, grabbed her new bangle and slammed in on her wrist with her collection and took a deep breath as she emerged from her room and began her journey to meet the mystery man. Fi was escorted into the lift and the gentleman said, "Whoops," as he pressed R, immediately followed by G and Fi was the one now wearing the wry smile, wondering what the hell R stood for as they began to go upwards in the lift but as the door opened she soon realised. In front of her was the rooftop of the hotel. Wow. The man gestured to her to emerge and she looked at him and said, "I thought we were going to the ground floor?" "I jested," he said and smiled. She stepped out of the lift as he held the door and as she turned to look at the man with a puzzled look on her face, the lift doors closed and he disappeared, smiling. There was nobody else visible. She gingerly stepped away from the lift area and took tentative steps along the wooden floor towards a large bright but elegantly lit space. There were giant wooden troughs to her right containing established bamboo, which were there to screen the view and she suspected, the weather, as she heard the rustle of the breeze kissing the bamboo. She was stood on an upper balcony area with a glass balustrade. There were huge sumptuous cushions on the low level seating with mirrored top tables, reflecting the light coming from candles of varying types, with the sensual oil aromas wafting from them and filling the air. Additional ambience was provided by giant candles in huge lattice and bird-cage style candle holders. She could see a large green space of mature trees in the process of their early spring foliage and glorious blossoms, out in front of her and in the far distance she could see the sea, cushioned between the left and right land masses lit against the evening sky. It was a beautiful site. She walked towards the end of the upper decked balcony and as she descended the stairs to the main bar area, she thought it looked familiar to her. There was a central white circular bar with illuminated glass panelling adding to the evening ambience, with high white circular bar stools surrounding it, gigantic plant pots containing mature palm trees were also illuminated, adding to the atmosphere of softness as she heard the gentle sound of the breeze, mixing with the soft music which she recognised immediately as Air, Ce matin la. It was one of her favourites and it always evoked feelings of 'a journey' whenever she heard it and as she turned around to look towards the upper decking she immediately recognised two things, the tiled wall behind the man who was sat in front of it! She was at The Angels Bar and Carl was sat on the low level chairs with two drinks on the table in front of him. She stood and stared at him as he smiled a beautiful smile at her. Fi lifted her right hand to her mouth and bit her finger to stop herself from crying as Carl walked over to the steps and walked down them towards her. He attempted to take her hand and she pulled it away saying in a quivering voice, as she fought back tears, "Carl, you are married, I cannot be here," and she turned to walk away. He gently took her arms and held them whilst looking into her eyes, as he replied, "Fi, I am not married, my wife died of Leukaemia five years ago" she gulped and asked, "then who was that woman I saw you with in Bologna?" He smiled and said, that is my Sister-in-law, she is my wife's sister and she has been a huge part of my life and that of my children since Maria died. I have needed her so much and she is always there. The children are all moving on in their own journeys now and it is my turn to continue on mine," he said. "Come and sit down," he added, as he took her hand and took the steps with her to the upper decked area. "Before we have our date if you agree to it, I have to say, absolutamente incrível," he said, before continuing, "sorry, habit, bilingual mode coming into play, I'm sorry, I said, absolutely amazing, you really do look amazing, what a transformation!" She smiled but inside she felt quite sad as she took a seat, "Carl, do you have any other secrets? Because this is an all too familiar scenario for me, secrets and lies at the beginning!" before adding, "and in all honesty, for me, secrets are just lying by omission, which is another strand to the lying definition for me." He sighed and said, "I have people I want you to meet today before we go any further and everything will all make sense to you," he said before adding, "and then it is all yours to decide." She felt sick inside, what the hell was he going to reveal now. He walked to a doorway and she saw him gesture, as if beckoning somebody to come to him and then she heard footsteps and watched four people walk towards them as she felt the waves of shock, confusion and sheer terror all battle a storm inside her body and her head. There in front of her were Julie, the old gentleman

William Carter, Pedro Cruz and another man whom she had no recollection of ever having met before. Carl took her hand and cupped it in between both of his hands to stop her from shaking, as Fi caught Julie's eye and her friend winked at her and mouthed, 'It's okay'. Carl said, I would like you to meet once again, my father William Carter (Mendes) or Bill to you," and he put his hand on his Father's shoulder adding, "Dad, Fi, Fi, Bill", I am Carlos Carter Mendes or Carl Carter, (Mendes is my Mothers name), he said, as he touched his own chest, "this is Pedro Cruz my cousin and business partner (Mr. Antique)" and he shook his cousin's hand too, "Pedro, Fi, Fi, Pedro," and this is his partner Luis Pinto and again he took the man's hand and shook it, "Luis, Fi, Fi, Luis" before finally introducing Julie by saying, "and this of course is Julie Sullivan (as he kissed her on each cheek) and she knows everything, I have involved her all along, since I decided that I would like to ask you on a date and she is also here for your safety and reassurance, which is paramount to all of us here tonight, after what you have experienced." Fi was visibly shaking and she could not yet get to grips with all the connections and how this was even possible. She walked over to the elder gentleman and said, "Hello Bill," and he hugged her and she sighed before smiling at him, next she took Mr. Antiques hand and she shook it before hugging him and kissing him on both cheeks, saying, "Hello Mr. Antique, at last we meet and yes you really are as gorgeous in the flesh, as in your images" and he laughed, a loud but friendly laugh, just as she had imagined he might, as he said, "it is so lovely to meet you Fi but you and I could never have fallen in love online or otherwise because I was already in love and this is my partner Luis," and he gestured towards the man stood next to him. Fi held out her hand and then hugged Luis before kissing him on both cheeks too and saying to him, "You are a lucky man," and he and Pedro laughed, as they understood her joke! Next in line was Julie and as she saw her friend, they held hands and Julie said, "It's okay, honestly Fi, it really is okay," and as she hugged her friend, a tear rolled down Fi's cheek as she turned to face the others and said, "now can somebody please explain to me what the hell is going on?" Everybody laughed at her bolshiness and Carl said, "Well I can do that with everybody present or I can do it in private as we continue our private date, if that is what you chose, it is up to you Fi!" She laughed and replied, "Am I the last to know again! This better be the last 'crazy' I am going to have to experience, no more, please, I cannot take anymore!" she said firmly and everybody laughed with her before she added, "I would like to have my private date now please," and everybody hugged and said their goodbyes and Julie reassured her friend once again that it was all okay and that she would see her tomorrow. They all waved to each other as the four of them walked into the hotel to leave Fi and Carl to their date.

Fi took a couple of deep breaths before slipping on her jacket as the night chill was now emerging and she took a seat next to Carl on the sofa and felt the warmth of the overhead lamps comforting her chilled soul. She sipped at her drink, which was her favourite Gin and Tonic and it was exactly how she liked it. "Cheers," she said to Carl, "now PLEASE, tell me the story!"

Now it was Carl's turn to take a deep breath. "Well," he said, as he relayed the story of how it began for him when he was having dinner one night with his children over at their Uncle Pedro and Luis's house. Pedro showed him a letter he had received from England that day, from yet another woman, claiming to have been scammed on a dating site using his images. He told him that he gets them all the time but that this particular one he found humorous and captivating, in that she was a writer and aspects of his career involve writing too. Pedro showed Carl her Facebook page and Carl had thought she was a beautiful woman but that was it. They had dinner and continued on with their family evening. A few weeks later he was over in the UK for business and pleasure and whilst he was visiting his father in Bowness, he happened to be on his boat on Lake Windermere one day and he saw a woman sat alone at a cafe on the edge of the lake. He admitted that he had a taken a peek at her, through his binoculars and saw a beautiful woman with quite a sad face, sat drinking alone and he didn't know why but thought that she looked familiar. Later that day he went to meet his father for their early evening glass of whiskey in the Old England Hotel, when a woman literally bumped into him as he was entering the hotel and she was exiting. He knew it was the same woman he had seen on the lakeside a couple of hours before. He continued his evening with his father as he told him all about his afternoon tea with this beautiful charming woman and of their conversation of ghosts and art. A few weeks later when he was visiting his father in his art studio, he discovered there was an open image of a side profile of a woman's face displayed on his Father's desktop computer and he recognised her immediately as the woman from the lakeside, who had bumped into him in the hotel foyer. He jokingly asked his father if he had a new woman and his father informed him that her name was Fi and she was the charming woman he had shared an afternoon tea with. He noticed his father had emailed her. A few days later he had a shared link from his Facebook friend Lisa who was a marketing expert. A Facebook friend of hers was initiating a new 'first' project and was interested in contacting a first time publisher. Upon investigating the woman's Facebook page further he suddenly realised that she was Fi, his father's art subject. He contacted her and through her own selection process she had chosen to work with him on her first book. When Carl had later travelled over to the UK with Pedro, to show him their publishing venture HQ in Salford, he had introduced him to some of the new clients work already underway, in the various aspects of the business. Amongst them were the illustrations for Fiora Burton's first book and having recognised the unusual name, Pedro had pointed out it was the same name as the woman who had written to him, who been scammed on the dating web site. They had checked Fi Burton's Facebook page again and Pedro confirmed to his cousin, that it was definitely Fi. What an incredible set of circumstances and coincidences had been in place to create this unbelievable tale. Carl knew that he really liked her and he had been contemplating asking her out on a date but when he realised who she really was and being aware of brief details of the complicated recent events in her personal life that she had chosen to share with him, he knew she was far too fragile and that she needed time, respect and space and so he had given her that. He had decided to speak to Julie in confidence at Fi's event in the Copper room, to ascertain if Fi was ready to begin another relationship and how he could approach it with Fi's best interests at heart, whilst ensuring he 'protected' her heart. He had chosen to get her to The Angels Bar as a surprise, as he was now aware through Julie and Pedro of the significance of the place to her and he also wanted to get her to Portugal without her suspecting anything. He wanted surprise, he wanted intrigue, he wanted fun, he wanted suspense, he wanted excitement and he wanted romance and he had to keep it a mystery and so he had created the TMM email address and contacted her. "Who is TMM?" Fi asked, "The Mystery Man, TMM is me!" he laughed and she joined in with the laughter too, finally realising the simplicity of the clue!

"Why could you not have just asked me face to face for a date?" Fi asked. He paused before replying, "Because it is such a bizarre and yet beautiful story that has literally come full circle, that I wanted all the characters to have a surprise part to play in our beginning, if that is what you want this to be, our beginning!" She paused before she eventually nodded and let the tears slowly descend, as she asked herself could she really try again? Could she trust this man because she felt that she really was running out of people she could trust. Her circle was small and tightly knitted together for a reason, she had cast off the crap from her life and she would always be very selective about who was allowed into her world from now on. Carl took her hands and lifted her off her seat and took her over to see and absorb the magnificent sea view, in the darkened horizon, with the twinkling lights of the properties in the distance, the reflection of the moon upon the sea and with the gentle breeze embracing them, he held her while she cried, "no more Carl, no more, I would not survive anymore pain in my heart!" she said, as she shook her head and the silent tears dripped onto her outfit, seeping into the fabric. He took her face in his hands and looking into her eyes he said, "If you want this Fi, then I promise you, that if you care to take the 'Do not disturb' sign off your heart, it will never feel pain again."

He kissed away her tears, before very gently finding her lips and giving her a single tender kiss.

The End.

Fi became Mrs. Carlos Carter Mendes 12 months later and amongst their wedding gifts were two paintings from Bill Carter, one, a side profile painting from the image taken in the Old England Hotel in Bowness and the other was her copy of the Jack Vettriano painting, which was now complete, she really was, 'Dancing to the end of love' just like the couple in the original image by the great man himself. There she was in the painting, in the arms of her very own Mr. Tuxedo.

Fi had left Robert in Devon knowing that she would be dealing with boulders of grief, as she attempted to cross the almost nigh impossible canyon of emotions now facing her but little did she know, that the boulders would continue to rain upon her as she attempted to cross the canyon alone. Yet here she was two years later, having taken on the might of that emotional journey, sat in a place called Boulders Beach, with her new husband watching some of nature's wonders. As they sat together, facing the ocean and watching the penguins, they had their arms around each other, heads touching, not needing to speak. Not only had she survived by inviting Karma into her world, simply by being herself, (if you live your life the right way, the universe listens, she pondered) but she could finally acknowledge

that she was on her final journey of love with Carl and she knew that she could toss the 'do not disturb, healing in progress' sign from her heart, into the ocean. As she looked into her husband's eyes, she knew she had found, her long lost trust in love and that this beautiful man sitting beside her, would make sure that the only sign hanging on her heart from now on, read, 'healed with love.'

Dedication:

This novel is a story of survival for women.

When your heart has been shredded and you are left to pick yourself up to recover from lies, betrayal, trauma, emotional and financial abuse, (to name just a few of the list of effects) bestowed upon us by partners who chose to be unfaithful and betray us, be it in reality or online, I just want you to know you WILL survive, you CAN do it.

It takes the seconds which seem like they are as long as a day, to eventually turn into manageable minutes, that then become a goal of an hour, followed by aiming to survive the never ending days and nights, when you don't want daytime to come and you cannot wait for night time to fall once more, to allow you the peace of knowing you have survived another day. Believe me, you do have it in you. Dig deep and do what is required to get through those seconds, minutes, hours and days. It could be screaming as loud as you can, it could be dancing and singing like nobody can see or hear you, it could be power walking like you have batteries inside you, refusing to die, it could be a peaceful soak in the bath, it could be crying until you can cry no more, it could be grabbing precious time with your children, it could be choosing to drink a fruit drink and eat a yoghurt because that's all you can face eating, it could be writing in your journal, explaining how you feel about those who chose to hurt you, it could be snatched moments of laughing with your friends until the tears roll down your legs. Whatever it is that helps you. Do it.

Just believe. Have faith in yourself, trust your craziness, trust your recovery, trust your relapses, trust that you are doing great, as you are able to tick off another day in your head, knowing that your life is going to be so much more fulfilled without having somebody difficult in it, who just did not deserve to be there. I am a firm believer in Karma and the law of attraction. Whilst sitting in my garden watching the recent eclipse, it made me realise the level of the precision of the alignments of the planets, which brought such a spectacle of nature and how infrequently that alignment happens. I believe our lives are also about precision and alignment and that we are meant to be on the journey we are on and that better things are coming our way.

Make sure that you have taken the time to ask yourself what you have learnt from the nightmare you have just emerged from first. There was a lesson to learn. Make sure you understand what it was and prevent yourself from reliving the nightmare.

Don't let somebody who chose to walk out on your dreams let you believe that your dreams are over. Create a new dream, a new goal. What have you always, always wanted to do? Go out there and do it. Right now. Start your dream machine.

Be good to YOU, all day, every day and goodness will come your way. Only you can mend you. Not your doctor, not your friends, not your family, not your work colleagues, not your neighbours and not your children. They might all want to be there for some of the journey, to help you recover but ultimately it is you and only you, who can do it. Look yourself in the eye, in the mirror and tell yourself nobody is worth keeping you in that place of pain and despair. Choose to smile and feel the wind in your hair, choose to laugh, choose to bath, choose to eat, choose a treat, choose a new look, choose a new book, choose the gym, choose to be slim, choose a walk, choose to talk, choose tears, choose to dispel your fears, choose whatever it is you need to get through the seconds, minutes, hours, days, nights, weeks, months to the 'you' that was there all along. You can do it and you will do it.

When you know you are finally mended, spread the word, hold out your hand, share some love from your heart and some laughter from your soul and be there for a new member of the sisterhood who needs your help. Let's all help all our sisters worldwide to stand tall and know, they can and they will recover, survive and thrive, to live the life they deserve.

To all the sisters who reached out and held my hand in whatever way you could, who cried my tears with me, and laughed my laughter too, I thank every one of you. I survived.

Jayne.

Acknowledgements:

I would like to thank the following people for being a part of this journey to publishing my first novel:

James Coupe my editor. Thank you for your support, your efficiency, your editorial suggestions, your encouragement and your sense of fun. I have had so many giggles whilst perusing our reams of correspondence. You really did a perfect job.

Kate Ainsworth who inadvertently became my co-editor and was so valuable as her editing style was completely different to James' and so my writing got a 'double sweep' of editorial experiences. Thank you for your support in both these and my real life chapters.

To Julie, Kate, Tanya, Jackie, Debbie-Jane, Tracey, John, Jennifer and Pauline. My perfect review team who made me believe in myself and my skills, as you 'eagerly queued,' for each new chapter to be emailed to you. I am grateful for your editorial suggestions, plot changes and review comments but most of all I am grateful for the varied parts you all play in my life.

To my children. Nathalie and George. You have been the foundations of my soul at times, literally keeping me alive, as you have watched me deal with some of life's curve balls repeatedly whacking me in my gut. I wasn't always able to be a fully functioning mum but you were both always stalwarts in your support of me, to get me through some of my journeys, but especially this one. Thank you Nathalie for your 24 hour visits from London on the bus, to make sure I was okay. George, thank you too for your subtle little ways of making sure your mum was all right. I believe in Karma and as a good mum I acknowledge that I have good children. I am so proud and I love you both.

To my friends, near and far, thank you for your support throughout the emotional and physical pain, for your cards, flowers, texts, emails, phone calls, coffee shop treats, gifts, champagne, food parcels, shoulders to cry on and for the never ending supply of giggles and hysteria that not only provided material for the book but also let me know that I was loved and cared for. Your enthusiasm for my writing gift spurred me on to the end. I have the most amazing friends. Thank you all.

To Jennifer. My 'Geordie' cousin. Thank you for your love, your support and your kindness in sharing my highs and lows and for your feedback on my writing journey too. Boy, did we laugh? Lots 'o love to you pet!

To Julie. My Bestie. Very few people are blessed with a friend such as you. I will never be able to thank you enough for your often perfect timing in giving me your 'own time'. Thank you for your patience, for your unbelievable kindness. From making sure I had food or a drink, to making sure I showered so I didn't stink! Thank you for the shopping trips and the cafe treats, in your efforts to help me survive. You listened to my hysteria in both my painful and joyous episodes and you held me when I cried. You never let a day go by, without some form of contact, to make sure I was okay. All of that, whilst being a very busy working mum and wife too. Most of all Julie, I feel like I have been on the most fun filled road trip ever, without even going out of our front doors! It has been hilarious and if they could bottle the fun, laughter and tears of hysterics you and I have had this past few months, then this world would be a much happier place. Thank you Bestie.

To Sarah Ollis, my cover designer. Thank you for taking the trouble to read my book and interpret the main character so brilliantly.

To all my readers, wherever you are and whoever you are. This book was borne out of traumatic events stemming from betrayal and lies in its very many guises and I have had the most amazing time researching, writing and rewriting it. I thank you for buying it, reading it, borrowing it, sharing it and recommending it. However you have come to have it in your possession, I am humbled that the words that I wrote made their way into your life. Thank you.

Web links:

Central Library Manchester UK

www.manchester.gov.uk/centrallibrary

Chorlton Bookshop Manchester

info@chorltonbookshop.co.uk

Freds Ladies' Clothes Shop, 518 Wilbraham Road, Chorlton, Manchester, Lancashire M21 9AW. 0161 881 1101

Swan with Two Nicks Pub, Little Bollington

www.swanwithtwonicks.co.uk

Betty Etiquette Creator of whimsical cards and stationary

www.bettyetiquette.co.uk

Greenwich Market

www.greenwichmarketlondon.com

Goddards Pie Shop Greenwich

www.goddardsatgreenwich.co.uk

The Old England Hotel Bowness

www.macdonaldhotels.co.uk/our.../macdonald-old-england-hotel-spa

Jack Vettriano Artist

www.jackvettriano.com

Coordinates Collection

www.coordinatescollection.com

Nespresso

www.nespresso.com/uk/en/home

Sex And The City Candace Bushnell

www.hbo.com/sex-and-the-city

The Lead Station Chorlton

www.theleadstation.co.uk

The Lloyds Chorlton

www.thelloydschorlton.co.uk

Green and Blacks Organic

www.greenandblacks.co.uk

Tower of London

www.hrp.org.uk/TowerOfLondon

Slatterys Whitefield

www.slattery.co.uk

Hawes and Curtis

www.hawesandcurtis.co.uk

Zaibatsu

www.zaibatsufusion.co.uk

Heaps Sausages

www.heapssausages.com

Fallbarrow Park Holiday Park

www.park-resorts.com

Little Moo Cakes Award winning cake designs

www.littlemoocakes.com

Sarah Ollis Artist (Book cover designer)

www.kaleidoscopiccreations.com

Music listing:

Pink. Just give me a reason

Madonna. Power of goodbye.

Hard Fi. Watch me fall apart.

Joshua Radin. A brand new day.

Redbone. Come and get your love.

Avalanches. Since I met you.

Pet Shop Boys. Se a vida E.

Tegan and Sarah. I was a fool.

Air. Ce matin La.

Agnetha Faltskog. Dance your pain away.

Tegan and Sarah. Closer.

Eric Clapton. Wonderful tonight.

Libera. Sanctus.

Andy Burrows. Because I know that I can.

Labrinth and Emile Sande. Beneath your beautiful.

BWO. Sunshine in the rain.

Aroma ft Katerina. The children of Piraeus.

Andrew Johnson. Pie Jesu.

Gary Go. Wonderful.

Altered Images. Happy Birthday.

Cinematic Orchestra. Arrival of the birds.

Pharrell Williams. Happy.

Adele. Make you feel my love.

Chris de Burgh. Lady in red.

All for one. I swear.

Phylis Nelson. Move closer.

Elton John. Candle in the wind.

Don Williams. Turn out the light and love me tonight.

Michael Bolton. Missing you.

Boyz II men. The Color of Love.

Kim Wilde. You came.

Tommy Sparks. She's got me dancing.

Pet Shop Boys. Always on my mind.

Abba. Our last Summer.

Animal Kingdom. Two by Two.

David Guetto. Dangerous.

Shayne Ward. Breathless.

Ariana Grande. Love me harder.

Michael Jackson. You Rock my world.

Wretch 32. 6 words.

Michael Buble. Close your eyes.

Ed Sheeran. Thinking out loud.

Michael Jackson and Justin Timberlake. Love never felt so good.

Lightning Source UK Ltd.
Milton Keynes UK
UKOW05f2054300317
297944UK00001B/15/P